'It would be sweet to know you better, Catherine,' said Nick.

'I am not sure that would be right or proper,' she replied.

'Ah, there you have me,' Nick admitted. 'But love takes no account of these things. I would make you forget the foolish morality of a maiden's world, my pretty wench, and give you more pleasure than you have yet known, I'll swear.' He was breathing hard, and she felt the force of his passion as his mouth moved against her hair. 'I burn for you, sweet Catherine.'

His words and his looks were making her feel strange, and somewhere inside her there was a swirling heat that threatened to consume her.

'I think you are a rogue, sir...!'

Author Note

It has been a delight and a privilege to work on this Elizabethan series with Paula Marshall, an author I respect and admire. The Elizabethan age was a time when light began to penetrate the darkness of ignorance and suspicion, but it was also a time of danger and intrigue.

Each book is an individual love story but with a continuing undercurrent of mystery linking them. Through the eyes of young lovers, we have tried to portray the pageantry and ceremony of the four seasons of Elizabeth I's reign, from the spring of her joyous coronation through the summer of her life to a glorious autumn and finally to the chill of winter. We hope that you, the reader, will enjoy these stories as much as we enjoyed writing them.

These are the novels which make up **The Elizabethan Season:**

Spring	–	MAID OF HONOUR
Summer	–	LADY IN WAITING
Autumn	–	THE ADVENTURER'S WIFE
Winter	–	THE BLACK SHEEP'S BRIDE

Love to you all,

Anne Herries

The Elizabethan Season

LADY IN WAITING

Anne Herries

*First published in Great Britain 2004 by
Harlequin Mills & Boon Limited,
Eton House, 18-24 Paradise Road,
Richmond, Surrey TW9 1SR*

© Harlequin Books S.A. 2004

Special thanks and acknowledgement are given to Anne Herries
for her contribution to The Elizabethan Season series.

ISBN 0 263 84086 7

148-0404

*Printed and bound in Spain
by Litografia Rosés S.A., Barcelona*

Anne Herries lives in Cambridge but spends part of the winter in Spain, where she and her husband stay in a pretty resort nestled amid the hills that run from Malaga to Gibraltar. Gazing over a sparkling blue ocean, watching the sunbeams dance like silver confetti on the restless waves, Anne loves to dream up her stories of laughter, tears and romantic lovers.

Other novels by
Anne Herries

THE ABDUCTED BRIDE
CAPTIVE OF THE HAREM
THE SHEIKH
A DAMNABLE ROGUE

and in the Regency series
The Steepwood Scandal

LORD RAVENSDEN'S MARRIAGE
COUNTERFEIT EARL

Chapter One

September 1560

'Come, Mistress Catherine, a visit to the fair will do you good on this bright day. And besides, I do not like to see you downcast, sweet Cousin. My good Aunt Elizabeth would have driven you out into the sunshine before this, I dare swear.'

Catherine Moor laid down her embroidery with a sigh. She would as lief have sat quietly over her work, though others had already left for the delights of the fair that had come to visit, but she knew only too well the determination of her cousin Willis Stamford. Both Willis and her aunt, Lady Helen Stamford, were concerned for her, believing that it was time she put aside her grief for her beloved mother. Lady Elizabeth Moor had died of a putrid inflammation of the lungs in the spring of the year 1560, and it was now September of that same year.

Catherine no longer spent hours weeping alone in her bedchamber, but the ache of loss was constantly present and she had no real wish to visit a fair, even though she had always loved them when her parents had taken her. However, Willis would give her no peace until she acquiesced, which she might as well do with a good grace since she knew him to be a kind-hearted lad, some five years her senior. Most lads of his age would not have concerned themselves with a girl of barely eight years.

'Will you wait a moment while I fetch my cloak and purse, Cousin?'

'Martha has your cloak ready in the hall,' Willis replied, smiling at her. 'And you will have no need of your purse, as it is my pleasure to treat you to whatever you desire. You shall have sweetmeats, ribbons and trinkets, as many as you shall please.'

'Then I can only thank you, Cousin.'

Catherine stood up, brushing the stray threads of embroidery silk from her grey gown. Her dress was very simple, the full skirts divided over a petticoat of a paler grey, and the laced stomacher braided with black ribbon. More black ribbons attached the hanging sleeves to a plain fitted bodice and were her only ornament apart from a tiny silver cross and chain that her mother had given her just before she died.

Martha, her nurse and comforter since Lady Moor's death, was waiting to fuss over her in the hall, clucking like a mother hen with a chick as she tied the strings of Catherine's cloak and warned her not to stand in a chill wind.

'You take good care of her, Master Willis, and don't let her overtire herself.'

'Trust me, good mistress,' he replied and planted a

naughty kiss on Martha's plump cheek. 'I shall let no harm befall my cousin, I do promise you.'

'Get on with you, you wicked boy!' cried Martha, blushing at his teasing. 'Or I'll take my broom to your backside.'

The threat was an idle one, as both Catherine and Willis were well aware. Martha's heart was as soft as butter straight from the churn, and Willis knew exactly how to twist her round his little finger.

'I hope it will not tire you to venture as far as the village,' Willis said after they had been walking for some minutes. He glanced anxiously at Catherine's pale face. She had been ill with the same fever that had carried off her mother, and though long recovered, he knew his mother considered her still delicate. 'Perhaps we should take a short cut through the grounds of Cumnor Place?'

'Do you think we ought?' Catherine turned her eyes on him. They were wide and of a greenish-blue hue that made Willis think of a clear mountain pool he had drunk from on a visit to the Welsh hills as a young boy…deep and mysterious and deliciously cool. 'Will the lady of the house not mind us using her grounds as a short cut?'

'Poor Lady Dudley never leaves her bed they say. She has a malady of the breast and is like to die soon enough…' Willis stopped abruptly, wishing he had cut his tongue out before saying those words to his cousin. He hastened to repair his slip. 'Though I dare say that is merely gossip and the doctors will make her well again.'

'You need not protect me, Willis.' Catherine's serious eyes turned to him and he thought how lovely she was; the wind had whipped a few hairs from beneath the neat Dutch cap she wore so that they clustered about her face in dark red curls. 'I know that people sometimes die when they are ill, no matter how hard the physicians try to save them, as my dear Mama did. If we take this short cut you know of we must be very quiet, for we do not want to disturb the poor lady.'

'As to that, I daresay she would be glad of some company, for it is certain that her husband is often at court and seldom visits her...but it is this way, Catherine.' Willis stopped and held out his hand to her. 'See the gap here in the hedge? If we squeeze through it will save us half an hour of walking.'

Catherine looked at the gap doubtfully. She could see that it was well used and realised that local people must often take this route rather than walking around the perimeter of the grounds. Willis was beckoning to her and she followed him through, looking about her guiltily as they began to walk across an open sweep of grass. The house was some distance away, and she was relieved to know that they could not possibly disturb the sick woman if she were resting on her bed.

Ahead of them was a small wood, and once inside it they would lose sight of the house altogether and would soon rejoin the common ground grazed by pigs and cows belonging to the village folk. Catherine glanced back at the house and paused for a moment, her eyes narrowing as her attention was caught.

What was that? She shaded her eyes, puzzled by what seemed to be happening close to the house.

Something odd had occurred, causing an icy chill to fall over her. She could not see clearly enough to be sure, but it was like a creeping black mist that appeared to hover just above the ground. Where had it come from so suddenly? It had not been there a moment ago.

'Willis!' She called out to her cousin, pointing back towards the shadow, which had become more upright, looking almost like a man's form now but less defined, not quite substantial enough to be human. A shiver of fear went through her. She was not a girl given to superstition, though she knew the common folk believed in all kinds of evil spirits and demons that stalked the night, but this was broad daylight! 'What is that…back there…near the house? Do look, Willis.'

She tugged at his arm to make him look back.

'What? I see nothing.'

'There…' But she had taken her eyes from it and when she looked again it had gone. 'It was by the house. I cannot describe it…a strange shadow. It was sinister, evil. I felt its evil, Willis.'

'A trick of the light, no more. I can see nothing, cousin.' His eyes studied her with concern as she shivered. 'Come, Catherine, you have let your imagination lead you astray. There is nothing there to disturb you. We must hurry or the pedlars will have sold all their best wares before we arrive.'

She knew he was right, and yet for a moment her feet seemed almost glued to the ground and she felt as if she were unable to move. A sense of some evil having taken place here seemed to hang in the air, making her throat tight so that for a moment she could scarcely breathe. Catherine felt cold all over, her skin covered in goose-pimples. The feeling of terror was so strong in her that she was afraid she might faint. She had seen something that had frightened her but she did not know what it could be.

'Come along, Catherine!'

There was a note of impatience in Willis's voice. Catherine found that her feet were no longer leaden and she hurried after her cousin. Since whatever it was had gone, there was no point in trying to explain to Willis. Besides, all she wanted now was to leave this place.

She would make sure that they returned home by another route.

April 1571

'Do not look so at me, Catherine,' pleaded Sir William Moor as he saw the mutiny in his daughter's fine eyes. She was a beautiful girl of almost nineteen years, her long red hair flying about her face as she came in from some hard riding that morning. 'Your aunt is determined on this trip to London, and, God forgive me, I have neglected the question of your marriage. It is time a husband was found for you, my dear child.'

'Why must it be so?' Catherine asked, fire sparking in the bottomless depths of those green eyes. Her life had been so peaceful and serene these past years, and now it seemed that all must change. 'Why may I not stay here to take care of you for always, Father? Why must I marry and leave all that is dear to me?'

'It is true that my estate is not entailed…' Sir William hesitated as he sensed the mutiny in his much loved child. He had put this same argument to his sister the previous evening and been roundly scolded for his trouble. 'But it would be selfish of me to keep you here, Catherine. You must be presented at court— and a husband must be secured, if one can be found to please you.' He looked at her doubtfully, knowing her stubbornness of old.

'You will not force me to a marriage I cannot like?' She seized on his hesitation like one of the little terrier dogs the bailiff used for chasing rabbits from their holes. 'Promise me only that, dearest Father, and I shall go with a willing heart.'

'When have I ever forced you to anything you did not like?' He gave her a chiding look, for they both knew that he had spoiled her these last years, never remarrying after his beloved wife's death as most widowers did to gain an heir. Catherine was child enough for Sir William and he would miss her when she married. 'I swear I should not mind if you never married, my dearest Cat, but your aunt is determined you shall have the chance…and I believe my Elizabeth would have wanted this for you.'

'Then of course I shall go,' Catherine said, for any mention of her mother's wishes was sure to soothe her rebellion. Their mutual respect for a woman still loved and missed was a bond between father and daughter. 'But I wish you were coming with us, Father.'

'I shall join you soon enough,' he promised, eyes warm with affection. His Catherine was a high-spirited girl with a temper upon her when she chose, but he knew the sweetness and goodness of her true nature. 'Go up and tidy yourself now, Daughter. Your aunt awaits you in the best parlour.'

Catherine nodded, walking slowly up the wide staircase of the manor house that was her home. It was a sturdy building erected in the early days of King Henry VII's reign by her great-grandfather: half-timbered, with overhanging windows above good red bricks, it had a large open hall with stairs leading to a gallery above. Some of the walls were hung with bright tapestry, which lent colour and warmth to the rooms. Recently, Sir William had had the small parlour and the principal bedchambers panelled with good English oak in the latest fashion, and the new wood glowed with a rich golden colour.

Catherine's own bedchamber was furnished with an elaborately carved bed, which had two posts and a tester overhead; below the tester was suspended a canopy of silk tied with twisted ropes. Heavy brocade curtains could be drawn about the bed at night if the room was cold, though she seldom used them, preferring not to be enclosed.

At the foot of the bed there was a planked chest, and there was a counter beneath one of the small windows. This was a plain chest on joined legs that had once been used by the stewards for counting and storing money; but having found it lying neglected in a store, Catherine had had it removed to her own chamber, because the extra height made it useful for her personal items. She had spread an embroidered cloth over its scarred surface, and her beaten-silver hand mirror, combs and perfume flasks lay on top together with gloves, a string of amber beads and some feathers for a hat. Inside the cupboard were stored gloves, hats and various articles of feminine attire.

A number of triangular stools stood about the room, one by a harp, another in front of a tapestry frame, her much prized table desk set on a board and trestle with yet another stool near by; these, her virginals, several items of silver set upon the board and rich hangings proclaimed this the chamber of a privileged and favoured woman.

Taking a few moments to wash her hands in cold water from a silver ewer stored in a curtained alcove, Catherine finished her ablutions and then glanced in her mirror to tidy her wayward hair. Her careful work had restored the damage of a mischievous wind, and she was now neat enough to meet her aunt. Lady Stamford was a fastidious woman who always dressed richly, as well she might, having survived three wealthy husbands.

She was standing before the fireplace in the best parlour when Catherine entered, holding her hands to the flames of a fire that had been lit for her benefit. It was now April of the year 1571 and fires were seldom lit until the evening once the worst of the winter was over, because Sir William and his daughter, being busy about the estate, had no time to sit here during the day.

'I hope I find you well, Aunt?'

Lady Stamford turned as she spoke. Eyes that had once been described as sparkling were a little faded now, as was the complexion she embellished with paint, and the sparse grey hair she hid beneath a wig as red as Catherine's own hair. Painted cheeks and lips were the fashion for ladies of the court who needed a little artifice to aid their looks, but seemed strange to Catherine, who was used to fresh-cheeked country-women.

'Well enough, Catherine,' Lady Stamford said and smiled thinly. It was more than four years since she had seen her niece, for they lived some many leagues distant and travelling was hard enough in summer, almost impossible in the depths of winter. She was pleased to find that Catherine had matured into a beauty. Taller than some men of the age, she was perhaps too slender to please those who found more roundness their ideal, but child-bearing would no doubt change that soon enough. 'You look even prettier than when I last saw you. I had feared that at almost nineteen your looks would have begun to fade, but I see it is not so. I think we shall have no problem in establishing you at court, and then who knows? If Her Majesty is pleased with your conduct she may arrange a prestigious match for you.'

'You are kind to trouble yourself on my account, Aunt.'

Catherine thought it wise not to impose her own thoughts and wishes too soon. She had her father's promise and did not wish to quarrel with Lady Stamford for nothing. Her aunt had shown her great kindness over the years, especially when she had gone to stay at her home in Berkshire after her mother's untimely death.

'I have often wished for a daughter, but most of my babies did not survive their first year. Willis has given me my heart's desire in part, for Margaret is a good wife to him, and they have a son already. A beautiful boy and strong, praise God.'

'You must be thankful for it,' Catherine agreed, only too happy to change the subject. 'I trust the child will continue healthy and that they will have more fine babies.'

In an age when babies were fortunate to survive their infancy, the need to produce strong sons was often paramount, second only to the importance of marrying for wealth and position.

'I pray it may be so—but to other matters, Catherine. Your gown is sufficient for country wear but will not do in town. Before you can be presented at court you must be properly dressed. It is my intention to leave for London on the morrow. We shall have time to visit the silk merchants and my own dressmaker—a Frenchwoman of some skill—before we are summoned to attend the Queen.'

Catherine hid her sigh. Since both her father and her aunt were determined on this she must accept with a good heart. Yet she was aware of regret and an unease she could not name. Given her choice she would have remained at home, but perhaps no gentleman would be brought to offer for her and then she could return to her old pursuits in peace.

Catherine eased her aching limbs. They had been on the road for hours now, the unwieldy carriage lurching and bumping over deep ruts carved out by the frosts of the past winter and as yet unrepaired. Lady Stamford had insisted on travelling this way, with an entourage of servants in train, their baggage following behind on another even more cumbersome coach together with Martha and her ladyship's maid.

Feeling bruised herself, Catherine pitied her elderly nurse, who had insisted that she must be the one to accompany her young mistress to town. Out of consideration for her age, Catherine had suggested taking one of the other maids, but Martha would not hear of it.

'And who is to put warm cloves in your ear when it aches?' she demanded, though it was many years since Catherine had complained of the earache. 'Only Martha knows how to make you a soothing posset when you have a putrid throat, my sweeting. Of course you cannot go without me.'

Listening to her devoted nurse, Catherine could not deny her, though once she went to court Martha would no longer be able to stay near her.

Catherine would have preferred to ride, being used to travelling that way with Sir William when they visited the county fairs, and she was sure that Martha would have been more comfortable riding pillion behind their trusty groom Jake. However, Lady Stamford would not hear of it, and so they were being shaken to bits in the uncomfortable carriages for league after league.

It was a relief when they saw signs of a busy inn ahead. The road had certainly improved for the past few leagues, and Lady Stamford told her that it would be much better now that they had at last joined the main highway for London.

'Country roads are always the worst,' she said as

the jolting ceased at last and their groom came to open the door and let down the steps. 'And I believe Cambridgeshire is worse than most.'

Refraining from answering her aunt's comments on her home county, Catherine followed her through the inn yard. A grinning urchin, who ran up to them holding out his hand, had swept the yard clean of horse droppings and straw.

Catherine placed a farthing into his grubby paw, and then, noticing the hubbub and crowd to the rear of the inn, asked him what was going on.

'Why, 'tis the mummers, mistress,' the urchin said. 'They be giving a performance of a play.'

'A play?' Catherine's interest quickened. She had seen strolling players perform religious plays at Christmas in the village square at home, and sometimes her father asked roving minstrels to come to the house at that season to entertain them and their friends—but this seemed different.

Leaving her aunt to enter the inn alone, Catherine walked under the archway to the large courtyard at the back. There was a raised dais at the far end in a position that gave watchers from the upper windows of the inn an excellent view. For those watching from the inn yard the view was somewhat obstructed by the milling crowds.

However, Catherine found a space at the back, and by standing on a metal anvil often used as a mounting block she had a clear view of the stage. One of the players was declaiming a speech in a loud voice, while another rolled about the ground at his feet clutching himself and groaning awfully.

'He has been poisoned,' a voice said close to her. 'It is a Greek tragedy, mistress, and he is dying. He should lie still now, but methinks he enjoys the part too much.'

It was clear the audience agreed, for there were shouts of 'Die! Die!' from the more rowdy elements, and as Catherine watched someone threw what looked like a rotten cabbage at the actor rolling on the floor.

'Oh, the poor man,' Catherine said moved to pity. She glanced at the boy who had spoken to her. He was a lad of perhaps six years or so, but with a bright intelligent look and a precocious manner. 'Do you like to watch plays, young sir?'

'If they are good plays.' His mouth curled in scorn. 'This is a very bad play. When I am older I shall write much better ones. People will not throw rotten vegetables at my actors.'

Catherine smiled to hear such a proud boast from one so young.

'I shall remember that,' she said. 'May I know your name, sir? Then I shall know when one of your plays is being performed in the future.'

'I am Christopher Marlowe, known as Kit to my friends.' He bowed elegantly to her, showing more presence than any actor now performing on the stage. 'Come to the theatre when my play is being performed and I shall remember you.'

'I shall not forget, Master Marlowe...'

She was about to tell him her name when an uproar from near the front of the audience drew her attention. The group of rowdy gentlemen was throwing things in earnest now and shouting out rude remarks to the actors, and the man who had been rolling about was up on his feet and throwing something back at his tormentors.

Catherine's eyes were drawn to one of the young men in particular. So far she had not seen him throw anything, and he neatly avoided what was thrown in his direction, but he was clearly enjoying the ruckus, his generous mouth curved in a smile, his eyes glinting with what she thought malicious amusement. It was unkind of him to mock the poor actor so!

He was dressed in a brown jerkin of leather with breeches of the same material slashed through to show a lighter coloured woollen cloth beneath. His boots were thigh high and looked well travelled, and the cloak slung over his shoulder was dusty and slightly shabby. Yet he looked a gentleman, tall, broad-shouldered, with a powerful air around him. He was an attractive, distinguished man, who ought to have known better than to associate with the clearly intoxicated young rogues about him. If they did not know better then he certainly ought, which was perhaps why she had picked him out for particular censure.

It looked very much as if the play was about to become a riot. Catherine was turning away when she heard her aunt's voice calling to her.

'Come away, Catherine. There will be a fight 'ere long. It is not a fitting entertainment for a young lady of your breeding. When we are in London we shall see something better than this mummery.'

Catherine looked about for the young lad she had spoken to earlier and saw that he too was being led away from the trouble by a man who looked as if he might be his father. She smiled to herself as she recalled his boast and wondered if young Kit Marlowe would achieve his ambition. And whether fortune would be kind to him if he did.

Travelling players were at the mercy of their patrons, as were ambitious playwrights. Rich men were sometimes moved to support a group of players they admired, but those less fortunate were forced to tramp the country performing where they could for whatever was given them.

Following her aunt into the inn, where a meal of cold meat, pickles and a dish of hot buttered turnips was being served, Catherine frowned over the behaviour of the young blades who had turned the performance into a brawl. It was monstrous unfair to treat the unfortunate players so, and had she been a man she would not have hesitated to tell them so. Indeed, had her aunt not arrived to take her away, she might have been tempted to speak sharply to the man in the brown leather jerkin.

It was growing dusk when Catherine heard the horrible snapping sound and their carriage jerked to a sickening halt. She was thrown from her seat, and after recovering her position scarcely had time to glance at her aunt before the flaps at the windows were pulled aside and the groom was apologising.

'The leading pole has snapped, my lady.'

'Can it be mended, Jake?' Lady Stamford asked.

'Not right 'ere, it can't, my lady. We shall need to find a blacksmith and 'ave 'im make a metal splint...'

'Then what are we to do? How far is it to the next inn?'

'Five miles or more, my lady.'

'I cannot possibly walk that far…' She glared at the hapless groom. 'Go and fetch the blacksmith or a carpenter. And be quick about it. It cannot be long before darkness falls and I do not wish to be sitting here all night.'

'No, my lady.' He looked at her hesitantly. 'Could you not ride in the baggage coach? We could mend the pole in the morning…'

'Pray do as you are told, sirrah. Go and see to it at once.'

'We shall need to lead the horses off the road, my lady—and the carriage is blocking the road. No one can pass until we move it to one side.'

'Well, do so then!'

'Yes, ma'am—if you and Mistress Catherine would be good enough to get down.'

'Get down?'

'It will make things easier, Aunt,' Catherine said, seeing that Lady Stamford was outraged at the idea. 'And the carriage might overturn if they have to rock it to move it.'

'In that case we shall oblige.'

Catherine smiled inwardly as her aunt was helped out of the carriage. The look of dismay on Lady Stamford's face as she stood at the side of the road was amusing, but after some minutes, while the coachman and groom attempted to move the cumbersome vehicle, the situation became less diverting. Catherine had begun to feel uncomfortable herself, for it turned a little chilly and looked as if it might rain soon.

'Where is the baggage coach?' Lady Stamford demanded irritably, as her servants showed no sign of moving the cumbersome vehicle. It was obvious that she was beginning to think riding with the maids might be more desirable than standing by the side of the road. 'Have all my servants deserted me? I am not accustomed to being so ill served.'

'The coach is slower than our carriage—and poor Ben and Jake are doing their best, Aunt.'

'Then their best is not good enough!' She looked set for another angry outburst when they heard the sound of horses' hooves approaching. 'Ah, perhaps it…Oh, it is merely a rider.' Lady Stamford's face registered her disappointment, but in another moment she was smiling as the rider dismounted and came towards them.

'You are in some trouble, ma'am?'

'Indeed, sir, as you see.' Lady Stamford threw out her hands. 'These incompetent fools of mine make no progress and I fear a storm is imminent.'

'I believe you may be right.' The stranger glanced at dark clouds gathering overhead. 'You need help, for it will take more than two men to move that carriage.' He made her a little bow. 'May I introduce myself, ma'am. I am Sir Nicholas Grantly and I have relatives living just a short distance away. If you would consent to accompany me I am certain they will offer you and the young lady shelter and refreshment while their servants assist yours to clear the road.'

'Sir, I shall be delighted to accept your friends' hospitality, for I declare I am weary of standing here and turning chill.' Lady Stamford turned to Catherine, beckoning her to follow as Sir Nicholas offered to lead the way. 'Come along, my dear.'

Catherine hesitated, feeling oddly reluctant to go with him. She had recognised their rescuer as being the gentleman she had noticed at the inn. He had been in the midst of the rowdy element and laughing as heartily at the discomfiture of the poor players as the rest.

'You do not know him, Aunt,' she whispered, darting a glance of disapproval at Sir Nicholas's back. 'He might be anyone—a villain set to trap unwary travellers. Might it not be better to wait for the baggage coach, which cannot now be long behind us?'

'Nonsense!' Lady Stamford frowned at her. 'Sir Nicholas is clearly a gentleman and you should be grateful he came this way and chanced upon us, for in another ten minutes we should have been caught in a downpour.'

As a steady drizzle had begun to fall, Catherine was unable to contradict her aunt, though she continued to feel doubtful until the house was reached. For who knew what kind of a man he was or where they might find themselves lodged for the night?

The house was, however, as Sir Nicholas had stated, but a short distance down the road, and proved to be a simple but sturdily built country home of good proportions. One long building had a sloping thatched roof, and ivy growing up its walls; it made no pretension of grandeur but was the home of a gentleman of some substance, glass windows having replaced the older shutters which were still in evidence but permanently nailed back.

They were welcomed at the front porch by an apple-cheeked housekeeper, who drew them in and clucked over their misfortune, promising to send Jed and Seth with the farm horses to sort the matter out.

'For them fine carriage horses will be frettin' themselves to a lather by now and nobody be better with horses than our Seth. He'll see you right and tight, milady—and Seth can mend that pole of yours in a trice.'

'I'll take our guests into the parlour, Jessie,' Sir Nicholas said. 'Will you send in some wine and biscuits in a moment?'

'Aye, that I shall, Master Nicholas. The mistress be always pleased with company.'

'Ladies—this way.' Sir Nicholas waved them through the rather narrow hall into a large and comfortable parlour. The wooden floor had been recently swept with sweet herbs that cast a delicate fragrance. The main wall had been hung with a fine carpet, and there was a court cupboard at one end set with burnished pewter. An elbow chair was placed to either side of the fireplace, which had a good blaze to welcome them, and there was a Gothic oak settle that looked as if it might have come from a monastery at the time of their dissolution. Stuffed cushions, embroidered possibly by the lady of the house, had been placed against the carved back. Clearly the mistress of this home was accustomed to being indulged, for there were several precious items that showed that her husband had used his wealth to bring pleasure and comfort to his wife.

'Ah, Sister Sarah Middleton,' Sir Nicholas said, and held out his hands as a young and comely woman came flying towards him. 'I find you well, I hope?'

'Nick, my darling! At last you come,' Sarah Middleton cried. 'I have been expecting you two days and more.' She turned sparkling dark eyes on Lady Stamford and Catherine. 'But who have you brought to see me? You said nothing of guests, you wicked one.'

Her scolding tone was belied by an affectionate smile as she hung on to his arm. She was a pretty, plump woman of perhaps twenty, with soft dark hair that streamed from beneath a cap of fetching lace.

'You must not scold your brother,' Lady Stamford said, going forward to greet her. 'For he found us stranded on the road after our carriage unfortunately broke down and took pity on us, which was exceedingly kind of him. I hope we do not trespass on your hospitality too much, ma'am?'

Sarah's face glowed as she replied, 'No, indeed, ma'am, for it is just what I should do myself and Nick knows it. He was perfectly right to bring you here and only just in time.' The rattle of rain against the small panes of grey glass at the windows was quite fierce. 'You must not think of leaving this night. Jessie can easily put a hot brick in the best guest room and Nick can spend the night in the nursery.'

'Where my nephew will ensure that I sleep not at all,' her brother replied. 'I thank you for your attention to my comfort, Sister, but you are perfectly right to offer shelter to these ladies, and I shall be happy to give up my room for their sakes.'

His grey eyes seemed to dance with wicked laughter for a moment as they rested on Catherine. Unwilling to be charmed so easily by a man she suspected of being a rogue, she gave him a cold look and saw the sparkle die from his eyes, which became rather serious and thoughtful.

Catherine's attention was drawn away by Sarah Middleton, who was insisting that Lady Stamford take the place of honour in the chair to the right of the fire. Rather than take the lady's own chair, Catherine went to the settle and sat on its hard seat. She was grateful for the cushions at her back after hours of wearisome travel and longed for the familiarity and comfort of her own bedchamber.

Lady Stamford and Mistress Middleton were talking easily to one another. The introductions made and refreshments brought by the smiling Jessie, they passed on to the topics of the day.

'You may depend that Her blessed Majesty will never be properly secure while the Catholic impostor lives,' Sarah declared. 'They do say that wicked plotter Norfolk would marry Mary of Scots if he could, and there is even talk that he planned to have our Queen murdered…' She looked at her brother appealingly. 'Have you heard aught of this, Nick?'

'There is much talk,' Sir Nicholas said. 'And everything is not yet clear, but fear not, Sarah, while Her Majesty has men like William Cecil about her such plots will always fail. Besides, the Queen likes not to hear criticism of Norfolk and for the moment he escapes the punishment he deserves. I should not let the gossip disturb you, Sister, for I dare say it will all come to nothing in the end.'

'You always make me feel so much better,' Sarah said and gave a little shiver. 'I should not want to see another Catholic Queen on the throne of England.'

'Forgive my impetuous sister if she offends.' Sir Nicholas shot her a warning look. 'Our family has reason to distrust such a regime, for my father suffered many setbacks and fines while Mary reigned, and was lucky to escape being burned as a heretic—but there are Catholic men I claim as friends.'

'Oh, you need not fear to offend,' Lady Stamford assured him. 'Queen Mary of England burned my first husband's elder brother as a heretic. To see our glorious Elizabeth replaced by a woman brought up amongst the Catholic French would go against all I have been taught to believe. I have heard she is a vain, flighty creature and would cause nothing but harm if she ever came to power. Besides, when I was young I was lady in waiting to Anne Boleyn—God rest her soul! In my eyes her daughter Elizabeth is our true queen and shall always be so; though others may deny her I shall remain loyal.'

'Amen to that,' Sir Nicholas said. 'For myself I would see no other than Gloriana on the throne.' His eyes flicked towards Catherine, sitting silently on the settle. 'What say you, Mistress Moor?'

'I can only echo your sentiments, sir. I am persuaded you are wiser about such matters than I…' She sent him a haughty look that would have disconcerted many a man, though he gave no sign of having noticed except for a faint gleam in his eyes.

However, the coolness of her tone brought a frown to Lady Stamford's forehead. 'Come, Catherine, you can give Sir Nicholas a fairer answer than that. Your father is staunch in his support for Her Majesty and you must have heard his opinion often enough.'

'Indeed I have, Aunt, and my father is most loyal to Her Majesty. I meant no offence to anyone. I must blame my lack of courtesy on the long hours of travelling. Forgive me...' She avoided looking at Sir Nicholas, making her apology to the room at large.

For a time there was silence, and then their hostess stepped in to the awkward moment with a little tutting cry of dismay.

'You look exhausted, Mistress Moor,' Sarah Middleton cried. 'I am thoughtless to keep you talking when you must be longing to rest. Jessie shall take you to your chamber. We dine when my husband returns at seven. I pray you will forgive the lateness of the hour, but Matthew has been to inspect a distant field with his neighbour and was not expecting company.'

'You are very kind, ma'am. My father often keeps late hours himself.'

Catherine blushed the more because she knew she had been rude to Sir Nicholas. She had come close to insulting her generous hostess's brother and it was very bad of her.

She was taken to task for it when she was alone in the bedchamber with her aunt.

'I do not like to see such manners in you,

Catherine,' Lady Stamford said, looking at her with disapproval. 'Sir Nicholas has been all that is good. You might at least be polite if you cannot do better. If you behave like this in London you will never catch a husband.'

Catherine accepted the rebuke in silence, acknowledging it to be fair. Indeed, she was not sure why she had taken against Sir Nicholas, for he had done no more than laugh and call out to the actors. Perhaps she had been a little too harsh in her judgement.

If Sir Nicholas asked her opinion again on some point she would answer him with the consideration he deserved. She need not go out of her way to be friendly but there was no occasion to be impolite.

Chapter Two

Catherine would have liked to spend some time alone in the garden before joining the others that evening, but since it was raining it was barred to her and she did not want to go down too soon for fear of any inconvenience to her hostess. Lady Stamford took a long time over her toilette, and in consequence they did not go down until summoned by a maid. If she had hoped for a quiet moment alone it was not granted her.

Over supper she was given no opportunity to reveal her mellowed mood, because Matthew Middleton was a big, bluff man who talked and laughed a great deal. He had much to say for himself, and wanted to hear what his brother-in-law had to contribute on many topics, his loud voice dominating the conversation. However, Catherine found it interesting to listen, for in this way it was revealed that Sir Nicholas had but recently returned to England after some eighteen months of travelling on the Continent.

'You wrote of your visit to Italy,' Matthew Middleton said, attacking the good roast goose set in front of him with gusto. He ate with his fingers and a knife in the time-honoured way, using a trencher of bread to soak up the rich sauces, though all the ladies had been provided with both a knife and a spoon, a luxury not always to be met with in country houses. Besides each plate was a bowl of scented water for washing the fingers, and a napkin of soft white damask. 'I hear it is discouraged to visit the country now in some circles, for folk do say it is a place of devils and would have none of these canting Papists.'

'You know I hold no love for Papists, Brother—but it does a man's mind good to behold the wonders of Rome. There is beauty beyond imagining to be seen there, and it would be a sad day if religious prejudice ever prevented our experiencing such things.'

'Well, well, I suppose you are right, Nick. I say only what is the opinion of many these days.'

'Wait until you see the marble statuary I have brought for your beloved garden,' Sir Nicholas said, smiling at his brother-in-law with obvious affection. Despite their banter there was clearly a good understanding between them, and Catherine found herself envying the warmth of this family circle. 'And somewhere amongst the baggage that follows me I have a crystal posset set for Sarah that came from Venice. When you have seen these and more of the treasures I have brought back from my travels I'll wager you will sing another tune.'

'I trust you have not brought Matthew any indecent ladies?' Sarah said, and then giggled at the mocking look in her brother's eyes. 'You will have our neighbours denouncing us as wicked pagans before the pulpit on Sunday.'

'Only ladies swathed in folds to cover their charms—and a cherub or two, sister mine,' Nick replied and blew a kiss to her. 'Though for my own estate it is a different matter, and I have some fine Greek gods in all their maleness—but I had best not tell you more lest I offend those innocent ears.'

Sarah dimpled and shook her head at her unrepentant brother, turning her bewitching smile on Catherine.

'You will forgive us for neglecting you, Mistress Catherine, but it seems an age since my brother was here with us. He has sent messages and gifts from his journeying, but to have him here is a gift beyond price.'

'Yes, I imagine it must be so. I have only my father, my aunt and cousin. It must be pleasant to have brothers and sisters.'

'I have another sister,' Sarah told her. 'Agatha is some fifteen years older and has a different mother, but Nick and I are true brother and sister. We had another brother, Harry, but he died when travelling in Italy with friends. It was some years ago and I was but a child, so I hardly remember him, but Nick adored him of course.' Following her gaze across the table, Catherine saw that the laughter had faded from Sir Nicholas's eyes and wondered at it. What could cause him to look like that? There was bleakness and anger in his face, a kind of haunting sadness that somehow touched her heart.

'That was sad for your family,' she said. 'It is always hard to lose someone you love.'

'Yes, but much harder for Nick than me,' Sarah said, seeming to become aware of her brother's silence. 'And Matthew has three sisters and two brothers, of course.' She looked fondly at her husband. 'We are truly blessed with our family in having many of them close by.'

Her husband smiled at her and addressed some trifling remark to Nick about his journey. After that, the talk was turned to politics, touching briefly on the plot concerning the Duke of Norfolk's alleged attempt to arrange a marriage with Mary of Scots without seeking the Queen's permission, and then veering to the shocking prices of wheat and wool, before coming round to family matters. Catherine found the time passed very pleasantly, and though she said little herself she enjoyed the conversation of others.

She was aware that Sir Nicholas had given the evening a touch of spice with his stories, many of which she was sure he had invented purely for his sister's amusement. That he was a clever man well able to hold his own in any company she could not doubt. However, she clung stubbornly to her picture of him as an idle rogue who wasted his time with feckless companions and thought it amusing to throw rotten fruit at a hapless actor.

It was past nine when Sarah took the ladies to her parlour for a sweet tisane, which she said would give them ease and aid their rest in a strange bed.

'Matthew and Nick will talk long into the night,' she said, 'and my day begins at cockcrow. I shall bid you good night now, ma'am—Mistress Catherine. I wish you both sweet dreams.'

'How fortunate we were to find such hospitality,' Lady Stamford said, as they retired to their chamber to discover everything in readiness for their comfort, a warm brick passed between the sheets and a small fire in the grate. 'Such open kindness is not often met with in strangers, Catherine. It has quite lifted my spirits and restored my faith in my fellow beings.'

So saying, Lady Stamford removed her wig, climbed into bed and fell asleep within seconds of her head touching the goose-feather pillow.

Catherine lay wakeful at her side for some time, listening to her aunt's gentle snoring and the creaking in the eaves. The moaning of a dying wind was not disturbing, for in such a solid house as this there was a feeling of safety. It must have been late into the night when she heard the tread of boots along the hall and Sir Nicholas's voice calling a cheery goodnight to his host.

And then she slept.

Waking at cockcrow, Catherine thought longingly of her day at home. She would have been out even now with her horses and dogs, riding the estate while the dew was still upon the ground.

Rising from the bed in which her aunt slept on, Catherine dressed quickly and went downstairs. It was a fine day, the only signs of the storm some debris strewn upon the ground, and with luck she would be able to escape into the gardens without being seen.

Sarah Middleton kept a good kitchen garden, with

lots of soft fruit bushes, and spring vegetables beginning to push their way through the soft earth. Everything smelled so fresh and sweet after the rain, and Catherine stooped to pick one of the herbs used for cooking, rubbing it between her fingers and holding them to her nose to catch the fragrance of rosemary.

'You are abroad early, Mistress Moor. I had not thought to see you here this morning.'

Catherine jumped, swinging round guiltily to face the man who had spoken to her.

'I hope I do not intrude,' she said. 'Perhaps I ought to have waited until we were summoned, but I looked out and was tempted. It is always my habit to rise early at home.'

Sir Nicholas looked at her, his eyes narrowing as they moved over her with slow deliberation. His study brought a flush to her cheeks, making Catherine catch her breath. There was something so essentially masculine about him then that she was aware of a feeling that disturbed her, though she did not understand it. Why did he look at her so? It was almost as if he were undressing her with his eyes! No man had ever looked at her that way before.

'Do you ride, Mistress Moor?'

'Yes, every day at home.'

'You will miss that at court,' Nick told her. 'When in the country Her Majesty sometimes hunts and those ladies skilful enough to keep up with her may be invited to join in, but in London you will find scant opportunity for a good gallop.'

'I believe I shall miss it a great deal,' Catherine

replied. She raised her head, a challenge she was unaware of in her lovely eyes. He should not look at her
so! 'You also keep early hours, sir—though I think
you went late to bed last night.'

'Did we disturb you?'

'No, no, of course not. I was not asleep,' Catherine
said quickly, a flush in her cheeks. She could not meet
his eyes. He would think she was criticising him again,
and indeed she had not meant to. 'I dare say it was all
the excitement of the day.'

'Yes, I dare say.' His brow wrinkled as he looked
at her. 'Perhaps…' Whatever he was about to say was
lost as Matthew Middleton appeared. 'Ah, my good
Matthew comes. I must bid you adieu, Mistress Moor,
for I have promised to ride with him. I wish you a
safe journey onwards.'

Catherine inclined her head but made no comment.
She envied them their early morning ride, and the
thought of yet another long day in the uncomfortable
carriage did nothing to raise her spirits. She found herself wishing that her aunt would be forced to delay
their journey for a few more hours, and watched wistfully as the men rode out of the courtyard together.

There was, however, to be no such delay. Their
smiling hostess greeted them with a hearty breakfast
of coddled eggs and fresh muffins to eat with her own
honey—and the news that the carriage was repaired
and awaited their pleasure.

'We must thank you for your kindness,' Lady
Stamford said. 'Should you ever wish to be presented
at court you must call on me to help you.'

'Lord bless us, ma'am, what should I find to do at

court?' Sarah went into a peal of good-natured laughter. 'Our Nicholas can play the fine gentleman when the occasion calls for it, though I have always thought him a countryman at heart, but I am mightily content with my life here.'

'And a very good life it is too, Mistress Middleton.' Lady Stamford bit into a third muffin oozing with creamy butter. 'You are fortunate in your cook, ma'am.'

'Oh, I made those myself,' Sarah said, and turned to Catherine. 'So beautiful as you are, you'll be certain to find a handsome husband at court, mistress—but make sure you choose a kind man, for in the end a peaceful, loving home is what makes a woman happy.'

'I thank you for your good wishes, ma'am.'

Catherine wondered if Sir Nicholas would return before they left, but in the next breath Sarah told them that the men would not come home before the evening. Catherine was conscious of a feeling of disappointment; though she did not know why she should feel anything for a man she had met but briefly and would probably never meet again. He had been pleasant enough when they met in the kitchen garden, but the image of him amongst those drunken idlers remained with her.

'Well, Catherine,' Lady Stamford said when they were settled in their carriage having said farewell to their hostess, 'I do hope that we shall have no more adventures on the road, fortunate as this one turned out.'

'We were indeed fortunate, Aunt. Sarah and Mr Middleton were generous hosts.'

'And Sir Nicholas.' Lady Stamford looked at her hard. 'I hope you will be more disposed to greet him kindly should he decide to call upon us in London.'

'I was not aware he was intending to visit London.'

Catherine's heart had begun to throb rather oddly as she waited for her aunt's reply. It was most unaccountable! Why should she be so affected by the rogue?

'Indeed yes. Mistress Middleton told me that the Queen's most trusted adviser had summoned him there. Sir Nicholas was named for his father, who was a friend to Cecil. Unfortunately, the father died some three years back, having never quite recovered from a lingering illness he contracted while a prisoner in the Tower for some months during Mary's reign, and then the untimely death of his eldest son, Harry. It was because of that friendship between Cecil and Sir Nicholas's father that he may have a brilliant future open to him at court.'

Catherine wrinkled her brow in thought. 'Do you think Sir Nicholas an ambitious man, Aunt?'

'All men of sense are ambitious.'

Lady Stamford had settled into her corner, cushions at her back and a rug over her lap. She closed her eyes, leaving Catherine to stare out of the window at the countryside. Some of the land to either side of the high road was commons and grazed by animals belonging to village folk, but more often now enclosure was encroaching on land that had once been open to all. The walls of large estates had altered ancient boundaries, often causing hardship to the poor.

'It is so unfair,' Catherine had complained to her

father when one of their neighbours took away a stretch of land that had previously been common land. 'He has so much, and they have so little.'

'It is the fault of rising prices,' Sir William explained. 'Land owners can get no more rent for the land they have let to tenants for years past, but they must find more coin for everything they buy. Therefore, they must take more land into enclosure, and if they have title to it…the right is theirs.'

Put like that, Catherine could understand why some landowners felt justified in enclosing land, but she knew that their actions caused much suffering for others.

Were the Middletons like other farming gentry and forced to take land that had once been free for all? They had seemed prosperous to Catherine—and judging by the supper talk the previous evening, Sir Nicholas was a man of some substance.

Catherine's thoughts returned once more to the man who had rescued them the previous afternoon. Why could she not dismiss the incident from her mind? It mattered not if he thought her a cold, mannerless wretch. As indeed she had been the previous afternoon and evening, though she had tried to be more conciliatory in the garden—at least until he had looked at her so oddly.

He was charming, but undoubtedly an ambitious rogue and it would be better for her peace of mind if she instantly forgot him, as no doubt he had already forgotten her.

'What think you?' Matthew looked at his brother-in-law as they surveyed the stretch of good land by

the river. 'It has always belonged to my family, but
we thought it well to keep it as it is, a pretty stretch
of sweet grass that all may graze. In summer I may
have a few sheep here myself, though 'tis oft flooded
in winter.'

Nick's eyes were serious as they rested on the
strong, rather craggy features of Sarah's husband. It
had been a good match for his sister, one that he had
approved soon after his father's death. He knew
Matthew to be a good man and understood he was
troubled by his conscience. He had waited for Nick's
return before making any decision, simply because he
found it a thorny problem.

'You have the right to erect your fences,' Nick said,
knowing that Matthew would be guided by his opinion. 'But it will cause hardship for the villagers.'

'Aye, I know it,' Matthew replied heavily. 'It goes
against the grain with me, but I need more land under
cultivation…'

'Why not take that piece of scrub to the north bor-
der?' Nick suggested. 'It will need more work to bring
it round, but you may call upon the village folk to
help you. Make it clear that you need more land and
ask for their help in preparing the scrub in return for
keeping this wash open for all.'

The frown cleared from Matthew's brow and he
smiled in gratitude. 'Aye, I'll do it. I've not asked for
the accustomed days in labour for many a year, for we
all pay in coin these days—but I'll take the labour in
lieu of the land, and all may be satisfied. Sarah told
me to consult you, and as usual she was right.'

'My sister flourishes,' Nick replied with a soft chuckle, affection and warmth in his eyes. He was fond of Sarah and she of him. 'You have spoiled her and yet she is less fiery than of yore. Tell me, what kind of magic have you used to tame her?'

''Tis love, nothing more,' Matthew answered with a smile. 'Speaking of fiery wenches…what of Mistress Moor? Think you she was an uncommon beauty? That red hair and those eyes, and the whiteness of that skin…such a woman might tempt any man to madness.'

'Do not let Sarah hear you,' Nick warned, his eyes full of wicked laughter. 'She will take a broom to you, I swear! But you are right, Matthew, Catherine Moor is a beauty, though she seemed overly proud and a little cold to me.'

'Cold?' Matthew raised his brows incredulously. 'No, Brother, you cannot be serious? I would swear there was fire simmering beneath the ice. She has a haughty bearing I'll grant you, but that is but a façade I dare swear. I vow it would be entertaining to see what lies beneath that cool manner, and would be tempted to probe for it right lustily were I not a married man.'

'I'll admit that a wench of that ilk is tempting to any man,' Nicholas said, a smile on his lips as he remembered the way Mistress Catherine had glared at him. Even in the garden she had still seemed reserved and cool, though she had blushed when he first caught her amongst the herbs. It was probably true that there was fire beneath the ice, and in other circumstances he might have been tempted to breach the walls of the citadel, for he was a man of lusty habits and had taken his first wench when but fourteen in the hayloft of his home. Unfortunately, he had other more important matters on his mind and could not spare the time for dalliance.

'When do you leave for London?' Matthew asked as they remounted their horses, setting out to inspect further pastures that Matthew had a mind to plough up and put down to grain that year. The export of wool was frowned on these days, and the call was for more grain to keep down the price of bread, which like everything else had been rising of late. 'Sarah is hoping you will stay a while.'

'A few days at least,' Nicholas replied. 'I must be in town within a fortnight, but I have someone else I would wish to see first and it will take me some days to ride to Leicester and back. I may go tomorrow, then join you at the weekend again for a couple of days before I go on to London.'

'You know your business best,' Matthew said. 'Sarah wishes you would marry and settle down, but I've told her you'll find your own way when you're ready. But we'll say no more on the subject, for I see it vexes you.'

Nick was frowning to himself as his companion fell silent. He would have liked to confide in Matthew, for he was a good man and true to his principles, but in knowledge lay danger and Nick would not involve his sister's husband in this.

There were but few men he would trust with the problem that was taxing his mind. The court was alive with intrigue, and one could never be sure where others stood. This business of Norfolk had seemed settled after the failure of the Northern Earls in their uprising of November 1569. The Queen, reluctant to punish her cousin, had allowed him at least partial freedom—but there was treachery afoot, and if it were not for the vigilance of men like Francis Walsingham and Sir William Cecil England might even now be at war with a foreign invader.

Nicholas's business in London was important but not urgent. There was time enough for him to speak to the man he trusted most outside his family. Oliver Woodville was his late brother's closest friend, and the man who had brought them the news of Harry's death. He had broken the news first through a letter and then had come in person on his return to England.

Oliver had been very distressed by Harry's death, but though he assured the family that it had been caused by a common fever, which affected many travellers, Nicholas had always retained a faint suspicion that Oliver himself was not convinced. Or perhaps it was merely Nicholas who refused to be convinced, because his grief was too terrible to bear, his sense of loss too deep for a younger brother to accept. However, his reason for seeking Oliver out was only partially to do with his brother's death all those years ago; he had other concerns that nibbled at his mind, troubling him with a half-forgotten memory. More pressing perhaps was his secret work for Walsingham.

The Italian banker Ridolfi had most certainly been behind this latest plot, but was there also another hand involved? Walsingham was uncertain, though he suspected something…something hidden beneath the layers of intrigue and deceit.

'Ridolfi would seem the prime mover in this plot, for it is certain Norfolk hath not the stomach for it,' Walsingham had told Nick privately in Paris at their last meeting. 'Had he grasped the nettle in 'sixty-nine he might have raised the country and swept Elizabeth from the throne. There is much love for Norfolk, amongst commoners and nobles alike. Even Cecil likes the man, though they be on opposite sides in this matter, but he would not see him dead, and Her Majesty protects him. I believe him dangerous but not the prime mover in these plots.'

'But once his true perfidy is proven? Surely Her Majesty will see he is a traitor and must be dealt with as such?'

'As yet the final pieces have still to be found,' Walsingham had told him. 'We know much, but Her Majesty is no weakling to be directed against her will in this. She asks for absolute proof of his guilt and will not return Norfolk to the Tower until we have it.'

Nick nodded, looking thoughtful. He knew well that Elizabeth was made of stubborn material, and given now and then to sudden rages like her father. Despite gossip and the harm done by malicious tongues that had slandered Anne Boleyn, there was no doubt in those closest to Her Majesty that King Henry VIII had fathered the courageous, determined lady many called Gloriana.

But this was not the problem that Walsingham was currently trying to grasp. Nick looked at him for a moment, trying to fathom the working of this clever mind. 'And you think there is still another traitor involved in this plot—someone we do not yet know?'

'I sense him…smell him,' Walsingham declared. 'There is the stench of evil about him, Nick, but I cannot name him. Nor can I say for sure that he exists outside my imagination.' He shook his head sorrowfully. 'I have my suspicions of John Dee, but he is Her Majesty's astrologer and trusted by her. I do not like the man and think him a bad influence on the Queen, but without proof my hands are tied.'

'You think Her Majesty's astrologer may be involved in some plot against her? Surely not?'

'Some writings came to my hand, from Dee to a man who had sought his advice on workings of the occult. There was nothing of treachery in them, but something…' He shook his head. 'I do not trust the man nor any that treat with him.'

'But you have no proof,' Nick asked and Walsingham shook his head. 'Nay, I need not ask, for you would have moved against him had the evidence been in your hands.'

'In my business I glean crumbs from time to time and in this way my bread is baked. If the man be in league with the Devil I shall find him out one day.'

Absolute proof was hard to find and must be sought thread by thread until the tapestry was complete. And that would be all the harder if, as Nick suspected, he himself had been followed to and from his last meeting with Walsingham. Could their conversation have been overheard—and who was the man he had caught a glimpse of in the shadows?

He could not be certain. Indeed, he had seen the

man in the shadows only briefly as they walked together in the gardens of Walsingham's house at dusk.
That brief sighting had touched a chord in his memory
when he recalled it later, taking him back to a time
when he had been much younger. Yet was it possible?
It seemed unlikely. He was most probably mistaken;
it had more likely been a trick of the light or a face
long forgotten remembered wrongly, but it would do
no harm to ask Oliver for a name.

The remainder of Catherine and Lady Stamford's
journey to town was uneventful, though they had to
accomplish it without the baggage coach, which having somehow missed them on the road had continued
on to London and awaited them at Lady Stamford's
town house.

The house, situated just off St James's and convenient for the Palace of Whitehall, which was the
Queen's main residence in London, although she had
many other palaces within a short distance, was a tall,
narrow building with overhanging windows and a tim-
bered frame.

Catherine was surprised at the closeness of the
houses through which they passed on their way to
Lady Stamford's home. The streets were filthy and the
smell that came from the rubbish-strewn gutters in-
describably foul. She had expected her aunt's house
to be larger, but Lady Stamford explained that as she
came to town only occasionally she did not need anything grand.

'We shall be out most of the time, and I do not
entertain lavishly in town, merely a supper or two if I

feel inclined to invite close friends. Indeed, if it were not for Willis I might be tempted to sell it altogether. My second husband, who had ambitions at court, bought the house as a gift for me. Unfortunately, he caught the pox and died before he had a chance to make his name. And then of course I married again, and when the young king was taken from us my husband felt it prudent to retire to the country. We did not come to town again for a long time.'

Many Protestant ladies and gentlemen had done as much during the reign of the Queen some named Bloody Mary. It had been safer and more prudent so.

The London house had been reopened after Elizabeth came to the throne amongst scenes of rejoicing by the common folk, Lady Stamford having attended the Coronation and been present in the Abbey. Her third husband had unfortunately died soon after of a putrid fever, and once again she had retired to her house in Berkshire. Now she had returned to London for Catherine's benefit.

Inside, the furnishings were good solid oak, some of it worn to a mellow softness by time and wear. The unwarranted use of English oak for anything but shipbuilding was frowned on these days, because it had been over-used, and imported woods were beginning to take its place, walnut being a favourite for good furniture. However, there were rich hangings on the walls and a set of six beautifully carved elbow chairs with padded backs covered in a bright tapestry. The stuffed backs made them more comfortable than any Catherine had ever used before and she remarked on it to her aunt.

'They were a special present to me from my third husband for our wedding,' she told Catherine. 'He asked me what would please me most and I told him of chairs I had seen in Her Majesty's bedchamber so he commissioned these for me. I liked them better than any jewel, and they have given me ease on many a weary night. There were ten of them in all but I gave four to Margaret when she married Willis, and I shall give you two as a wedding gift.'

'They are indeed most handsome,' Catherine said and thanked her.

She must be grateful for her aunt's consideration. Such chairs were seldom found in even the best houses, and it was a generous gesture to give such a valuable gift. Clearly her aunt expected her to make a good marriage and Catherine hoped she would not be too angry if her plans came to naught.

The scolding she had received after her coldness to Sir Nicholas had chastened her and she had found herself quite unable to put the incident from her mind. But now that they were in London, she imagined it would be easier for there was so much to see and do.

Lady Stamford had talked constantly of the silk merchants they would visit, and over the next several days Catherine was shown a dazzling display of wonderful silks and velvets. So many that she found it difficult to choose and spent an enormous amount of her father's money.

'My brother can well afford it,' Lady Stamford told her when she wondered what he would say at their extravagance. 'And you cannot go to court looking like a pauper.'

The merchants' shops had signs hanging above them, often brightly painted and in many cases depicting the nature of their trade or guild; they swung backwards and forwards in the wind, making a creaking noise and adding to the general hubbub. The market stalls abounded everywhere, crowding the narrow streets; meat, fish and vegetables were open to the elements and flies in the heat of the day, and sometimes the smell was enough to make Catherine retch.

At home she would have ridden to a local market or fair, but in London they found it more convenient to summon a chair to carry them about the city. Walking was out of the question, because the gutters were choked with filth and one had to watch for housewives throwing the contents of their chamberpots from an upstairs window with only a brief warning, which caught many unawares. She had seen more than one fine gentleman raise his fist in anger when slops splashed his hose or trunks, as he was slow to dodge the deluge from above.

It was often almost impossible to pass through the narrow, congested streets, which quickly became choked with the press of traffic. Sitting behind an overturned wagon that had spilled its load on the ground did not find favour with Lady Stamford, and the best chairmen were adept at avoiding such disasters.

Catherine was in turn delighted and appalled by the sprawling city, which had spread out beyond its medieval walls, despoiling the countryside about it. The ditch outside those walls, which had once been a part of the city's defences, had become a narrow, silted channel that stank in summer and had been built over in places. However, the curving banks of the Thames were still green and pleasant in many areas, gentle, spreading trees gracing them with their tranquil beauty, and flocks of swans frequenting the clear water. Within the city itself it was possible to come upon orchards secreted behind walls or pretty private gardens, and the houses of the rich were sometimes very grand, often situated close by the river with long sloping gardens to the rear. Catherine thought how pleasant it would be to walk there on a warm evening, and regretted that her aunt's house had only a small walled courtyard.

The streets of the city were mostly dark at night, though lanterns hung outside the better houses and inns. It was, however, a risk to venture out late at night, despite the efforts of the watchmen.

'We shall be well escorted if we go out in the evenings,' Lady Stamford told her niece. 'But we must wait until your father arrives before we go to court.'

In the meantime Catherine was content to be taken about the city, visiting the newly opened Royal Exchange, the beautiful parks, so many shops that her head went spinning at all the frills and trinkets she was shown. What she enjoyed most was being rowed down the river on a pleasant day to watch some sport or a play given in the courtyard of a superior inn.

Catherine was pleased to discover that the particular players she was taken to watch were under the protection of the Earl of Leicester, and vastly more talented than those she had seen on her way to London. While watching them she recalled the young Kit

Marlowe, and thought he might have liked to be present for the performance. The behaviour of the audience, which was made up of richly dressed ladies and gentlemen, was better than that she had witnessed on the road, but there was still a rowdy element who called out occasionally, using the poor players as the butt of their wit.

'It is always so at a public performance,' Lady Stamford told her. 'But you will see better manners at court.'

Catherine found herself looking about the audience. She scolded herself for her disappointment at not seeing the person she sought. How foolish she was! Sir Nicholas was undoubtedly still in the country with his sister. Besides, why should it matter to her? She would do best to put him from her mind!

It was as they were being rowed back up river that Catherine saw the heads on spikes outside Traitor's Gate and shuddered. Public executions were not uncommon, and she had been forced to witness a hanging when on her way to a certain silk merchant Lady Stamford had praised for the quality of his wares, their chairmen having been unable to make a way through the press of the crowd. However, the sight of blackened heads left to rot and be pecked at by the crows was one she would rather not have seen.

'You must accustom yourself to such things and learn to ignore them,' her aunt told her with a frown when she spoke of the barbaric behaviour of some in the crowd at the hanging. 'Those men were enemies of the state and must be punished. After the attempted uprising in 'sixty-nine Her Majesty's advisers are determined that this latest plot shall come to nothing, and she must be protected from those who would harm her.'

Catherine nodded, knowing her aunt spoke the truth, but the sight had cast a shadow over the afternoon and she was conscious of coldness at the back of her neck. The unease between Catholic and Protestant was a source of constant tension in England, and seeing those blackened heads upon spikes she could not help but feel sorry for the men who had died such a cruel death and for their families, who would naturally suffer grief and deprivation.

It was at moments like this that she longed for the peace of the countryside and wished that she might be back at home with her father.

However, her mood was soon altered, for when they entered her aunt's house it was to find a bustle and a stir that could mean only one thing.

'My brother has arrived at last,' Lady Stamford said with satisfaction. 'That means we may attend the court tomorrow. Her Majesty is to give a masque at Hampden and we are bidden to attend…'

Catherine paid little heed to her aunt, giving a cry of delight as her father came into the hall and rushing to hug him. The shadows receded as he embraced her, then drew back to study her closely, taking in the richness and modish style of the gown she was wearing.

'I see Sister Helen has been busy spending my money—and to good effect. You look beautiful, Catherine, though to my eyes you always have.'

'Thank you, Father.' She smiled at him as they went into the best parlour together. 'Oh, I am so very glad that you are here…'

Chapter Three

'So you have come back to us, Nicholas.' Lady Fineden looked at her son with approval. She was a woman long past the bloom of her youth, though still considered handsome. 'I hope you found Sarah well?'

'Blooming and as lovely as ever,' Nick said, giving his mother a smile warm with affection. He kissed the hand she offered gallantly, saluting her as both mother and friend. Although into the autumn of her life, she was a healthy, energetic woman who had married again after his father's death to a gentleman of the court. Sir John Fineden was one of Sir William Cecil's staff and a very busy man who seldom had the leisure to entertain his wife, expecting her to make her own pleasures, which she was very able to do having a large circle of friends at court. 'It is good to see you looking well, Mother.'

'By that you mean stout,' she replied, pulling a wry face. 'But I feel well and I am always entertaining so must keep up a good table. Sir John has been away again, but I am expecting him home soon. He asked in his last letter when you would return and will be pleased to see you, I make no doubt.'

'As I shall to see him. I have something of importance to tell him.'

Lady Fineden nodded, her grey eyes studying the clean-shaven, handsome features of a man who seemed to have grown in stature in the matter of a few months. Her son had been a careless, seemingly light-hearted fellow given to the pursuit of pleasure when he set off on his travels, but had returned a confident man with the maturity of his nine-and-twenty years upon him. The change was marked and she wondered what had brought it about, though to be fair to him she knew he had not travelled merely for his own plea-sure. She alone of her immediate family was privy through her husband's trust to her son's mission.

'No doubt you will be summoned shortly—but we shall say no more of that. I have you here for a while at least, and you will do me the kindness of escorting me to court tomorrow evening, I hope?'

'It would be a pleasure, dearest Mama,' Nick as-sured her. 'But I pray you will excuse me this eve-ning? It is a while since I was here and I have people I must see.'

'You must do what pleases you, Nick. I am content with your promise for the morrow. Now I must tell you about your sister Agatha. She joins me in town next month, and I believe she is hoping for another addition to her family, for her daughter is with child.'

'Sarah was asking after her, but I had no news. She will be glad to hear that Agatha does well.'

'I shall be writing to Sarah soon. But you may be

more interested in something I heard at court the other evening…'

Apparently listening as Lady Fineden recounted some of the latest gossip from court, Nick's mind was elsewhere. His detour to the estate of Oliver Woodville had been unnecessary because the man he sought was in town, and he must waste no time in speaking with him, for Nick was once again certain he had been followed. This time he had caught sight of the fellow several times, and knew it was not the man of shadows he had seen so briefly in Paris but another, clumsier fellow who had possibly been paid to watch him.

There was always the chance of an attempt at assassination, for these were dangerous times and a man such as he who worked in secret ways was liable to meet a violent end. He had known it when he took on the work, but his life had seemed an empty charade, with nothing for an able mind to discover but pleasure, and that palled after a while. He had been at the point of deciding to leave London and return to his estates when he was offered the chance to broaden his mind and serve Queen and country in one.

His travels in Italy had not been only for the purpose of discovering the beauty of which he had spoken so compellingly to his sister and her guests, but for another, more important.

His Holiness the Pope considered Elizabeth of England a usurper, and there were many of that faith who spoke openly of excommunication and of sweeping the impostor from the throne. He had been asked to discover as much as he could about the mood in Rome and to report to Walsingham in Paris, and this he had done, but he could bring no good news. Though other foreign rulers were inclined to treat with England's queen, the Pope seemed set in his determination to damn her.

Nick had been kept constantly on the move as a courier for Walsingham these many months, returning in secret to England for an interview with Her Majesty before setting out again. It was at this meeting that he had been knighted for services to Elizabeth, though the reason he had given his family for the honour was very different from the truth.

Nick's face was grim as he recalled his last conversation with Walsingham, who was presently in Paris as the Queen's ambassador. It was a position Francis had not desired, for he felt he was needed here in England at such a tense moment, but his own mission had been placed upon him by his masters and was an important one. Walsingham's thankless task was to arrange a marriage if he could with the Duc d'Anjou, but he had confided to Nick that he doubted either party could be brought to the match. However, his diplomatic skills were such that his very presence in France at this moment might prevent an alliance between Her Majesty's most dangerous enemies.

The situation was to say the least fraught with tension, for the mood here in England was uneasy, Norfolk having many supporters who might rise to help an invasion if it came. When questioned, Norfolk had naturally denied any desire to marry Mary Queen of Scots, saying that his earlier plans had been a passing fancy that he had never intended to carry to a conclusion. But such an alliance might still be popular with those who would see England returned to Rome and the Catholic faith.

Cecil and Walsingham believed that the throne would be safer if Elizabeth had a husband by her side, but convincing the Queen was not an easy task. She was skilful at avoiding the subject, and at turning the tables on those who opposed her.

The Queen's marriage was indeed a thorny problem, but for the present Nick had other matters in mind...

'You have been away overlong, Nick.' Annette Wiltord gave him a speaking look from eyes that had been described as being like sapphires. Her pretty mouth was pouting as she waved her fan of painted chicken skin with its handle of polished horn embellished with silver. 'More than eighteen months I have languished for sight of you—and now you come to me and say only that you need to find Oliver Woodville. Now is that the behaviour of a lover, sir?' Her tone was teasing but her eyes showed that she was annoyed.

'Forgive me, Annette,' Nick kissed the hand she offered, smiling at her in the way that had always melted the ladies' hearts and made them his easy conquests. Annette was a widow of some means and had been his mistress before he left on his travels. He had assumed their affair was at an end and that she would have replaced him. Indeed, he was certain that she had not lain in an empty bed these many months pining for him, but the look in her eyes told him that she was prepared to continue their relationship now, should he wish it. 'Perhaps another evening we may spend some time together? However, I would be grateful if you could tell me where I might find Oliver. I was told he had come to London but having tried his house and found it closed I am at a loss and unsure where else to look.'

'I believe he stays in lodgings, having come only for a brief visit—and you may already have missed him, for he did not wish to be long parted from his wife.' The look in her eyes suggested that she had tried to tempt his friend, but he knew Oliver too well. Having settled for marriage he would not lightly betray his love.

'Then if you would give me the direction of his lodgings I may hasten there and hope to catch him before he departs.'

Annette pouted again. 'Only if I have your promise that you will give me your attention soon, Nick.'

'Tomorrow after the masque,' Nick promised, moving to take her in his arms and kiss her full ripe lips so competently that she was near to swooning when he let her go. 'I escort my mother, but later I shall come to you—if you wish?'

'You know I wish it, devil that you are,' Annette said and ran her finger down his cheek. 'No one makes me feel as you do, Nick. The others are merely diversions, to fill the empty hours you refuse to spend with me. No other man can satisfy me as you do.'

'No one man would ever satisfy you,' Nick said a smile on his lips, as he pressed her against him so that she could feel the burn of his arousal. 'But you are a lusty wench and I have been away a long time, and it would be no hardship to lie with you, Annette.'

'Then stay…come to bed,' she said, her eyes willing him to give her the satisfaction she craved. 'Surely your business can wait a little longer?'

'You tempt me mightily,' Nick told her. 'But if I should miss Oliver it will mean a trip into the country. Let me go now, my hot wench, and I shall please you another night.'

With that she had to be satisfied, though she pulled a wry face as he left her with indecent haste once she had supplied the direction he needed. He had never been easy to manage, though often through indolence rather than indifference in the past, but she was aware that something had changed. There was a new purpose, an alertness and eagerness that she had not noticed before…a certain hardness of character that she found fascinating.

In the past Annette had been content with the time Nick was willing to give her, but now she found that she wanted more…much more.

'I vow that you will be the most beautiful of all the ladies at court this night,' Sir William Moor said to his daughter as she twirled for his benefit just before they left for the masque. 'That gown becomes you well, Catherine.'

It was beautifully fashioned in the latest style, with a heavy damask overskirt of white embroidered with gold and sewn with tiny seed pearls. The petticoat was of a pale rose, the hue of which matched a tiny ruff of lace about her neck, and the sleeves had little pink silk rosebuds pinned to them where the shoulders puffed out in the exaggerated style now so popular with the courtiers. From beneath the skirts of her gown, the toes of her tiny satin slippers were just visible; fashioned of white, they had rosettes of pink silk that complemented her toilette.

Around her neck she had twisted a long string of freshwater pearls, which had been coiled twice and then allowed to fall to her waist just above the V of her stomacher. Her hair was dressed in curls across her forehead, but the heavy mass of it tumbled down her back in soft waves that had taken much brushing and pomade to straighten them from their usual unruly state. She wore only a thin net of gold wire encrusted with pearls over her hair, the colour of which rivalled burnished copper that night.

'You flatter me, dearest Father,' Catherine said and kissed his cheek. 'I thank you for it, though I dare say there will be other more beautiful ladies present at court.'

'Not in my eyes,' he assured her. Then, seeing the footman at the parlour door. 'Are the chairs here, Simon?'

'Yes, sir. I summoned them as you ordered…' He hesitated uncertainly. 'Thomas wondered if you wished him to accompany you, Sir William?'

'No, no, I think not,' he replied. 'I accompany the ladies, that should be sufficient, I believe.' He touched the sword at his side confidently.

'Why not let Thomas come with us?' Lady Stamford asked with a little frown as the footman bowed and went out. 'I vow the streets have grown worse these past few years, brother. You have not been to London in an age and the number of beggars and rogues has vastly increased of late.'

'I dare say I can manage a beggar or two,' Sir William replied, stubbornly refusing to listen to his sister's advice. 'Are you ready, Catherine?'

'Yes, Father.' Catherine looked at her aunt's dubious face and wondered if she ought to endorse Lady Stamford's warning. There were many beggars on the street, their limbs encrusted with sores, dressed in rags and often quite wretched creatures. She and Lady Stamford had witnessed more than one attempt at robbery in broad daylight since coming to town, and been glad of Thomas's stout arm, never leaving the house without at least two footmen to accompany them. However, her father was wearing a sword and the presence of a gentleman with such a weapon must surely be protection enough. She smiled at him. 'Yes, quite ready.'

Catherine took her father's arm, Lady Stamford following behind them. Catherine noticed that her aunt stopped to speak with her footman before leaving the house, but no one followed them outside so she imagined that Lady Stamford had decided to be content with her brother's escort.

Catherine was feeling excited by the prospect of her first visit to the court of which she had heard so much. She was also a little nervous, because despite her father's compliments she was certain that there would be more beautiful ladies, who were far more worldly and clever than she could ever hope to be, and she prayed they would not laugh at her for her country ways. However, she knew that her education at her father's hands was second to none, for he had encouraged her to read widely and helped her with her studies himself.

Her aunt had schooled her in the manners expected of her at court, and she knew how to curtsey to the Queen, should that great lady deign to look at her. Lady Stamford was hoping that Her Majesty would do much more than merely speak to her in passing, but Catherine was sure she would not be noticed amongst so many.

Wherever the court chanced to be, in one of the London palaces, at various great houses about the country or at Windsor Castle, where Queen Elizabeth had taken her stand when the uprising was expected, men and women flocked to the royal presence in the hope of being noticed. Why should Catherine Moor be favoured above so many others?

Catherine's thoughts fluttered nervously from one thing to the other as she wondered if Sir Nicholas Grantly might be at the masque that evening. Lady Stamford had told her he was bidden to London but she had seen no sign of…her thoughts were abruptly suspended as she heard a cry from her father. As the chair came to a shuddering halt, she glanced out from behind the curtains that sheltered her from the elements to see that several rough-looking individuals, who appeared to be demanding money, surrounded them.

Sir William had drawn his sword and was facing them fearlessly, clearly intending to fight rather than surrender his family's jewels to these ruffians. The chairmen had put down their burdens, but had made no move to aid Sir William, and it looked to Catherine as if they might take flight at any moment.

'Cowardly dogs!' Sir William lunged at the ruffian nearest to him. 'I'll teach you to attack my family.'

'Give over yer gold and we'll let the women pass…' One of the men, who appeared to be the rogues' leader, seemed undecided whether to rush at Sir William and glanced about uneasily, as though wondering if the chairmen would fight. 'If yer gives us any trouble we'll crack yer 'ead open!'

'Be damned to you, sir. I'll see you in hell first!'

Sir William lunged at him again, nicking his arm with his sword blade and causing him to back off. The man swore fiercely as he caught at the wound, which was bleeding profusely.

'Get 'im!' He yelled his orders and three more of the ruffians advanced on Sir William, who stood his ground, striking out to left and right boldly. But there were more of them than he could manage alone and one of them struck him a blow to his sword arm with a heavy cudgel that made him cry out with pain and drop his weapon.

'Help him,' Catherine cried to one of the chairmen, but from the look on the man's face she could see that it was hopeless to apply for assistance. The two men who had been carrying her aunt's chair had already retreated to a safe distance. Angered at their cowardice, Catherine scrambled from the chair and threw herself into the fray, beating at the back of one of the ruffians with her fists and then hanging on his arm in an attempt to even the odds for her beleaguered father. 'Help us! Someone please come to our aid! Will you not help us?' she screamed desperately. 'In God's name help us or they will kill my father…'

The ruffian she had attacked whirled on her, knocking her backwards with such force that she staggered and fell. It was at that moment, when she lay gasping for breath in the gutter, that she heard shouting from just behind them. Even as she began to recover her breath and look about her, several men came charging up, laying about the ruffians with cudgels and sending them scattering into the night. Catherine glanced up as a helping hand was extended to her and her heart caught as she recognised the gentleman who had come to her rescue. This was the second time he had done so within a month!

'Mistress Moor?' Nick's look of surprise was echoed by his tone. 'Forgive me. I believe we were tardy in coming to your aid and you have suffered some harm.'

'You came in time for me, sir,' she said as he helped her to rise. 'But my father…'

'I am well, Catherine.' Sir William came to them, rubbing at his arm where he had been struck a heavy blow. 'It is mightily sore but not broken, I thank God. We were fortunate that this gentleman brought his fellows to our aid.'

'They are my mother's servants,' Sir Nicholas said. 'She never travels abroad in the evening with less than three footmen, even though I was her escort on this occasion. I think it wise in these dangerous times to employ a stout arm to aid you, sir.'

'As my sister warned me,' Sir William frowned as he saw Lady Stamford's man Thomas standing close by his sister's chair as if to protect it, and realised she must have given orders for the fellow to follow them. 'I thought myself sufficient but now I see the folly of my ways.'

Catherine had become aware that debris was clinging to the skirt of her gown and glanced down at herself in dismay. Her rescuer was elegantly dressed in black slashed with silver on the court breeches, a ruff of silver lace about his throat, and a black cloak slung across one shoulder. A diamond pin nestled in the folds of his lace, and he wore sapphire and ruby rings on his left hand, though she saw that his sword hand was unadorned, as if ready for action.

'I fear your gown is ruined, Mistress Catherine,' Sir Nicholas said as she brushed ineffectively at the skirt. 'It is stained where you were knocked to the ground and the mark will not brush off, I fear.'

'You were foolish to get out of the chair, but very brave.' Catherine's father looked at her in concern. 'Will you not introduce me to this gentleman, daughter, since you appear to know him?'

'This is Sir Nicholas Grantly, of whom my aunt has told you,' Catherine said, with a little blush at being reminded of her manners. 'And this is the second time he has come to our rescue, for he came to our aid when my aunt's carriage suffered an accident on the road.'

'Ah yes, my sister has spoken warmly of you,' Sir William said and offered his hand at once. 'I thank you for your good offices, Sir Nicholas—not just for what you did this evening but your earlier kindness to my sister and daughter.'

'It was my pleasure on both occasions...' Nick was interrupted by the arrival of Lady Stamford's servant, who coughed and looked awkwardly at the ground. 'Yes—you wish to speak to us?'

'My mistress asks if Sir William and Mistress Catherine intend to continue to court?'

'It is not possible this evening. I feel too shaken and Catherine's gown is ruined,' Sir William replied. 'I will have a word with your aunt, Cat. We must not rob her of this evening's pleasure. I shall take you home and she may continue on her way and make our apologies to the Queen.'

'If I may offer Lady Stamford the safety of joining our party this man may see you safely home, Sir William. I would escort you both myself, but my mother has need of me this evening.'

'You are kind to offer your protection to my sister, sir. I am sure she will accept. And since our chairmen have decided to return now that the danger is over, there is nothing to delay her once I have advised her of our plans.'

Catherine glanced shyly at Sir Nicholas as her father walked off and they were left alone together for a moment. 'I must thank you for what you have done this night,' she said. 'Had you not come when you did, sir, I fear my father might have been murdered.'

Nick looked at her but said nothing. Her father's murder might not have been the least of it if he had not come this way, and he blessed his mother for her habit of never going about the city without sufficient escort.

'It is fortunate that we were here,' he said at last.

'I am sorry that your evening has been so rudely spoiled, Mistress Catherine. And it is a shame that beautiful gown has been ruined by your fall. It is most becoming for a lady of your rare colouring; the court will be the poorer for your absence this evening.'

'A gown is neither here nor there, sir,' Catherine replied with a toss of her head, her cheeks warmed by his compliment as her heart beat faster. She breathed deeply, her breasts rising as she fought her agitation, aware that his eyes moved over her and rested for a moment on the creamy mounds partially exposed by the dipping neckline of her gown. 'It may clean and if it does not I shall not repine—for my father's safety is of far more consequence.'

'Indeed.' He smiled over her flash of spirit. 'But 'tis always a shame to despoil beauty. Forgive me, I believe my mother summons me to her. I must leave you and tell her of our altered plans…'

'Yes, of course. I thank you again for your kindness.'

Catherine watched as he walked away, feeling the disappointment sweep over her. Had her gown not been ruined they might have spent some time together at the masque that evening. It was an opportunity lost and she did not know when the chance might come again.

She had climbed into her chair once more by the time her father returned to her. 'Your aunt is most annoyed with me, Catherine,' he told her. 'And indeed she is right. Had we been better protected I think this incident would not have happened. I apologise to you for the loss of your enjoyment this evening, daughter.'

'Oh, Father,' Catherine said gently. 'Please do not blame yourself for what happened. Had I not been so impulsive my gown would not have been spoiled.'

'And perhaps your friend might have been too late to help me. Your brave effort undoubtedly caused those villains pause, Catherine. I dare say your aunt will scold you for it on the morrow, but I can only thank you for what you tried to do.'

'My concern is only for you, Father. I fear you must be in pain. Let us go home so that I may bathe your arm and rub a healing unguent into it or you will not be able to use it by the morning.'

'Yes, child. We shall go home, for I must confess that I feel sore and shaken by what has happened.'

Catherine was glad of her aunt's servant walking beside them on the way home. He was a large, burly man and she knew that her father was not feeling well, though he had not said it in as many words. For him to admit that he was shaken was enough to tell her that he was not his usual self, and she was not surprised when he went straight to his bedchamber.

'Do not trouble yourself, Catherine,' he said when she asked if he would let her tend his arm. 'My man will do whatever is necessary. Forgive me for deserting you. I promise that you shall have a treat another day to make up for your disappointment this evening.'

She shook her head at him, kissing his cheek and assuring him that it was nothing to her, but later, when she was alone in her own bedchamber, she could not help but regret the loss of what might have proved an entertaining evening.

Sitting in the little window embrasure, looking

down at the street below, Catherine heard the watch calling the hour.

Why could she not put Sir Nicholas from her thoughts? Catherine wondered. It was not just that he was an attractive man, but there was something about him that touched a chord within her.

She shook her head, mocking herself for allowing her thoughts to become so foolish. Her first sighting of Sir Nicholas had convinced her that he was a rogue and she would do better not to forget it.

In the morning Sir William sent word that he had decided to spend the day in his chamber, resting. When Catherine hurried to his side, he smiled at her and repeated that she was not to worry, giving her his hand as she sat on the edge of his bed and looked at him anxiously.

'I am not a young man, Catherine,' Sir William said. 'My foolish pride made me think I could protect my family without help, but I shall know better in future. However, this incident has made me aware of my vulnerability. I am well enough for the moment but there cannot be so many years left to me, dearest child, and your aunt is right concerning your marriage—as she is about so many things. If I were to die and leave you unprotected...'

'No, Father!' Catherine's voice held a tremor as she interrupted him. 'I pray you will not talk so. You feel a little unwell this morning but you are still young and I would not have you speak of dying. I pray that we shall have many long and happy years together.'

'No, Catherine,' he said with a shake of his head.

'We must face the truth, daughter. I am not yet failing but my health is not what it once was. We must hope that a suitable marriage presents itself. I shall not force you to a match you cannot like, my word is given on that—but I shall pray most earnestly that a man you could be happy with is moved to offer for you.'

'Let us not quarrel over it, Father,' she said. 'I shall marry if I meet a man I can love as I love you.'

'You may meet someone you could love far more,' her father said and smiled gently. 'When he comes along, Cat, you will know it. Believe me, you will know—and you will glory in his love, for you are very like your dear mother and she was a woman made for love.'

'You loved her very much, Father.'

'So much that no other could ever take her place when I lost her.' There was sadness in his face as she carried his hand to her cheek and she felt the sting of tears. Elizabeth Moor was much missed by them both. 'Go to your aunt now, my dear, and see what plans she has for you today.'

Catherine was thoughtful as she went in search of Lady Stamford. She had never considered marriage until her aunt had insisted that it was her duty to marry, and that had made her rebel against the idea, but her father's words had softened her heart. Perhaps she might want to marry one day if she found a man she could like well enough. After all, her parents had been truly happy, why should she not be as fortunate?

If there was another reason for the softening of Catherine's heart, she was not yet prepared to admit it, but her memory of a man's smile might just have something to do with it.

'Ah, there you are,' Lady Stamford said as she went into the back parlour and found her aunt labouring over her accounts. 'I trust William is being sensible and keeping to his bed this morning?'

'Yes, Aunt. My father feels a little shaken after what happened.'

'The foolish man…' Lady Stamford began, but subsided as she saw Catherine's look. 'Well, well, I shall not scold. We were fortunate that Sir Nicholas happened along. I do hope you thanked him properly for his kindness, Catherine?'

'Yes, of course, Aunt. I could not but be grateful for what he did last evening. Without his timely arrival my father might have been fatally hurt.'

'Yes, indeed. We must thank God for it,' Lady Stamford said. 'Now I must apologise to you, my dear. I had thought your father would take you out today and have made prior arrangements to meet a friend— a very old and wearisome friend whom you would find quite tiring. It was not my intention to ask you to accompany me, though you may if you wish?'

'I think I would rather stay here, Aunt—if you will forgive me? You have been good to take me everywhere these past two weeks and a day spent quietly at home will not hurt me. Besides, I would rather be here if my father should need me. He says he is feeling better, but I am still a little concerned.'

'You are a good girl,' Lady Stamford said. 'It was a shame that your gown was ruined last evening. I have sent it to my seamstress and asked her to take out the panel that was spoiled and replace it if she can so you may yet be able to wear it again. However, your other gowns will be ready soon and Her Majesty understands why you were unable to attend. She commended your courage and said that if she has as brave men about her she can count herself fortunate.'

'Did Her Majesty truly say that, Aunt?'

'I believe she found the tale diverting,' Lady Stamford said, looking thoughtful. 'I naturally apologised for your absence, for a royal invitation is a command, Catherine, and I believed she might be angered, but not so. You will I am sure be commanded to her presence again soon.'

'I thank you for your good offices on my behalf, Aunt.'

'You repay me with good manners, Catherine. Remember them should Sir Nicholas or his mother call on you. Lady Fineden did say she would ask us to dine another night, but we shall see…'

Left to herself after her aunt had gone out, Catherine spent half an hour or so at her needlework but found that it palled and laid it down, venturing into the small courtyard at the back of the house to take a turn about it in the sunshine. Her inactivity irked her, for she had been told that her father was sleeping and she had nothing to do but wait for her aunt's return.

It was as she was about to return to the parlour that she turned to see one of the footmen waiting to see her.

'Your pardon, Mistress Moor—but there is a visitor. A gentleman has called to inquire after Sir William's health.'

'A gentleman?' Catherine stared at him, her heart racing frantically. 'What name did he give?'

'Sir Nicholas Grantly, mistress. I asked him to wait in the small parlour but Sir William's man has given orders that he is not to be disturbed.'

'I shall come at once,' Catherine said. 'The gentleman is known to me. I shall receive him myself. Please request Mistress Pike to bring refreshments to the parlour—some wine and biscuits I think.'

'Yes, of course.'

The footman bowed and went away. Catherine took a deep breath before walking into the parlour. Sir Nicholas was standing by the small window, looking out at the street, his back towards her, but he swung round as she entered, a slow smile spreading across his mouth—a mouth that could only be described as sensuous—and into those grey eyes. Oh, what that smile did to her foolish heart. It was beating so fast that she was sure he must see her agitation.

'Mistress Moor. Forgive me if I intrude? But I came to inquire after your father. He seemed much shaken last evening. My mother was most concerned and scolded me for not accompanying you both home myself. And indeed, I regret that I did not do so, for your need was surely the greater.'

'You do not intrude, sir. I thank you and Lady Fineden for your concern on my father's behalf. He was indeed much shaken by what happened, and I believe his arm pains him a good deal though he denies it. He is resting in his chamber today and may not be disturbed, but I shall tell him of your kindness in coming to inquire.' Catherine smiled as she took a seat in a chair by the fire and gestured to its pair at the other side of the hearth. 'Will you not sit down? I have ordered refreshments, as I am certain my aunt would wish to return the hospitality that was shown us at your good sister's house.'

Nick did not hesitate, sitting at his ease in the chair she indicated, his long shapely legs stretched out in front of him. She noticed that he was again dressed in black that morning, his white shirt showing through the slashing of his handsome velvet doublet. As on the previous evening, his clothes were much finer than he had worn when they had met on the road and at his sister's house, and he looked every inch a courtier of some degree. But there was more than that about him, some indefinable quality that Catherine could not name, but which she found fascinating.

'I hope your father's health will not be long impaired? It would be a shame if we were not to have your company at court, Mistress Catherine. Her Majesty was pleased to ask me for the truth concerning your absence last night, and much entertained when I told her you were as fierce as any bear in defence of its young, hanging on to the ruffian's arm until he threw you off by superior strength. I told her that a lady of your beauty and courage must be brought to court, for we should all be the poorer for the lack. You must know that Gloriana admires spirit more than anything, and she was intrigued by the story.'

'My aunt assured me that Her Majesty would invite me to attend her again, but I feared I might have offended. I am glad that it was not so.' Catherine blushed as she met his look, which seemed almost to burn her with its heat. Why did she find her eyes drawn to his mouth so often! She looked down, feeling slightly breathless, and was a little relieved when the housekeeper brought in their wine. 'Ah, thank you, Mistress Pike. You will take a glass of wine, Sir Nicholas?'

'I thank you, Mistress Catherine.' Nick bestowed his warm smile on the housekeeper. 'Did you make those delicious-looking biscuits yourself, ma'am?'

'Why yes, sir.' The woman dimpled at him and placed the dish of almond comfits on a small board set on a stand close to his hand. 'Should you need anything else, Mistress Catherine, you have only to ask...'

'I have never seen Mistress Pike dimple before,' Catherine said after the door was safely closed behind her. She smiled, her green eyes unconsciously alight with teasing laughter. 'I think you are a rogue, Sir Nicholas. Do you charm all the ladies so?'

Nicholas chuckled softly in his throat, amused by her show of spirit. He had been trying to charm her and she knew it—no fool then, the little Moor. Yet he would swear Matthew was right and there was fire beneath the ice. Indeed, the ice had already begun to melt several degrees.

'How is it that you have found me out so swiftly, Mistress Catherine?'

'I saw you on the way to London—you were watching a play with those ruffians who caused the trouble...' She broke off and frowned at him. 'That was not well done of you, sir. The poor man was doing his best to entertain us.'

'And making a poor show of it.'

'You and your friends did not make his task easier, sir, for you taunted him dreadfully.'

'Nay! I beg you acquit me of the charge, Mistress Catherine. I am guilty of many things, but I am not so ill-mannered—though I admit to being amused by their jesting. He did take so very long over his dying. You must admit it was overlong?'

'Yes, I shall not deny that,' Catherine said. His tone was teasing and his eyes were full of gentle mockery, and she responded in kind. 'But I saw you laughing and calling out insults to that poor man—though I do not believe you threw anything at him.'

'Nor was I a part of the company who did,' Nick said, his smile warm with merriment. 'But I will admit that I was not kind to the poor fellow—and I did not know that I was being watched by a lady of your tender heart.'

Catherine's cheeks were on fire as she met his look. Was he flirting with her? She was confused and yet pleased by his teasing looks, her heart fluttering like a dove in a cage.

'Do you claim you would have behaved less unkindly if you had?'

'To win your approval? Indeed, I should have beaten off those who taunted him. I was a fool else, Mistress Catherine, for a lady of your beauty and sweet nature is seldom met with.'

'My nature is not always sweet,' Catherine said, pouting at him. 'I have claws, sir, and may use them when minded to do so.'

'Ah, I might have known such a rose would have

its thorns,' Nick said wickedly. 'But a scratch from thorns that adorn thee, sweet rose, would be sweeter than a kiss to me…'

'Are you a poet, Sir Nicholas?' Catherine laughed at his words, which were clearly designed to flatter and cajole. 'You have a way with you, sir. None could deny it in truth. But despite your silver tongue, I still think you are a rogue.'

'Every man must have a silver tongue at Gloriana's court,' Nick replied. 'And it is as well to be able to pen a few lines to the mistress you would court. A true troubadour never lets the sun go down without a poem for his love.'

'I dare say your flattery goes well with the ladies of the court,' Catherine said, standing up to take a turn about the room. His looks and words had brought a flame to her cheeks and she felt a little giddy with excitement. For the first time she was aware that she was flirting with danger by entertaining a gentleman alone. Did he think her fast—would he attempt to seduce her? Indeed, he was succeeding without trying too hard, for her foolish heart was beating like a drum. 'But I am…'

She turned and discovered that he had come up behind her and was standing close to her, his eyes intent on her face, burning her with their heat, setting her whole body aflame. His mouth was soft and somehow tempting to her, and her lips parted on a sighing breath as something stirred within her—some desire or longing she had never felt until this moment.

'You are lovely, perfect…' Nick said huskily. 'I

vow you have bewitched me, Mistress Catherine. I languished all night for thinking of you.'

His words were true enough, for he had forgone his tryst with Annette because he could not get a picture of Catherine Moor out of his head, and he had lain sleepless in his bed thinking of her. The glimpse of her white breasts above the revealing neckline of her gown had set him to wondering about the softness of her skin and the gentle curves of her lovely flesh. How sweet it would be to lie with her!

'Fie on you, sir!' Catherine laughed. 'You flatter me but I...' She caught her breath as he moved towards her, certain that he meant to kiss her and not sure what she would do then, but even as she trembled inwardly she heard her aunt's voice calling in the hallway and knew that she was saved. 'Ah, my good aunt is home. She will be delighted to see you, sir.'

'And I to see her, of course,' Nick replied but looked so disappointed that Catherine could not hold back her laughter.

She was laughing as Lady Stamford swept into the room, her eyes sparkling like precious jewels as she turned to greet her.

'Sir Nicholas called to inquire after my father. Was that not kind of him, Aunt?'

'Exceeding kind,' Lady Stamford said. 'I hurried home lest you were fretting, Catherine, but now I see you have been well entertained.'

'Mistress Catherine was good enough to see me in your absence,' Nick said coming smoothly to her rescue. 'And we laughed over Her Majesty's comments last even. Now, I must come to the second purpose of my visit, ma'am. My mother Lady Fineden begs that you will bear her company at a picnic tomorrow by the river—if such a pastime is agreeable to you?'

'Thank your mother for her kindness,' Lady Stamford replied looking pleased. 'We shall be delighted to come, sir.'

'Then I shall take my leave of you, sweet ladies.' Nick's eyes dwelt on Catherine for a moment. 'I look forward to seeing you tomorrow, and shall send an escort for you so that you may easily find the appointed place.'

'We shall look forward to seeing you, sir,' Catherine replied, a little flush of pleasure in her cheeks.

Catherine's aunt gave her an odd look but said no more as Nick bowed and went out, merely remarking a little later that it was a kind thought on Lady Fineden's part to invite them to a picnic.

'I have heard that her home has a splendid garden that leads down to the river,' Lady Stamford said. 'I imagine we shall be somewhere nearby.'

'We must hope the weather keeps fine.'

'Yes, indeed,' her aunt replied. 'And now I must go up and see how William is, for it would be a shame if he were not able to accompany us tomorrow.'

'Father would not wish us to give up our pleasure, even if he did not feel able to come with us.'

Lady Stamford looked at her thoughtfully for a moment, then inclined her head. 'I am sure you are right, Catherine.'

'Besides, we have promised to go.' Catherine's cheeks flushed as her aunt was silent.

'I know a little of the family,' she said at last. 'Lady Fineden is a woman of some influence, as is her husband, and Sir Nicholas comes from an old family. I shall say no more, Catherine, but he has a reputation for being a charmer…'

The morning dawned fine and bright as Catherine had hoped, but though her father came down to the small parlour when she and her aunt were being served some coddled eggs and fresh muffins with butter and honey, he told his daughter that he preferred to stay at home and rest for another day.

'If you feel unwell I shall stay with you,' Catherine offered, though her heart sank at the prospect of missing the promised treat.

'You have already suffered a loss of pleasure because of my foolishness,' Sir William said smiling at her. 'I shall not ask another sacrifice of you, Catherine. You must go to your picnic and Helen must accompany you. I shall do well enough here with a book of poems to keep me company. If it is fine I may sit in the garden for a while.'

Catherine kissed her father and thanked him for his thoughtfulness on her behalf, for which she received an affectionate pat on the cheek.

She spent some time sitting with him in the best parlour until their escort arrived. Within minutes they were ready to leave, setting out with Thomas walking beside their chairs as well as the escort Sir Nicholas had sent to show them the way. Despite seeing a few beggars standing or lying at the street corners, they met with no trouble and were eventually taken to a pretty spot on the riverbank.

Lady Fineden's was a handsome house situated down river from the Palace of Whitehall, and sat on the opposite bank in a pleasant spot that had not yet been encroached on by the press of building that was springing up all around the city.

However, they did not enter the house itself and were taken through the gardens to where a picnic had been set out a little distance from the water's edge.

Sir Nicholas had clearly been awaiting their arrival, for he immediately left a group of ladies and gentlemen with whom he had been conversing, and came to welcome them, taking Catherine by the hand to introduce her to his mother.

Lady Stamford was already slightly acquainted with her hostess and many of the guests, but they were all unknown to Catherine and the first half an hour or so was taken up with meeting and greeting strangers. She was asked her opinion of London, and whether or not she had been to court, but after a while the conversation became more general. Most of the ladies seemed to prefer gossip from the court, but there was also some talk of politics amongst the men.

In February of that year the Pope had excommunicated Elizabeth by means of the Bull Regnans in Excelsis, by which he hoped to see the Queen deposed and Mary of Scots raised to Queen in her place. This had given cause for fears amongst those loyal to Elizabeth that the Catholics would see this as a reason to rebel, though with the failure of the uprising the previous year others thought it unlikely.

The talk of politics held no interest for Catherine, who, once left to herself, was more than content to look about her and enjoy the sunshine. She sat on large soft cushions while Lady Fineden's servants served the meal, tasting the delicious cold fowl, pies and pastries, which were accompanied by wine cooled in the river. It was after the food had been consumed that everyone began to stroll about the gardens, admiring the splendid view.

Catherine stood up and went down to the water's edge, where a pair of swans and five signets were leisurely swimming by. A dragonfly skimmed over the surface of the river, and swallows were swooping on the warm current to catch their food.

'I have often thought this a pleasant spot,' Nick said, coming to stand by her side. 'Especially on such a day as this.'

'Yes, almost idyllic,' Catherine replied, turning her head to look at him. 'One would hardly think the city is all around us.'

'Building goes on apace,' Nick said. 'I dare say much of this open land will be eaten up in years to come.'

'Yes, perhaps.' Catherine's heart raced as she glanced at him and saw the warmth in his eyes.

'Would you care to stroll for a while?'

'I thank you, yes,' Catherine said, the sudden drumming of her heart making her a little shy, giving her the appearance of being reserved. 'Tell me, sir, are you pleased to be home in England—or shall you soon be off on your travels again?'

'I do not know for sure,' Nick replied, looking se-

rious for a brief moment. 'It is as the fancy takes me.'
He could not tell her that he must do as he was ordered, for his work was secret and must remain so.
'For a while I hope to be here in London.' He smiled
at her. 'Perhaps I may be of service to you, mistress?
I should be happy to escort you about the city at any
time, should you wish it.'

'You are very kind to offer, sir.'

Why did he look at her so particularly? They had
wandered towards a small copse, and now Catherine
realised they were away from the rest of the company,
suddenly alone.

'It would be my pleasure, sweet Catherine,' Nick
said, his voice husky and compelling as he looked at
her. 'You are very lovely…so lovely that you tempt
me sorely.'

'I do not know what you mean, sir.'

Catherine's cheeks were heated as she gazed into
his eyes and found herself mesmerised by what she
seemed to find in them.

'Do you really not know, Catherine?'

His eyes seemed to hold her like a trapped bird in
the palm of his hand. He trailed a finger down her
cheek, following the line of her throat down, down to
lie in the valley between her breasts, and she could
almost feel the touch of his fingers against her skin
though the material of her gown lay between them.
She swallowed hard, her mouth suddenly dry, as she
felt an explosion deep within her and knew all at once
what ailed her. Her heart raced as he reached out for
her, drawing her close to him, and she felt that she
could scarcely breathe.

'I can feel your heart beating, Catherine. I think it beats for me.'

'Sir, I do not know what…'

'Then I must show you, my sweeting.'

Nick bent his head, touching his mouth to hers in a soft, gentle kiss that made her want to swoon for pleasure. She could scarce prevent herself from moaning for sheer joy, pressing her fingers to her lips as he released her at last. She stared at him, shocked and yet thrilled by what had passed between them.

He was courting her! Surely it must be so. Catherine was as yet completely innocent of the ways of men, having never been kissed until this moment. As her father's dearest companion, she had never found the time nor had the inclination to indulge in light flirtations, and this sudden attention from a man of Sir Nicholas's stature was like heady wine that made her feel a little dizzy.

'I do not think you should have done that, sir,' she said breathlessly.

'Perhaps not,' Nick agreed, a teasing smile on his mouth. 'But did you not find it pleasant, Catherine?'

'Perhaps,' she said, unwilling to let him see how much it had affected her. She might be innocent but she was not foolish. 'Yet still I think you took too much liberty.'

Nick's hand caressed her cheek, one finger lingering for a moment at the base of her throat. 'It would be sweet to know you better, Catherine.'

'I am not sure that would be either right or proper.'

'Ah, there you have me,' Nick admitted. 'But love takes no account of these things. I would make you forget the foolish morality of a maiden's world, my pretty wench, and give you more pleasure than you have yet known, I'll swear.' He was breathing hard, and she felt the force of his passion as his mouth moved against her hair. 'I burn for you, sweet Catherine.'

His words and his looks were making her feel strange, and somewhere inside her there was a swirling heat that threatened to consume her.

'I think you are a rogue, sir. You assault my proper modesty.'

'Catherine, sweet rose of many thorns…'

'Catherine—are you there, Niece?'

Lady Stamford's voice came to them, bringing Catherine from the trance into which she had fallen and breaking the spell that held them both in thrall.

'I must go,' she whispered, breaking away from him. 'My aunt calls me.'

'I shall take you to your aunt,' Nick said, realising that he had almost let himself be carried away by her sensuous allure and his own desires. He had forgotten for a moment that she was an innocent girl of good family, and must be treated accordingly. 'Forgive me if my teasing went too far. You must blame it on the sweetness of the day, and your beauty, Mistress Catherine.'

Catherine smiled and shook her head, feeling too confused to answer. Such passionate lovemaking must surely mean that he cared for her? It was too soon to think of arranging a match between them, of course, but he would speak to her father before very long, she was sure of it. Why else would he have spoken to her the way he had?

'Indeed, there is no need, sir. I am sure Lady Fineden wishes you to remain and entertain her guests.'

'The guests are leaving,' Nick replied. 'And it is my pleasure to see you and Lady Stamford safely home.'

Catherine could say no more on the subject, and her aunt seemed well content to accept his offer of an escort.

There was no opportunity for them to be alone on the return journey, though Sir Nicholas insisted on coming in and paying his respects to Catherine's father.

'I shall hope to see you again soon,' he said, looking most particularly at Catherine. 'I believe my mother has invited you to dine with her one evening next week?'

'Indeed she has,' Lady Stamford said, 'and I have accepted on my brother's behalf for us all.'

'If I may be of service at any time…' Nick left the invitation open as he bowed over her hand. 'Mistress Catherine. Perhaps you might like to see a play one afternoon?'

Catherine intimated that she would enjoy such an outing, and Sir Nicholas took his leave.

Catherine was about to go upstairs and change her gown a few minutes later when her aunt came after her.

'A word of warning, Niece…'

'Of warning, Aunt?' Catherine's heart quickened as

she met Lady Stamford's look. 'I fear I do not understand you.'

'Lady Fineden was telling me that she despairs of her son ever taking a bride. I believe he is accustomed to take his pleasure where he will, and that, my dear, makes him a dangerous young man for you to know.'

'Why, Aunt, I thought you liked him?'

'Indeed, I like him very well, but I am not a young virgin with much to lose,' her aunt replied. 'I know you to be a girl of sense, Catherine, but it is as well to be on your guard.'

'Sir Nicholas helped my father,' Catherine replied with dignity. 'I am merely doing as you bid me in being polite to him.'

'Then I shall say no more. It was for your own sake that I spoke.'

Catherine went on up the stairs, her cheeks warm. What would her aunt say if she knew that Catherine had allowed Sir Nicholas to make love to her that afternoon? Her heart raced as she recalled his wicked, teasing looks and the words that had hinted at a pleasure she had never known. She was not so innocent that she did not know what he meant, and though she had rebuffed him, she had allowed him to become too forward. And yet her heart told her that he had been serious in his intent, his looks too warm to be merely flirtation.

He had been intent on seducing her! How could she doubt it? But he must love her to have spoken to her so passionately. It was the urgency of his love that had caused him to make love to her so wantonly that afternoon. It must be so.

Lady Stamford would change her tune when Sir Nicholas spoke to her father, as he surely would. Catherine nursed her secret happiness to herself as she continued to her chamber.

She had thought herself immune to love, but how quickly her heart had succumbed to a man's smile. It was foolish to be so sure on such short acquaintance, but how could she doubt when he had kissed her so sweetly that her insides turned to liquid honey?

Chapter Four

A little smile touched Nick's mouth as he walked towards his mother's house. He was thinking of that moment when he had seen a spark of fire smoulder in Catherine Moor's eyes, the moment he had been tempted to take her down to the sweet grass with him, to posses her utterly and throw caution to the devil. Truly, he had burned for her, desiring her in a way that he had not felt for a long time—if ever.

He had held back only because his mind told him that she was not a wench for an easy bedding, to be treated lightly as he might some other women who surrendered too easily, with a careless charm that could sometimes hurt without his meaning it. In the past he had taken his mistresses for their beauty and spirit, giving generously of his wealth but little of himself. Though his body had clamoured to possess Catherine, his senses had told him that she was different from the women he had known in the past, and he had hesitated at the last second, both relieved and disappointed by Lady Stamford's untimely arrival.

But perhaps it was a welcome respite, he reflected,

a rueful smile about his sensuous mouth. An affair once begun with Catherine Moor, a girl of impeccable virtue and good family, could sensibly have but one ending, and Nick was not yet certain he was ready for marriage. Lady Fineden often spoke of his marriage, sometimes with a touch of impatience, reminding him that it was his duty to provide an heir for the estate. And indeed, he knew that it was his duty to marry, though perhaps not just yet.

Sarah had told him more than once that he knew not what he was missing by staying single. She had often tried to tempt him in the past by bringing young, pretty girls to his notice, but he had disappointed her by ignoring their coquettish smiles, preferring the sophisticated women of the court who were willing to entertain his games of intrigue and passionate love-play. Yet he knew that Sarah had his interests at heart, and he had considered taking a bride in the future simply to please her.

'I want to see you happy, Nick,' Sarah had said, giving him a hug as he took his leave of her this last time. 'It is not good to be always alone, my Brother.'

Sometimes Nick wondered if his sister, to whom he was closer than any other these days, had guessed that there was a lonely place inside him that no woman had yet been able to fill.

He had been this way since Harry's death, afflicted from time to time with a melancholy concerning the brother he had worshipped from afar as a young lad. Perhaps it was because Harry had died in a foreign land, without his family about him, that his death still haunted Nick's mind in the dark hours. He had never been able to rid himself of the idea that there had been something unnatural about the fever that robbed Harry Grantly of life. Yet Oliver Woodville had assured him that an eminent physician had been called and everything possible had been done that might have saved him.

'It is an illness named Roman fever,' he had told Nick and his family. 'An illness that often afflicts visitors to the city, and one that is too often fatal.'

'But Harry was so strong…' Nick had thought that for a moment doubt flickered in Oliver Woodville's eyes, as though he too had had his doubts, but if he had he had kept them to himself, perhaps thinking to save the family more grief.

Nick's father had also grieved for his eldest son, and his sorrow may have helped to hasten his death, though the months he had spent in the Tower for a treasonable offence he had not committed had ruined his constitution. Because of his father's ailing health, Nick had taken over the running of the estate, going to court only after his death.

He had spent just over a year there, idling his time away, taking his choice of women eager to be his mistress and discarding them at will, and earning himself the reputation of a heartless flirt, until his chance came to do something useful with his life.

In his heart, Nick knew that he had seized his opportunity to travel abroad, retracing the journey his brother had taken on the grand tour with Oliver Woodville and one other youth, in the hope of discovering what had truly happened to Harry. Of course it had been impossible after so many years, even though he had spoken in length to the physician who had treated Harry in his last illness. The fever had apparently been a virulent one, but quite common in travellers, and the leech had assured him that he suspected no foul play. Yet still Nick had the uneasy feeling that something was not right about his brother's death.

It was perhaps because he was conscious of having unfinished business that he had been unable to find for himself the content and happiness Sarah had discovered within her marriage. But now there was Mistress Catherine Moor, and Nick knew that she had affected him powerfully in a way no other woman ever had. So much so that he was unable to put her from his thoughts. But he must do so!

There were other things with which he ought to occupy his mind. His search for his brother's close friend Oliver had so far proved fruitless, since he appeared to have left for Leicestershire the very morning Nick had arrived in London, and he had decided to give up his quest for the time being.

Perhaps after all he had been mistaken about the identity of a man briefly glimpsed in the shadows after his last meeting with Walsingham. It was unlikely to have been the person he had thought he vaguely recognised. It was years since he'd last seen the rather weak and effeminate youth his brother and Oliver had spurned so scornfully.

Nick had seen all three young men talking together shortly before they left for the grand tour with their bear leader, a man much trusted by all the families concerned. Though Oliver and Harry had been the best

of friends, Nick had seen at once that the third youth
felt left out, inadequate because of their superior
height and strength, and as a younger brother himself,
Nick had understood. He had wondered that his
brother seemed not to realise that he and Oliver had
upset the other youth with their careless jests. It was
strange that Nick could recall the quickly hidden look
of anger in the youth's eyes but not his name.

By what name had he been called? Nick was
damned if he could recall it, try as he might.

If he could but put a name to the face his mind
might be at rest. But why let it tease him? It was
unlikely that the youth who had accompanied Oliver
and Harry on that grand tour years before was the man
who had followed Nick in Paris. But could the man
he had glimpsed in the shadows have been that youth?
Nick remembered him as being slight and ineffectual
and there had surely been something sinister about that
man of shadows. Something odd that had caused Nick
to be uneasy for some time afterwards. Yet mayhap
all was in his mind! Perhaps he should put these things
behind him and begin to think of the future, and of
taking a wife…

Walking into the house, he was met by his mother's
steward, who told him that Lady Fineden wished to
speak to him as soon as he came in and was awaiting
him in her private parlour.

The message was clearly urgent, and Nick wasted
no time in going to his mother, all other considerations
pushed aside as he was alerted to the possibility of a
meeting with the man he most needed to see.

'You are summoned by Cecil urgently,' she told

him when he entered her parlour. 'The summons came an hour ago, Nick. Where have you been this age?'

'Seeing Mistress Moor and her aunt safely to their home.' He smiled at her. 'Did you think I had fled the country?'

'You are pleased to jest,' she said, shaking her head at him. 'I would not have thought your errand would take so long, but your business is your own. I was merely anxious because the message was urgent, Nick—and Cecil does not like to be kept waiting, as you know.'

'Then I shall not keep him longer,' Nick replied. The smile died from his eyes as he left the house once more. Sir William Cecil must have some mission for him, which meant that he might not be able to call on Mistress Moor as soon as he had planned…

Catherine's heart quickened as she heard the knocker and then her aunt's housekeeper speaking to someone in the hallway. Was it Sir Nicholas come to call at last as he had promised?

She was disappointed when the gentleman was shown into the parlour. Lord Branwell was an elderly friend of her aunt's and had called twice before this. She managed to greet him with a smile, walking away to gaze out of the window as he was welcomed effusively by Lady Stamford. It was hard to hide her feelings when her mind was in such turmoil. Why had Sir Nicholas not come? Had something befallen him, or had he never meant to come at all?

More than a week had passed now since his last visit, and they were due to dine with Lady Fineden that evening. Catherine had made all manner of excuses to stay at home each day, even though her father was quite recovered and had offered to take her about the city, saying that she must have a new gown to replace the one that had been spoiled in his defence. When forced to go out at her aunt's insistence, she had been on thorns until they returned to the house lest Sir Nicholas should have been and gone in their absence, but although others had called and left messages there was none from him.

'Are you listening, Catherine? Lord Branwell has just told you something of importance.'

'Forgive me.' Catherine turned apologetically as she heard the sharp note in her aunt's voice. 'My mind was elsewhere I fear, sir. I did not hear you address me. Pray tell me again what you said, if you please.'

'Of course, my dear,' he said smiling kindly at her. Too old to desire her for himself, he was still aware of her exceptional beauty. 'Her Majesty has charged me with the task of seeing you and your family safe to court next Monday. There is be a banquet and I am to provide an escort so that there is no mishap this time, Mistress Catherine.'

'You are kind, sir—and I am grateful to Her Majesty for her graciousness in inviting us so soon.'

If she was to go to court she might see Sir Nicholas there! But she was foolish to let herself hope. If he really cared for her he would have kept his promise to take her to a play one afternoon, which must mean that he had merely been flirting with her. How painful that thought was, Catherine realised, pricking at her pride as well as her heart. What a simpleton he must have thought her! She had been near to surrender that afternoon by the river, and only the presence of others had prevented her from giving herself to him.

Foolish, foolish Catherine! That she who had considered herself unwilling to marry could have allowed her heart to be so easily stolen was beyond understanding.

She went to sit down on a stool near her aunt, giving her mind to the present company and determined not to think of Sir Nicholas again. Perhaps they would meet at Lady Fineden's that evening, and if they did not—why, she was sure it did not matter to her!

'We had thought we might see Sir Nicholas this evening.' Lady Stamford said the words that had hovered on Catherine's tongue since their arrival at the Finedens' house but which she had not dared to utter. 'Is he not to dine with us?'

'My son left on some business of his own almost a week ago,' Lady Fineden said waving her hand in a vague manner. 'I fear Nicholas is apt to disappear without telling anyone of his intentions. He has always been unpredictable and easily bored. No doubt he grew tired of London and went off somewhere with a friend. He will return when it pleases him, as he always does.'

Lady Fineden cheerfully maligned her son, not realising that every word she spoke was like a dagger in the heart of the girl who had pinned her hopes to seeing him at dinner. That Nicholas had gone on some urgent business for Cecil, his mother did not doubt, but the very fact that he had left no more than a curt note for her saying he was not sure when he would return meant that it was secret and must not be revealed by careless talk. Nicholas had been known for his casual behaviour at court in the past, and it was better to prolong the myth that he was still interested in seeking only pleasure …less dangerous for him and confusing for his enemies.

'Mistress Annette Wiltord was asking after him only yesterday. I believe they have some understanding, though of what kind I dare not think—but he went off without bidding her farewell and I fear she was not best pleased.' Lady Fineden beamed at her guests. 'But come, let us repair to the dining table, for the meal is ready to be served. You must sit by me, Mistress Catherine, and tell me how you like being in London. I believe it is your first visit, my dear?'

Sir Nicholas had gone away without a word to her! Oh, how could he do such a wicked thing after the way he had made love to her?

'I like it well enough, ma'am,' Catherine replied, forcing a smile to her lips. She did not know whether her feelings were more inclined to anger or distress. How could Sir Nicholas flirt with her the way he had when he had an understanding with another woman? He had led her to think…but no, she had allowed herself to believe that he liked her. It was clear now that he had been merely flirting with her to while away an idle half an hour. She had flattered herself into thinking that the way he'd looked at her meant something more. 'The attack on my father was distressing, but no harm was done—due entirely to your servants,

Lady Fineden. I must thank you for what they did that night.'

She would not praise Sir Nicholas, even though she knew that it was his commanding presence that had made the villains take instant flight. But he was himself a rogue, for he had harmed her more than those robbers, taking something far more precious than mere jewels. Oh, she had been such a fool to be taken in by his smiles and his teasing kisses!

He had made her love him, but she would not let him break her heart. She would fight the tears that threatened her so shamefully, and she would put him out of her heart and mind. He was not worth one single tear!

'I do not know what might have happened had you not come along when you did, my lady.'

Lady Fineden nodded and smiled but made no further comment on the incident. Her servants had begun to serve the first of many rich courses, which the taster first tried himself, then served to his mistress and her guests. Bewildered by the sheer volume of the food, Catherine managed a mouthful of the baked carp and a morsel of the suckling pig, which had been roasted on the spit to perfection. She picked at the boiled fowl but refused the neats' tongues and the pigeons in wine, tasting only the merest trifle of jugged hare with a side dish of onions and greens.

'You eat very daintily, Mistress Catherine,' her host said, looking anxious as she refused yet another dish of creamed neaps. 'Is the food not to your liking?'

'It is delicious, ma'am,' Catherine assured her hastily. 'But I am not accustomed to such rich and varied fare.'

'I do pride myself that I keep a good table,' Lady Fineden said with a smile of satisfaction. 'My husband is a hearty trencherman, and I like to feed my guests well—but perhaps you will taste a sweet junket or a syllabub?'

'Thank you, I shall have the syllabub if I may.'

Catherine sipped her wine, which was strong and gradually easing the pain and shock she had felt on hearing of Sir Nicholas's desertion. For he had deserted her! He had promised to visit her soon and he had broken his word. What a wicked rascal he was! Would he were here now. He should feel the rough side of her tongue if she but had the opportunity.

Anger had been growing steadily inside her throughout the evening, for Lady Fineden's conversation was freely spiced with anecdotes of her son. A picture was building up in Catherine's mind of a very spoiled young man who had showered his favours on half the ladies at the Court, if his mother's words could be trusted. It was clear that Lady Fineden was proud of her handsome, devil-may-care son, and thought his exploits a great jest with which to entertain her guests.

For Catherine the evening was lengthy and painful and she longed to be able to escape to the privacy of her bedchamber. But by the time she was at last alone, the burning desire to weep had left her. Now a cold anger had taken root, and she was determined not to pine for the handsome young man who had so wantonly stolen her heart.

She would not allow herself to be hurt by his careless behaviour. She would forget that she had found him attractive, and that his kisses had made her near to swooning.

Indeed, she would not think of him again, Catherine decided. It was as she had always suspected, men were not to be trusted—apart from her father, and her cousin Willis, who were both good men. She had known that Sir Nicholas was a rogue from the start, and it was her own fault for letting him break down the barriers between them. He should not do so again!

She blew out her candle and settled down in her goose-feather bed. Instead of pining for a man who did not deserve her regard, she would make the most of her time at court, and when it was time to go home she would do so with a good heart.

She had been a fool even to think of marriage. It would be much better to stay quietly at home with her beloved father, who despite his words of caution would live to a long and contented old age with his daughter to care for him.

Her eyes closed and she slept at last, though her dreams made her cry out a few times, and tears to trickle down her cheeks, but when she woke she had no memory of them.

Staring out into the moonlit gardens of the British Embassy in Paris, from the bedchamber in which he was staying for the night, Nick's thoughts were far away from his surroundings. His stay here was to be a temporary one, for in the morning he must be on his travels again. He had been asked to return to Italy for a purpose that he had been warned to keep secret to himself alone.

At their meeting in London, Sir William Cecil had told him only that Walsingham had requested his services urgently, and Nick had been obliged to leave the city immediately. He had ridden to Greenwich, where he took ship for France, making his way to Paris with all speed.

His instructions had been to tell no one where he was going, his mission strictly secret. Forbidden to tell even his mother of his plans, Nick had been unable to send word to Mistress Moor of his departure.

It was as well, he thought, that he had not begun a serious courtship, for she would else have thought him a careless flirt for abandoning her. The temptation to seduce her that day by the river had been strong in him, and he had flirted with her a little. Yet he was in no position to begin a courtship for the moment. His life could be at risk, snuffed out like the flame of a candle at any second. Should he decide in the future that he wished to marry, there must be an end to these dangerous missions, but for the moment he believed he was needed and therefore all thoughts of self and the fascinating Mistress Moor must be put aside.

Walsingham was convinced that Ridolfi was not the only plotter behind the move towards a Spanish invasion. He had caught wind of another man he wanted Nick to discover if he could—a man of shadows.

'He has something of the look of an Italian,' Walsingham had told Nick at one of their recent meetings. 'An agent I trust described him to me in his report as slight of build, a little effeminate in his manner—the kind of man you would not give a second glance. My agent thinks his hair is dark and yet his beard had a slight touch of red. Others say he is fair, and yet all these reports seem to be of the same man—what think you, Nick? I value your opinion.'

'You think he assumes a disguise at will?' Nick looked thoughtful as Walsingham nodded. 'A dangerous man indeed, sir, if your suspicions are correct. And yet, if I am right, I seem to remember that you had some doubts concerning John Dee?'

'Mayhap I was wrong on this occasion, though it is possible that the man we seek has dealings in secret with Dee. I believe he has consulted Her Majesty's astrologer on matters of the occult. My opinion of Dee has not changed. He will bear watching, but recent communications from my agents lead me in another direction for the moment. As I told you before, I have but crumbs to feed my theories on for now.'

'And what of Ridolfi?'

'Cecil believes that Ridolfi was the prime mover in this affair, and I was of the same mind until this latest report—but now I have this picture building in my mind. I sense a brooding shadow that menaces the future of this realm and its Queen, and I shall not rest until I have the truth.'

'I shall do my best to discover what I can,' Nick promised. 'But how do your investigations go otherwise?'

'Slowly but surely. I swear we shall have all the proof we need to send Norfolk back to the Tower before the year is out.'

'Surely the root of the present threat to Her Majesty

lies with Norfolk? He is the head—cut it off and the body is powerless. Without him I think Spain would hesitate to invade England, even for the prize of the duel crowns of Scotland and England.'

'If only it were so easy. I fear the monster hath many heads, and as fast as we cut one off it will grow another like the Gorgon of ancient mythology.'

'Mayhap you are right.' Nicholas frowned. 'I shall follow the lead your man gave you, though if this man of darkness is as clever as you believe, it will not be easy to pick up his scent.'

'You name him aptly,' Walsingham said. 'He is truly a man of darkness and may well seek to enhance his powers through the occult—I vow this business has the stench of sulphur about it.'

'Nay, sir,' Nicholas said, a mocking twist to his lips. 'Tell me not that you believe in such practices?'

'It ill behoves a man to mock the practice of al-chemy and other black arts that those who worship Satan indulge in, Nicholas. Witches have used a mix-ture of medicine and prayer to cure the sick for cen-turies past, and been forced to desist from their wicked ways. It is no more than thirty years at most since they were allowed to go free with a payment of a fine. Now such creatures are more harshly punished for their crimes and unfairly, so I have thought, when they seek only to heal—but there are those who act in secret, more for their own gain than for the good of others. Men who call demons up at will to help them in their wicked work. I believe our man may be of their num-ber.'

Nick had smiled inwardly, for he had ever taken

matters of religion lightly, believing that a man was entitled to worship in his own way as long as he did no harm to others. He had always suspected that Satan was no more than a myth the clergy used to confound the common folk and keep them in their place. This talk of satanic powers seemed to him very like the tales that his old nurse had told him of Jenny Greenteeth when he was a lad. The nurse had vowed that if he did not behave the ogress would come up from the depths of the bottomless pool in which she lived and devour him for her supper.

Nick believed in a power for good and a power for evil, but was not as superstitious as many of his contemporaries, who most certainly considered demons to be both real and powerful. He had never sought the help of an astrologer nor been tempted to have his chart cast, sure that his future lay in his own hands. But there were many amongst commoner and noble alike who believed completely in the power of demons, and that they could inhabit a person's body, taking them over and destroying their lives. To Nick, a man fiercely independent of mind, that had always seemed unlikely. He believed in the power of a man to shape his own destiny, to fight the temptations that came to haunt his darkest hours.

Now, standing alone in the darkness, Nick found himself thinking once more about his brother's death. Italy had the reputation of being a country of subterfuge and subtle poisons, intrigue and treachery long woven into the fabric of the ruling elite. Was it possible that his brother Harry could have been poisoned or that his death had been due to some black spell?

And if so, who had been responsible? Not Oliver Woodville or their tutor, a man trusted by Nick's father—but possibly another. A youth so jealous of his companions that he might kill…

What nonsense was this? Nick mocked himself for his thoughts, which were surely foolish, letting them turn once more to Catherine Moor. He smiled, finding these thoughts vastly more pleasing, though also frustrating. He would have liked to continue what he had begun by the river that day. She had stirred his senses, arousing a feeling so intense that for a few minutes he had forgotten himself. She was a tempting wench and he found her both exciting and desirable. However, it would be some months before he could return to England and she would most like have forgotten him.

Would she have found a husband to her liking and left the court by then? Nick found the idea unacceptable, though he was not certain why it should matter. He hardly knew the wench.

Her looks were such that he knew she would have no lack of suitors, and her father would no doubt provide her with a reasonable dowry, though for him such considerations were of no import—if he wished to marry. She was a considerable beauty, and a fiery wench, but did he wish for the settled domesticity of wedded life?

Laughing at his own indecision, Nick left the window and turned back towards the bed. He was like a mooncalf, he thought with a wry twist of his lips. Time to put such thoughts away and concentrate on the task ahead. He needed some sleep if he was to keep his

wits about him, for tomorrow at dawn he must be on
his way.

In the shadows of the Embassy gardens while Nick
slept, a watcher yawned and thought of the gold he
would receive when he made his report to the master
who owned him body and soul—a master so terrifying
and fearful that he might be the devil himself.

Catherine was wearing a gown of cream silk over a
petticoat of cloth of gold when they left for the court
that evening. Her shoes were of fine leather embroidered with gold thread, and her ruff was of stiff gold
lace, which was wired to stand up at the back of her
neck, and opened at the front to reveal the beauty of
her costly necklace against the whiteness of her throat.
Because of the height of the ruff, she had asked
Martha to put up her hair into an elaborate style of
curls, allowing one curled lock to fall forward against
her shoulder.

'That style becomes you well,' Lady Stamford said
when she saw her. 'But I think it makes you look
older, Catherine. It is more youthful to wear your hair
loose as you did before.'

'It would not sit right with this ruff,' Catherine said.
'Besides, I do not want to look like a country maid
just out of the nursery.'

Lady Stamford nodded and said no more. There was
a new crispness about Catherine's manner that she approved but did not understand, almost as if she had
put up a barrier to protect herself. Now why should
that be? The girl could not have been slighted in love,
for she had met no one who had paid her any particular

attention as yet, though for a while she had feared that Sir Nicholas might be dallying with Catherine. That had come to nothing, and since then they had met no one who might have attracted the girl's attention, though her aunt was hopeful that that would change this evening.

Catherine was not aware of any alteration in her manner. Indeed, when with her father there was no change in her, but she had decided that she would resist all attempts to woo her. Marriage held no attraction for her, and she hoped that at the end of their stay in London she could return home as she had come, a maiden. She would spend the rest of her life quietly at home with her father, and in time the memory of a man's teasing smile would fade from her mind.

They were escorted to the palace by men provided by Lord Branwell, and met at the main entrance to Whitehall by the man himself. He smiled with approval as his eyes went over Catherine and offered her his arm.

'Her Majesty wishes to see you privately before the banquet begins, Mistress Moor. She has instructed me to bring you to her so that she may see for herself what manner of woman you are.'

Catherine's heartbeat was heightened as she laid her arm on his, nervous now of meeting the woman who ruled England. Elizabeth Tudor had the reputation of being clever, able to converse in several languages with the ambassadors who came to her court, and of having a sharp tongue when she chose. Cecil had once said of her that he had never heard anyone speak such flawless Latin as Her Majesty.

Catherine was escorted to a small chamber, where Lord Branwell left her and told her to wait until she was summoned. Catherine contented herself with studying a magnificent tapestry hanging on the wall until a pleasant voice made her turn.

'Mistress Catherine Moor?'

Catherine turned to look at the woman who had spoken. She was diminutive in size, pretty, with pale hair and vivid blue eyes.

'Yes…' Catherine raised her head. 'Forgive me, I do not know— Whom do I have the honour of addressing?'

'I am no one in particular.' The woman smiled and shook her hair back from her face. 'I am Lettice Williams, a lady of the Queen's dressing chamber— and I have come to take you to her now.'

'Oh…' Catherine took a deep breath. 'Do I look tidy? Is my gown creased?'

'There is no need to be nervous,' Lettice said. 'Her Majesty is well disposed towards you and she is in a good mood this evening. Be fearless, though not over bold, and you will do well enough. The Queen likes spirit in those she has about her.'

'Yes, someone else told me that, though I am not sure he was to be trusted.'

Lettice motioned to her to follow, looking at her curiously. 'May I ask who the gentleman was who made you less than trustful of his words?'

'I know him only slightly, of course—Sir Nicholas Grantly…'

'Oh…' Lettice looked at her curiously. 'Did he flirt terribly with you, Catherine? I hope that I may call you by your name?'

'Yes, you may—and no, Sir Nicholas did not flirt with me, but I believe he is a gentleman given to such ways.' Catherine crossed her fingers behind her back as she told the small lie, for Sir Nicholas had certainly flirted with her, though it did not suit her pride to admit it.

'Oh yes, very much so,' Lettice said and smiled. 'I believe there is scarcely a lady at court who has not swooned at his smiles—to the annoyance of Annette Wiltord. They say she is his mistress, though no one knows for certain. However, since Her Majesty shows her little favour I would say she believes the tale. He has always been a favourite with her, and she knighted him for his services to her entertainment—for you must know that he is considered skilled in all the arts of the minstrel, and his poetry is enough to melt the hardest heart.'

Catherine nodded, making no comment on this but returning to something Lettice had said earlier. 'Mistress Wiltord is a widow, is she not? And as such has more licence in her behaviour than a maiden, I believe. Does Her Majesty expect high moral standards of her ladies?'

'She frowns on any match between one of her ladies and a gentleman of the court unless she has sanctioned it. Indeed, some have been sent to the Tower for daring to marry without her permission. And it would be a foolish lady who flirted with a man the Queen favoured herself. Such behaviour might lead to a sojourn in the Tower.'

Catherine did not have time to answer, for Lettice put a finger to her lips and motioned her to enter the next chamber alone.

Catherine had never seen the Queen, but the magnificent personage standing alone just inside the small room Lettice had indicated could be no other. The colour of her hair was lighter and brighter than Catherine's own, and fashioned in what looked like tight curls over her head. A jewelled net partially covered her hair and her cheeks had a high colour which Catherine thought was artificial. Her ruff was similar to Catherine's but even taller and encrusted with pearls, matching those she had curled several times around her throat. Her sleeves and overskirt were of black, thickly embroidered with gold and pearls, and her petticoat was of purple damask. Her hands were covered with huge rings of flawless emeralds, sapphires and rubies, and a wonderful jewelled cross was pinned upon her bodice.

Catherine made a deep curtsey, remaining with her head bent until she was told to rise.

'I see you have been well schooled in manners, Mistress Catherine. By Lady Stamford, I make no doubt.'

'My aunt has been kind in teaching me much,' Catherine replied, gazing up now, 'but my father has always taught me to show respect for others, and I try to follow his example in all things.'

'Sir William was foolish to escort you alone in our streets at night—but brave and courageous. I have heard that you are also brave. Let us hope that you are wiser than your father.'

'I hope to become wiser in time, ma'am. My endeavour is always to improve my mind, if given the opportunity.'

'An agile mind is worth more than an able body,' the Queen replied. 'I have the body of a frail woman but the mind and heart of a prince.'

'This I have been told, ma'am. For myself I think that a woman is oftimes stronger in all things than a man—for I do not think that many men could stand the rigours of childbearing.'

Elizabeth laughed, giving the young woman a shrewd look. 'It is as well for you that you speak so frankly to me alone and not to mixed company, for your words are almost heresy. Do you not realise that it is not so long since a woman could have been put to the fire for less than you have just said? Womankind is inferior to man—do you not accept that?'

Catherine took a deep breath, for to offend the Queen could be dangerous, leading to disgrace and worse. Yet she could not pretend to believe in things against her nature.

'No, Your Majesty—for I think you superior to most men of my acquaintance. The accident of your birth is neither here nor there, for as a man you could not have done better since you came to power...' Catherine halted, her heart jerking with fright as she saw the Queen's gaze narrow as it dwelt on her face. 'Forgive me if I speak too boldly. I meant not to offend.'

'Nor have you, Mistress Catherine,' Elizabeth said

at last. 'Had my own belief not been much as yours I should not now be England's Queen. I tread a thin line between glory and disaster, and need able wits about me. If you seek to flatter be sure that I shall find you out—but if your sentiments are honest I think we shall deal well together. Go now and enjoy the evening as you will. You are welcome at my court.'

She waved a hand in dismissal, and Catherine curtsied deeply once more before backing out of the chamber into the even smaller one where Lettice, who had waited for her, took her in hand.

'There—that was not such an ordeal, was it?' she asked, her eyes merry with laughter. 'Now you are free to enjoy yourself, Catherine. Come with me and I shall introduce you to other ladies and show you where to sit this evening.'

Elizabeth stood without moving or summoning a maid of honour to attend her, her face a mask that revealed none of her thoughts to the casual observer. The little Moor was interesting, bold but not in such a way that made one think her wanton. She seemed to have a good mind and would make stimulating company if she continued in this way—and there were times when Elizabeth stood in much need of diversion. The cares of state weighed heavily upon her, and she had much to do to keep the Commons in line, for they grew too bold in their demands for her marriage.

Such demands made Elizabeth angry, for *she* was not to be told whom or when she would marry nor even if. Such concerns were solely hers, as she had made plain on more than one occasion—but it was necessary to keep these men sweet, for her crown was not so secure upon her head that she could ride rough-shod over their feelings. She must play upon them like a minstrel plays upon his harp, bringing forth smiles and sweet words of compromise to soothe the angry breast.

This latest in a long line of marriage negotiations was like to come to naught, despite all Walsingham's skills as an ambassador. There were good reasons why she should push for the marriage, and perhaps even better ones why she should not. Given her personal choice…but Fate had conspired against her and the love that had blossomed in the spring of her first months on the throne was forbidden to her. Yet the innocent joys of loving and dalliance were not denied her, merely the fulfilment and fruits of the natural coupling of man and wife.

Elizabeth shook her head, casting off the mood that had threatened to spoil her pleasure in the evening. She had sacrificed much for the office she bore and would sacrifice all before she renounced it. And as for this fancy that sometimes held her mind…it must be dismissed, along with all the bad memories and nightmares of her childhood.

If it seemed sometimes that she was doomed to lose all that she loved—that those she cared for were struck down and taken from her—then it was merely sad co-incidence. This business of Norfolk, a man she admired and had once felt warmly towards, could be dismissed for now. They would have her condemn him out of hand, but no matter how much her ministers persuaded, she would have absolute proof before she

committed him to the fate they demanded as his punishment for treason against her person and the state.

Casting off her fit of the sullens, which had been
brought about because Catherine Moor reminded her
so much of herself when she was the same age, she
summoned her ladies. It was time for the banquet to
begin, time for her to take her place, to become the
adored and flattered Gloriana.

Neither she nor the ladies who had left her but
minutes before could know that in their midst the ser-
pent lay coiled, ready to strike when the moment of
his vengeance came.

It was a night of merriment and laughter, the company well entertained as they ate by a troupe of tumbling fools; this was followed by a short play, and
afterwards by music and dancing.

Catherine particularly liked the love songs sung by
a minstrel with dark, romantic looks that tugged at her
heart.

I saw my lady weep.
And sorrow proud to be exalted so
In those fair eyes where all perfections keep.
Her face was full of woe;
But such a woe, believe me, as wins more
hearts,
Than mirth can do with her enticing parts.

It was a song much enjoyed by those who listened,
though when Catherine asked who had written the
beautiful lyric no one seemed to know.

'It is anonymous,' Lettice told her. 'Mayhap the writer does not want his love to know that he wrote it for her.'

After the minstrel had entertained them, one of the Queen's ladies sang 'Who But My Lady Greensleeves' and another played the harp. Then the dancing began and for Catherine the evening really came to life, for like most young women of her age she loved to dance.

She was asked by various gentlemen to dance with them, and was pleased to accept those to whom her aunt gave the nod, though she kept a cool distance about her and was not familiar as some of the ladies were, flirting wickedly with their partners at every chance. It seemed to Catherine that evening that there was much licentious behaviour at court, and she was aware that many of the ladies had lovers who took the place of dull husbands in their beds.

Marriage, it seemed, was arranged for reasons of wealth and prestige, and only a foolish heart would hope for love. That was to be found in the arms of a handsome lover when a wife's duty was done and the heir safely delivered into the care of a nurse. Catherine was fast losing her naïvety, beginning to realise that flirting and seduction was the main amusement of the courtiers.

'And so, Catherine,' her aunt said when they were at home again after the night's feasting and merriment. 'What think you of your first visit to the court?'

'It was very interesting, Aunt.'

'Interesting?' Lady Stamford's brow rose at her choice of words. 'Have you no higher praise for what no one would deny was a brilliant occasion?'

'There are many words to describe such a feast and all that followed it,' Catherine replied. 'The food was exceeding rich, but often cold before it reached us. The wine only passing fine—but the company was interesting, and the music enjoyable. The players gave us an excellent performance of their piece, though it was rather short and the words a little trite…'

Lady Stamford hissed through her teeth. 'Most young women would give their eye teeth for the chance to be present at such a banquet, miss!'

'Do not think me ungrateful, Aunt. It was pleasant enough, but I have spent as amicable an evening at home with my father and his friends—though I must admit that the conversation was sometimes wittier than I have met with before.'

And extremely bawdy! Catherine had been shocked by some of the remarks by gentlemen concerning the other ladies. If they were to be believed, many of the fine ladies were little better than strumpets with no morals to speak of and the habits of an alley cat, and the gentlemen themselves no better.

'You seemed to have a good time,' Lady Stamford said, her eyes narrowed and shrewd. 'I saw that there was usually a crowd of young men about you, ready to fetch and carry whatever you required from further down the table. And you danced often enough later in the evening.'

'I enjoyed the dancing. But as far as the fetching and carrying is concerned it was at their own insistence,' Catherine said with a wry smile. 'I asked for nothing but a cup of cold water, for mine was warm and stale and I like not too much wine at supper. It makes me restless when I go to bed and then I cannot sleep.'

'I find the right wine helps me to rest,' her aunt replied. 'But you are right, Catherine. The palace wine is seldom of the quality your father keeps. I must ask him to stock my cellars for me before he returns to the country.'

Catherine looked at her in alarm. 'He does not think to go home yet?'

'Not yet, no—but should Her Majesty take you as one of her ladies your father will not want to remain in town. Indeed, you may not do so yourself for long. It is often the Queen's pleasure to go on one of her progresses during the heat of the summer, when the stink of London oftimes becomes unbearable. It is better to leave for a while then to avoid the diseases that come to strike us down when it grows too warm. Pomanders stuffed with sweet herbs and spices do much to reduce the stench, but I think they do not ward off the sickness, though it is said they are efficacious for the plague. I should say rather that a trip into the country would be of more use. Should Elizabeth wish it, you will accompany her on her travels, Catherine.'

'Oh…' Catherine stared at her in surprise. 'I had not realised that—though I knew Her Majesty likes to journey about the country sometimes.'

'As to that…she scarcely ever goes too far from London, but there are many great houses where she may stay for a few days or weeks at the homes of rich nobles. I dare say it helps her purse, which is always stretched, and allows her a little longer before she need go to the Commons for more money. But she never stays in one place more than a few weeks. None but the very wealthy can afford to keep the court for too long; the cost of the food alone would be huge. One of her favourite nobles, with whom she often stays, told me that twelve hundred chickens, a cartload of oysters and four hundred and thirty pounds of butter had been consumed the last time the Queen stayed with him.'

'It must have cost the poor man a small fortune. I dare say even the wealthy are happy to see the court move on,' Catherine said, 'for so many must put a strain on any resources.'

'For those who covet a title or preferment at court it is a small price to pay,' Lady Stamford replied. 'But we digress. I saw that you showed no particular favour to any of the young men about you this evening, Catherine—and while that reflects a proper modesty, was there no one you liked more than any other?'

'No, Aunt, none. All were acceptable to me as companions.'

'Well, I suppose it is early days yet, and a certain coolness is always to be admired—but make sure that you do not acquire a reputation for coldness, niece. It will not help your marriage prospects, believe me. Men look for warmth and docility in a wife.'

Catherine nodded but made no answer. She had found the flattery heaped upon her tedious and, having enjoyed long, serious conversations in the evenings with her father, wished that someone would find something more original to say. However, any attempt to turn the conversation to more erudite subjects was met with blank stares. They seemed to have nothing to say about the works of Archilochus, a Greek poet of the seventh century, or of Peter Abelard, scholar and theologian of France, and their eyes positively glazed over when she mentioned Aristotle. Though they had much to praise in modern poets like Barnabe Googe, Richard Edwardes, Stephen Hawes and others.

Catherine sighed. 'I shall try not to appear cold, but I cannot flirt as some of the ladies do. I have not been used to such behaviour—which my father would describe as lewd in some instances.'

'You must not be too pretty in your manners at court,' her aunt said with a frown. 'A certain modesty is well enough in a maiden, but you are not a child, Catherine, and prudery will make you the butt of others' wit.'

'I shall try to behave modestly but without being a prude,' Catherine said. 'You must forgive me if I choose not to drink too much and flirt with every gentleman who comes my way, Aunt. I do not think the matter of my marriage so urgent that I must throw myself at the first to show an interest.'

Lady Stamford looked at her through narrowed eyes. 'I hope you do not intend to be stubborn over this, Catherine. It is your duty to marry—as a woman and as your father's heir. A woman must have a husband to run her estate for her. Besides, the position of a spinster is not a happy one. If you choose wisely you may live to become rich and respected in your own right, as I have.'

It was on the tip of Catherine's tongue to make a sharp reply, but she held her peace. Her aunt was thoughtful for her sake and it was better to tread carefully until the need for confrontation arose.

'If the time comes when a man asks for me, I shall speak with my father and be guided by his opinion—and yours of course, Aunt.'

'I am not a fool, Catherine.' Lady Stamford gave her a speaking glance. 'I know that your father can deny you nothing—but that does not mean you have the right to be wilful. William worries over your future, if you do not, and you owe it to him to be dutiful in this matter.'

Catherine did not reply, for to deny her aunt would seem churlish. Instead she smiled and yawned.

'The evening has tired me, Aunt. With your leave I shall retire.'

'Of course. I am weary myself. I came to London only for your sake, Catherine. Please remember that, and think before you leap.'

Catherine felt a little guilty as she made her way to her bedchamber and allowed the maid to help her out of her gown. Her aunt had gone to a lot of trouble to introduce her to the court, and it was wilful in her to set her face against marriage.

Perhaps she would relax her guard a little, for there was clearly much pleasure to be had at court with the ladies and gentlemen who attended Her Majesty. Yet still she would hold herself slightly aloof, for she was in no hurry to be wed, though it might be that she was forced to it in the end. Why was it that women had so much less freedom than men?

Even Catherine's mother, though dearly loved, had always considered it her duty to put her husband's wishes first. No doubt Catherine was not the first young woman to feel rebellious at the constraints put upon her, nor would she be the last—but she would not marry unless she believed there was a chance of happiness with the man who would be her husband, and in effect her master.

As she lay in her bed, weary and yet somehow unable to sleep, a picture of a man's face came unbidden to her mind. Had Sir Nicholas been less careless and more honest in his wooing, she might have been ready to listen to her aunt's urging. But it was useless to think of him—he had gone without a word, leaving her easily and without regret.

Surely it must be possible to find someone who could make her heart respond as it had to Sir Nicholas? Yet she had found herself indifferent to flattery and cajoling smiles alike, untouched by several declarations of undying love from men who were attractive and skilled in the art of courtship.

Lettice had told her in a whisper that her apparent indifference had set the courtiers to wagering against her being won by at least three of the men who had aspired to be her suitors.

'They are calling you the Lady of Ice,' Lettice had told her, much amused. 'But some swear there is fire beneath the ice and that they will have you within three months.'

'I do not think I care to be the subject of such a wager.'

'But it will make you,' Lettice said. 'Nothing is worse than to be ignored and for as long as you resist without alienating your suitors, you will be much admired and courted.'

Catherine had smiled at her friend's teasing, for already she liked the other girl and found her friendship welcome.

'It might be amusing to play such a game,' she said. 'But much depends on Her Majesty—for if I am not bidden regularly to court I dare say I shall soon be forgotten.'

'The Queen will have had a dozen reports of you this evening,' Lettice said. 'She loves a contest and I believe she will find your behaviour both admirable and amusing.'

'We shall see…'

Catherine slept at last with her friend's words echoing in her mind. If she remained at court it might be that Sir Nicholas would return in time and it would do no harm if she had a reputation for being unobtainable.

Chapter Five

Catherine's recall to court was not long delayed, for the summons arrived the following morning. Sir William was asked formally to give his permission for Catherine to be become one of Her Majesty's Maids of Honour and a room was to be provided for her use within the palace.

'Once you are settled I shall return home,' her father told her after reading aloud the letter that had come from a palace official. 'I shall see that your belongings are brought to you and provide an escort myself to see you safely there.'

'You will not come with me, Father?'

'I think not, my dear, for partings are odious and I prefer that we should say ours here away from prying eyes.' He opened his arms to her, enclosing her in a warm embrace. 'Be happy, my dearest child. You know that I hope for your comfort and security in marriage. Choose wisely and do not let your aunt bully you into something that does not please you. You must know that my home is always open to you should you wish to return.'

'Of course I know that,' Catherine said, 'but a request from Her Majesty is tantamount to a command and I think it may be pleasant to be a part of the court for a while. The subject of my marriage is another matter. You know that I would not marry unless I love and believe that I am truly loved in return.'

Her father gave her a grave look. 'I hope that you may gain your true wish, but even love can sometimes lead you astray, Cat. Be sure that the man you give your heart to is worthy of that honour, and then I shall have no need to worry for your sake.'

Catherine assured him that she would be very careful not to give her heart away lightly, but in truth she was not sure that it had not already been lost to a man who by all accounts was not worthy.

Dismissing her doubts and fears, Catherine prepared to leave her aunt's house a little later that same morning.

'I know I have no need to warn you to uphold your virtue,' Lady Stamford said before she departed. 'We have spoken of these things and I know you to be a good, modest girl, Catherine. I hope your pride will not be a stumbling block to your success, but we need say no more. I shall remain in town for some weeks, but when the court leaves on a progress I shall return home. You know that you may write to me at any time should you need me.'

'I believe I shall be content enough in my new post, Aunt,' Catherine replied and went to kiss her cheek. 'I have to thank you for your kindness and good offices on my behalf, for I am sure I should never have come to court had you not put yourself out for me.'

'Well, well, it was no trouble,' her aunt said, softened by the pretty speech. 'But do not be too stubborn in your choice of husband, Catherine. Your father may not say it, but he does worry about your future.'

'I know it,' Catherine said. 'If the right man should ask, Aunt, I shall not deny him.'

'As to that, remember that while at the court the Queen is your guardian. Should a man speak to you of marriage, you must direct him to Her Majesty before giving your answer. Disobedience in this may carry a heavy penalty.'

Catherine had thanked her for her advice, but Lettice Williams had already warned her of many pitfalls that awaited the Queen's ladies, and she would no doubt guide her in the coming days.

When she arrived at the palace, Catherine was greeted immediately by her new friend, who told her that they would be sharing a room.

'It is very small,' Lettice confided as she led the way. 'But there is space enough for our clothes and a place to sleep. Some nights I sleep elsewhere—Her Majesty occasionally asks one of us to wait in the antechamber where a pallet is provided, and I am often chosen.'

'Does Her Majesty have nightmares?'

'She is sometimes restless and cannot sleep, then I talk to her or read poems or play a game of chance. Her mind is so active and she has so many cares that there are times when she needs a companion while others sleep. We do not speak of it outside our own ranks, but since you are to become a lady of the bedchamber and may be called upon to amuse her, you must know these things.'

Catherine was surprised that she had been chosen to be one of the ladies closest to the Queen, for the post offered her had not been mentioned in the letter and she had expected to be just one of many who waited at court. Some of the ladies and gentlemen required to attend had very little to do unless asked to perform a specific service, but to wait on the Queen in her bedchamber was a high honour.

It meant that she would often see Her Majesty when few others were present, and would share an intimacy not granted to many.

The Queen sent for them half an hour after Catherine arrived, which Lettice said was proof that Elizabeth's intelligence service was working as normal.

'Her Majesty likes to be kept informed of everything that happens, and someone will have been told to watch for you and tell her of your arrival.'

'I had not thought it was so important.'

'Her Majesty leaves no detail to chance,' Lettice told her. 'She has the ablest mind of any person I have ever known, and can switch in an instant from matters of state to something frivolous you would think she had not even noticed. And she demands that her advisers are as sharp and clever as she is herself. She does not suffer fools about her.'

'Does Her Majesty have many advisers—apart from her ministers, of course?'

'Her chiefest councillor is Sir William Cecil, but there are others she trusts. Lord Dudley is very close to her—and her personal astrologer and magician, Dr John Dee. He cast her horoscope before she was Queen and told her that she would have a long and happy reign—and that Queen Mary would die soon. He was thrown into prison for it, because it was thought he had cast a magic spell to bring about his prophesy, but after she came to the throne, Elizabeth took him as her personal adviser on such matters.'

'I believe many great men and princes rely on their astrologers,' Catherine said, feeling a little trickle of ice run down her spine. 'But my father was against such things, for he believed the practice of dabbling in the occult was dangerous.' A long-forgotten memory stirred unbidden in her mind. 'Was it not thought at one time that the Earl of Leicester would marry Her Majesty?'

They were walking along a narrow passage that led from the bedchambers of the female courtiers to rooms of state, and it was dark and chilly, the heavy velvet drapes that concealed alcoves and doors to other passages stirring in a sudden wind that made Catherine shiver and turn cold.

'We do not speak of that,' Lettice warned her. 'When Lord Dudley's wife died so…unfortunately… many things were rumoured and though all was proved innocent, it is better to forget.'

'Amy Robsart.' Catherine nodded and crossed herself. 'God rest her soul.'

Catherine understood what Lettice meant, for the death of Lord Dudley's wife in mysterious circumstances would always cast a long shadow. If the Queen were to marry him, scandal would attach to her name and it might be thought that she had played some part in poor Amy's death.

'You mean because Amy Robsart fell down the stairs?' Catherine said frowning. 'It was thought that she might have been pushed, wasn't it? I did not hear it at the time, for I was a child and my mother had just died. I dare say they kept it from me, but I saw something that day, in the grounds of Cumnor Place…'

Lettice stopped walking and looked at her, a kind of fascinated horror in her eyes. 'You were there? On the day that Lord Dudley's wife died? How can this be?'

'My cousin had taken me on a short cut to the village,' Catherine explained. 'We were going to a fair and he was in a hurry. I saw…it was very strange and I have never spoken of it. I saw a shadow leaving the house, though when my cousin looked it had gone.'

'Was it a man or a woman?'

'I do not know for sure. It was odd, at times shapeless, at times seeming to take the form of a man, but I could not be certain. I only know that whatever it was it frightened me. I felt a sense of evil…a sense of something bad having been done, though I did not know that the poor lady had fallen down the stairs. God rest her soul!'

'May God protect us!' Lettice cried and crossed herself fearfully. 'It was a demon conjured up to murder the poor lady…' She clapped her hand to her mouth and looked at Catherine in dismay. 'No, I didn't say that. You must never tell anyone that I said such a wicked thing, Catherine. And you must never, never tell anyone else what you have just told me—it is too dangerous.'

'I shall never tell anyone what you said,' Catherine promised because she saw that Lettice was really frightened. 'And I had almost forgotten what I saw that day. I dare say it was nothing but imagination after all. Willis said it must have been a trick of the light, and I dare say he was right. It was your speaking of Dr Dee and his powers of astrology and magic that put me in mind of it.'

She smiled at Lettice, turning the conversation to the subject of the evening's entertainment, for there was to be a masked ball and Catherine was intrigued at the prospect.

As the girls hurried on, talking and laughing together, neither of them glanced back to see the man step out of the shadows and stare after them with a frown on his face. He was a thin man, of medium height and build, his beard neatly trimmed, dressed in a style no longer fashionable at court. A man that no one would give a second glance. Unless that is, they happened to look into his eyes when he was angry.

Nick was aware that he was being followed once more. The man had been his shadow since he left Paris, never far behind him as he travelled. His purpose was what? Had he planned robbery or murder he would have surely attempted it before this—so why follow? Unless it was to discover Nick's purpose, which meant that Walsingham was likely right in believing they had stumbled on some dark secret.

His shadow was there to report on him. He was

merely the monkey at the command of a master and therefore not a threat. A smile touched Nick's lips as he reined in, slowing his horse to a walk. The stranger in the shadows was unable to make an immediate adjustment and drew closer. Nick halted, turning in the saddle to look at the fellow.

'Have I not seen you somewhere before, friend?' he asked in a polite, deceptively mild tone. 'Come, sir, if you travel my way, let's us go on together.'

Hostile eyes greeted his sally and he knew that he was right. The man had been following him for weeks.

'You are mistaken, sir,' the man grunted. 'I have never seen you before and our ways part here.'

With that he put his horse to the spur and rode off at speed.

For the moment Nick was free of his shadow. It was unlikely that the same man would seek to follow him again, but he was in little doubt that another would take his place. It was dangerous work that he had embarked on for Walsingham, for if as he suspected there was yet another scheme afoot, the men who plotted against England and its Queen would stop at nothing to achieve their aims.

Nick would be advised to keep his wits about him! It was as well that he did not have a wife, for she might become a widow at any time.

The purpose of a masked ball was to hide one's identity, which would be revealed at midnight when the ball ended. Since Catherine knew only a few courtiers, and those but slightly, they were all a mystery to her.

Lettice was very clever at piercing the disguises of various gentlemen, and whispered behind her fan whenever someone approached them, advising her whether she ought to dance with a particular gentleman or not.

'Sir Alan Dovedale is a terrible rogue,' she told Catherine as a gentleman wearing the mask of a stag made a beeline towards them. 'But he sings like an angel and his poems are divine.'

Catherine laughed, for Lettice was clearly teasing her, and accepted the gentleman's hand when he begged her to be his partner. His success was noted, and for the rest of the evening she went from one gentleman to the next, laughing and refusing to answer as they tried to pierce her disguise, though she suspected that in some cases they were already well aware of who she was.

All were clearly gentlemen, and although one tried to be a little familiar with her, brushing his hand as if by accident across her breasts, and another begged her earnestly to meet him in the gardens at midnight because he was dying of love for her, there was only one she found an uncomfortable partner. He was wearing black and gold and a rather terrifying bull mask, and he was silent for most of the time, speaking only to ask her for the dance, and then to thank her.

Catherine found the touch of his hand cold and a little damp, and there was an odd smell about his clothing that she found unpleasant—a heavy perfume that seemed to mask another, more unpleasant smell.

After the dance Catherine asked Lettice if she knew the identity of the man wearing the ugly bull mask.

'No…' Lettice sounded uncertain. 'I cannot say that I know him. Why do you ask? Was he over-familiar?'

'No, not at all. He barely spoke to me. It was just…' A shiver went through her. 'There was something I did not like about him; he smelled odd, for one thing.'

She could not explain the fear that had suddenly taken hold of her, nor the feeling that she was in some kind of danger. It had passed as swiftly as it had come, and she knew that it was merely imagination.

Lettice laughed and shook her head. 'Then that explains why I did not know him. He must be one of those gentlemen who rarely come to court. He keeps his fine clothes in a trunk with herbs and spices to ward off the moths, and that is what you found so peculiar, Catherine.'

'Yes, perhaps you are right,' Catherine said, relieved at her friend's explanation. 'It is so expensive to buy court clothes, and I dare say the less wealthy never wear their best clothes except for those rare occasions when they feel it is time to visit the court.'

The next moment Catherine forgot the odd incident as another gentleman approached her. This time she knew him, for it was Sir Alan, and despite his reputation as a flirt, she found him a pleasant companion.

'Meet me in the rose arbour at midnight,' he begged, in a voice husky with desire. Coal-black eyes glinted amorously behind his mask. 'There we shall discover each other's identity and the delights of love, sweet mistress.'

'You are a wicked flirt, sir,' Catherine replied. 'I cannot meet you, for I shall be in bed and asleep long before then.'

'You might sleep in a sweeter place,' he suggested. 'But I shall not tease you, mistress, for I know you to be a lady of virtue, though I shall lie lonely this night for want of you.'

'Fie on you, sir!' Catherine laughed, tossing her head at him. 'You are a wicked flirt and I dare say you have already asked a dozen others to meet you in the garden.'

Sir Alan laughed but did not deny it, kissing her hand as he led her back to her friends when the music ended.

Catherine glanced around the hall, but there was no sign of the man in the bull mask. The Queen had retired half an hour earlier, which meant that Catherine could also go to her chamber when she was ready. She yawned, behind her fan. The evening was late and she was tired, but at least she would sleep tonight.

Catherine was dreaming, thrashing restlessly on her pillows, her mind possessed by the fearful images. The dark shadow hovered over her, filling her mouth and her nose with its suffocating evil. She could not breathe, and the stench was beyond bearing, the stench of death and sulphur from the pit of Hell. She knew that she must fight off this dark shadow or die.

'Wake up, Catherine!'

She was startled back to reality by a hand shaking her shoulder, bringing her back from the depths of that black pit.

'What happened? Where am I?'

Catherine stared at Lettice in bewilderment.

'You were having a nightmare. You screamed and

cried out but I could not hear clearly what you said. Your words were jumbled and indistinct.'

Catherine sat up, shaking her long, heavy hair from her face as she fought off the drugging haziness that still seemed to claim her mind.

'I cannot recall my dream, but I know it frightened me.' She looked at the other girl apologetically. 'Did I wake you? Forgive me.'

'I was not asleep. I had stayed late with Her Majesty, but she sent me to fetch you. She wants you to keep her company.'

'Me? I must dress at once!' Catherine frowned as she began to pull on her petticoat. 'It is very odd. I have never suffered from bad dreams before—or none that I recall.'

'I dare say you ate too much cheese at supper.'

'Yes, perhaps I did.' Catherine threw off her doubts as she tied the strings of her overskirt at her waist, hurrying over her toilette. 'I ate more than usual last night, but it was very good cheese.'

Leaving the chamber she shared with Lettice, Catherine made her way quickly to the Queen's apartments. It had merely been a bad dream, nothing to worry about. She would put it from her mind. No doubt Lettice was right, she had eaten too much for her supper.

The dream did not return in the weeks and months that followed. Whether it had been due to too much supper or because she had not yet become used to sleeping in a strange bed, Catherine did not know, but her sleep was usually sound thereafter. Unless she was summoned to keep Elizabeth company when the Queen was restless.

It surprised Catherine that she should be chosen to sit with her mistress so often during the dark hours when Elizabeth could not sleep. However, she soon became used to it and found that she enjoyed their conversation, which was always stimulating.

Elizabeth would set her hypothetical questions about a set of circumstances and ask what she would do if she were Queen. It was only after several of these conundrums had been presented to her that Catherine realised Elizabeth was voicing her private anxieties, but in such a way that her true purpose was concealed.

Once, when she had been asked whether she would be afraid if she were sent to the Tower accused of treachery, Catherine guessed that her mistress was thinking of those dark days when she had herself been imprisoned and had been close to losing her own life.

'It would depend on whether I was guilty or innocent,' Catherine replied. 'The guilty must expect the worst—but the innocent must have the courage to stand up and fight for justice, even if by doing so it seems they walk at the very edge of danger.'

'You remind me of myself when I was your age, before the cares of state were placed upon these frail shoulders. Tell me, Catherine. What would you do if they told you that you must condemn a man you have liked and trusted to a traitor's death?'

'I should want absolute proof, ma'am—and then I should pray for guidance in such a grave matter.'

'As must I—very well, that is enough teasing for

this night, Cat. Now, tell me, who amongst my court-iers is most to your liking?'

'Why all are equal, ma'am. I enjoy their banter and nonsense, but I have no wish to marry just yet.'

'That pleases me,' Elizabeth said and smiled. 'I would keep you with me for the moment. I need pleas-ant companions about me, for the coming months may test my strength to its limit.' She waved her hand in dismissal, sending Catherine to her own couch.

Catherine sometimes wondered at the secrets locked in her mistress's mind, for she knew that Elizabeth was often sorely troubled.

For herself the days flew by so fast that she scarcely had time to mark their passing. Much of her day was given to attending Her Majesty, but in the evenings there was almost always some amusement to pleasure the Queen and her court.

The Queen loved dancing. Sometimes she danced with one of her gentlemen. It might be the Earl of Leicester or perhaps the handsome and accomplished Christopher Hatton, who was one of Her Majesty's personal bodyguards. Christopher was a favourite of the ladies at court, for he was a master of the art of courtly love, and though none dared to flirt too openly with him for fear of offending Elizabeth, his manners were greatly admired and whispered of behind fans.

But many great gentlemen, both from the far corners of England and the wider world, came to Elizabeth's court wherever it happened to reside. Catherine was often amongst those ladies present when ambassadors from foreign princes made their bow. Able to under-stand and converse in French and Latin, though not as fluent as the Queen, Catherine was privy to much that some of the other ladies did not share.

She knew that some were jealous of the position she held, but none dared speak out against her. Catherine had acquired a reputation for being clever and sometimes sharp of speech. It was well known that no one had come close to seducing her, despite many an attempt to breach the citadel of her maidenhood, and yet she remained popular with the gentlemen and most of the ladies.

Catherine knew that she was fortunate to have been given so much. It would be ungrateful of her if she let herself dwell on something that was never meant to be. She must forget a man's teasing smile and the thrill of his kisses.

Yet night after night before she slept, the last thing she saw was the laughter in his eyes as he bent his head to kiss her. And when she slept, it was most often of a sunlit garden where a man and woman lay together beneath a scented rose arch, locked in the embrace of love, that she dreamed.

But sometimes as she slept, the sweet dreams of courtship faded and she saw again the dark shadow that had seemed to glide from the house on the day of Amy Robsart's death, and in her nightmare it seemed to be hovering over her.

Elizabeth was comfortably placed in her favourite chair, several of her ladies about her, most perched on cushions on the floor, one or two standing near the open windows conversing with one of the few gentlemen in the room. It was high summer, and they had moved to a palace outside London, away from the stench of the city and the fear of disease.

'I wish for music,' Elizabeth said. 'Will you play for me, Lettice? I am in the mood for something sweet and soft to banish the sullens.'

'Yes, of course, ma'am.'

Lettice got up at once to take a seat by the harp, which had been provided. She had a clear, sweet voice, and her plaintive song was of a young woman who had pined too long for a faithless lover, and having born him a child and been denied, was about to throw herself into the cold water of a bottomless pool.

Catherine got up to gaze out of the open windows. The view was of a pleasant park, which she had already explored on one of the long walks she took whenever she was free to please herself. There was a small lake, a wood and an extensive knot garden, also a large mews where hawks were kept. She could hear the faint mewing sounds made by the hawks on their perches, and realised that they too were suffering from the heat, poor things. Like her, they would prefer to be out in the air, flying free in pursuit of their prey.

Hunting was one of the chief pursuits in the country, and the Queen enjoyed riding out in the early morning. She was an excellent horsewoman, and in the excitement of the chase few of her ladies could keep up with her.

Catherine was one of those who managed it, and was therefore often included in the party. She wished that they might have gone riding today, but it was far too hot and even Her Majesty was feeling languid, despite the fact that they were staying with one of her favourites.

Some of the gentlemen had roused themselves to play sport in another part of the grounds. The occasional shout of triumph told Catherine that they were playing stool ball or perhaps shooting arrows at a barrel in competition with one another.

It was the heat that was unsettling her, not Lettice's song, Catherine told herself. She certainly was not pining for anyone!

Her memory of a man she had met briefly in the spring that she had first come to court was less sharp than it had been, her disappointment over Sir Nicholas's desertion tempered by the flattery and consequence her closeness to the Queen had brought her. Yet she could not quite forget the moment when Sir Nicholas had kissed her, or the way she had felt that she would melt for sheer pleasure.

So much time had passed that she had given up hope that he would ever return to court. No doubt he had forgotten her, as she had forgotten him! She would not think of him again, and could not imagine why her thoughts had returned to that day by the river, except that it was so hot and it would be pleasant by the water.

'Do you wish for a walk, Catherine?'

She turned as she heard herself addressed by the Queen, her cheeks flushed as she realised that she had given herself away.

'It is just that it is so very warm indoors, ma'am.'

'Indeed, the heat is stifling,' Elizabeth said. 'I believe I shall walk in the gardens and those of you who wish for it may join me. Come, Cat, you shall walk beside me, and tell me why you look so sad. Can it be that you were dreaming of your lover?'

Catherine smiled and shook her head. 'I have no lover, ma'am.'

'I am sure you might have a dozen an' you wished it,' Elizabeth said, clearly in a teasing mood. 'Walk with me, Catherine. Tell me which of my gentlemen you prefer and I shall command him to pay attention to you...'

Catherine felt her mood lifting as there was a general movement outside. It would be foolish to fall into a decline over a man she might never see again.

By September of the year 1571 enough proof had been found that the Duke of Norfolk had indeed been plotting to marry Mary Queen of Scots and, with a Spanish army of six thousand men, incite an uprising that would sweep Elizabeth from the throne of England. It was sufficient to force Elizabeth to send Norfolk back to the Tower.

'I own I am glad that this foul conspiracy hath been laid bare,' Catherine heard the Queen say to one of her ministers. 'But it grieves me sorely that many of my nobles have been drawn into Norfolk's scheming.'

Catherine knew that her mistress was restless. She was called often to spend an hour or two with Elizabeth, and she knew that the Queen was haunted by dark thoughts during the winter that followed the Duke's arrest. Elizabeth was unsure of the loyalty of many of her gentlemen, even some of her favourites were under suspicion, and she gathered her truest ladies about her as a cloak.

In the January of 1572 Norfolk went before a council of his peers at Westminster and the verdict of his trial was never in doubt. Yet still Elizabeth hesitated over signing the warrant that would take his life.

In the dark hours that tormented her, Catherine was most often the one to comfort her mistress.

It was June before Elizabeth at last consented to an act that filled her with dread, and she steadfastly refused those who bayed for Mary of Scots to die in like manner.

Only Catherine and a favoured few of her ladies would ever guess what these decisions had cost the fair Oriana—or Gloriana as many called her.

'It is good to have you back, Sir Nicholas.' Walsingham greeted him with a smile. 'Though these are dangerous times for us here in France.'

'Something disturbs you?' Nick sensed the other's unease. It was the evening of the twenty-second day of August 1572. 'You are concerned about another plot? I had hoped that with Norfolk's death there would be an end to such treachery.'

'For the moment I believe England to be safe from the threat of invasion,' Walsingham replied. 'It is here in France that I suspect treachery.' He glanced over his shoulder as if fearing to be overheard. 'I have learnt nothing specific, you understand. Rumours have reached me concerning the Medici…'

'The Queen Mother—Catherine de' Medici?' Nick nodded his understanding of Walsingham's unease.

The lady was known for her love of manipulation and conspiracy, and there were many rumours of darker matters concerning her. 'Tell me—what has happened? I came straight to you on my arrival and have heard nothing.'

'This morning an attempt was made to murder Admiral Coligny, who I make no doubt hath angered the Medici by meddling and defying her at every turn…'

'You think the Medici may have been behind the attempt?'

Walsingham shrugged expressively. 'It may be but a part of a larger plot. I sent for you to return some weeks ago because I feared that all my work here might be ruined by some disaster. Troubled in my mind, I consulted with an astrologer of some repute, though you know that as a general rule I distrust men of this ilk. However, I was minded to consult the man who had been telling others of his prophecy, and he forecast a black cloud that would descend on France and remain as a bloody stain for all time.'

'You have no idea what this terrible disaster may be?'

'There is much unrest in France,' Walsingham replied. 'The Huguenots are hated by many, and I fear this assassination attempt may incite riots and worse.'

Nick looked at him thoughtfully. Walsingham was not a man easily swayed, and he must indeed have been troubled to have consulted the astrologer.

'Then I shall pray that it will not happen, sir. As to my own business, I wrote to you that I was minded to return and our letters must have crossed. My presence in Rome was to no purpose, for I learned nothing new of any consequence. Your trusted agent was dead of a fever before I arrived and the trail was cold. If your man of darkness was ever in Italy, he is not there now as far as I can discover.'

'For the moment he is of little matter. Mayhap he never existed other than in my mind, though further papers have come into my possession, cryptic messages that disturb me, for they seem to call on the powers of the Devil and his minions. Yet no matter. For the moment I have other concerns. More important is the matter of the treaty I recently concluded with France and the marriage negotiations. Anjou was always doubtful because of the religious difficulties, but Her Majesty seems more inclined to Alençon, who would be easier to manage.' He sighed. 'I am uneasy, Nick. I can feel something bad coming and it is very close—but I do not know what comes and it worries me.'

'I had thought to return to England…'

'You must be anxious to do so—yet I would ask you to stay for a few days longer.'

'Then of course I am at your service.'

Nick was only half listening as Walsingham expounded his theory of some dark treachery. He had been travelling for too long and was impatient to be at home again.

He imagined Catherine Moor would be betrothed by this time or at least courting a man she loved. When he'd left England so hastily in the spring of 1571, he had never expected to be away more than a year. Nor had he expected that the memory of her would linger in his mind. There had been many women before her, but none had stayed with him, haunting his dreams as she did. He felt a surge of frustration at so much time wasted.

It was probably useless even to think of seeing Catherine. She might be married and living happily in the country and far from court, and himself long forgotten. Just someone she had once met briefly who had faded from her thoughts these many months.

'You look so sad,' Lettice said, coming upon Catherine as she was reading her letter. 'Has your latest admirer deserted you for another? Or do you have the toothache?'

Catherine smiled at the other girl's teasing and slipped the letter into the small writing box that resided in an alcove by her truckle bed.

In truth she did not know what ailed her, aware merely of a sense of unease that came to her, most often when she was alone in her bed. She seemed haunted by dreams—dreams of the day she had seen that dark shadow hovering—the day that poor Amy Robsart had died.

Why should she be haunted by that memory now when she had forgotten it for so many years? Was it possible that she had seen more that day than she realised—that some forgotten thought was trying to make itself known?

No, no, that was nonsense. There was no reason for her dreams or for her sense of unease, almost as though she was watched, secretly and from a distance. Yet she wished that there was someone she might talk to—someone in whom she could confide. Lettice was not that person, though she loved her dearly as a friend.

'Neither thing ails me,' she replied throwing off her mood. 'The letter was from my father. He wrote it some weeks ago but it has only just reached me.'

'It is always thus when we travel,' Lettice said with a little sigh. 'I shall be glad when we return to London, for I weary of this constant moving, a week or so here and there is most unsettling.'

It meant more work for the ladies who waited on the Queen, for there was constant packing and unpacking of her possessions, and some things were too precious or important to be entrusted to servants.

At the moment they were staying at Kenilworth as guests of the Earl of Leicester. It was not by some standards a large house, and as was often the practice, some of the courtiers had been forced to seek lodgings outside in the village or surrounding district.

Catherine preferred it to some of the larger and often older manors at which they had stayed over the summer months, for it was more like her father's house and made her think nostalgically of the past. She enjoyed her life at court, but at times longed desperately for her home and the peace of the countryside.

'Away with the sullens,' Lettice said as Catherine got to her feet. 'It is a lovely day, Cat, and we are not on duty until later. Let us go walking by ourselves. I saw a wood where we might wander, and a sweet meadow filled with flowers.'

'Why not?' Catherine knew that her friend's request answered a need in herself, for sometimes she grew tired of the rather artificial atmosphere of the court, where one must always watch one's words for fear of a careless remark being seized upon to make mischief. 'Yes, a walk would do us both good.'

They slipped away from the house by a side door, not wanting to be followed by anyone, linking arms as they left all danger of discovery behind and entered the ancient meadow where a variety of flowers grew wild. It had been cut for hay earlier in the year, but now that summer lay upon them in all its glory, the grass was high again. Finding a sweet spot where they could lie unheeded, they sat down to enjoy the sun and gossip.

'What do you think of James Morton?' Lettice asked. 'I think he is very handsome and he seems to favour you, Catherine.'

'James Morton?' Catherine considered the new-comer. He had presented himself to Elizabeth two months earlier, having come from estates in the north, and had been kindly received because he brought a letter of recommendation from someone Her Majesty had known years ago, when she was not yet Queen. 'He is well enough, I suppose. I had not particularly noticed him.'

'He has spoken to me several times of you,' Lettice said, her eyes guileless as she leaned over to tickle Catherine with a blade of grass. 'I think he is in ear-nest, Cat. This one means to wed you.'

'Then I fear he shall be disappointed,' Catherine said. 'I like him well enough but no more than any other—and several of my suitors have expressed a desire to wed me, though most have seduction in mind, I think.'

'You came to court in early May last year,' Lettice said, 'and it is now August—fifteen months on. Tell me, is there no one in all these many months who makes your heart beat a little faster?'

'None,' Catherine replied, and then groaned as she heard the sound of laughter and chatter. 'It seems we were not the only ones to think it a pleasant day to walk...'

Lettice had jumped to her feet, waving as she saw the group of young men and women, amongst whom she had noticed Catherine's latest admirer.

'Mistress Lettice, and Mistress Catherine,' James Morton said, moving a little ahead of the others. 'Why do you hide yourselves here? Will you not join us by the river for a picnic?'

'We came for a little bit of peace,' Lettice said. 'It is good to be alone sometimes.' Her words seemed to warn him to go and yet her manner was all invitation. 'But if you care to sit with us...'

'What are they all talking about so earnestly?' Catherine asked as she watched the group of courtiers walk on. 'Has something happened?'

'Have you not heard?' James Morton came to sit on the dry grass beside her. 'There has been a terrible night in France—I heard only a few details before we left, but a messenger arrived to tell Her Majesty that the Huguenots are being massacred in Paris.'

'Massacred?' Lettice looked alarmed, her hand flying to her throat. 'I have an uncle there, my mother's brother...he is a Huguenot...'

'Is your uncle a Frenchman?' Catherine asked, looking at her in sympathy. 'You are not of their religion, I think?'

'No, nor was my uncle as a young man—but he married a French girl, took her faith and went to live with her family some ten years back,' Lettice replied. 'He brought his family to visit us the year before last. He has three children.' Her eyes were dark with fear as she looked at James. 'Pray tell me, sir—are they killing children as well?'

'I heard no details,' James answered. 'But do not distress yourself, mistress. It may be all rumour and no substance. These things are often made worse by rumour than they truly are.' He looked at Catherine. 'Is that not so, Mistress Moor?'

'Yes, it is oftimes the case,' Catherine said, seeing her friend's distress. 'You should not worry too much just yet, Lettice.'

'Those dear children…' Lettice choked back a sob. 'I pray God they are safe.'

'Perhaps there is more news if we return to the house,' Catherine said. 'At least we may discover how serious the news is there.'

'Yes, perhaps.' Lettice looked at her gratefully. 'I think I shall go back, but you need not come, Cat. Stay here and talk to Mr Morton.'

'No, indeed I shall not when you are in distress,' Catherine said, getting to her feet. 'Mr Morton may accompany us or he may join the friends he was with just now.'

'Oh, I shall come with you,' James said at once. 'Mayhap I may be of some service to you and Mistress Williams.'

Nick saw the young girl being tormented by those who had captured her and rushed to the rescue, his sword drawn at the ready. There had been a night of bloodshed and terror the like of which he hoped never to see again, men, women and children torn from their beds and massacred where they stood, their homes and possessions seized or burned. It sickened his stomach, and though he had tried to stay clear of it, he could not stand by and see a young woman raped, for that was surely what the brutes were about.

Like the cowards they were, two of them turned to flee as soon as he charged down upon them, their courage gone when faced with his sword. The third, armed with a thick cudgel, stood his ground, but within seconds Nick had sliced through his arm and the rogue retreated, following his friends with blood pouring from the deep wound.

The girl had fainted, her strength all but gone as Nick knelt beside her. He reached out to touch her face, smoothing back the damp hair, and pulling up the bodice of her gown to cover the pale flesh the brutes had uncovered in their eagerness to despoil her. Her eyes fluttered open and she gave a cry of fear.

'No, no, do not be frightened,' Nick said, speaking to her in her own language. 'I shall not harm you, and the rogues who did this have gone. I am English, mademoiselle, and my Queen supports your cause.'

'Yes, I have heard of the English Queen,' she whispered in a faint voice, clearly fluent in his own language. 'I have been told that it is safe there…'

'Hush now,' Nick said, touched with pity for her. She could not be more than seventeen! 'I have friends and I shall take you to them—but I do not know your name.'

'It is Louise Montpellier,' she said. 'I am alone, monsieur. They killed my family, burned my father's house and they would have killed me when they had had their fun.'

'They are gone now,' he told her. 'I shall take you to a safe house.'

Louise shuddered and turned her frightened gaze on him. 'Nowhere is safe here now. Our people are hated. Take me to England, sir, I beg you. Take me with you or I shall die…'

Alone in her room, Catherine was thinking of the terror in France. The news was bad, and it made her sorrow for all those who had suffered on that terrible night. For a moment she thought of the man who was seldom from her thoughts.

Was Sir Nicholas in France and had he witnessed the horror of that wicked massacre? In her heart she whispered a prayer for his safe deliverance and all those who had been in such peril.

Why was it that she felt herself in danger sometimes? Safe in England, she could have no need to fear such terrible events. No, her own danger lay elsewhere, in some private secret manner that she could not name.

Chapter Six

'I thank God to see you well and safe,' Walsingham cried when Nick walked into his office the morning after the massacre. 'After such a terrible night I feared that you might be amongst the victims.'

'No, I am safe enough,' Nick replied, a grim line about his mouth. 'But I dare say I shall never forget what I witnessed last night. Women and children dragged into the street and beaten to death. It was madness, sheer madness, the like of which I hope never to see again.'

'Amen to that,' Walsingham agreed and crossed himself. 'You must return to England now, my friend. For the moment it is not safe for you to remain here. Even my own position is uneasy, though the Medici assures me that I have her personal protection.'

'It was to tell you that I intend to return that I came,' Nick replied. 'And to ask a favour of you, sir. Last night I rescued a young gentlewoman from the mob that had burned her home and was intent on violating her. Her whole family was murdered, and she is left with nothing. I am minded to take her to my mother, who may know what best to do for her.'

'And you wish me to provide papers for you to take her to England?' Walsingham nodded. 'It is a small thing you ask, Nick, for you have served me well. The papers will be ready for you this afternoon.'

'I thank you on behalf of Mademoiselle Montpellier,' Nick replied. 'At the moment she is in a state of shock, but I have hopes that she will recover completely once she is in England. At the moment she has nothing but the gown she wears and I must do what I can to provide her with clothes and all that she might need for travelling. I shall return this afternoon to collect the papers.'

'Take care about the city,' Walsingham warned. 'The madness has not yet cooled, for when the blood of man becomes heated it takes time for sanity to return.'

The two men shook hands, and Nick took his leave. He was thoughtful as he left Walsingham's apartments and began to walk towards the lodging house where he had found temporary shelter for Mademoiselle Montpellier.

The papers Walsingham would provide would give Louise English citizenship, and as she spoke the tongue well enough providing she was not long questioned, Nick saw no reason why they should not pass safely through the city.

He was determined to do so, for then he would have had the satisfaction of saving at least one Huguenot from the night of evil that would evermore be known as St Bartholomew's Eve.

* * *

It was at Woodstock that Elizabeth kept the French ambassador Fenelon waiting for an audience, that he might give his version of the terrible events of St Bartholomew's Eve. The Queen was furiously angry, but before she dared to show her displeasure she wanted to make sure that all her agents in Paris were safe.

'How can *that woman* have done this wicked thing?' Elizabeth raged as she paced her bedchamber. 'She will surely burn in Hell for such an evil act. So many killed when the death of one man lies heavy on the conscience…'

'Is it certain that Catherine de' Medici ordered the assassination attempt which sparked off the massacre?'

Catherine watched her mistress's angry pacing. She knew that this terrible act had caused much consternation amongst those closest to the Queen, and would make the marriage negotiations with the Duke of Alençon impossible for the moment.

'My spies tell me so and I must believe them.' Elizabeth's eyes sparked with anger. 'She must be rejoicing at what she hath so easily achieved. Think yourself fortunate that you have not our burdens to carry. Go! Leave me, I would be alone.'

Elizabeth's mood had been angry for days, and Catherine, like others of her ladies, had borne the brunt of her temper. Lettice whispered that she believed the Queen had truly wished to wed the young French duke, and that this time the negotiations had been serious. If so, Catherine could understand why her mis-

tress was in such a mood, for she was no longer young
and would soon be too old for safe childbearing. Yet
Catherine was not sure Her Majesty had ever intended
to wed; she enjoyed the negotiations and the wooing
but seemed to draw back before a contract could be
agreed.

Lost in her thoughts, Catherine walked towards the
back stairs that led down to a small walled garden. It
was still light and she was not ready to retire. It would
be pleasant to walk a little in the fresh air.

'Annette Wiltord is furious,' Lettice said the moment Catherine entered their bedchamber. 'Her lover
has returned to court after all this time, but accompanied by a beautiful French girl he rescued from the
streets of Paris when she was being attacked by a
mob.'

Catherine's heart stood still. She stared at Lettice
for a moment, her mouth suddenly dry.

'Are you speaking of Sir Nicholas Grantly?' she
asked, feeling her chest tighten. Sir Nicholas had returned at last! She had begun to think that she would
never see him again. Yet what could it matter? He was
a faithless flirt and could mean nothing to her.

'Yes. Do you know him?' Lettice stared at her for
a moment. 'Oh, yes, I remember that you once spoke
of him as untrustworthy. He had done something that
upset you, I believe?'

'I hardly know him at all,' Catherine said. 'We met
but briefly—when he helped my father as some ruffians were attacking us.' And he had made her heart
respond to his wilful flirting! She tried to control the

rapid drumming of her heart. Sir Nicholas was back in England! She had prayed for it and now it had happened. 'But you said that he has rescued a French girl?'

'Yes, so they say. It seems that Lady Fineden and Mademoiselle Montpellier accompanied him to court, which is why Annette is so very angry. I remember when he was last at court there were some that thought he might marry her. Mind you, if rumour be true she has had several lovers since then.'

'What of the French girl?' Catherine asked, feeling a curious ache somewhere about her heart. Sir Nicholas had come back at last, but he had not come alone. 'Is she very beautiful?'

'I have heard that she is lovely, though I have not yet seen her for myself. Annette whispered to me that Her Majesty has taken pity on her and told her she will take her as one of her Maids of Honour.'

'Then no doubt we shall meet her.' Catherine breathed deeply. Why should it matter to her who Sir Nicholas brought to court? Of course it did not! 'What is her first name, do you know?'

'Louise, I believe.' Lettice gave a little sigh. 'It is rather romantic, is it not? Sir Nicholas was brave, do you not think so? It would be exciting to be saved from certain death by a handsome man and then brought to a new life at court. I dare say she is in love with him. Who would not be in her situation?'

'Perhaps it is Mademoiselle Montpellier that Sir Nicholas intends to wed,' Catherine said, turning aside so that Lettice could not see her face. 'If he brought her to England he must care for her, would you not say so?'

'Yes, perhaps,' Lettice agreed. 'Annette is no match for a young, beautiful and innocent girl. He would naturally prefer to marry Louise Montpellier. And he is of an age when he must be thinking of taking a wife to secure an heir.'

Catherine nodded, making no immediate reply. Sir Nicholas here at court! She had thought about it so often, imagining their meeting, and now he had brought a beautiful young French girl with him! She wondered why she found that painful, when she had told herself a thousand times that he was not worth one tear. He had flirted shamelessly with her when she first came to London, but by now he would have forgotten her.

She must not let anyone see that she was in the least interested in Sir Nicholas or his affairs. Resolutely pushing all thought of him from her mind, she looked thoughtfully at Lettice.

'Have you heard anything of your uncle or his family?'

'Not yet,' Lettice said. 'I have sent a letter, which I hope will reach him and I must wait and see what happens.'

'I pray that you will be successful, and that your family is safe.'

'Do you think that perhaps Sir Nicholas might know something?' Lettice asked. 'Would he mind my asking him for news?'

'I do not see why he should.'

'It is only that I refused him once when he tried to

make love to me. If you know him, Catherine…' Her voice trailed away as she saw Catherine's look. 'But if you do not wish to ask it does not matter.'

'Should Sir Nicholas speak to me I will make your request.'

'Thank you.' Lettice's face lit up. 'It would be such a relief to me to know that they are safe.'

'I cannot promise anything,' Catherine said. 'And now we must hurry or we shall be late…'

Released from her duties with the Queen, Catherine made her way towards the Presence Chamber, where Her Majesty would shortly make an appearance. She had some few minutes to spare before she need attend, and wished for a time alone to settle her thoughts, which had been in turmoil since she had learned that Sir Nicholas had returned to court.

'Mistress Moor, pray wait a moment…'

The voice sent a tingle through Catherine. She had known he was here but she had not expected him to seek her out. Surely it could not be…and yet something in her remembered too well. She turned slowly, letting her eyes wander over the face and figure of the man who had called her name, a face she had seen often in her dreams. She knew him instantly, would have known him even if no one had told her he was here, but her instinct was to deny him.

'You spoke to me, sir?' Her tone was cool, her manner a little haughty, but her heart quickened. His look, his voice, that smile were all as devastating as ever. Wretch that he was! She would not let herself be another of his foolish conquests. 'I am not certain I know…'

He came towards her, the smile she remembered instinctively on his lips. 'Forgive me. I know we met only three times, but I had hoped you might remember—Nicholas Grantly.'

'Ah yes.' Catherine wondered why she felt almost ready to swoon at the sight of him. He did not deserve that she should smile at him. 'I do recall you, sir, though it was a long time ago. You helped my father one evening. I seem to recall you spoke of visiting my aunt?'

It was not that vague promise she remembered, but the way his eyes and kisses had offered a glimpse of paradise, before it was cruelly snatched away.

'I was summoned abroad on business.'

'Indeed?' She raised her fine eyebrows. He claimed his business had taken him away, but according to Lady Fineden he had none other than pleasure. Catherine ignored her racing pulses as best she might, her tone deliberately cool. 'And are you settled in England now, sir—or is your business like to take you away again?'

Nick frowned as he caught the flash of temper in her eyes. It was clear that she had felt herself slighted by his neglect. He wished that he might explain, but it was no more possible now than it had been then.

'It was important work, Mistress Catherine.'

'Then no doubt you had no choice but to attend it.'

'None.' She turned away and he followed, suiting his stride to hers so that they walked side by side. 'May I be forgiven if I have offended, mistress?'

'To offend one must have caused offence,' she replied, struggling for indifference. 'Why should I have been offended? You owed me nothing, sir. Rather my family was indebted to you.'

It was the truth, yet he sensed she felt herself wronged, and indeed he had flirted with her that day at her aunt's house, and again by the river. Oh, yes, he recalled that moment by the river when he had felt inclined to cast all caution to the wind and make her his own. He had spoken in a light flirtatious manner, but she must have thought him serious in his intent and been more distressed by his desertion than he had imagined. Of course she had been very young and innocent that day. She was not quite as naïve now.

'I meant no offence.'

'Then I am not offended.'

She walked ahead of him into the garden. The scent of night-flowering blooms was heavy on the air as he followed, and somewhere a thrush trilled its evening hymn. It was a warm, sensuous evening, a night made for lovers and for loving. Catherine felt its pull and realised she had been unwise to venture out here alone with him.

'I have just returned from France…'

'Yes, I heard you were there, that you had rescued a young French woman from the terror.' Her eyes narrowed, and her head went up, her manner proud and unbending as she fought the burgeoning desire within her—the desire to be in this man's arms. 'You must have seen what happened to those poor people. I believe it was terrible?'

'Yes, more horrible than you could imagine.' Nick's

expression was serious now. 'I had been summoned there to meet someone. My friend feared that something of the kind was about to happen. It was a night of wickedness and will be long remembered for the shame it brings on those most concerned. Something like four thousand souls were murdered all told.'

'We had heard that there were many women and children killed. Her Majesty is beside herself with anger and grief.'

'As would any right thinking person be,' Nick said. 'This will do untold harm here in England. Already there are calls for Mary of Scots to be sent to her death, and it makes for yet more unease between Catholic and Protestant. Her Majesty has always sought to keep the peace and persuade those who oppose her rather than use force...but now her hand may be forced to move more harshly towards those who will not conform.'

Catherine nodded her agreement. The night of St Bartholomew's Eve had brought a trail of bitterness in its wake, and it was little wonder that Elizabeth was angry. She herself preferred the path of tolerance and peace, but there were many who called for harsher measures.

'I had wondered if you might have tired of the court by now,' Nick said, his change of subject causing her to look at him again. 'You have not married, Mistress Moor?'

'I am of use to Her Majesty,' she replied coolly her eyes glinting. Did he imagine she had had no offers? Or that she had languished for love of him? 'Marriage does not attract me for its own sake. I have not yet met a man to whom I would entrust my heart.'

This flighty, foolish heart that had gladdened at the sight of him!

'Your words are sweet music to my ears. I had feared you would be wed before I could return to claim…' He paused as he saw the way her head went up, her cheeks flushed with temper.

She could not believe her ears! What was he saying? Did he think to take up where he had left off so many months ago, as though he had never abandoned her without a word? Her sense of outrage was sharp as she stared at him in disbelief.

'Your fears are of little matter to me, sir. I have no interest in them—or you. And now I beg you to excuse me. I came out for a little air because I wished to be alone.'

'You are asking me to leave you to your walk?' Nick bowed, unsurprised by her answer. She had altered not one whit and he was conscious only of relief. He could bear her anger, for he had feared her indifference. She would take some wooing but he hoped this time he would have time enough. 'Then of course I shall obey, sweet Catherine.'

She caught the mocking note in his voice and it did nothing to improve her mood. She watched as he walked away, feeling a little disappointed that he had taken his dismissal so easily. She would have liked to quarrel with him further, to test out the claws her time at court had sharpened.

How dare he imagine that he could simply walk back into her life so easily? She was not to be won by a few smiles and careless words—and so he would learn!

As she turned to go back into the house, Catherine was unaware that a man who stood in the shadows of some dense shrubbery had overlooked the interlude. Of medium stature, he was a man that few would notice unless they happened to look into his eyes. Eyes that were at this moment cold as ice and filled with malice.

He was frowning as he watched her. The problem of Mistress Moor had lingered at the back of his mind these many months, though alone she was of little importance. She had once seen something that troubled her but it was a long time ago; she was probably too frivolous of mind to understand it or what it might mean. In *his* experience women were most often foolish, vain creatures who seldom looked beyond their pleasure.

She might, however, present a danger if she became too involved with the man. Anger and hatred festered in his heart as he lingered on in the courtyard.

His mind returned to that day in childhood when his mother had told him of his father's unjust death in the Tower for a crime he had not committed. Tortured and then most cruelly put to death while *he* was carried in his mother's womb, his father had been betrayed by a friend's indifference. How his mother had screamed and wept before they took him from her—a woman driven mad by her grief.

'Remember, my son,' she screamed, as they restrained her with chains while he struggled to free himself from the hands that held him back. 'Remember and hate those who destroyed your father—the Tudor tyrant and Sir Nicholas Grantly. He might have stood your father's friend and saved him had he tried.'

He had remembered and he hated; he hated all those who bore the name of Tudor and the son of the man who had sought favours for himself at King Henry's court while his supposed friend died for an imagined crime against the ageing King.

Oh yes, he hated. The girl was nothing to him beside the man. She had seen something she did not understand the day Amy Robsart died—the day *he* had so cleverly contrived that Elizabeth's hope of marriage to the man she loved foundered on the rock of scandal. A woman sick near unto death and wandering in her mind; it had been an easy task to arrange a little accident. 'Twas a sweet revenge, but not enough, not near enough.

Nothing would stand in the way of *his* grand design. He had waited for this, planned for it, and no one would be allowed to stand in his way. One day he would take full revenge for the harm done his family and in doing so would snatch back all that had been stolen from him. Yet he must be patient, the time was not yet.

While he waited for his moment he must take care not to be unmasked. Able to come and go at court without notice, he lingered in the shadows while his power grew. His interest in the occult had become an obsession, feeding his thirst for revenge on those who had wronged him.

Sir Nicholas had come too close for comfort more than once, but even he had failed to make the connections that would have solved the mystery he sought to unravel. Yet was it not always so? *His* luck held, and he went undetected, coming and going without hindrance. Perhaps it was not merely luck, but the right and just order of things. He had been granted a power known only to the chosen ones. Besides, few could rival *his* superior mind and so he was safe to carry on his work, the work that must be done.

He smiled as he considered how much *he* had achieved in France. Let the Medici take the blame, *he* knew how easy she had been to persuade, how much malice and envy had worked in her at his instigation to bring about the act of terror and destruction that had thrown horror into the lives of so many. It was but one small piece of *his* grand design, a design that would see that upstart Elizabeth Tudor brought to ruin in the end.

Nothing must stand in his way, nothing prevent England's return to the true faith—and the greatness that must fall on the shoulders of the man who had achieved so much. *He* had the blessing of the Pope himself, who had declared it the duty of all good Catholics to bring about the bastard's ruin.

Whether His Holiness would care for the way in which the work was carried out...but there were great secrets to be learned through the occult and the practice of alchemy: the secret of the Philosopher's Stone but one. A man who could discover that might rule the world—or at least control those who ruled in name. For unlimited gold was every man's desire.

If *he* could discover it, ah then...then his revenge

on all those that had sneered at and slighted him, all the hurts to his family, would be complete.

But he was tired after so many months of scheming and plotting. He cursed the body that could at times be frail. His physical strength had never been the equal of his mind, holding him back when victory seemed close. Had *he* not been struck down by a fever that left him wasted and unable to move for months, that fool Norfolk might have seized his chance and even now be king—a puppet who danced to *his tune*.

Norfolk was dead. Another tool must be honed to take his place, though it might take years of careful planning to bring about the desired result. Yet there was time for one who hated as he hated, time to plan and scheme, to enjoy small triumphs like the destruction of the marriage plans with that foolish French duke.

For the moment there was the minor matter of Mistress Moor. Something must be done to make sure that she did not become too closely involved with Sir Nicholas Grantly.

Catherine looked at the French girl, who had been invited to join the courtiers standing about Her Majesty. She was certainly very lovely, with her pale blonde hair and blue eyes, and her gown was extremely stylish, more so than many of the other ladies present that night.

If she had barely escaped with her life, how was it that Louise Montpellier had jewels and expensive gowns to wear? Unless of course, Catherine thought, someone had given them to her—a lover perhaps?

Catherine's gaze travelled round the room, coming to rest on the man she sought at last. Rumour had it that Sir Nicholas had swelled the fortune he had inherited to twice or thrice its size by clever investments.

She recalled that he had bought expensive presents for Sarah and her husband. He was modest in his dress, wearing black laced with silver for his court appearances and one very fine emerald on the middle finger of his left hand. He did not cover every finger with jewels as some men did, nor did he wear any other adornment on his person. Despite that, he stood out as a man of distinction, and was undoubtedly very wealthy.

He had seen her staring at him and was coming towards her! Catherine's heart raced, though she gave him a haughty look that would have kept many a man at bay.

'You look more beautiful than ever this evening, Mistress Catherine.'

'I thank you for the compliment, sir,' she replied coolly. 'I think Mademoiselle Montpellier very beautiful. Her gown has such style it puts most of us to shame.'

'It came from Paris,' Nick replied carelessly. 'She had nothing when I rescued her from the mob, for her home was burned to the ground and she barely escaped with her life. My mother did what she could to rectify the matter when I brought her home by giving Louise some of her own gowns, but this one is new. It seemed the least I could do in the circumstances.'

'You are generous, sir. Mademoiselle Montpellier is fortunate that you show such an interest in her comfort. But I hear that she is high in your estimation, and that you have taken her beneath your wing?'

Jealousy was burning her like a torch. An emotion she felt unworthy and struggled to overcome. What could it matter if he cared for the French girl? He was naught to her!

'I do what I can for a young girl who has no one to care for her,' Nick replied, his eyes narrowed. 'But you must not believe all you hear. My interest is no more than friendship.'

'Then rumour lies,' Catherine said, made a little uncomfortable by the look in his eyes. Was she misjudging him? 'I wondered if perhaps you might be able to help Mistress Williams? Her family are Huguenots and she fears that they may have become caught up in the violence.'

'I shall make inquiries,' Nick said. 'Perhaps you would care to give me more details?'

'It is Mistress Williams you must speak to,' Catherine said. 'It would be a kindness in you, sir, for she is very worried.'

'Of course, as all who have family in such a situation must be. You will excuse me if I seek out Mistress Williams?' He bowed his head to her, preparing to depart.

'Naturally. And I must speak with Sir Alan Dovedale…'

Nick watched as she moved away, her gown swaying gracefully, her head high. She was not the only one at court to imagine that he was captivated by Louise. He must do something to make his feelings clear before Louise herself listened to the rumours and began to believe them, for he had no intention of marrying the French girl. His interest was, as he had told Catherine, merely compassion for a girl who had lost everything in a night of such savagery it had shocked all that witnessed it.

Yet Catherine's little outburst had cleared up something that had puzzled him. If she believed that he was courting Louise Montpellier it might explain her coldness to him. He smiled at the thought, well pleased with others that followed it. If Catherine was angry, it might be that she was jealous.

A month had passed since Sir Nicholas's return to court: a month in which Catherine had been irritated to see them always together. It seemed that whenever Nicholas was at court, Louise would find him, monopolising his company to the exclusion of all others.

Louise was often with the Queen, for she had been favoured above many as Elizabeth sought to show her sympathy for the cause of the Huguenots. To Catherine it seemed that she could not go anywhere without bumping into the other girl these days.

It was on the day of the archery competition that she saw Louise clinging to Sir Nicholas's arm and smiling up at him in a way that showed how confident she was of his approval. She had given him a favour to wear tied to his sleeve, and it was clear that he was her champion for the contest.

Catherine was aware of the little smirk that came her way when Louise left Nicholas and came to join a group of ladies, which included Catherine and Lettice.

'Do you not think Sir Nicholas is very handsome?' she asked Lettice, choosing to sit beside her on one of the cushions that had been placed on the dry grass. 'They say he is clever with the bow and will win the contest with ease.'

'I have heard that Sir Alan is more likely to win,' Catherine said when Lettice did not immediately answer.

'I think you are both wrong,' Lettice said. 'I have been watching James Morton practise and I believe he may be the surprise champion of the day.'

'Shall we have a wager?' Louise asked. 'I will wager my pink scarf against your green spangled one, Mistress Catherine, and a silver pin against your pewter bangle, Lettice.'

'I do not care to wager,' Catherine replied and got up to move away. She was irritated that Louise had joined them, and wandered off to stand amongst a group of ladies and gentlemen who were also wagering on the winner of the contest.

'Who do you favour, Catherine?' Annette Wiltord asked. 'I hope it is Sir Alan. It will do Sir Nicholas Grantly good to tumble down from his pedestal for once.'

Seeing the spite on the other woman's face, Catherine was silent. She knew that Annette was bitterly jealous of the French girl and not above showing it. There had been more than one quarrel between the two, which was the fault of Sir Nicholas, of course. He was faithless and a wicked flirt and she was sure she did not care who he favoured with his attentions as long as it was not her!

Unwilling to be drawn on whom she supported, after a moment or two Catherine walked away to where a group of tumblers were performing their antics. Several pedlars had set up stalls at the edge of the field, selling ribbons, small items of jewellery and trinkets, and many spectators from the town had come to watch the various sights. As well as the archery contest there was to be a display of hand-to-hand fighting in the tiltyard that had been set up earlier, wrestling, and other sports. There was also a small group of gentlemen gathered in a corner to watch cocks fighting, and a man was forcing a bear to dance for coins.

It was quite amusing to see the great bear lumbering to the direction of his master's tune on the pipes, but then, happening to catch sight of sores upon its back, Catherine realised that he had probably been beaten to make him perform. The careless cruelty of some men made her angry and sick to her stomach. She turned away, knowing it was beyond her power to stop the man tormenting his bear, wandering back again to watch the archery contest begin.

From the very beginning it was obvious that only three men had any chance of winning, as their arrows hit the target again and again. Sir Alan's aim was true, but so was Sir Nicholas's, and a little to her surprise, Catherine discovered that Lettice had been right about Master Morton, who was matching the others arrow for arrow.

At the last it came down to just Sir Nicholas and Lettice's favourite, Sir Alan's last arrow having gone wide. For a moment Catherine thought Sir Nicholas would win and she hoped that Lettice had not wagered her favourite bangle against the other girl's pin, but then a groan broke from the watchers, most of whom had backed Sir Nicholas, and she realised that Master Morton had won. It was very unfair of her, but she was secretly pleased and hoped that the French girl had lost her silver pin.

When she returned to Lettice it was to find her congratulating Master Morton, who had brought his prize, a silver drinking cup, engraved around the rim and set with small gemstones, to show her.

'Ah, Mistress Catherine,' James turned towards her with a smile. 'I was looking for you. I wanted to present you with my prize.'

'For me?' Catherine was surprised. 'I could not possibly accept, sir. Indeed, it would be very wrong of me, for you must know I did not believe you would be the winner. My own favourite was Sir Alan Dovedale.'

'I do not mind that you did not favour me in the contest,' James Morton said. 'I dare say there were many present who did not know that I am a skilled archer.'

Catherine declined to answer, merely smiling and shaking her head when he offered the cup to her. She had heard that he was a gambler and spent much time with the men who diced in the corridors at court, but she believed he was not a particularly lucky gambler.

'Still, I shall not take your cup, sir. If you wish to give it to a lady, you should present it to Lettice, for she was brave enough to venture a wager that you would win.'

She walked away again before he could answer,

though she saw that he made no move to give the cup to Lettice and realised that he might have bethought him of its likely value.

'Are you enjoying the day, Mistress Catherine?'

She had not been aware of Nick until he came up behind her. Swinging round to greet him, her heart pounded as she saw the way his eyes danced with amusement as he looked at her.

'It is a fair day for the tournament, sir.'

'You did not accept Master Morton's prize?'

'He was not my choice of a likely winner,' Catherine replied.

'I trust that you did not wager on me?'

'No indeed, sir. I wagered on no one, though I thought Sir Alan might win, for he has won the last three contests in a row.'

'But that was when neither Master Morton nor I were at court,' Nick pointed out. 'It might have gone either way between us, but in the end he was too good.'

'You speak of victory too easily, sir. Yet I thought your last arrow careless,' Catherine remarked. 'One would almost think you had had enough and wished the contest over. Perhaps you had other, more important matters on your mind? You do not care to waste your time in such trivial pursuits.'

'You wrong me, mistress,' Nick said and frowned. 'I always try to win, and but for a faulty arrow I might still have done so.'

'Ah, it was the arrow.' Catherine nodded. 'It puzzled me as to why your aim had suddenly lost its surety.'

'I saw you watching the entertainment in the field earlier,' Nick said. 'You looked angry. Did it not please you?'

'I see no pleasure in watching an animal being forced to act against its nature, especially when it has been cruelly treated to make it do so.'

'Ah, the bear,' Nick said looking thoughtful. 'I do not care for such sports myself, though many think it fine amusement. For myself I see no sport in baiting a poor creature. Shall I buy the bear for you, Mistress Catherine?'

'What should I do with a bear?' She was astonished, but in another moment her mind raced on seeing the possibilities. 'Could you do so? And what would you do with the poor creature then?'

'It is impossible to set it free, for it has become used to captivity. There are, however, places where it might be housed in comfort for the rest of its days, where it would no longer be beaten and half starved. I could arrange for it to be transported to a place of safety, if you wished?'

'I should think that kind in you, sir,' Catherine said. 'If you could persuade the man who owns it to give up the beast?'

'I think it entirely possible that he will sell to me,' Nick replied; his eyes lost their serious expression, beginning to spark with mischief. 'Frown no more, my lady. This is a day of pleasure and I would see you smile. There must surely be something here that pleases you? I could offer you entertainment of another kind if you find none in the maypole dancing.' The look in his eyes left her in no doubt of the nature of his offer, and she knew he was mocking her as usual.

Catherine rewarded him with a soft laugh, the shadows lifting from her face. 'You are a rogue, sir, but I am grateful for your intervention with the bear. I would have rescued the poor beast myself, but I feared the man would not listen to me. I am a mere woman.'

'A woman certainly,' Nick replied, a little smile. 'But a woman of rare beauty and compassion. The two qualities are not always found in one.'

Catherine's heart fluttered as she looked into his eyes. For a moment she felt that she was back on the riverbank on the day of Lady Fineden's picnic, a young and foolish girl about to fall in love.

'So there you are.' Louise's voice was bright and false as she came up to them. 'I must scold you, Nick, for you have cost me a silver pin. You assured me you would win, and I believed you.'

'I apologise, Louise.' Nick smiled at the French girl. 'I shall make it up to you, I promise—but for now I must beg you both to excuse me. Mistress Catherine, Louise, I have some pressing business to attend.'

Louise watched him go, her eyes sharp with annoyance as she looked at Catherine. 'You were wise not to wager your scarf,' she said. 'For you would have lost it.'

'But not to you,' Catherine said. 'And Lettice is my friend. If she wishes to wear my scarf she may do so whenever she wishes. If you will excuse me, mademoiselle, I must go to Her Majesty.'

She walked away with her head high. She would be a fool to be taken in by Sir Nicholas's smiles again, for it was evident that the beautiful Louise Montpellier had made up her mind to have him, and he did not seem to object.

James Morton watched her in frustration. It seemed that Sir Nicholas had little more success with the fair Catherine than he—but his own case was urgent. He must win her if he could, for his life and fortune might depend upon making Mistress Moor his wife. Sometimes he thought that her life might also hang in the balance, for there were times when he was very afraid.

'I have heard something that might interest you.'

Catherine was surprised a few days after the contest to be stopped by Louise Montpellier as she was on her way to the Queen's apartments.

'I do not understand you, mademoiselle?'

'Sir Nicholas told me that you were making inquiries on behalf of the family of Mistress Williams?'

'Yes, that is true. Do you have any news?' Catherine looked at her expectantly.

'I can tell you that they are not amongst the official list of the dead, though many more are missing. They may have gone into hiding, of course.'

'Lettice will be relieved to know that at least they are not on the list of the dead. Thank you for telling me, mademoiselle.'

'She is fortunate that hope remains for her family.'

Catherine saw a suspicion of tears in the other girl's eyes and her heart was touched. She had never cared for Louise, but she could feel sympathy for her in this case.

'There is none for your own family?'

'No…' Louise raised her head, her eyes sparkling as she fought back her tears. 'None. I saw them killed that night and the house burned around them.'

'I am sorry. It must have been dreadful for you.'

'Do not give me your pity,' Louise said, anger driving out the grief. 'I want nothing from you, Mistress Moor. Except that now I have given you the news you sought you will stop plaguing Sir Nicholas at every turn! He does not find it amusing, though he is too much of a gentleman to say so.'

'I beg your pardon?' Catherine stared at her, surprised by the girl's sudden change of mood. 'What can you mean?'

'You are perfectly aware of my meaning.'

'This is ridiculous!'

'Do you deny that you deliberately provoke him because you want him to notice you? I have seen the way you look at him!'

'I do deny it,' Catherine said, a flash of temper in her eyes. 'Indeed, you insult me, Mademoiselle Montpellier. I have no interest in Sir Nicholas. None whatsoever. And I certainly do not seek him out at every turn.'

'Then why were you talking with him so earnestly last evening?'

'We had some private business to discuss, and I do not see that I must share it with you.'

Catherine raised her head proudly. Sir Nicholas had

come to her to tell her of the bear, which he had successfully released from its cruel master.

'I fear it must remain in captivity for its remaining days, for it could not live else,' he told Catherine. 'But I have a friend who rescues such animals and I know that he is prepared to nurse it back to health and care for it until it dies a natural death.'

'I thank you for your consideration,' Catherine replied. 'Perhaps one day I may be permitted to see the bear?'

'He is yours,' Nick replied with an odd smile. 'My friend will be glad to let you see him whenever you care to, but you would have to travel to my estate in Devon to do so, I fear.'

'Oh, well, perhaps one day…' She smothered a sigh.

'Yes, perhaps one day.'

'Why do you smile so?' Louise demanded now, infuriated by the look of satisfaction on Catherine's face that she herself did not know was there. 'You may think he dances to your tune like a tame bear, but I shall have him in the end.'

The simile was so apt in the circumstances that Catherine could not help laughing. Naturally Louise was affronted, and stalked off, leaving Catherine to stare after her.

Now why was Mademoiselle Montpellier so very angry?

Lost in her thoughts, Catherine was not aware that she was being followed until the man caught up with her. She turned at last as his voice broke through the mist that seemed to hold her mind.

'I have been calling you an age, Mistress Catherine.'

'Sir,' she said, looking at James Morton with impatience. 'I am on my way to the Queen and must not delay.'

'Will you allow me to walk with you?'

'If you please, sir,' she said. 'But you must walk quickly, for I would not keep Her Majesty waiting.'

'I saw you speaking to Mademoiselle Montpellier just now,' he said. 'They are saying that she will soon be wed to Sir Nicholas. I think it a good match, for she is grateful to him for saving her life.'

'Is gratitude a reason for marriage?' Catherine asked. 'I would have thought other considerations more important.'

'Do you speak of love?' He was suddenly eager.

'Excuse me, sir. I must hurry on.'

Catherine left him staring after her, a prey to his frustration once more. Time was slipping away, for him and perhaps for Mistress Moor though she little knew it.

Chapter Seven

'Louise Montpellier is determined to have him as her husband,' Lettice said behind her fan that evening. 'They are laying bets that she will get him in the end—but I do not think he wants her.' She gave Catherine a sly look. 'I think he is interested in someone else.'

'Do not look at me when you say that,' Catherine cried and pulled a face. Her foot tapped in annoyance beneath the skirt of her magnificent court gown, which was of a pale rose silk stiffly embroidered with silver thread and beads. As a rule she did not mind Lettice's teasing, but she did not want anyone to guess her true feelings in this matter. 'I care not whether Sir Nicholas marries Louise or another. He is of no interest to me.'

'I am not so sure.' Lettice laughed, unable to resist her teasing as Catherine's eyes took fire. 'I have seen you looking at him sometimes when you thought yourself unobserved…'

'I may look at many gentlemen,' Catherine retorted. 'That does not mean I care for them. I would as soon take any other man as he!'

Oh, but it was not true, it was not true. Catherine

admitted in her heart that none other could make her feel as he did with just one look from those wicked eyes of his, eyes that seemed to set a fire running deep within her. But she was foolish to think of him! Why could she not accept that he was faithless and be done with it?

'What of James Morton?' Lettice asked casually after a short silence between them. 'He comes this way. No doubt he means to ask you to dance. He is more constant than any other of your suitors, Cat. Perhaps you should marry him?'

'Perhaps I should,' Catherine replied with an impatient shrug. She did not mean it but she was tired of being teased about Master Morton. He was beginning to weary her with his attentions, for it seemed that whenever she turned round he was there behind her, hovering. He was always trying to please her, but she found his manner irritating, and did not quite believe in his profession of admiration for her. 'If I wished to marry he would suit as well as another— but I do not wish to dance with him. Nor shall I stay to be asked.'

Catherine moved away, threading her passage through the throng of courtiers until she reached the little cluster of privileged ladies and gentlemen that had the right to be near the Queen.

Lettice waited for James Morton to come up to her. She smiled as she saw his little frown of annoyance. He must realise that Catherine had deliberately avoided him.

'Have you come to dance with me, sir?' She invited with a pout of her pretty lips, her manner flirtatious.

James looked at her, his frown lifting. Mistress Williams was a woman much to his liking, good-humoured, pretty and obliging. Indeed, if the choice were his alone…but he had lost the power to choose when he had thrown away his fortune at the fall of the dice. If he wished to avoid disgrace and a debtor's fate he must do as he was bid. Mistress Moor was heir to a considerable estate. He must win her and her fortune—and serve the master who had bought him body and soul.

Yet the look in Lettice's eyes was enticing and he felt his blood stirring; it would do no harm to dance with her this once.

'Will you give me that honour, mistress?'

'Indeed, I should be delighted, sir.'

Catherine, glancing round at that moment, saw Lettice give him her hand. Something in the other girl's manner made her realise for the first time that her friend was much taken with James Morton. She cursed her careless tongue, for she had no intention of encouraging Master Morton, and did not wish to hurt Lettice. Though she did not want him for herself, Master Morton seemed a pleasant, harmless fellow and she would be glad to see her friend settled.

Lettice had been at court for five years. She had served the Queen well, and it was time she was allowed to marry and make a life of her own. She had spoken wistfully of having children more than once, but although quite popular with the other courtiers she had shown no sign of forming an attachment.

Catherine decided that she would be more careful when speaking of James Morton in future. Lettice clearly liked him and the match would be a good one for her—and for him, since Lettice had a fortune of some substance in trust for her when she married.

It was a wonder that a match had not been arranged before this for Lettice, but this was because she was an orphan and the Queen's own ward.

'I cannot marry unless Her Majesty approves,' Lettice had told her once in confidence. 'I have no one to speak for me in the matter—and I believe I shall die an old maid.'

It would be a pity if Lettice were not to marry, Catherine thought with a little frown. She must do what she could to encourage the affair.

Nick's frown deepened as he watched Catherine moving about the great chamber. Her every movement was gracious, sensual, the swaying of her hips turning more than one man's head, and he knew that he was not the only one who counted her a prize worth the winning. He had already attempted to approach her several times this evening, but she had seemed to anticipate his every move and had gone out of her way to avoid him.

Now what had he done to upset her? He had thought she'd warmed to him a little when he'd told her of the bear he had rescued for her sake, but now she had retreated into her former coldness.

Why did she dislike him so? Nick could not understand. What had he done to cause this new reserve in her?

'You frown, Nick. Have I done something to make you angry with me?'

He turned as the lovely young French girl spoke, smiling at him intimately. He was aware of a slight sense of irritation, for he knew that Louise wanted more from him than he was prepared to give. His consideration for her welfare had led her to believe that she might expect more than friendship, and he was aware of both guilt and frustration: the wench was at his elbow every time he turned.

'My frown does not concern you, Louise. I was thinking of something else.'

'Or someone else.' Louise pouted at him, her lips red and soft with the freshness of youth but somehow less enticing than the lips he longed to taste. 'You waste your time with that cold fish. They say she has had every man at court dangling on her string and none can win her, for she hath no heart.'

'I have heard something of the sort, but I do not believe it to be so.' Nick's eyes had followed Catherine and he saw that she was speaking to a man who was often at her side. 'I do not like to hear such unkind words from you, Louise. It does not become you.'

'I am sorry, will you forgive me?' Louise flushed, knowing that she had made a mistake.

She looked so downcast that Nick smiled. 'Of course. I should not take my ill temper out on you, Louise. Come, dance with me?'

'Willingly.'

Louise's face lit up as he led her out to join the dancers. Nick noticed that Catherine had given her hand to Sir Alan Dovedale, and appeared to enjoy dancing with him. Nick was puzzled. Why did she smile on Dovedale, who was a wicked flirt and had had affairs with almost all the presentable ladies at court, and yet have only frowns for him?

He was thoughtful as his eyes continued to follow Catherine about the room while he performed the dance with his own partner, and then a little smile began to hover on his lips. She had not meant to, but Louise had given him an idea that might just break through the barrier of coldness Catherine had erected between them, and at the same time lay to rest the rumours concerning his relationship with Louise herself.

'What are you reading?' Lettice asked, looking curious as she entered their bedchamber to find Catherine frowning over what appeared to be a letter. 'Is something wrong?'

'It is a poem,' Catherine replied. 'A foolish trifle, nothing of consequence.'

'A love poem,' Lettice cried. 'How lovely. Who sent it to you, Cat?'

Catherine screwed the scrap of vellum into a ball.

'I told you it was nothing.'

'But someone must have sent it.'

Lettice swooped on the crumpled note, smoothing it out as Catherine tried to snatch it back and failed.

'Why, it is from Sir Nicholas,' Lettice said, surprised. 'He wrote this for you, Catherine. He has addressed it to *A Rose of Many Thorns*. That is you, Cat. It describes you perfectly when you are on your high horse. He writes of the unrequited love that burns him, giving him no peace while he lies in his bed at night.'

Lettice giggled as she read the impassioned words. 'This is so wicked and so clever, Cat. I vow it puts my cheeks to the blush to read it.'

'Then do not do so,' Catherine said and snatched it from her. 'He makes fun of me!'

'I would say rather he makes fun of himself—of his passion for you that plagues him so.'

'He has no passion for me. He is faithless. Look how he deserted Annette…'

'But she took lovers as soon as his back was turned. He would not have her back then, why should he? Besides, she is going to marry Lord Ramsden.'

'He is old enough to be her father!'

'Well, he has managed to father a child on her, or so Annette says, though I would not swear to it being the truth.' Lettice giggled and Catherine smiled. 'But since he needs an heir and his last wife could not give him one, God rest her soul, poor thing, he may as well accept the brat and have done with trying.'

'I am glad for Annette's sake that he will marry her, but that changes nothing. Sir Nicholas cares for someone else. He is always with *her*…' Catherine blushed as she realised that she sounded jealous.

'You mean Louise Montpellier, I suppose. It is certain that she wants him, but I am not sure he wants her—especially after he sent you this. You do know what the words really mean—what he is suggesting?'

'Of course. It is salacious and sly.' Catherine glared at her. 'He wants to seduce me. He speaks of lying with me in a leafy glade, of the pleasure to be found in drinking a nectar known only to true lovers. I should like to hit him, Lettice.'

'That would not be my reaction if he had sent the poem to me.'

'You may have it. I give it to you with pleasure.'

'That would not be the same.' Lettice gave her a knowing look. 'Do you really not like him at all?'

'He is faithless and a flirt,' Catherine snapped. 'If I never see or speak to him again I shall be happy.'

Even as she spoke she knew that she was lying. Nick made her angry sometimes, and she did not trust him, but when he looked at her with those mocking eyes, then…oh, then, she melted inside.

But his poem was wicked, the more so because it raised such pictures in her mind! But she was angry with him for sending it to her, when it was meant only to torment and tease, and she would show him her displeasure when next they met. And this after he had told Louise that she plagued him at every turn! If he dared to approach her that evening, he should feel the rough edge of her tongue!

'Why do you look so serious, Mistress Catherine?'

She jumped as the voice whispered close to her ear, recognising the fragrance he wore about his person without needing to see. It had the freshness of cedar-wood combined with the mystery of ambergris and was wholly enticing. Inside, she was trembling, the heat rising like sap in a young tree, but outside she remained cool and remote.

'Perhaps I was aware that you were nearby, sir.'

'Come, Catherine,' Nick chided. 'Are you so unkind as to dash my hopes of winning a smile?'

'Why should I smile for you, sir?'

'Did you not like the love poem I sent you?'

'I found it indifferently worded,' Catherine lied, for it had been beautiful, neither effusive nor sickly sweet but simple and true. Perhaps the rhythm was not perfect, the structure unusual, but it would have touched her had she not closed her heart against him. 'I fear you must try harder, sir.'

'Will you listen to a further piece I have composed to your beauty?'

Catherine fluttered her fan, pretending to hide a yawn.

'How tiresome these pretty pieces become when one has heard too many…'

Nick gave her a look of reproach, a hint of mockery in his eyes. 'You are cruel, mistress. And after I have laboured all day to bring it to you.'

Catherine's eyes flashed green fire. 'Save it for your mistress, sir, I dare say she may appreciate your piece of flattery.'

'Alas, I have no mistress, for the one I adore spurns me. How can you accuse me so falsely when I have eyes only for you?'

'You have a honeyed tongue, sir, but I do not believe you.'

'What does she say, Christopher?' The Queen's voice was light and teasing, more so than it had been since the terrible news had come from France. 'What does Sir Nicholas want that she denies him?'

'Sir Nicholas hath written an ode to Mistress Catherine's beauty,' Christopher Hatton replied. 'He has laboured all day for it but she will not let him read it to her. She declares she is bored with such tributes.'

'Shame on you, Cat!' Elizabeth teased. She was in a merry mood, having at last shaken off the shadows that had haunted her for weeks. 'Come, Sir Nicholas, we would hear you. If Cat will not listen you shall read it to another.'

'It shall be for you, ma'am,' Nick said making her an elegant leg. 'For, failing Mistress Catherine, who has stolen my heart and will not give it back, there is no other lady I love so well—nor one so fair as Gloriana.'

'You are a rogue, sir,' Elizabeth retorted, a flash of amusement in her eyes. 'Your flattery will gain you nothing. Yet I shall hear this poem. Pray begin, sir.'

Nick went down on one knee before her, his hand on his heart, a smile upon his lips as he began to declaim in a voice that carried clear and sweet to all about them.

> *As night is still, so is my love;*
> *The morning mist no sweeter dew,*
> *Than her breath that so scorneth me*
> *When I my lady dare to woo.*
> *No sun can warm my heart as she,*
> *No moonlight give my sleep the ease*
> *That her gaze doth bestow on me*
> *When I my lady strive to please.*

There followed several more lines about his burning desire, his frustrated love, and other foolish things that brought a blush to Catherine's cheeks and set her foot tapping with annoyance, but at last he was done.

Silence followed his recital and then Elizabeth inclined her head in approval.

'Not one of your best efforts perhaps, but 'tis well enough. Mistress Catherine speaks truly, sir. If you would win her I think you must try harder.'

Her words seemed to criticise and yet her manner was teasing. The poem had been spoken in such a way that it breathed reverence for the object of the writer's love and few at court could have spoken them so beautifully that they made the throat go tight with emotion.

Catherine's cheeks were on fire, for everyone's eyes were upon her as they waited for her to speak. She lifted her head a little, her eyes bright with pride and perhaps the merest suspicion of tears.

'A pretty poem, sir,' she said. 'You should direct your words to a lady who would wish to receive them.'

'I can write poems only as my heart directs. It is my rose of many thorns who holds me in thrall to her, holding me prisoner to her beauty so that I can neither sleep nor eat.'

'Then you must find some new outlet for your talent,' Catherine retorted and fluttered her fan. 'Why do you not write a play for us, sir? We all enjoy a comedy of manners. I dare say that might be to your taste, since you like to mock at life and love.'

She was mocking him, and the duel of words between them was causing much amusement amongst the courtiers, but Nick was not so easily defeated.

'If I write the play will Mistress Catherine consent to take a part?' he asked, his eyes holding a cool challenge that made her pulses race and her breath quicken.

'Now he has you, Cat,' Elizabeth said, clearly much diverted by this discourse. The air about them seemed to crackle with tension, which was clearly sensual, at least on Nick's part, and everyone was waiting with baited breath for the next development. 'For if you refuse he wins the contest. If Sir Nicholas writes his play you shall take the part he offers you.' She clapped her hands and laughed as she saw the expression of frustration in Catherine's eyes. 'I declare that you shall both take up this challenge. It will help to while away the dull winter hours. You shall perform your play at Christmas, Sir Nicholas—and Cat shall be your heroine.'

Neither could refuse what was now a royal command. Catherine curtseyed to the Queen, while Nick made her a gallant salute by kissing the tips of his fingers to her and assuring her that he had known she would support his cause.

'It shall be my pleasure to write something that will amuse you, ma'am. Now I shall consult further with Mistress Catherine—if you will permit.'

Elizabeth inclined her head graciously, having brought about a situation that was guaranteed to bring them more amusement over the coming weeks. Sir Nicholas and Mistress Moor were well matched in this fierce contest and it would be interesting to see who would emerge the victor from their battle. Elizabeth loved nothing better than a little mischief-making, especially when it concerned those courtiers she liked about her.

Nick took a firm hold of Catherine's arm, leading her away from the courtiers and the Queen to stand by a window looking out at a sheltered courtyard, where roses still bloomed despite the first frost of autumn. The sky was curiously white, which meant the frost might be a hard one.

'You think yourself mightily clever, sir.' Catherine glared at him. 'Do not suppose that because I must spend more time with you I shall like you any better.'

'You might like me if you stopped being angry with me, Cat.'

'Who gave you permission to call me that?'

'It suits you. Sometimes your tail wags when you are angry—just like the cats at my home. As a boy I used to watch them about the garden when they were denied something, and you have their very manner.'

'You are impudent, sir! I do not have a tail but I should warn you that I do have sharp claws. Be careful that I do not scratch you with them!'

'My sweet Cat,' Nick said, laughing at her evident outrage. 'The tail you do not have is swishing at this very moment—and I need no warning of your claws, for I have felt them before now. You showed me their velvet the first time we met.'

'I did not!' Catherine flushed as she met his gaze. 'Well, perhaps I was a little unfair to you—but you deserved it. You are a wicked flirt, sir, and a rogue as I first thought you. You should address your poems to your mistress.'

'If you mean Annette Wiltord, she was once my mistress; I do not deny it—but that was a long time ago. She has taken other lovers since, and if she would have me in her bed again I cannot oblige her, for I no longer desire her. Nor would her future husband be pleased if I were to court her.'

'She was not the only lady to show you her favours. I dare say a dozen more languish for a smile from you and it is clear that Mademoiselle Montpellier has a *tendre* for you, sir.'

'Louise has no call on me other than friendship. I made her no promises and our arrangement was always meant to be merely that. I have never offered her more.'

'She may think differently.'

Nick's eyes gleamed. She was so lovely when she was agitated, her bosom rising and falling, the neckline of her gown cut so that he was privileged to catch the merest glimpse of the sweet white flesh he burned to feel close to his own.

'Are you jealous, Catherine? Do you want me to swear that I have forsworn all others for your sake?'

'Pray save yourself the trouble, sir. It is of no matter to me. I am indifferent to your affairs.'

'Methinks the lady doth protest too much. Come, admit you like me a little, sweet Cat.'

'I dare say there are things to like about you, sir. If one has the time and the inclination to discover them.'

'But you have not—or is it merely that you will not admit the truth? You are determined to be cold to me, but I shall win you, my little kitten.'

She glared at him. 'I am not your anything! Do not imagine I shall purr if you stroke me.'

A wicked smile curved about his sensuous mouth, his voice soft and husky as he said, 'Ah, but you do not know how sweetly I should stroke you, Catherine.

Would you like me to show you how pleasant it could be? I swear I could make you purr with pleasure and take much joy from it. You were made for loving, Cat. I could prove it to you an' you let me…'

Catherine's cheeks were burning. His words and the caressing looks he gave her made her feel weak inside, and that mouth—oh, that mouth! She wanted to feel his mouth possessing hers, his body pressed hard against her so that they became almost one, but she was determined not to show it. He had flirted with her once before and then he had gone away for fifteen long months, leaving her to nurse her hurts alone. She would not let him serve her so again!

'You insult me, sir!'

'You think I meant to insult you when I spoke of love?' Nick smiled oddly. 'The love I offer you is the most precious gift a man can bring his woman, a thing of beauty and of pleasure. To me your body is a shrine that I would worship and adore. You are beautiful, Catherine, and a passionate woman. Few have as much fire, though you hide it as best you can. But you cannot hide from me, for I feel your thoughts even before you have them. Why will you not trust me—just a little?'

'Because I know you are not to be trusted.'

'Who has so maligned me? Point him out and I shall challenge him to prove his accusations.'

'You cannot duel with a lady, sir.'

'Annette…' Nick's mouth curled in scorn. 'You would take her word above mine?'

'It was not Annette…'

'Who then? She must be a very viper to have made you hate me so.'

'Indeed she was not. She spoke in jest of your careless behaviour, but it was said in affection. Lady Fineden is a fond mother. She saw nothing wrong in what she said of you, rather I think she meant us to think you a fine fellow who had half the ladies at court languishing after you.'

'My mother? But she would not malign me. You mistook her meaning, Catherine. Shall I have her come to you and tell you that I am not the heartless monster you imagine?'

'You shall not!' Catherine could not look at him. It was true Lady Fineden had spoken merrily to entertain the company, but, hurt by Nick's desertion without a word, Catherine had taken her words literally. Besides, she had never meant to tell him, never meant to let him see that he had hurt her. 'This is all nonsense! Why will you plague me so? Can you not believe that I have no wish to be courted by you?'

'Then why do your eyes invite even while your lips deny me?'

'They do not! You are impossible, sir.'

'Come into the courtyard with me, Cat. I shall prove that I do not lie about my love for you. In my arms you shall become a woman who knows herself worshipped and adored.'

'And lose my virtue for a careless few kisses I suppose?' She gave him a scornful look. 'I shall listen to no more of this, sir!'

Catherine walked away from him angrily, her gown swishing like the very cat's tail Nick had accused her of having. She was aware that half the court was watching and laughing behind their hands. Sir Nicholas had suddenly become her most ardent admirer, and after this evening's charade everyone would be laying bets for or against his seducing her by Christmas. It was very annoying to be the object of so much merriment, and she could have slapped Nick for making his courtship so public. Indeed, she would have done so had it not been bound to cause more scandal and speculation.

'Your pardon, Mistress Moor. I believe you dropped your kerchief.'

Catherine hardly glanced at the kerchief that was offered her or the man who had handed it to her. She might have seen him at court before, but he was merely one of the hangers-on, not part of the inner circle, and had made no impression on her.

'Thank you, sir.' She tucked the kerchief into the waist of her bodice.

'Bevis Frampton at your service, mistress.' Catherine nodded and made to move on, irritated by this intrusion into her thoughts. She was detained as he laid a hand on her arm, keeping her a moment longer. She caught a glimpse of a flawless ruby ring on his right hand: a ring such as that one was rare and worth a fortune. Yet everything else about him was modest and slightly old-fashioned. 'A word of warning. Be careful of Sir Nicholas. He is not a man to be trusted.'

'What do you mean, sir?' Catherine looked at him properly for the first time. There was nothing to mark him out from a hundred others, but she sensed some-

thing beneath the surface and for some reason felt
chilled by those strange eyes…rather dead eyes, like
a reptile, she thought. And there was an odd smell
about him, as though his clothes had been stored in a
chest for a long time and were a little musty. 'Why
do you speak thus of Sir Nicholas?'

'For your good, Mistress Moor. And now you must
excuse me. I have work to do.' He pressed a lace kerchief to his lips and she noticed a beading of sweat
upon his brow, as if he were not quite well, and to
prove her right he coughed harshly. 'Forgive me…'

Catherine frowned as he moved away from her
abruptly, staring after him. Who was he? He had said
his name was Frampton but it meant nothing to her.
She could not recall having met him or even having
heard him spoken of at court. Yet there was something
at the back of her mind that made her feel she might
have met him before, though where or when she had
no idea.

'Who was that gentleman?' she asked as Lettice
came up to her a moment later.

'What gentleman?' Lettice looked puzzled and yet
there was a little gleam of excitement in her eyes. 'I
saw no one in particular.' She gave a giggle. 'Everyone is talking about you and Sir Nicholas, Catherine.
Did I not tell you that it was you he wanted? Louise
is furious. You should have seen the way she looked
at you. If looks could kill…'

'Do not say that!' Catherine shivered suddenly.
Something had made her turn cold. She took out her
kerchief and was about to use it to blow her nose when
the scent stopped her. It was not hers, and she did not

like the heavy perfume. She dropped it on the floor, kicking it to one side with the toe of her shoe.

'Are you getting a chill?' Lettice looked at her oddly. 'You've dropped your kerchief.'

'It was not mine. Someone handed it to me—but I think it was just an excuse. He wanted to warn me that Sir Nicholas was not to be trusted. I did not like him very much.'

'He must be jealous,' Lettice said. 'That trick with the kerchief has been tried many times before. Besides, half the gentlemen of the court wish that you would look at them as you do Sir Nicholas.'

'Do not be foolish, Lettice. I do not look at him any differently than I do at anyone else.'

'You cannot see yourself.' Lettice laughed as she scowled. 'Do not pull a face, Cat. There is no shame in finding such a man as Sir Nicholas attractive. I vow that almost any woman at court would change places with you.'

'But not you,' Catherine said, looking at her with affection. 'I think there is someone else you care for— isn't there?'

Lettice blushed. 'I have tried to hide it…'

'Why should you? I promise I do not want him, Letty.'

'But he wants you. He means to ask you to marry him, Cat. He asked me if I thought you would listen to his proposal.'

'I hope you told him not to be so silly?'

'How can I?' Lettice asked and sighed. 'He must be in love with you, Cat.'

'Perhaps he has heard I am an heiress. He may need

money. You should let him know you have a fortune in trust for you, Lettice.'

'That is unkind! To accuse him of only wanting your money...' Lettice looked upset and a little angry.

'Half of my suitors have courted me for my fortune,' Catherine reminded her. 'You know it to be true, you have told me so yourself these many times. And warned me to be careful!'

'But James is different. I don't believe it is just the money. He...he seemed almost desperate when he spoke of you just now, as if he could not bear it that you might be interested in another.'

'If it is for love of me then I am truly sorry. I cannot marry a man I do not love. Besides, you care for him and I would see you happy, Letty—which you could not be if I married him without love.'

'I should be happy married to James even if he did not love me.' A wistful sigh escaped her. 'But he thinks only of you.'

'Be his friend,' Catherine advised. 'Be there when he is sad and make him smile. He may turn to you when he sees his cause with me is hopeless, and I shall make certain that that is soon. I had not thought him so serious, but now I shall discourage his attentions more than I did before.'

'He might turn to me if he realises he cannot have you.' Lettice summoned a smile. 'I have been told of an astrologer who can cast fortunes that will come true. Will you come to visit him with me, Cat?'

'I do not know...perhaps.' Catherine shook her head decisively. 'No, I do not care to. You go if you wish, Lettice. I know my fortune. I shall stay here at court until I go home to live with my father.'

'You say that because you are determined not to marry unless you fall in love—but you may not have a choice. James told me that he has written to your father of his regard for you...' she broke off with a sigh.

'How dare he!' Catherine was angry now. 'To write without my permission! It is unfair and impudent and I shall tell him so when next we meet.'

'Pray do not for my sake,' Lettice begged. 'I was told in confidence. Besides, it is often done that way. Most would approve his approach to your father before addressing you.'

Catherine made no answer. Lettice spoke the truth, but it was most provoking for her father, would be sure to inform Lady Stamford that an offer had been made. What could have possessed James Morton that he had done such a thing?

'You make little progress, sir. I vow my master will not be pleased when I report that you have not managed to win the lady.'

They were in a small courtyard beyond the banqueting hall which was little used by others, for it was dark, and the flagstones were overgrown with moss, slippery on a night such as this when the frost was hard.

'Then do not tell him,' James Morton said, trying hard not to shiver in the chill wind that echoed about the palace. He had been summoned to this meeting and hated the situation in which he found himself. 'For by my faith I have tried everything I know to please her, yet she scarcely looks at me.'

'You must find other methods of persuasion…a way to bring the lady to heel and make her more amenable.'

'I have written to her father of my wish to wed her.'

'Then perhaps all is not lost. If your suit pleases him, the girl must do as she is told.'

'You will stay your hand yet awhile?' James gave the other man a look of appeal. 'Grant me a little more time, I beg you.'

'You must redouble your efforts. If she should promise her hand to another my master would not be pleased.'

'You think I do not know that?'

James shivered as the trickle of ice slid down his spine. He had met the man this one called his master but once and that in darkness, never seeing the face of the man who had paid his debts and now owned him. At that meeting he had been told the price he must pay to redeem himself, a task that had seemed easy enough at the time, but had proved more difficult than he had imagined. Mistress Moor was a woman of some spirit and all his careful wooing had come to naught.

'Then take care you do not push his patience too far. I think you know what fate awaits should *he* decide to call in his debt?'

James nodded mutely. His orders were given to him by this creature—a poor thing he would scarcely look at twice if it were not for the other one. There had been something evil about the *other* one; he would swear he had caught the stench of sulphur that night, while this one smelled only of old clothes kept too long in a camphor chest. The night he had met the *Master* the scent of evil had filled his nostrils and his lungs, seeming to make it almost impossible for him to breathe—yet perhaps that had been merely fear.

That there were men who had dealings with Satan and were able to summon demons at will, James had no doubt. The Church itself spoke of all the demons of hell and threatened sinners with eternal damnation. And there had to be a source of evil to explain all the ills that afflicted mankind. For why else should the good be struck down with the bad? The sciences that governed the forces of light and darkness were beyond James, but he had been brought up to fear those things that were secret and beyond the powers of a normal man.

'There is something more you might do...if you were willing.'

James was brought back to the present as he looked at the other man. 'I have spoken to Lettice Williams about the astrologer as you bid me. She is intrigued and she will try to persuade Mistress Moor to go with her to have her fortune read.'

'A love charm might win the lady to you.'

'Lettice will persuade Mistress Moor to visit the astrologer if she can,' James said.

'Then we must hope for your sake that your friend hath a silver tongue.'

James nodded, his mouth set grimly as he watched the creature walk away coughing. This one was a weakling and could be disposed of with ease, but it was hardly worth the effort.

It was the *other* one who frightened him, the man who had trapped him into this invidious position. James wished desperately that he had never taken his money. Better to have applied to his uncle for payment of his debts.

Yet he knew the old skinflint would never part with a penny on his nephew's behalf, and it had been such a large amount. Only on his uncle's death would James inherit the estate that was entailed on him—and he wouldn't put it past the old goat to take a young wife and cheat him at the end.

Before his uncle died he might be ruined—or dead himself if he did not manage to carry out the promise he had made that fateful night. He cursed the ill fortune that had caused him to ruin himself at the throw of a dice. Until then he had been without a care in the world, and now he was at his wits' end.

Yet his anxiety was not all for himself. There was a fear in him that if he did not achieve what had been demanded of him, Mistress Moor herself might be in danger.

Somehow—somehow!—he must persuade Catherine Moor to marry him.

Catherine woke with a start and lay shivering for some minutes as the dream lingered. It had been more frightening than others that had disturbed her sleep, for she had been alone in a strange place, alone in a mist that seemed to surround her. And somewhere in the mist there was a menacing figure threatening her.

'You shall not be permitted to live…death is coming soon…'

The whisper seemed to linger in Catherine's mind, like a dark shadow hovering.

'No…' she whispered and jumped out of bed.

She was foolish to let such dreams haunt her and she would put it from her mind.

Chapter Eight

Catherine had spent a very trying morning, for Her Majesty was in one of her moods again, and she had refused to be pleased with anything her ladies did for her. Some whispered that she was displeased with the Earl of Leicester over some rumour that had reached her regarding his affair with one of her ladies, but no one dare mention the subject within the Queen's hearing.

Released from her duties for a few hours, Catherine walked slowly back towards the chamber she shared with Lettice. She frowned as she saw Louise Montpellier coming towards her, a gown she had fetched from the sewing room over her arm.

'I hope you know that everyone is laughing at you?' she hissed as they passed in the narrow corridor. 'He will never marry you. He merely wishes to seduce you, and then he will tire of you as he has others.'

Catherine refused to answer her, merely walking on by with her head high. She knew that the other girl was jealous because she wanted Sir Nicholas for herself, but that did not mean she was wrong. Catherine knew only too well that he was capable of cruel desertion. Why should she care what he did?

But she did, of course, she did despite all her denials.

She went into the bedchamber, finding Lettice in the act of putting on her cloak, and remembering belatedly that her friend had spoken of visiting the astrologer that afternoon.

'Are you sure you will not come with me, Cat?' Lettice paused as she tied the strings of her cloak. She gave Catherine a persuasive look. 'Do you not think it might be fun?'

'Perhaps… No, I do not wish to have my future told,' Catherine said, making up her mind finally. 'I know it seems foolish, but I have a horror of such things.'

'It is merely a game.' Lettice looked at her uncertainly. 'It cannot mean anything.'

'Then why go—if you do not believe?'

Lettice shrugged. 'I don't know. I just want to hear what he has to say. Besides, James told me about him. He thought you might like to have your horoscope cast.'

'Well, I should not.' Catherine smiled. 'Take no notice of me, Letty. I dare say I am in a mood. I expect you will enjoy the experience, and I know that many people do believe in the power of a good astrologer to foretell the future.'

'The Queen hath consulted Dr John Dee many times. I have heard that he is a very clever man, much skilled in the art of mathematics and other sciences. There are those that would condemn him for his work in many of these areas, which they think dangerous, and they say he dabbles in the occult—but she protects him, for she finds him useful.'

'I know it, for I have seen them consulting together, and I dare say it is foolish to hold back on my own account—but I shall not ask what is ahead for me. It might be something bad and then I should be afraid.'

Catherine did not know why she feared to ask about the future, but she was aware of an iciness in her blood whenever Lettice mentioned the astrologer she intended to visit.

'Oh, they never tell you bad fortune,' Lettice said and laughed merrily. 'For else you would not pay them nor recommend them to your friends. Well, if you will not come I shall go by myself.'

Catherine sat alone in the chamber they shared after Lettice had gone, brooding over her own thoughts. In a way she regretted not having gone with her friend and yet she hesitated to dabble in things she did not understand.

Perhaps it was because of what she had seen that day at Cumnor Place. Even now the thought of that shifting, formless shadow could send a cold shiver down her spine. What had she seen? Could it have had anything to do with that poor lady's mysterious death—or was that evil shadow Death itself?

The Grim Reaper come to claim another victim? Is that why she was haunted by menacing dreams? Or was she being warned? Was she in some danger herself?

Feeling the now familiar coldness steal over her, Catherine jumped up in an agitation of spirits. Either way it was something she did not wish to dwell on, for if it had been human it might mean that Amy Robsart's fall had not been an accident, and if it were not of this earth… But no! She was foolish to let her thoughts drift this way. She would go and walk in the gardens. Although it was cold out it would be better than sitting here alone with such morbid thoughts.

Catherine had known she would not be long alone in the gardens. She was not the only lady to brave the cold and soon came upon a group of ladies and gentlemen taking the air. They greeted her with cries of welcome, and James Morton being one of their number, he immediately attached himself to her side.

'You do not find it too cold for walking, Mistress Catherine?'

'No, not at all, sir. At home I am used to walking and riding in all weathers.'

'I think you miss your home,' he said, catching a wistful note in her voice. 'Can it be that you prefer a country life?'

'Sometimes I wish myself at home,' Catherine admitted. 'I miss my father too. He writes to me now and then, but I fear he is oftimes lonely, though of course he has many friends.'

'If you were married he might come to you for long visits…' he dangled the temptation before her, but was disappointed in her answer.

'Or if I were to return home I might be with him always,' Catherine replied with a flash of spirit. 'For the moment my place is here, sir. It pleases Her Majesty to keep me with her and I must not think of marriage yet. Nor do I wish for it!'

'Her Majesty might be brought to consent if she thought it would please you, Catherine.'

'But it does not please me, sir. I believed I had made myself plain?' Catherine gave him a speaking look. 'Excuse me, I go another way…'

She turned off from the main party, following a path through the shrubbery which she knew led to a small, often sunny courtyard, where she might sit protected from the wind. For a moment she feared that James might follow, but after a while she realised that he had continued with the others, her snub having left him chastened for the moment.

'Whither goest thou in such a hurry, sweet kitten mine?'

Catherine heard the voice call to her and knew who was now following in her footsteps. Her heart began to thud in her breast, making her feel breathless. Oh, why must he follow her now, when she was feeling so low in spirits? She did not look back, but walked on at a faster pace, hoping he would give up and leave her be.

'Nay, I shall not be shaken off like a troublesome puppy,' Nick cried as he caught her as she reached the sheltered arbour. 'I saw that Morton had annoyed you. If the fellow is a nuisance I shall warn him off—just say the word and he troubles you no more.'

Catherine looked at him, eyes flashing. 'Master Morton is merely a nuisance, sir. I vow there are others I find more troublesome.'

'Meaning myself, I dare swear,' Nick replied, laughing at her as she stood there defying him, the wind catching her hair. 'You are so beautiful when you look like that. 'Tis no wonder I lose sleep for thinking of you! You drive a man to madness, Cat…'

Catherine found herself mesmerised by the expression in his eyes. She stood without moving as he reached out, drawing her close to him, so close that she could feel the throb of his heart and the heat of his manhood burning her. The flame in his eyes, and the soft, loose slant to his mouth that spoke volumes of his desire, made her feel that he had stripped away the barriers between them, laying her bare to him, exposing her vulnerability where he was concerned.

'Let me go,' she whispered hoarsely, but she could not struggle as he lowered his head, taking urgent possession of her mouth. It was as if the heat of a furnace possessed her, turning her to molten fire, and her body melted into his, desire sweeping over her in a great wave that made her almost faint. 'Let me go…I must go…' Her words were smothered as he kissed her again, his tongue inserting itself into her mouth, flicking at her, teasing her into further submission. She was drowning in a sea of flames, the fire raging down inside her, in that secret feminine place that had known no man's touch yet now longed for his…his hand touching her, caressing her where it burned and trembled for him. 'Please, I beg you…'

'What do you beg of me, sweet Cat?' Nick whispered as his lips moved against her throat, making her moan with sheer need. 'Do you want me to love you? Shall I take you here? Shall I thrust myself into that secret place that burns for me? You can feel the need, can you not? It throbs against you, begging for entry to the temple of love to which you alone possess the key. You want to be mine, my precious rose of many thorns, I sense it. Why resist when you long for the love I can give you?'

His hand was caressing her breast, his fingers insinuating themselves beneath the lace at her neck, stroking the white flesh that trembled and burned for his touch. Her back arched as his mouth followed where his hand had been, thrusting her closer to him, the aching need inside her almost slaying her will to resist.

'No! No, you must not,' she whispered weakly, knowing she was near to capitulation. 'If you deflower me I shall hate you for it, Nick. I swear I shall hate you until the day I die.'

'I would have you love me,' he murmured. 'Fear not, darling kitten, I would not use you so, though I burn for you, need you even as you need me inside you—but I honour you too well to force you to something that might shame you.'

'Then let me go,' she begged, raising her eyes to his in a desperate appeal. 'You have come upon me at a time when I am vulnerable...' A little sob escaped her.

'What ails you?' Nick asked, letting her go as he saw that she was neither angry nor defiant, but truly distressed. 'If something or somebody has hurt you, you may safely tell me.'

'No—it is nothing,' she said, her throat tight with emotion. Her body was still aching for his touch and in truth she longed to be back in his arms, but she dare not trust him. She had come too close to the point of no return to risk another moment in his arms. Besides, he had deserted her once before and she knew him for a rogue. 'Just a bad day…a shadow that sometimes haunts me.'

He reached out to touch her cheek, his touch gentle, caressing but without the heat of their earlier embrace. 'Is it this foolish contest between us, Cat? I shall call it off and admit I cannot write a play worthy of Her Majesty's notice if you wish it.'

'Can you not write it, sir?'

Catherine was recovering, her breathing easier now than it had been when he had held her so close that she felt they had almost become one.

'It is almost done. It was to tell you this and ask if you would like to read it with me that I followed you, but then you looked so beautiful that I was minded to…but now I have upset you and it was not my intention.'

'It was in your mind to seduce me?' Catherine's voice had regained its acerbic quality, a flash of pride in her eyes as she gazed up at him. 'I know well that you are minded to make me your mistress, sir.'

'My mistress, Catherine?' Nick smiled in amusement at her flash of pride. 'But do you not know that you are already the mistress of my heart, mind and body? What more can you want—unless it is to be mistress of my home, my wife in name as well as love.' His expression was teasing and wicked, making her angry.

Catherine tossed her head. 'It is as well I know you mean not one word of this, sir—else you might find yourself being thrown into the Tower for making promises to one of Her Majesty's ladies.'

'But if I mean this promise, Cat? What would you say then I wonder?'

'I should say that I have no wish to wed you, sir. I shall not take a rogue for my husband. I mean to marry only a man I can respect and love.'

'But I know you love me,' Nick replied in a voice so husky that it nearly took the legs from under her. 'You are bound to me with every look and every breath you take. What may I do to gain your respect? For I swear I do not know what I must do, my lady.'

'Do not look at me that way,' Catherine breathed, a catch in her throat. 'For I almost believe you. It will not do, sir. I believed once before and...'

She turned away, angry with herself for revealing so much of her private thoughts to him. If he had guessed that she felt so much for him, he would use his knowledge against her, breaking her will little by little until she surrendered to him. And then, when he had tired of her, he would leave her.

'If I hurt you once before, I swear it was not with intent,' Nick said to her back. 'I left England and you because I was ordered to it, Catherine. I cannot tell you more—indeed I risk much by telling you this, but if it will give you back a good opinion of me it is worth the taking.'

Catherine looked back at him. Her heart was beating madly and she did not know how to answer him. 'I must not stay,' she said. 'We shall talk another time. Forgive me. I would be alone...'

Nick stared after her as she walked away. He had begun his public courtship of her out of a mixture of pique and a sense of desperation that she would give him no chance to make his case with her. Now he knew that it was not what he wanted—to win her, to break her, would only cause more bitterness. The only way he might win her was to be seen to lose himself...

Alone in her room once more, Catherine paced the floor. She knew that she had come close to surrendering her will to his, and that she would have gloried in doing so. Indeed she longed to be back in his arms, to lose herself in them. But that would only lead to more hurt and humiliation. What a fool she was to have given her heart to a man who would surely break it!

And yet he had tried to explain that he had left her not from wilfulness but from duty. If she could but believe him! How she longed to believe, to give herself the chance to love and be loved.

She had thought her life at court satisfied her, but now she knew that it did not, nor could it ever. She wanted a home of her own, a husband and children about her.

Foolish, foolish Catherine, she scolded herself. Her pride had made it impossible for her to find a husband amongst all the gentlemen who had courted her, for she had been so sure that she did not wish for marriage, and all the time her wilful heart had been waiting.

Waiting for Nick to return and claim her.

But no, she would not let him win her so easily. His smiles charmed her, and his kisses made her want to melt in his arms, but they meant nothing. For all she knew, he had made as many promises to Louise Montpellier.

He was a wicked rogue and she would do well not to forget it.

Catherine listened to her aunt's lecture in silence, staring out into the gardens where the trees had shed their autumn glory, the branches bare against a sky that hinted at more frost. Her thoughts strayed despite her efforts to keep them from doing so, and she wondered where Sir Nicholas was and what he was doing, as she always did when he did not come to court for a few days. She had not seen him since their meeting in the garden, when she had so nearly given all for love.

'This is very foolish of you, Catherine. You have been at court nearly eighteen months and your father has received but one offer for you. If you refuse James Morton you may not be asked again. Pray think carefully before you turn your face against this marriage.'

Catherine sighed inwardly. She had known her aunt would lecture her ever since she had been told that Lady Stamford had arrived and was asking for her. It was clear that her aunt thought she should accept Master Morton, indeed she had intimated that she thought it an excellent match.

'This offer has not been the only one made me, Aunt,' she replied as calmly as she could, her nails turned into the palms of her hands, reminding her not to lose her temper or her dignity. 'I have discouraged others from addressing my father. Master Morton did so without my knowledge or consent.'

'That is very proper of him.' Lady Stamford frowned at her. 'And no reason to refuse Master Morton. If this is a fit of pride, Catherine, it ill becomes you and I beg you to reconsider.'

'It is neither pique nor pride, Aunt. Master Morton is pleasant enough as a companion but I do not wish to marry him. I am quite content as I am for the moment.'

'If you think Sir Nicholas Grantly will marry you, you may be disappointed, Catherine. Oh yes, I have heard of this stupid wager or challenge, whichever you wish to call it, but the man is a flirt and a seducer. Once you have given in to his persuasion he will look elsewhere for his amusement. I warn you, niece, this man will not bring you happiness even if you should wed him. My first impression was I admit favourable, but I did not know then that he was a careless flirt. Such men do not make good husbands.'

'Thank you for your advice, Aunt,' Catherine said icily. She had to bite back the angry words that sprang to her lips. How dare her aunt presume like this! 'But it was unnecessary. I am neither a fool nor a wanton to be taken in by a man's flattery. And besides, Sir Nicholas may not be as bad as you paint him.'

Catherine did not know why she was defending him, but her aunt's attitude had angered her.

Lady Stamford stared at her in silence for a moment. Catherine had in her opinion been spoiled. As a child she had been headstrong and wilful, and her temperament had not improved during her stay at court. Indeed, she seemed to have grown in pride, and there was a new authority about her. Clearly she was not to be easily persuaded.

'I find your attitude selfish, Catherine. Your father worries for your future and his health is not what it once was…'

'My father is ill?' Catherine looked at her in alarm. 'He writes always that he is perfectly well.'

'I do not say that he is precisely ill…' Lady Stamford sighed. 'You cannot expect that either my brother or myself will live for ever, Catherine. How do you expect to manage for yourself? Or would you rather become a ward of the court and languish here for the rest of your life?'

'That will not happen.'

'It might. If the Queen decided you were too vulnerable to manage your estate alone, she might decide to make you her ward. Do not frown at me so, Catherine. I say these things only for your own sake. You are young yet and the life here is still exciting, but when your beauty faded and you were no longer the centre of attention you would find it was less amusing.'

'I shall return to my home long before that happens.'

'Unless Her Majesty decides to keep you here. Be careful, niece. I would not see you spend the rest of your life in regret.'

'I thank you for your care of me, but I shall never marry Master Morton—nor any man I cannot love.'

'You try my patience severely, but I shall leave you to think about my words, Catherine. Be sure I do not say them lightly.'

Catherine inclined her head and they parted. Lady Stamford having been summoned to an audience with the Queen, Catherine made her way slowly to the room she shared with Lettice, her thoughts twisting and turning in confusion.

As she went into the small bedchamber, she saw that Lettice was bending over her bed. The girl turned with a guilty start as she became aware of Catherine watching her.

'I thought you were with your aunt,' Lettice said, moving away from the bed.

'What were you doing just now?'

'Looking for a scarf I have mislaid. I thought it might have fallen under your bed and I was merely straightening the covers, having dislodged them in my search.'

'Oh, I see.' Catherine accepted the explanation though she was not quite certain it was the truth, but it was not important enough to press Lettice further. 'You did not tell me how your visit to the astrologer went. Did he have good news for you?'

'I did not tell you, because I thought you were not interested in such things.'

'Only for myself. I should like to hear what he said to you.'

'Well…' Lettice wrinkled her forehead in thought. 'It was a little strange. The room was very dark. I could not see his face, for what light there was fell on me while he remained in the shadows. And there was a curious smell that was not particularly pleasant.'

'What kind of a smell?'

'It was fusty…like old clothes that have not been

used in a while. It made my head ache and I was glad
to be out in the fresh air again.'

'Were you not frightened?' Catherine looked at her
curiously.

'Yes, just a little,' Lettice confessed. 'His voice was
soft…and he spoke in riddles. He said that if I obeyed
my heart it would bring me close to danger. But he
also said that if I bought his love charms and used
them according to his instructions I would get what I
most desired, so I am not quite sure what he meant.'

He had said a lot of other strange things to her that
Lettice was not prepared to disclose, things that concerned her best friend—and that meant Catherine. She
had not really understood him, but she had done what
he bid her and placed one of the charms beneath
Catherine's pillow.

'And did you buy the charms?'

'Yes. It was worth a few silver pennies, Catherine.
If I can turn James's thoughts to me I would pay far
more.'

'Do you suppose these charms work?'

'Perhaps…I do not know.' A smile touched
Lettice's mouth. 'James has sought me out once or
twice of late.'

'My aunt tried to bully me into accepting his offer.'

'You did not give in to her?' Lettice looked
alarmed. The charms would not help her if Catherine
were forced into accepting James's offer. 'You will
not change your mind, Cat?'

'I have no intention of marrying James. I've told
you so, Lettice—but my aunt will not accept my re-
fusal so easily. I hope she does not speak to Her

Majesty of this marriage, but I fear she will attempt it. For if it were to be made a royal command…' Her voice died away. Lettice did not need to be told the consequences.

'You would be forced to marry him then.'

'I should beg her to change her mind,' Catherine said, her expression defiant. 'And if she refused…I should run away. My father would not force me to a marriage I cannot like. He gave me his word and I know he will not renege on that.'

'You are brave to speak of defying Her Majesty,' Lettice said. 'I am not sure I would dare.'

'If the choice was to run away with James or be forced to marry a man you did not love—what would you do?'

Lettice stared at her in silence for a moment, then lifted her head. 'If James asked me to run away with him I believe I would…even though it might mean punishment for us both.'

'Then I know you must truly love him. Do not despair, Lettice. When he understands I will not have him he will turn to you,' Catherine said. 'Then he must approach Her Majesty and ask for your hand.'

'Supposing she will not grant her permission? I have sometimes thought it suits her to hold the strings of my fortune. Once I am married she would have to hand the estate over to my husband.'

'But she cannot mean to keep you here for ever?'

'It has happened before with other women who were made wards of the court,' Lettice said. 'I think in the past it was quite often the case that an heiress would be kept languishing at court until she was no

longer young enough to marry. If I were to die unwed
my estate would become the property of the Crown.'

'Then you must run away and marry. You may be
punished but I am sure Her Majesty will relent in time,
for she is not a cruel woman by nature.' Catherine
laughed. 'But first you have to make James fall in love
with you.'

'What does Mistress Moor have to say on the matter?' Elizabeth looked without favour at the woman
standing before her. Lady Stamford was inclined to
presume too much at times because of her service to
Anne Boleyn in the past, and Elizabeth did not care
to be reminded of her mother's unhappy fate. For as
the child of an adulteress she had been set aside, forgotten and despised by all but the few who had remained loyal. It was only through the grace of God
and her own skills at diplomacy that she had survived
the dangerous times that followed. 'I have not remarked that Catherine has a particular liking for
Master Morton. Indeed, it would surprise me to learn
that she wished to marry anyone.'

'Catherine is stubborn,' Lady Stamford said with a
twist of her thin lips. 'She does not know what is good
for her. I am here to ask for your approval, ma'am. I
am of the opinion that it would be a good match for
my niece. The young man may inherit a fortune and
a title if Lord Aldborough does not marry again.'

'The match would be well enough if Catherine had
less wit or beauty, but I think Master Morton too dull
for her. Besides, it does not please me that she should
marry just yet.'

'She is past twenty, ma'am. Her father worries that her chances may soon be gone and she will wither into an old maid.'

'You think her too old at twenty? You surprise me, Lady Stamford. You married three husbands, which is an inordinate amount for any woman, and yet I seem to recall that you were never a beauty.'

Elizabeth's manner was icy cold, and it soon became clear to Lady Stamford that she had made a mistake in implying that Catherine might soon grow too old for marriage. She had touched a raw spot with the Queen, who was still smarting at the ruin of her marriage negotiations with Alençon. Her foot was tapping, her anger barely under control as she glared at the other woman.

'I merely meant that another chance might not come Catherine's way, ma'am. It is not the case for all ladies, of course.'

'You made yourself plain the first time. Your request is denied, madam. I shall not give my approval to the match. Indeed it does not please me. I forbid it. Master Morton hath already approached me and received the same answer. Let me hear no more of this, for you try my patience sorely.'

Elizabeth made an impatient gesture of dismissal. She was angry and weary of these endless marriage negotiations. Why must the ladies about her be constantly talking of marriage? Had they nothing else to amuse them? She was irritated beyond measure by her ministers, who plagued her to take a husband or name an heir, and then refused to endorse her choice. It was always that she must do this, or must not do that, for the good of the country. Was she never to be allowed personal happiness? But she would not be bullied or harassed by those who demanded too much of her!

She alone was queen. *She* alone knew what lay in her heart and mind, and for the good of England—for the safety of her realm, for which she had sacrificed so much—so it must remain while she yet had breath in her.

Catherine feared the worst as she answered a summons from her mistress not half an hour later. She had not seen her aunt since their earlier interview, and her heart was beating very fast as she entered the Queen's presence and curtseyed deeply.

'Pray, come and sit by me,' Elizabeth invited, indicating a stool. It was not the first time Catherine had been permitted to sit in the Queen's presence, though she would never dream of doing so in public, for she had not officially been granted the privilege of the stool, nor would her rank permit it. 'I wish to talk to you, Cat.'

'Thank you, ma'am.' Catherine perched on the stool, which was padded and covered in silk tapestry. 'I believe my aunt has been with you?'

Elizabeth inclined her head. 'Lady Stamford was here. She requested that I give my approval to a marriage between you and Master Morton. What say you to that?'

'I say only that I earnestly pray Your Majesty did not give your approval to the match.'

'Is the fellow not to your liking?'

'I would not like to marry him.'

'Is there someone else you wish to marry?'

'Not for the moment, ma'am. I am very happy as I am, thank you.'

'That pleases me, Cat. I am not yet ready to lose you. You may rest easy in your mind. I have refused the match on your behalf.'

'I thank you from the bottom of my heart, ma'am.'

'We shall speak no more of Master Morton.' Elizabeth glanced at her, a hint of mischief in her eyes. 'How do you go on with Sir Nicholas? Has he shown you aught of his play?'

'I believe it is almost written, though I have not yet seen it. When last we met, he spoke of giving me a copy to read soon—though that was some days ago.'

'I have seen a few pages.' Elizabeth laughed softly. Her interview with Sir Nicholas had much amused her, but for the moment she had charged him to keep it private. 'I believe we have a talented playwright at court. It should be an entertaining piece. I look forward to seeing you play your parts.'

'Sir Nicholas is to act as well as write the play?'

'I believe that is his intention, yes.'

Catherine's heart sank. If he had cast himself as the lover in this play it would lay her open to his assault, for if the part called for them to kiss…her thoughts shied away from the possible result. It was impossible, unthinkable. She would have to take great care that she did not betray herself before the whole court!

'You may leave us now, Cat.' Elizabeth gave her an indulgent smile. 'I wish I was free to join you on a stroll about the gardens, but I fear I have matters of state to attend. Think yourself fortunate that you have not such cares. Go now! I must prepare for more important questions.'

Catherine left her mistress, making her way towards the gardens, as was her habit when she was free to please herself. She sought the solitude of the rose arbour in the shelter of the walled garden, where it was pleasant to sit even on a cold day, but she found that someone was there before her.

'I hoped you would come,' Nick said, coming forward to meet her. Catherine's heart stood still as she saw his smile of welcome, and she recalled the last time they had met in this place. Her wretched heart and body had betrayed her, making her near swoon with the torment of her emotions. Oh, but she must not let him make love to her like that again! 'I wanted to give you my play. It is finished, and if you will read it and consent to play the part I have written for you we may begin to rehearse by the end of the week.'

Catherine hesitated to take the rolled script from him. There were but half a dozen sheets, which meant that it was not lengthy and should be easy enough to learn.

'How many characters are there, sir?'

'But four,' he said. 'It is a mere nonsense, a comedy of manners as you bid me, Catherine. You play the fair Melodia and men will play the other three parts. The friend of Melodia is too ugly to be taken willingly by any other lady at court, and besides, it will be more amusing played by a man.'

As it was usually the custom for all parts to be taken by men or fair youths posing as ladies, except in private performances, Catherine was not surprised by his statement. Indeed, she would have thought long and hard about taking part herself had it not been a command from the Queen, which naturally removed all stigma.

'I shall read it,' Catherine said, accepting the script from him. 'As you well know, we are bidden to our parts by Her Majesty, but I shall not easily forgive you if you win this contest by foul means, sir.'

'Trust and believe,' Nick replied with an odd smile. 'I would not hurt you, Catherine.'

'Her Majesty has told me you play a part yourself?'

'Mine is the character of Sir Peabody,' Nick replied. 'But you will discover all for yourself when you read it, Catherine.'

'Will you leave me now so that I may read this alone?'

'If it is your wish. I apologise if the words do not please you. I have no real talent for such work. A poetic trifle is perhaps not beyond me, but this was more difficult.'

She could not know how long and hard he had laboured to please her. For he had had to take the greatest care that he would not offend her, and yet he had to make both her and others laugh. He thought that it would have been much easier to write a tragic love story, but she had commanded a comedy and he had done his best to oblige her.

Catherine waited until she was alone. Her hand trembled as she unrolled the script. Nick's handwriting was both bold and neat, showing strength and character. She began to read, tentatively at first and then with a growing eagerness. The first few lines made her

smile. It seemed that Melodia was a rich heiress who
had decided she would not marry until her ugly friend
Sybil had been found a husband. Enter Sir Peabody
and his friend Sir Trustworthy.

Sir Peabody it seemed was a vain, bragging fellow
who vowed that he would have the heiress in the palm
of his hand before a sennight was out. His friend Sir
Trustworthy begged to doubt that Melodia was to be
so easily won, and a wager was made between them.

There followed a series of scenes between Melodia
and Sir Peabody during which the rogue tried everything to win her and was rebuffed at every turn by the
clever heiress. This went on until Sir Peabody came
up with a scheme to abduct and seduce Melodia and
thereby force her into marriage.

Catherine's heart raced as she turned the last sheet.
Was this Nick's way of warning her that he would
have her in the end?

She read the last scene with bated breath and then
gasped, her frown turning to a smile as she realised
how cleverly he had played her and their audience.
For instead of Sir Peabody gaining his wicked intent,
with the help of Sir Trustworthy the heiress turned the
tables on the rogue and he found himself first abduct-
ing and then marrying Sybil at the point of a sword.

Catherine clapped in delight. It was sheer nonsense,
of course, but the ending was so delightful, with
Melodia marrying Sir Trustworthy and the bragging
Sir Peabody tied to his ugly wife. The heroine's
speeches were both witty and sharp, and she recognised some of her own rebuffs to Sir Nicholas.

But why had he cast himself in the part of the fool?

Surely he would rather have played Sir Trustworthy? It was what she had expected. This way it made Melodia the winner…and Catherine too.

She realised that he had fulfilled his challenge but in such a manner that he relinquished the honours. Why had he done that? She knew that if she had had to kiss Nick at the end she might have betrayed her true feelings for him. He must also be aware of this and yet he had deliberately given the part to another. Indeed, he had suggested that Christopher Hatton might play the part if both he and the Queen approved. A friend of Nick's had agreed to play Sybil.

Catherine knew that such a piece would delight and amuse the court. She found it exceedingly diverting and her former dread had been transformed to antici-pation. Had she wished to tease and punish Sir Nicholas for his attentions to her, this was the perfect opportunity.

She was smiling as she began to memorise the opening lines.

The rehearsals began almost at once. Christopher had declined with regret, having important business elsewhere, but another gentleman whom Catherine liked was found and sworn to secrecy.

No one was allowed to watch except Lettice, who had agreed to prompt those who forgot their lines.

She had been delighted to be included and promised faithfully to keep the plot secret. Only those involved and the Queen herself knew what the play was about, and at her own request the ending had been held back from Her Majesty that she might enjoy the performance the more.

Nick was superb as the arrogant, pompous Sir Peabody. Catherine had only to play herself, while the others threw themselves into their parts with eagerness.

Nick's friend Joshua Brundle was a good-natured fellow who allowed himself to be padded out with cushions and his face to be painted with so much rouge that he looked ridiculous. Sir Trustworthy was a kindly gentleman some years older than Catherine, and again had only to speak his lines as himself.

It was Nick himself and Joshua who bore the brunt of Nick's wicked cleverness, and each day he came up with some new trick or way to punish Sir Peabody. Catherine laughed so much when he accidentally tripped and landed on his bottom at her feet that he decided to include it in the performance.

'I vow I have never had so much excitement,' Lettice told Catherine when they finished their last rehearsal. 'I shall be sorry when it is over.'

'I also, in a way,' Catherine agreed. 'Yet I do not look forward to the performance itself.'

'Why ever not?' Lettice stared at her in surprise. 'You have nothing to fear. Sir Nicholas has done nothing that might harm you or make you appear foolish. You are shown as caring for your friend, for she is given a rich present at the end to settle Sir Peabody's petulance. I should have thought you would be pleased with the part he wrote for you, Cat.'

'I know it flatters me,' Catherine said and nodded. 'It is merely nerves, a fear that I may not acquit myself well. Sir Nicholas and Sybil will carry the play. They are quite wonderful and 'tis a most amusing piece.'

'I envy those who see it for the first time,' Lettice said. 'Yet I have enjoyed being with you all. Louise is furious that she has been excluded. She blames you, Catherine, and says that she might have been trusted to keep a secret as well as any other.'

'Mademoiselle Montpellier does not like me.' Catherine sighed. 'But what of you? I have been so caught up in the play that I have not had time to think of you, Lettice. Have you made any gain in your relationship with James Morton?'

'I believe he likes me,' Lettice said hesitantly. 'Yet he seems nervous and on edge, as though he is afraid of something. Sometimes he seems as if he wishes to tell me what is on his mind, but then he draws back.'

'It may be that he has debts,' Catherine said with a frown. 'I know you do not like to hear me say it, Letty—but if he is worried about money it might ease his mind to know of the fortune in trust for you.'

'You think I should tell him?'

'He must by now realise that he has no hope of me. Even my aunt gave it up as hopeless and went home after Her Majesty said she would not approve the match.'

'I know he is anxious about something.'

'Then speak to him,' Catherine urged. 'Tell him… Oh, I do not know, tell him that you wish to marry and leave the court. He must know that you have a feeling for him, let him see that you are not truly happy here, and that you will have an inheritance when you marry.'

'Yes, I suppose I might,' Lettice said thoughtfully. 'He has had business elsewhere for a day or so, but he should return tomorrow in time for the play.'

'Are you saying that you will not do as my master bids you?'

James Morton looked into the cold eyes of the other man and shivered. He had thought him a weak creature, but there was an underlying menace in him now. He could almost think master and creature but one.

Cold sweat broke out over James's body as he realised that he might have been fooled. If both were indeed one…it meant that *he* was a master of disguise and perhaps even more dangerous than James had imagined.

'You will regret this, Master Morton. You owe a great deal of money…'

'I shall find the means to repay your master. I give you my word that I shall pay my debt somehow.'

James licked lips that were suddenly dry. He was finding it difficult not to reveal his fear. He must not let this man guess that he had pierced the secret of his true identity. Nor that his hopes of getting money from his uncle had failed, as he had known in his heart they would.

'Money will not suffice. A bargain is a bargain, sir.'

'What else can I do? She will not have me and the Queen forbids the match. There is nothing more to be done.'

'You must find a way to change the lady's mind. Abduct her—carry her off and seduce her. She will marry you swift enough then, I'll vow.'

'But that is wicked! Even if I could do it I would not. By my honour, sir, you ask too much.'

'Then persuade her, if you have not the stomach for abduction. Surely you can find the way? Give more love charms to Mistress Williams to slip beneath her pillow.'

'They do not seem to work.'

'I shall give you something stronger. Here, take this, but remember it must go beneath her pillow.'

James took the small pouch he was handed reluctantly, slipping it inside his velvet doublet. 'Lettice will do as I ask, but I fear the case is hopeless. The best I can do is to repay your master the money I owe him.'

'He will not be pleased. For your own sake you would do better to abduct her, Master Morton.'

'I cannot do it.'

James quailed as he saw anger in the other's eyes. He was almost certain now that he had been duped into thinking that there were two men rather than one, and his skin prickled with fear. He fancied he caught the stench of sulphur and his mouth tasted foul, his stomach wrenching with sickness as the sweat ran cold down his back.

'I will think about it...'

He spoke out of fear, to pacify the anger he felt flowing from the other man. Never could he do such a wicked thing as this creature of Satan demanded. He respected Mistress Moor, and besides, there was Lettice. Of late he had found himself more and more attracted to her. Indeed, he had been on the verge of speaking his mind to her more than once.

'See that you do not fail my master.'

'I shall try.'

James's mouth was dry, his chest achingly tight as he struggled for control. Could this man see into his mind? No, surely not! If he had that power, James would probably already be dead.

He was racked with doubt and terror as he left the inn and had himself rowed back across the river. The mist swirled over the water, giving it an eerie feel and convincing him even more that he had been in the presence of evil. Why did the man, who called himself the *Master* and yet pretended to be a poor, sickly creature, want this marriage? James had asked himself the question a hundred times but was no nearer finding an answer. Did he mean Catherine Moor some kind of harm? It was a mystery that haunted him throughout the long cold journey.

If Frampton, or whoever the *Master* really was, wanted Catherine dead, why did he not simply have her killed? Or mayhap he would if his plan to have her removed from court went awry?

James's blood ran cold, his stomach turning. The thought that it might eventually come to such a thing horrified him. Rather than that, it might be better to force her hand. Supposing he did abduct her?

Could he bring himself to do it? While not precisely a coward, James knew his limitations. He could hire rogues to capture the girl, he supposed—but would he then have the courage to seduce her against her will?

If he did not he might be the victim of an assassin's knife one dark night, his body cast into the river to be eaten by the fish.

It was a stark choice and one that James would have to think on long and hard.

Nick frowned over the note that had just been delivered to him. It purported to come from Catherine, but he suspected it had been written by another. It asked that he meet Catherine alone in the courtyard at once.

The hour was late, and he was almost certain that she had long since retired to her chamber, but the writer claimed to be in some distress and Nick could not ignore it. However, he would be on his guard.

It was well his instincts had served him truly, for even as he entered the courtyard, which was in darkness save for the light of a crescent moon, he was set upon by three rogues.

'Damn you!' he muttered as the first blow landed. 'I should have known it was a trick!'

The rogue said nothing but struck him another blow with his cudgel. Nick seized it, wresting it from him and throwing it into the bushes. In the next instant he drew his sword. The first assassin fled into the darkness at once, but the other two lingered, circling him as if wondering whether to attack or not. When Nick gave a shout and lunged at them, they took to their heels and fled after their companion.

The attack had been ill planned, Nick thought, and wondered at its purpose. Surely the rogues could have killed him had they wished—or had it merely been a warning?

Nick grimaced as he felt the stiffness in his shoulder where the first blow had struck. Clearly he had an enemy who knew him well enough to be certain that he would come in answer to a plea for help from Catherine.

Was it a jealous lover? Someone who hoped to win her for himself—or was there something more sinister behind it?

Chapter Nine

The play was the success Catherine had known it must be. Her Majesty was much amused, and the courtiers entered into the spirit of the occasion by calling out to encourage Melodia to give Sir Peabody more of her sharp tongue.

Nick played his part with evident enjoyment, showing himself to be a fine actor. It would have been so easy for him to take the part of Sir Trustworthy, but no one else could have played Sir Peabody so well, combining the roles of fool and rogue so effortlessly.

By the time it finished, the courtiers were laughing and cheering at the arrogant fool's downfall. The Queen laughed so much that she was seen to hold her sides, and when she stood up to speak everyone looked at her expectantly.

'I vow we have been well entertained this night,' she said. 'It would appear that Melodia won the contest with Sir Peabody, but I would say that the honours are even between Mistress Catherine and Sir Nicholas. For she played herself while he hath given us a splendid buffoon to amuse us, and I think only a true heart and excellent talent could have done so well.'

It seemed that everyone agreed, for rapturous applause greeted her decision, and the dismissed courtiers drifted away to talk amongst themselves.

Catherine was surrounded by friends wishing to congratulate her, as was Nick himself. It was some time before she was able to escape for a few minutes of much needed solitude.

Her mind was a turmoil of confusion, for Elizabeth had spoken truly. Nick's performance as the fool had not led to his being mocked as she had feared. Indeed, she had sensed something almost noble in the way he had accepted his defeat at the end of the play. And the look in his eyes had seemed to tell Catherine that he had humbled himself before the court for her sake.

What had he been trying to tell her? Catherine had never asked throughout their time together at rehearsals. Was she afraid to ask? Afraid of the answer he might give, and of her response?

Her steps had taken her as usual towards the walled garden. It was a cold frosty night, but the sky had a curious whiteness about it that made the gardens almost as bright as day, and she thought that it might snow during the night.

Catherine looked into her heart and knew that she could no longer deny him, in thought or deed. She loved Sir Nicholas, far more deeply than she would have him know, loved him with her heart, her mind, her body. Yet her dilemma remained the same, for unless he truly cared for her she would betray herself at her peril.

'Mistress Catherine. Stay a moment. I would speak with you.'

Catherine sighed as she heard herself addressed by James Morton, and turned to face him.

'Why do you persist in this foolishness, sir?' she asked, her head high as her eyes swept over him with disdain. 'Have I not made my feelings clear?'

'You must know that I have a high regard for you? I did not mean to anger you, but wished to offer my congratulations on the play.'

'You should rather congratulate Sir Nicholas. His was the wit that conceived it, his the hand that penned those clever words.'

'They are saying that he will give up his pursuit of you now, that you have rebuffed him too often and that he has lost interest now the contest is over between you.'

'I do not care for what others might say, sir.'

James decided on one last try to win her.

'You know that I would never desert you if you would but trust me, Catherine? I would not seek to harm you in any way. You should not trust Sir Nicholas, for he will deceive you.'

'I thank you for your concern, but my affairs are my own.'

'Do you love him? Be wary of giving your self to such a man, Catherine. He will take your heart and crush it carelessly beneath his heel.'

'You are impertinent, sir. I care for no one—neither you nor Sir Nicholas,' Catherine retorted with a toss of her head. She was lying but she was not about to reveal her heart to this man. 'I shall marry only as I wish, and that will not be to you, sir. Or any other for the moment.'

James took a step towards her. For a moment he was tempted. They were alone and none was like to hear her cry out. If he acted boldly he might seduce her and…but no, he was not made of such base clay. No matter how extreme his need, he could not force her.

'You should speak to Lettice,' Catherine said as she read some part of his thoughts in his face. 'I believe she has something to tell you that might help you.'

James inclined his head stiffly. It was clear that she would never yield willingly, and he could not bring himself to act in the way he had been bid. He could do no more here, and for his own safety must think of leaving the court. He must put as much distance as possible between himself and the evil creature that had sought to use him.

'I beg your pardon, Mistress Moor. I shall trouble you no more. But for your own sake, I would beg you to take care, for there are some who would do you harm if they could…'

'What do you mean, sir?'

'I can say no more. Forgive me.'

He spoke in riddles! Why should anyone wish her harm? It was ridiculous, and she would give his warning no credence, for it plainly deserved none.

Catherine watched as he walked away. He was an odd man, and she had never believed in his protestations of love for her. Would he speak to Lettice? She hoped for both their sakes he would, because she had sensed desperation in him, and despite his annoying pursuit of her she wished him no ill.

Shivering as the coldness swept over her, Catherine retraced her steps towards the palace. The stone walls had an icy dampness about them that was unwelcome, and she thought longingly of her father's house with its oak-lined comfort. But how much of the cold that afflicted her was due to the ache about her heart?

In the outer corridors the torches were smoking, their flames flickering in a bitter breeze as she made her way back inside. Had she hoped that Sir Nicholas might follow her to her favourite place? If so, she had been sadly disappointed.

It was over, she realised. The play had been his way of telling her that he was no longer interested in continuing the contest between them.

Catherine was conscious of pain somewhere in the region of her heart. She had hoped for a different outcome to the conclusion of this night, but it seemed that Nick had become bored and wanted no more of her.

Well, it was her own fault. She had scorned him too many times but she had been afraid to love lest he leave her. And now it seemed that she had lost him anyway.

Catherine was unaware that she passed within a few paces of Sir Nicholas as she left the gardens.

Nick had come after her, hoping that they could talk at last, but he had been delayed again and again by people wishing to tell him how much they had enjoyed the play, arriving in time to hear Catherine say that she cared for neither James Morton nor himself, that indeed she had no wish to marry.

Could it possibly be the truth? Nick knew that there were women who truly had no desire to wed. Most retired to a nunnery, or they had before such places were closed by King Henry VIII. Now there was no shelter for women with an aversion to married life, except the soulless existence of a despised and unwanted spinster destined to live as a poor relation in someone else's home.

Surely Catherine could not truly desire such a life? Nick was revolted at the idea. No, there was too much fire in her. He was certain of it, and that she felt something for him. Yet she had resisted all her suitors, maintaining that she did not wish to marry. He had believed she was responding to him, that she loved him, and that only her pride prevented her from confessing it. He had hoped that his play would show her that he loved and respected her.

It seemed that his hopes were dashed, for she had accepted his tribute without comment. He had failed to reach her after all. A wise man would withdraw now, and yet he could not forget that moment in the gardens when she had yielded to him so sweetly.

He could not, would not give her up! He would go after her and somehow he would make her respond to him.

'Your pardon, Sir Nicholas. This arrived for you a few minutes ago.'

Nick took the letter from the equerry he met almost as soon as he entered the palace, recognising the handwriting at once and what it would most likely mean.

His mouth settled in a grim line as he read the contents and knew that he must leave for France on the morning tide. To leave at such a moment was impossible, and yet he must answer Walsingham's call.

But this time he would not leave without a word to Catherine!

'Stay a moment,' he ordered the equerry. 'I must write a letter and you shall deliver it for me.'

Catherine took the letter from the equerry, feeling a little surprised. Who could be writing to her? She had been given love poems before this, but they were mostly delivered by the author or passed to her by Lettice. Her heart jerked as she looked at the distinctive hand.

'Who gave you this, sir?'

'It was Sir Nicholas Grantly,' the servant explained. 'I believe he left the palace a few moments ago and he charged me to deliver this to you personally.'

'Thank you.'

Catherine's pulses raced. She was about to open her letter when Lettice came hurrying up to her.

'I must speak with you in private, Cat. Will you come to our room?'

'Yes, of course.'

Sensing her friend's excitement, Catherine slipped the letter into the bodice of her gown. She let the other girl hurry her away, looking at her expectantly as they were at last alone, the door firmly closed behind them. Lettice did not keep her long, the excitement tumbling out of her as she began to speak.

'James has asked me to go away with him!'

'Oh, Lettice!' Catherine rushed to hug her. Despite what had happened in the garden earlier, she knew that this was what Lettice wanted most in all the world and was happy for her. 'That is wonderful. I am so glad for you.'

Lettice laughed, her happiness mixing with some apprehension as she went on, 'He told me that he is leaving tonight. There is some trouble over money. A man paid his debts and James is afraid of him. He says he must leave at once, and I have agreed to go with him. We shall be married just as soon as James can arrange it. He says he loves me, has always loved me, but he needed money.'

'Did I not tell you it was so?'

'He is ashamed of himself for the way he pursued you when he knew you did not want him,' Lettice went on. 'But this man was forcing him to propose marriage to you. James does not know why, other than it might be because you are heir to a fortune. He was told to abduct you if you would not agree to marry him, but he could not bring himself to do it. Instead he decided to run away.'

'I do not understand. Who was this man—and why should he try to force James to wed me? It is very strange, do you not think so?'

'Yes, it is odd. James thought at first it was so that he could repay the money he had borrowed to pay his debts, but now he is not sure. I wish I could explain, but I know no more than that.'

'It hardly matters now. Tell me, have you told James you have money of your own in trust?'

'I tried but he wouldn't listen. He truly cares for

me, Cat. He says that money is no longer important, that he is not sure what the future holds but wants to be with me.'

'Then I am happy for you both. It is what I hoped might happen.'

'You have been a good friend to me, Cat. I wish you might be as happy as I am now.'

'I fear that is unlikely.'

'But why? Sir Nicholas loves you. You must know that?'

'Would that he did,' Catherine said and sighed. 'But I fear I have driven him away with my scolding. He has sent me a letter of farewell and left the palace.'

'Are you sure?' Lettice looked concerned. 'If he left in a hurry it must have been important. I would swear he loves you too much to give you up lightly.'

'Perhaps…'

'This will bring him back to you.' Lettice took something from her coffer by the window. 'It is a lucky charm. Place it beneath your pillow and you will gain your heart's desire.'

'Did it work for you?' Catherine laughed as she saw her friend's glowing face. 'Of course it did. Thank you for your gift, Letty. I fear it will not work so well for me, but I am grateful for the thought.' She placed it in her own coffer. 'But you said you were leaving tonight. What of your things?'

'James is waiting for me. I can take only a few small items. We shall send for the rest later, when we are safely married.' She looked at Catherine. 'Pray tell me I am doing the right thing!'

'You are taking your chance of happiness. It may

bring some danger, for the Queen will not be pleased, but I am persuaded that she will not punish you too severely. I shall speak for you if she will allow me.'

'God bless and keep you,' Lettice said and kissed her cheek. 'I should never have dared to do this if you had not encouraged me.'

'Hush,' Catherine put a finger to her lips. 'The less said now the better. Gather what you need. If anyone asks what you are doing when you leave here, tell them you are taking one of Her Majesty's gowns to be laundered.'

'Yes. I shall use the back stairs. James knows where to meet me. We shall be rowed across the river and on our way to his home by morning.'

'I shall cover for you as long as possible, Letty.'

'Wish me luck, Cat?'

'And happiness,' Catherine said. 'Go now, before you lose your courage.'

Between them they gathered Lettice's most precious possessions and placed them into a small bundle that looked as if it might be dirty clothes. Then they embraced for the last time and Lettice went out, a suspicion of tears in her eyes.

Catherine sat down on the edge of her bed. They had arranged Lettice's to look as if she were sleeping if anyone chanced to look in. Catherine's own nerves were ragged. She prayed that the Queen would not send for Lettice too soon, and decided that she would pretend the other girl was unwell if necessary. If she could manage at least a day's delay it would give the lovers time to get right away.

After a few minutes she was calm enough to think

of Sir Nicholas's letter and take it out. She stared at it in the light of the candle for several moments before slitting the wax seal.

It was brief and to the point.

> *I have been called away urgently. I ask you to forgive me, Catherine, and to believe that this was not of my choosing. We have much to talk about. I shall return as soon as I may and I shall speak with you then. This affair must be resolved for both our sakes. Do not condemn me without a hearing this time, Nicholas.*

Catherine's first impulse was to screw up the letter but in another moment she had smoothed it out and was reading it again.

What could he mean? This affair must be resolved for all our sakes? It sounded as if he cared for her, but if that were so why had he not followed her into the garden?

Perhaps he had been intercepted by a message calling him away? Yet what urgent business could he have? Unless…

Catherine recalled one or two remarks concerning the terrible night of St Bartholomew's Eve. Was it possible that Nick was working for Sir William Cecil or Lord Burghley, as the Queen had recently created her Secretary of State?

Nick had mentioned both Cecil and Walsingham after his return from France. Nothing very much it was true, but there had been a hint of something more…something hidden perhaps.

And there was the Queen's manner towards him. True, she liked to tease him as she did others of her gentlemen, but there was a degree of respect in her tone when she spoke of him. Would that be so if he were naught but an idle flatterer?

Catherine knew the Queen too well. Her Majesty did not suffer fools gladly. She liked bold men, men of action who would risk anything in her cause.

Sir Nicholas had not been knighted for a trifle. He must have performed a service for Her Majesty. Had he been abroad on some kind of spying mission?

Catherine recalled the Queen speaking of information her spies had given her, and she began to remember other little things that seemed to tell her much more than she had ever previously suspected. If Nick was truly in the service of the Queen, then she had misjudged him utterly.

Catherine's breast swelled with pent-up emotion. She had wronged him, not he her.

She got up to place his letter in her coffer and saw the charm Lettice had given her. For a moment she hesitated, then she picked it up.

No doubt it was all nonsense, but what harm could it do? She would place it under her pillow, but she would also pray that Nick came safely back to her.

'God keep safe, my love,' she whispered. 'Only come back to me and I shall listen to your words. Only say that you still want me and I shall show you that I too know how to love.'

Going to the window, she looked out as the snow began to fall softly, covering the trees and bushes. It looked heavy and by morning would be several feet deep where it drifted across the road. If it had only fallen sooner it might have prevented Nick from leaving.

It would be a cold journey for him, she thought, wishing he were here with her. She left the window and went to her bed, feeling cold as she slipped between the sheets.

Oh, how she wished that Nick was here to keep her warm.

'My spies tell me that as I suspected at the time, an Englishman was most certainly involved in the plot against Coligny,' Walsingham said as they shared a glass of wine in his private rooms. He rolled the deep red wine about the glass, frowning as he looked across the table at Nick. 'No one seems sure of what he looks like, but he is said to have Italian manners and to have a sinister air about him. Yet others think him a poor creature.'

'You think he may be your man of darkness?'

'I do not know. I believe he had a hand in the terrible events of St Bartholomew's Eve, but it cannot be proved. The Medici is blamed but few dare speak out against her. The massacre is said to have been spontaneous, yet I would swear someone stoked the fires of hatred.'

'But there must be more. You are not a man given to flights of imagination, sir.'

Walsingham smiled oddly. 'It pleases me that you know me, Nick. There was an incident some years ago at court—when a man was murdered. I was not at court then, but I heard rumours and I believe a dagger of Italian origin was used. Blame was placed on a young man in the service of the then Lord Dudley, but then another was arrested and confessed under torture—but there was something strange about that confession that has puzzled me. I have studied the report and believe that our man may have been active even then.'

'It is not unusual for a man to confess when tortured, sir.'

'But there was more—the man acted as if he were possessed, a puppet of the Devil. There have been other incidents over the years, unexplained, sinister. I have compiled a thick dossier and believe there is a dark force at work against our Queen.'

Nick felt a coldness at the base of his spine. 'What is it you want of me, sir?'

'Return to court. Watch for a man such as I have described to you. I ask only that you should observe. Do nothing more, Nick, for I would know more of him before I decide what action must be taken.'

'You think he may be a danger to the Queen?'

'My senses warn me there is a great evil hovering near her, but my mind dismisses the idea. How can one man have brought about so much? If he was involved in the Ridolfi affair, can he also have worked his malice with the Medici—and perhaps more to the point, why? What lies behind his plotting?'

'If you are right, he has some grand design.' Nick swore softly. 'The man would rule the world! Is he mad, think you? A man gorged on some vision of his own greatness—or is he driven by his hatred?'

Walsingham's eyes narrowed in thought. 'You have

spoken more truly than you know. If this master plotter exists, he must have some bitter reason for what he does. Some hurt he nurses like a festering sore inside his mind—or he is indeed mad. Deluded into believing himself the tool of a higher deity.'

'You do not say God?' Nick saw the answer in his eyes and nodded thoughtfully. 'No, he would worship the anti-Christ—Satan would be his master, though he might give lip service to a more acceptable form of religion.'

'From his Italian manners I would suggest a man who visited Rome when he was young,' Walsingham spoke his thoughts aloud. 'He took a liking for all things in the Italian style. Mayhap he studied the writings of Machiavelli or some other diabolical theory, and through these studies came to his interest in the occult.'

'We convince ourselves that he exists.'

'He is a dangerous man if we are right. A man who has perhaps little power in the conventional way.'

Nick's blood ran cold, and he was aware of a deep foreboding that he could not explain. 'Would he attempt an assassination, think you?'

Walsingham considered for a moment, then shook his head.

'He does not use physical force himself—mayhap he has an actual aversion to it because of something that happened to him in the past or perhaps he is not physically strong. His is the power of the mind, subtler than a knife thrust in the back, and less open to suspicion. If he is the master of some grand design, he cannot be involved in murder himself for fear of dis-

covery. Yet he can kill when he chooses, though in
his own way. If he thought you a danger to him, Nick,
he would not hesitate to dispose of you, or any other,
I dare say.'

'Does he know you suspect him? Are you in danger?'

'If he is the man I think him he would relish the
challenge, my mind against his. He needs flattery; he
needs to be admired and it would give him great satisfaction to know that his mind was superior to ours.
He would gain little from all this if no one knew he
had brought it about.'

'And yet he guards his identity.'

'Until he is secure or has achieved his purpose,
whatever that may be. He is a manipulator, Nick, a
man who waits in the shadows and enjoys the knowledge of his power.'

'I begin to see him,' Nick said, nodding thoughtfully as the man of shadows began to take sinister
shape in his mind. 'I shall be on my guard from now
on.'

'Return to court then.' Walsingham smiled. 'Am I
to congratulate you, Nick? I hear that you are about
to propose marriage to a certain young lady?'

'Your spies know more than I know myself,' Nick
replied ruefully. 'I am not sure that the lady will even
listen, let alone accept me.'

'I wish you good fortune. I hope not to call on your
services for a while. Indeed, I have hopes of returning
to court before long myself.'

Nick took his leave, relieved that he had not been
asked to make a journey of many months this time.

He could not wait to return to court and speak to Catherine. She haunted his dreams and every waking thought that was not dedicated to the service of his Queen. This time he must speak his mind, if only she would grant him a hearing.

The Queen was in a towering rage over Lettice's elopement. Catherine had been summoned and, realising that it would be useless to lie, confessed to her own small part in the affair.

'How dare you conspire against me!' Elizabeth demanded. 'You are well aware that Mistress Williams is my ward. She has no right to marry without my consent.'

'She is in love with Master Morton…' Catherine quailed before the fury in her mistress's eyes, her words dying away. 'He…he was in debt and had to leave the court in a hurry.'

'You imagine that excuses her behaviour? Or yours in covering up for her? You lied to us, telling us she was unwell to give her a day's start!' Catherine trembled as she saw the Queen's expression, knowing that her mistress was very angry. 'You encouraged her in her disobedience and are therefore as guilty as she. You deserve to be punished, Mistress Moor!'

'Yes, Your Majesty. I know it was wrong, but Lettice is my friend and I wanted to help her.' Catherine's legs felt weak as the Queen's eyes flashed with temper, yet she continued with her brave speech. 'She was afraid that she might never be permitted to marry and she longed for children. She was most distressed when she thought her young cousins lost in the massacre in France, though I understand she has since heard that they survived and are safe hidden in the country.'

Elizabeth's mouth pulled into a sour line. She did not care to be reminded of the events in France or what they had cost her personally.

'Be silent! You condemn yourself with every word you utter. I am very angry with you. Go to your chamber, mistress. You may remain there until I decide on the nature of your punishment.'

Catherine curtseyed and bowed her head as the Queen swept into her private chamber. It was clear that she was indeed very angry over Lettice's elopement, and Catherine was being forced to bear the brunt of her displeasure.

She returned to her chamber, feeling sorry that she no longer shared it with Lettice yet pleased that her friend had escaped to a chance of happiness. The Queen's anger was perhaps an indication that she would not have given her approval had she been asked, which was unfair to Lettice. At least she had taken her chance while she could, and Catherine did not regret her part in the affair. She could only pray that the Queen would not punish either her or the lovers too harshly.

Feeling the return of a headache that had been troubling her since she woke, Catherine went to lie down on her bed. Nick had only been away for a day and she was missing him terribly, but she must not give way to such foolishness. He might be gone months; more than a year had passed before he returned the last time.

Blinking back her foolish tears, Catherine closed her eyes. If she could sleep for a while perhaps this wretched headache would go.

The dream was terrifying. In the grip of the nightmare that held her mind, Catherine tossed and turned restlessly on her pillows.

'No…I beg you, no!' she cried and woke with a start of terror. Something was over her face, a cobwebby veil that seemed to suffocate her. If she could not remove it she would surely die. She clawed at it and discovered that it was merely her hair.

How foolish she was! Catherine got up as the dream faded from her mind. If Lettice were here she would say that Catherine had been eating too much cheese.

Catherine sighed and thought of her lost friend with regret. It would not be the same at court without Lettice. She could share her room with someone else. Indeed, she might be ordered to do so, for space was short in the palace. However, the close friendship she had enjoyed with Lettice was unlikely to come her way again.

Tidying her gown and hair, Catherine wondered what she was to do with herself while confined to her room. She could work on her tapestry, of course, or perhaps write a letter to her father. At least her headache had cleared for the moment.

She was about to begin a letter when there was a knock at the door, and then it opened to admit Louise Montpellier. The Frenchwoman stared at her with evident dislike.

'I have been sent to pack Mistress Williams's things.'

'Are they to be sent on to her?'

'I have no idea. It is being said she will be sent to the Tower if they are caught—and it is what they both deserve.'

'That is unfair of you. Surely Her Majesty would not be so cruel?'

'The Queen is justly angry—with you, too.' Louise smirked, clearly pleased by Catherine's fall from grace. 'It was your own fault. Did you imagine you were so high in Her Majesty's favour that you could get away with anything?'

'I have done nothing, except give my good wishes to a friend.'

'That is not what I heard. It was your own fault. You pretended that Lettice was unwell for a whole day, giving her time to get clear. Everyone knows you were involved. I dare say you will find yourself in the Tower by morning—or sent home in disgrace if you are lucky.'

'And that would please you, would it not, Louise?'

'He was mine until you took him.' Louise came closer to her, her face hard with malice. 'He would have married me if you had not set your cap at him, flirting with him so disgracefully and flaunting yourself before the court in that play! You are no better than a wanton, though you pretend to be so virtuous. I have seen the hot looks you give him, and I dare say more did we but know it.'

'I did not set my cap at Sir Nicholas,' Catherine defended herself against the other's bitterness. 'He was determined to have me from the first—and I was commanded to play a part whether I wished it or not.'

'But you encouraged him.' Louise's hatred glittered in her blue eyes. 'I wish that you might rot in the Tower until your hair falls out and your flesh is eaten by rats!'

The fury in her face warned Catherine that she was about to strike, her nails curled like claws as if she would rake Catherine's flesh from her bones. Even as she prepared to defend herself, the door opened once more to admit Lady Knolsworth, one of the Queen's most senior ladies.

'You are wanted, Mistress Catherine.' Lady Knolsworth looked from her to Louise, her eyes narrowing in suspicion as she sensed that she had interrupted something. 'Why are you here, Mistress Montpellier?'

'I came to pack Lettice's things.' Louise moved away from Catherine, but the look she gave her was full of menace. 'I am waiting for her trunk to be sent down.'

'Very well. I shall stay and supervise the packing. Go along now, Cat. Her Majesty must not be kept waiting.'

'Do I look tidy? I lay down to rest for a while and my gown is creased.'

'It cannot matter for the moment. You must go at once to your mistress.'

'Yes, ma'am.'

Catherine hurried away, her heart beating madly. The Queen must be very angry to have summoned her again so soon. Was she to be sent to the Tower as Louise had implied?

As she entered the antechamber next to the Queen's private apartments, Catherine heard the sound of laughter. It seemed that Her Majesty was amused at something.

'Wait here a moment,' Catherine was told by the lady sitting in the outer chamber. 'Her Majesty is talking with Christopher Hatton, with whom she hath been pleased to discuss some lengthy matters of business. She will see you in a moment.'

Catherine waited in a state of agitation, her pulses racing as she wondered what fate awaited her. She paced back and forth about the room, completely unable to admire the fine hangings. Elizabeth seemed to keep the captain of her bodyguard talking an inordinately long time. However, he came out at last, tidying his lace ruff as if it had been disturbed—perhaps by a passionate embrace or two? Seeing Catherine standing there nervously, he smiled in an encouraging way.

'I believe you may find Her Majesty better disposed towards you now, Mistress Catherine.'

'Thank you, sir.'

Catherine managed a smile for him, but her stomach was tying itself into knots as she was told to go into the bedchamber at last. She curtseyed to the Queen, who was gazing at a miniature portrait of a man, which she then tucked inside the bodice of her gown, a little smile of satisfaction on her lips. It occurred to Catherine that she looked like a woman who had been thoroughly kissed, but she dismissed the thought instantly, knowing it could be constituted treason.

'Ah, Cat,' she said and the stormy expression of earlier had cleared from her eyes. 'I believe I may have been harsh with you this morning?'

'I deserved your censure, ma'am. Lettice would have done well to ask your permission to wed.'

'Mistress Williams is another matter. *We* shall deal with her as *We* see fit. But you did nothing so very terrible. Christopher reminded me of the play and other things, and I am minded to forgive you this time.'

'You are gracious, ma'am.'

'I wish to hear no more of wilful ladies who disobey my command. We shall not speak of Mistress Williams. Nor do I wish to speak of marriage at all— do you understand me, Cat?'

'Yes, Your Majesty.' Catherine curtseyed, understanding very well.

'Then the matter is over. You are returned to your duties and may carry on as usual. I may send for you this evening to sit with me. Go now. You are free until I need you.'

'Yes, Your Majesty. Thank you.'

Catherine curtseyed once more and left the royal chamber. It seemed that she owed much to the intervention of Christopher Hatton. He had certainly lifted the Queen's mood, and Catherine knew Elizabeth was fond of the young man's company.

There were those at court who whispered about the nature of his relationship with Elizabeth, the more malicious amongst them slyly suggesting that he spent too much time in her chamber for it to be merely business matters.

That the Queen gained great pleasure from his company was not in doubt, nor that she had lately been displeased with her erstwhile favourite the Earl of Leicester. It was certain that the Earl had been conducting love affairs of his own, though not certain that the Queen knew the exact nature of these affairs. The Earl naturally denied that they were serious, declaring his undying love and devotion to Her Majesty, but he was a man who had waited a long time for a prize that an act of fate had cruelly denied him through the accidental death of his wife, and it was scarce to be expected that he would not take lovers. What was remarked was that the Queen had cooled somewhat towards the Earl, giving her warmer smiles to Christopher.

Catherine was as close to the Queen as any woman was ever permitted to be, and she was not sure that Elizabeth would ever have married, even if the Earl's wife had not died in mysterious circumstances. That the Queen would have loved children, and that she greatly enjoyed the flattery and attention of handsome young men about her, Catherine did not doubt. But would she ever have felt secure enough to have shared her throne with a man?

It was only by sheer determination that Elizabeth ruled. Her crown had never been truly secure. Many would have replaced her if there had been an heir with a claim that could be called rightful other than Mary Queen of Scots, who was of the hated Catholic faith. There were of course men of that faith who wished to see Elizabeth swept from the throne. Only by her wit and courage did Elizabeth defy them—and the loyalty of men like Lord Burghley, of course.

Pondering her thoughts, Catherine made her way slowly towards the garden. The remains of the headache were still bothering her a little, though it was nowhere near as bad as it had been earlier, and she felt that a walk in the air would do her good.

'Mistress Catherine, wait a moment if you will.'

Catherine's heart caught as she heard the voice she both longed and dreaded to hear. Pausing, she turned slowly to face the man as he came up to her, his stride confident and powerful. She had never quite understood before what a powerful man Nick was, she thought, realising that her image of him had been coloured by the idea she had created of an idle man who cared only for pleasure. Now that her eyes had been opened, she saw that she had been a fool to let herself believe in that false image. This was no creature of the court, but a man of action, his manner alert, his eyes serious as they searched her face.

'I was about to walk in the garden,' Catherine said. 'The air will clear the remains of a fuzzy head that has plagued me since I woke.'

'I am sorry you have been unwell.' Nick's look was concerned as he saw the signs of tiredness in her face. 'May I have your permission to walk with you, Catherine?'

'If it pleases you,' Catherine said, her manner still a little reserved but out of shyness this time. 'I thought you might be away some months, sir.'

'I made good speed,' Nick replied. 'Indeed you see

me in all my dirt fresh from the journey. I wanted to see *you*, Catherine.'

Catherine's heart jerked to a standstill as she heard the note of passion in his voice. 'I received your letter, sir.' Her voice was barely above a whisper, her heart racing like the wind so that she could scarcely breathe. 'I believe your business was urgent?'

'And secret,' Nick told her, moving towards her. His manner was intense, eager, as if he had waited for this moment. 'If you will trust me in this we shall not speak of it.'

'No, I think that best,' Catherine replied as they went into the gardens. 'I have thought long and hard, and I believe I begin to understand.'

'Then I have no need to explain,' Nick said and seemed relieved. 'Believe me, it is best you know nothing, Catherine. There are times when a little knowledge is dangerous.'

Catherine inclined her head, a smile on her lips.

'You little know how truly you speak, sir. I dare say you are not aware of what has happened in your absence?'

He frowned as he saw her expression. 'I came straight to find you. I have heard nothing.'

'Lettice has run away with Master James Morton to be married, and the Queen is furious because Lettice was her ward. She was very angry with me and said at first that I should be punished, but she has relented and I am to be allowed to continue with my duties.'

Nick stared at her in surprise. 'I thought Master Morton had paid court to you these many months?'

'Much to my dismay, for I did all I could to discourage him,' Catherine agreed. 'I knew that Lettice loved him and did my best to turn him her way, but he seemed determined to wed me, even going so far as to write to my father. However, Her Majesty refused the match, and when I made my feelings plain the other evening, Master Morton confessed to Lettice that it was my fortune he loved.'

'The rogue!' Nick looked at her as she gave him what he could only call a smile of more warmth than he had received from her for many a day. 'I am glad you were not fooled by Morton.'

'Not for a day, I assure you. I told Lettice long since that he was in some trouble, and he confessed he was in debt and, I believe, in some terror of the man to whom he was indebted. He decided his only course was to leave the court at once, and Lettice was persuaded to go with him. She has a fortune in trust for her, and will be rich enough once she is wed, even once his debts are paid.'

She decided to keep the curious story of the man of mystery who had tried to force James to abduct her a secret for the moment; it was surely not important and she would mention it another day. They had more urgent matters to discuss for the moment.

'If the Crown can be persuaded to release it,' Nick remarked concerning Lettice's fortune. 'It is not easy to pry money from royal hands, but in the end their lawyers may achieve it. Providing they do not languish in the Tower.'

'Lettice decided it was worth the risk,' Catherine said. 'And I do not blame her. Had she refused Master Morton she might never have married.'

'I thought you had an aversion to marriage, Catherine?'

Nick's eyes were very bright as he waited for her answer, bringing a blush to her cheeks.

'I...I wish to marry only if I love and am truly loved.'

'No one could love you more truly than I, Cat.'

The words were spoken so softly that she almost doubted she heard them, her eyes seeking confirmation, as she looked long and deep into his.

'Sir, I...'

'Catherine,' he whispered huskily. 'Tell me I may hope that you will learn to love me. I can be patient if you ask it of me. I ask only that you will try to care for me.'

'I do not need to try, sir.' Catherine moistened lips that were suddenly dry with the tip of her tongue, her eyes unable to leave his as he moved towards her, his hand reaching out to gently stroke her cheek. 'I have felt warmer feelings than were good for me these many months, sir. If I held you at bay it was because I did not trust you. I thought you would take my heart and body for devilment and then desert me.'

'Did it hurt you so much when I went away that first time?' Catherine nodded and Nick placed a finger at the pulse spot at the base of her white throat. She almost groaned with the pleasure she felt when he bent to touch his lips to that same spot. 'It was not of my choosing, Cat. I was ordered to leave in secrecy. Even my mother was only told that I did not know when I would return.'

'Then those things she said of you...'

'Were her way of covering my absence without arousing suspicion.'

'I was so foolish, and so naïve.'

'Say rather that you were young and innocent and my flirting had aroused a fire in you that I had hardly realised was there. I never meant to hurt you, Catherine. It was the beginning of a flirtation for me, and I did not know it would come to mean so much to me. Until I returned and you were so cold to me I never knew that I could love so much that it became a physical agony to me.'

'Your kisses that day by the river, the things you said—they meant all the world to me even then; though I have denied you again and again in my mind, my heart was always yours. I was devastated by what I saw as your callous desertion. I vowed that I would never give my heart to a man again, nor would I marry. If my aunt had not been so determined I might have returned to my home then.'

'And I should have found you there,' Nick replied with a smile. His voice was husky, caressing, the touch of his hand against her cheek setting a river of fire coursing through her. 'I was determined to search for you wherever you had gone. In my dreams I had irrational thoughts of snatching you from your husband's home and carrying you to my lair, where I would seduce you and keep you prisoner until you loved me.'

'The very rogue I thought you!' Catherine cried and laughed, sensing he was teasing her, thrilling to his words and his looks with every fibre of her being.

She looked so beautiful that Nick could not restrain

his passion. He swept her to him in a crushing embrace, his mouth devouring hers hungrily as they kissed. Catherine clung to him, letting herself melt in the heat of his desire, matching it with a raging flame of her own that threatened to consume them both.

It was Nick who eventually drew back to look into her face, his breathing harsh and ragged as he sought to control the fire she had lit with her response.

'If we are not careful I shall ravish you here and now,' he said croakily. 'Much as it would please me to take you now, my darling Cat, I have more respect for your virtue and your reputation.'

'And for your head, I hope?' Catherine raised a smile as she teased him, though she was as breathless and needy as he. 'Her Majesty has forbidden me to think or speak of marriage, Nick. Lettice made her so angry and I do not believe she will allow me to wed for the moment.'

'We must wait for her anger to cool,' Nick agreed. 'I am not minded to run away with you as Master Morton did with Mistress Williams. For the moment I shall try to be patient, though I would willingly wed you this day if the choice were mine.'

'Oh, Nick…' Catherine laughed as she read the impatience in his face and felt its equal. 'We must be careful. I do not wish to see you carried off to the Tower, nor to follow you there myself—though if we could be together there it might be worth it.'

'Depend upon it, we should be incarcerated in separate dungeons,' he replied, a wicked light in his eyes. He smoothed his finger over her lips and she sucked it, biting teasingly like the cat he had so often named her. He pulled her between his legs so that she felt the hardness of his maleness pressing into her, hearing his soft groan of frustrated desire as he held her for a moment before releasing her. 'No, we shall be patient, my sweet Catherine. I have a reason for wishing to remain at court for a while yet. I think it best if we continue as we always have in public, for it would not do to let everyone know our minds. There are those who might wish to harm you if they knew you were precious to me, and I would have you safe, my love.'

'Are you in danger, Nick?'

He recalled the letter that had lured him into a trap. He was almost sure that it had been meant as a warning—which could mean that he was closer than he'd thought to discovering the man of darkness. And the less Catherine knew of that the better for her own sake.

'I think not at the moment,' he lied. 'Yet I must take care, and it may be that I shall have to leave you at least once more—but when we are wed I promise an end to all this mystery.'

'You make me wish it could end now,' Catherine said and stepped closer to him. 'Kiss me once more and then we must go in alone.'

'When the time is right I shall speak to her Majesty. She knows my intention towards you and she was favourable to it at the time, but things have changed. We must wait until she is in a better mood.'

Nick drew her close to him, his hand stroking her hair softly. He bent his head to hers, kissing her lips so sweetly that her heart sang for sheer joy, and yet this time he did not demand anything from her.

Catherine sighed as he let her go. She had been willing to surrender to him, and she ached deep within

her femininity for his possession, but she knew that
they must be careful. Elizabeth was jealous of her
ladies, and Catherine had already been reprimanded
and warned. To flout the Queen's express command
openly would be to court disaster.

'Go in now,' Nick said as he let her go. 'And when
we meet be as you were to me, though perhaps a little
less cold. Her Majesty told me that she would consent
to our wedding if I won you. We must continue to
keep her favour and in the end she will consent.'

'If she does not?'

'Then I shall run away with you,' Nick said laughing down at her. 'But I think we shall win her consent
sooner than you imagine.'

Catherine nodded, content to play the game as he
had bid her.

'Then I wish you good day, sir.'

'God guard you well, my love.'

Nick watched her go in before taking a further turn
about the gardens. If Walsingham was right, he owed
it to his friend and the Queen to do what he could to
discover the man of darkness. And should it come
about that he in his turn was discovered, he would not
have Catherine involved in the danger that might befall him.

Fortunately for Nick and Catherine, no hating eyes
had seen their tryst, no malicious heart had stood
unobserved in the shadows and watched them speak
of love.

A putrid chill had laid their enemy on his bed, and
for the moment his mind was taken by fever, he himself unable to plot the downfall of the man who had
defied him by running away with Lettice.

Chapter Ten

Catherine was relieved to find that her bedchamber was empty when she returned to change for the evening. She did not wish for another encounter with Louise Montpellier, and besides, she wanted a little time to be alone, to think of what Nick had told her.

She began slowly to change her gown. She and Lettice had always helped each other with gowns that were difficult to fasten, and she was struggling with a tie at the back of her neck when someone knocked at the door. She hoped it would not be Louise, come to pick another quarrel with her.

'Come in,' Catherine called and turned to see a young, slightly plump but pretty girl in the doorway. 'Yes? What may I do for you?'

'Lady Knolsworth says I am to share your chamber, Mistress Moor—if you will permit me?'

The last few words were the girl's own, Catherine was sure. She smiled at her, making a gesture of welcome.

'Please, do come in. How are you called, mistress?'

'I am Jane. Jane Howarth. My parents died of a

fever last month and Her Majesty sent for me since I have no other living relatives. I am to be her ward and live at court.'

'Yes, I see, Jane.' Catherine felt sympathy for the shy young girl, who was clearly out of her depth. 'I shall be pleased to have you share my room. Perhaps you could fasten this tie for me? I cannot quite reach it myself.'

'Willingly, Mistress Moor.'

'Thank you,' Catherine said as the girl moved to help her. 'And of course you must call me Catherine. There is no need to be in awe of me, Jane. It is not so very long ago that I was new to court myself.'

'But you are beautiful and clever.'

Catherine laughed and shook her head. Jane was perhaps a little plump but she was also attractive, with soft brown hair and gentle eyes that reminded her of a doe in her father's park.

'Some call me beautiful,' Catherine admitted. 'But I do not pride myself on my looks. Do not be shy of me, Jane. I would have us be friends.'

'I should like that.'

'Has Her Majesty sent for you?'

'Not yet. I was told to stay close to you for this evening and I may be called upon tomorrow.'

'It will be my pleasure to show you what to do,' Catherine said, looking at Jane's gown, which was countrified and not at all suited to court. 'Have your trunks arrived yet?'

'I think they will be here on the morrow.'

Catherine considered. 'We are much the same

height. I have something that might fit you, though you will not be able to lace the bodice tightly.'

She brought out a gown that she had never worn because it did not become her, and helped Jane to try it on. The girl exclaimed as she saw herself in the hand mirror Catherine lent her.

'It is very fine, Mistress Catherine. I have nothing like it. Are you sure I may borrow it?'

'It becomes you,' Catherine said looking at her. 'You may keep it, for the bodice can be adjusted to fit you better. As it is, we must find a wide stomacher to cover the lacing, and then no one will know it was not made for you.' She rummaged in her coffer until she found what she was looking for, telling Jane to hold the wide embroidered band over the lacing at the front of the bodice, while she threaded the ribbons through the eyelets and fastened them in a neat bow at the top. 'There, that looks surprisingly well. Yes, I think you will do, Jane. Come, we shall go down now and join the others.'

'You are very kind. When Lady Knolsworth told me to come to you I was afraid you might not like me sharing your chamber.'

Catherine shook her head and smiled at her. The girl was shy and awkward but she would do her best to look after her. She would also hope that the Queen took a fancy to the newcomer. Perhaps then Elizabeth might be more inclined to forgive Lettice.

'Stay a moment.' Louise caught at Nick's arm as they met on their way to the Presence Chamber. 'You have scarce spoken to me in days. Are you angry with me?'

'No, I am not angry with you, Louise,' Nick said and sighed. He had not spoken out before because he did not like to hurt her, but it must be done. 'You must not expect me to dance attendance on you, Louise. There is another lady I care for, and in time, if she will have me…' He shrugged his shoulders. 'Who knows?' He left his intention unspoken, but it was clear enough.

Louise stared at him, two spots of bright colour in her cheeks.

'She has stolen your love from me. I hate her.'

'Do not speak so of the lady I love,' Nick replied, frowning at her severely. 'I have done my best to help you, Louise, and would provide a small dowry if a gentleman offered for you—but that is all you must expect from me. Forgive me, there is someone I must see.'

Louise stared after him, her eyes glittering with tears. She dashed them away, the bitterness settling in her heart. It was all the fault of Catherine Moor. She had set her cap at him from the first, and Louise would find some way of getting her own back if it was the last thing she did!

'Have you heard the news?' Louise Montpellier looked at Catherine, a hint of triumph in her eyes. Some days had passed since she had spoken to Nick, and at last the opportunity for revenge was hers. She had waited her moment to strike back and now it was here. 'Mistress Williams and Master Morton are mar-

ried and have been placed under arrest at his estate
while the Queen decides what to do with them. I dare
say she will have them brought back and imprisoned
in the Tower.'

'Oh, no,' Catherine cried, knowing that the other
girl spoke thus to punish her. 'I can only pray that you
are wrong, mademoiselle.'

'The pity of it is that you were not sent to join
them.'

Catherine ignored her taunt. She walked on, aware
that Louise was watching her with angry eyes. Seeing
Nick walking towards her, Catherine gave a little cry
of welcome and went to meet him.

'Have you heard about Lettice and James Morton?'

'That they have married and are now under arrest
at his home?' Nick nodded, looking at her thoughtfully. 'I think that perhaps it is not as bad as you might
believe, Catherine. Had the Queen really wanted to
punish them I think she would have had them brought
back to the Tower immediately. However, she must
make an example of them in some way, for she cannot
allow such flagrant flaunting of her command to go
unnoticed.'

'No, I suppose she must be seen to do something,'
Catherine agreed. 'I do wish she would forgive them
and then perhaps…' She sighed and Nick smiled at
her frustration.

'I know, my love. I know…'

'Mistress Moor! May I join you?'

Nick frowned as he saw Jane Howarth approaching
them.

'I believe I must leave you now, Catherine. Your

new friend approaches and I have urgent business elsewhere.'

'Nick!' Catherine protested as he walked away. She knew that he found the constant presence of Mistress Howarth irksome, but Jane was still so very unsure of herself and Catherine could not desert her. She turned as the girl came hurrying up to her. 'Where are you going, Jane? Have you no duties this morning?'

'There is so little for me to do,' Jane said. 'At home I was always busy, but I do not seem to fit in anywhere at court.'

'You will find a niche for yourself in time,' Catherine reassured her. 'But since you have nothing else to do you may join me. I am on my way to the sewing room. Her Majesty tore the hem of her favourite gown last week and the women have been repairing it. I am about to discover if they have finished their work, for it is requested for this evening.'

'You are kind to take me with you,' Jane said, her cheeks a little pink. 'I do hope I did not interrupt you just now? When you were talking to that gentleman?'

'Sir Nicholas, you mean?' Catherine shook her head. 'No, we merely stopped to pass the time of day.'

'Everyone says he once tried to seduce you, but you were too clever for him. I think he was wicked to treat you so!'

Catherine hid her smile. It seemed that she and Nick had managed to keep their secret, at least for the time being. She only hoped that someone would not go out of their way to bring it to the attention of Her Majesty.

Elizabeth was still very angry over Lettice's behaviour. If she learned that Catherine and Nick were hoping to marry soon there was no telling what she might do.

'Your female shadow does not approve of me,' Nick teased Catherine as he took her hand, leading her out into the throng of dancers one evening. 'I think she considers me a wicked seducer.'

'That is your reputation, which you may have once deserved,' Catherine said, her eyes bright with challenge. 'Why do you malign poor Jane?'

Her face was alight with laughter as she gazed up at him.

'She follows you like a little lapdog and I can never find you alone these days.'

'Jane is new to court. It is but two months since she arrived, and as yet the Queen takes little notice of her. The poor girl languishes with nothing to do. I feel for her because it was not thus for me—or for Mademoiselle Montpellier.'

'That is because Jane does not amuse Elizabeth. You have a ready wit and a sharp tongue, my sweet, and Louise Montpellier is clever in her way. Besides, the Queen showed Louise favour because she wanted to make her support for the Huguenots clear. Jane reminds me of nothing so much as a sweet dumpling. Plain fare when one has dined on swan.'

'You are unkind, sir,' Catherine reproved him with a frown. 'If you do not instantly apologise I shall not meet you later in the courtyard.'

'Mistress Howarth hath suddenly become a swan. How could I not have seen it before?'

'You change your tune too quickly, sir,' Catherine

teased. 'I think you must pay a forfeit. You shall dance with Jane and be nice to her.'

'You demand a high price, Cat.'

'If the prize is not worth the price...'

'You know I shall pay it and right willingly. But can we be sure that Jane will not follow you?'

'I shall arrange for her to be delayed,' Catherine promised. 'I noticed that a certain gentleman was looking at her with interest earlier. I shall introduce them after your dance, and then take the chance to slip away.'

'Your wish is my command, my lady.'

Nick made her an elegant leg as their dance ended. Catherine moved away from him, watching with a little smile as he sought Jane out. She was about to go in search of her own quarry when she noticed a gentleman looking at her.

He was staring in rather an odd way. Why did he appear familiar? She seemed to recall that she had spoken to him at some time, though she could not remember his name. He was just a very ordinary man with nothing in particular to mark him out, and she did not think that he came often to court. And yet for some reason she seemed to recall him.

Where and when had they spoken? The memory hovered at the back of Catherine's mind, but proved elusive. Clearly it had not been important or she would have remembered.

Dismissing the small puzzle, Catherine went in search of Robert Brooks. He was a gentleman of modest means, some years older than Jane Howarth, but

kindly and a man who might be trusted with the care
of a naïve girl.

He was flattered that Catherine had sought him out
and earnestly agreed that Mistress Howarth was a
sweet, innocent girl who ought to be protected from
some of the more unscrupulous flirts at court.

'I know that if you kept a protective eye on her she
would be safe,' Catherine told him. 'I cannot be with
Jane all the time and I am anxious that a less than
honourable man might seek to take advantage of her
innocence.'

'You may rely on me,' Master Brooks said, casting
a baleful eye in Nick's direction, which made
Catherine smile inwardly. 'I shall go to her side when
she has finished dancing and stay by her constantly.'

'You relieve my mind,' Catherine said, smiling at
him. 'I can rest more easily now that I know Jane has
you to protect her.'

Catherine made haste to introduce them after Nick
had excused himself. Then, glancing around to make
sure she was not particularly observed, she left the
great chamber, making her way to her favourite place
in the gardens.

The man she had remarked earlier had vanished.
Who was he? Catherine could not remember, though
she was certain she had spoken to him quite recently.
She puzzled over it for a few minutes, but then, hearing a firm, impatient step, she turned to greet Nick as
he came towards her.

'At last!' he cried and reached out to draw her close,
his mouth hungry as he sought for hers. Releasing her

at last, he sighed. 'I had begun to think the chance would never come for us to be alone.'

'Where is the patience you told me of?' Catherine teased. 'It is but two months since Jane came to court and you swore you would wait for ever if need be.'

'Two months too long if she will persist in following you,' Nick complained ruefully. 'How can I be patient if I cannot be with you like this sometimes? I long to hold you and kiss you, sweet Cat. Nay, if I am truthful I want much more…'

'Fie on you, sir! You waste time in words when actions speak more truly.'

'My sweet rose of many thorns,' Nick murmured, pressing her hard against him, her back to a tree, his knee between her thighs where he longed to lie. 'Your thorns are sharp enough, I vow. Sometimes I scarce believe you have promised to love me all your life.'

Catherine laughed, lifting her face for his kiss. She melted into his body, surrendering herself to him, her fingers stroking the back of his neck as she felt the heat of his passion flow into her, setting her aflame.

'How I want you in my bed,' Nick murmured huskily against her hair. 'I hunger for the taste of you; your lips are sweeter than honey to me, my lady. I cannot sleep for wanting you. My dreams are a torture, for I believe you in my arms until I wake and find you gone.'

'My poor darling,' Catherine murmured wickedly and nibbled at his ear. 'Sometimes I have dreams that terrify me, though sometimes they are sweeter—when I dream of you.'

'All your dreams should be of me. I trust no other man disturbs your rest?'

'Foolish, foolish, man,' Catherine chided. 'You should know that I want no other man but you.'

'As I want no other woman.' Nick touched her cheek with his fingertips. 'Shall I ask Her Majesty if she will permit our marriage at once, Cat?'

'I wish that I might think it possible,' Catherine replied. 'But she is still angry, Nick. I fear it is too soon to approach her.'

'Perhaps when I come back…'

'You are not going away again?' Catherine was alarmed at his news. 'Pray do not leave me. I am not sure I could bear it.'

'It is merely for a few days. I must travel to Leicester to see a friend. I should have visited Oliver a long time ago, but other things intruded. Last night as I lay wakeful thinking of you amongst many things, I remembered something I had intended to ask Oliver. I must make the journey.'

'I wish you would not go, Nick.'

Catherine shivered as a chill came over her. She was not sure why she suddenly felt frightened, but her instincts were to beg Nick not to leave her.

'It is important, Catherine. At the time I first thought of asking Oliver for help, I believed he might assist me to discover something about my brother Harry's death, and I had since decided that there was no point in clinging to the past. Whatever happened during that time in Italy cannot be changed. But I have been thinking of something Walsingham said to me in Paris…'

He broke off with a frown. 'I should not be telling you this. Some things are better left unsaid.'

Seeing the expression in his eyes, and sensing that he was anxious about something, Catherine knew she could not beg him to put off his journey. If he was troubled in his mind it was best that he go.

'You must do what you think right, Nick.'

'My sweet Cat.' Nick smiled and touched the pulse spot at the base of her throat. 'I hate to leave you again, but if my journey provides an answer I may at last be free of duty. Then I shall speak to Her Majesty and I am sure we shall be wed.'

'I pray you are right.' Catherine took his hand and placed it against her breast. 'Can you feel my heart beating? I think it would cease if I lost you, my love.'

'You need not fear to lose me.'

Nick pulled back the soft material of her gown where his hand had been a moment earlier, bending to kiss the sweet mound of her breast, his tongue circling on the rosy nipple until he took it into his mouth and sucked gently.

'I love you, Catherine,' he said huskily as she arched against him, her body surrendering to his so eagerly that he was hard put not to take her there and then against the tree. 'I swear I shall return to you within two weeks, and then we shall be wed.'

'I pray that you are right.' She shivered again. 'Hold me, Nick. Hold me close. I know you must go but it grieves me sorely.'

He chuckled softly, drawing her close once more, his lips seeking hers in a kiss that drove all thought from her mind. Wrapped in his strong arms, Catherine felt safe and protected.

It was only as she lay alone in her bed that night that she recalled the name of the man who had stared at her so oddly after her dance with Nick. He had once handed her a kerchief that was not hers, she recalled, and told her that his name was Frampton.

He did not come often to court. She was almost sure he had not been there for months, though she would not have noticed him that evening had his eyes not stared at her so particularly.

Why should he look at her in that strange way? Catherine pondered it for some minutes before she turned over to sleep. She had placed the charm Lettice had given her beneath her pillow again, for it had brought Nick back to her safely the first time and she prayed it would do so again.

She wished that Nick had not been forced to leave her. She had no doubt that he went on important, secret work, but still she regretted the need for his journey.

In the gardens she had felt such fear when he spoke of leaving. It was almost as if something…some evil presence had been near. She had felt as though they were watched, though she had seen nothing to disturb her.

Such foolishness! Catherine tried to dismiss her fears. She did not know why she should have become prone to such fancies. It was like the dream that sometimes haunted her, when she felt that cobwebby film cover her face and woke to find it was merely her hair.

There was no one watching her, no one haunting her dreams.

* * *

Louise was scowling as she left the great chamber and made her way towards her own bedroom. She had watched Nick follow Catherine outside, and she knew that she had lost him, but it did not make it any easier for her to accept defeat. If only there was something she could do to cause trouble for the other girl.

'Mademoiselle Montpellier?'

The soft voice sent a little shiver down her spine. She looked round for the source but could see nothing at first, and then she made out a figure standing in the shadows.

'Who are you, sir? What do you want of me?'

'It is not I who requires help. You wish to be rid of a certain lady, do you not?'

Louise's spine tingled. How could he know that? Was it possible that he had read her mind?

'I am not sure what you mean.' She took a step forward, but he held up his hand and she was halted, afraid now to see the face of this man who hid in shadows, lest it be hideous. 'Why do you seek me out?'

'Because I can tell you a way to gain your heart's desire.'

Louise's heart quickened. She glanced over her shoulder, afraid that someone might hear, and yet eager to know more.

'What must I do?'

'I shall give you something…' the voice said, its insidious softness terrifying her and yet holding her in thrall. 'Listen well now, for this is what you must do…'

* * *

Nick was thoughtful as he prepared for his journey. It was probably a waste of time, but at least it would settle his mind. For one brief second that evening he had seen a face in the crowd that touched a chord in his memory, and yet he could not be certain. One moment the man had been there and then he had gone. But it had been enough to trigger an alarm in his brain.

The fellow's name still eluded him, and yet he would almost swear it was the man he had seen in Paris, again briefly, and in shadow that time. Could the same man have been there at court, and was he right in thinking that there might be a connection with Oliver Woodville and Harry? If the man he had glimpsed was indeed the youth who had accompanied them on their grand tour so many years ago, what then?

It proved nothing even if his theory was right. It was hardly likely that he had discovered the man of darkness he and Walsingham had discussed that night in Paris. The youth he had seemed to recall had been a poor creature, insignificant beside the magnificent Oliver and Harry, who had both seemed so strong and full of life. Yet his bold, beautiful brother had died of a fever while the other had survived.

The old grief surfaced inside him, but Nick crushed it ruthlessly. Harry was dead; nothing could bring him back, and it was useless to spend his life in regret for his lost brother. But if this man were in truth the youth who had accompanied them on their journey and also Walsingham's man of darkness, what then indeed?

Such a man might be very dangerous, and perhaps Nick's instinct that his brother's death had not been the result of a common traveller's fever but of something darker, perhaps poison, could be very real. The nagging fear that Harry's death had been unnatural had haunted Nick for years. Oliver Woodville had seemed convinced it was but a fever and Nick trusted him. Yet still he had wondered.

What would he do if he felt sure that the two were the same? Once he would have had no hesitation in finding some excuse to fight his enemy, no matter what the consequences, but that was before he had met and come to love Catherine. She was more important to him now than an old score, and he would do nothing that might bring her into danger.

All he could do, Nick decided, was speak to Oliver, and then if he felt he had a case to put, seek an audience with Walsingham. He would then have done all he had been asked, and could devote his life to making Catherine happy.

Remembering the way she had clung to him, begging him not to leave her, Nick smiled. This waiting was impossible. He would speak to the Queen the moment he returned. He had served Her Majesty well, being instrumental in bringing the Ridolfi plot to a satisfactory conclusion, and he did not think she would refuse him a boon she had already promised.

Catherine had seemed a little odd in the garden, almost as if she were afraid of something. Nick wondered at it, then dismissed it as his fancy. His love was afraid of nothing. She had merely wanted to keep him with her.

Well, once they were married he would not willingly leave her side again.

Catherine woke with a fuzzy head. Her dreams had been growing worse of late and she was feeling far from well. She thought it might be the strong perfume Jane wore sometimes, for there was a heavy scent in the room that she had not noticed until recently. If she continued to have these bad heads, she might have to ask Jane if she would mind not wearing so much perfume.

Jane had been called to the royal chamber earlier, and Catherine dressed alone, washing in cold water. She might feel better if she went out for a walk in the air before she began her duties for the day. She closed the door behind her, putting a hand to the wall to steady herself.

What could be wrong with her? She had turned very dizzy of a sudden. For a moment she was frightened, but then the dizziness cleared and she straightened up. She must not give way to such foolishness. A walk in the air would help her recover from this faintness.

She just wished that Nick would return. He had been gone more than a week already and she was missing him so very much. But she must not be ill. She had never been ill, and she could not understand what ailed her. Those dreams had begun to disturb her sleep more often of late, and she found it difficult to wake up in the mornings, though as the day wore on she usually felt quite well again.

It must be Jane's perfume!

Catherine went out into the garden, turning towards her favourite place as she always did. She blinked as she saw something hovering at the end of an avenue bounded by a pair of close hedges. What was that? A shadow of some kind, formless at times and yet at others seeming to take shape. It was sinister some-how…very like that strange creeping mist she had once seen before.

Her hand flew to her mouth and she gave a little cry of fear. How could it be? Not here! Not here…

'Catherine, I was looking for you,' a voice called, and the shadow vanished as Jane came up to her. Perhaps it had been merely her imagination, a trick of the light? Or was she losing her mind? 'Her Majesty sent me to find you. She wants you to join her.'

Jane was wearing a sweet, light perfume that re-minded Catherine of spring flowers.

'That is nice perfume,' she said. 'I like it better than the other one.'

'But I always wear this,' Jane replied. 'It is all I have.'

'I thought you sometimes wore a stronger one?'

'No. I thought you did,' Jane said. 'I have some-times noticed it in our chamber of late.'

'I have not changed my perfume.' Catherine was puzzled. 'I do not understand, Jane, but it does not matter for the moment. I must hurry or I shall be late.'

'I am sorry to have kept you waiting,' Oliver Woodville said as he strode into the small parlour where Nick was seated. He was dressed for travelling and had not stayed to wash the dirt of the road from his person. 'My wife tells me you have been waiting to see me for two days. Is something wrong, Nick?'

Nick stood up, smiling as he went to take Oliver's outstretched hand. 'Mistress Woodville was most insistent that I should not leave without seeing you, Oliver. And indeed I did wish to consult with you. It is but a trifling thing, but it may be important.'

'Ask whatever you wish. It is good to see you after so many years, Nick.'

'And to see you, Oliver. Answer my question first and then I shall tell you why I ask it.' Oliver nodded his head as he paused. 'When you and Harry went to Italy there was a youth with you. A poor creature as I recall, and despised by both you and Harry.'

'Bevis Frampton,' Oliver replied with a scornful twist of his lips. 'A sly, unpleasant creature. Neither Harry nor I cared for him, but we were forced to accept him because his guardian provided part of the money for our tour. I doubt if I could have gone had he not accompanied us.'

'Bevis Frampton? You are sure?' Nick's eyes narrowed as Oliver nodded again. 'You spoke of his guardian—what of his father?'

'John Frampton died when Bevis was very young. In the Tower I believe, though I do not know the whole story. There was some talk of John Frampton having upset the King. Henry had a violent temper. I think that Elizabeth takes after him in that respect.'

'The Queen can be very like her father when she chooses.' Nick smiled wryly. 'However, we would not have her other than she is, God bless and keep her.

But I promised you an explanation. What would you say if I told you that I suspect Frampton of being an enemy of the Queen, of perhaps being behind at least some of the plots we have already uncovered against her?'

Oliver raised his brows at that. 'If you had asked me that when I came to see you after my return from Italy, I should have said I did not think he had the stomach for it. Now I am not so sure, for I know him to be sly and work in secret ways, and there was a time when I suspected him of being concerned in a plot against Her Majesty. I believe that he may in some way have interfered in Elizabeth's marriage plans, yet I cannot believe he would risk a traitor's death. But it is years since I have seen him, and who knows what he may be concerned in now?'

'You think him a coward?' Nick was thoughtful. 'The man I seek takes very little risk himself. Walsingham suspects him of working his evil through others. He believes him to be a man of darkness, and that he may even dabble with the occult.'

'Say you so?' Oliver was thoughtful for a moment. 'Now that I can believe, Nick. Frampton was ever secretive and Harry distrusted him from the start. I remember something he said just before he became ill— something about Frampton being evil.'

'My brother said that?' Nick felt his blood run cold. 'Could Frampton have heard him, do you suppose?'

'Who knows? He was always creeping up behind us, watching us. I believed he was jealous and envied us our friendship.'

'I met him but once, and that briefly, yet I thought him envious of you both.'

'I think you are right in that regard, Nick.'

'I have always wondered if Harry died of a fever or of some foul poison. I know you believed it was a fever often caught by travellers, Oliver, but if Frampton had reason to hate my brother...'

'He was such a weak creature, Nick, and had no interest in manly pursuits. It crossed my mind that he might have harmed Harry if he could, but I have never to this day been sure. When I came to tell your father of Harry's death, I dared not mention my suspicions, for I knew it was unlikely Bevis could have done the foul deed I feared. And later, when I suspected him of other things, I could not speak out, for I had no proof. Even now, I cannot say to you that Frampton would dare to do such a thing. He would be afraid for his life should he be discovered.'

Nick nodded, accepting that Oliver had his doubts but could not point the finger of blame at Frampton with any certainty. And it no longer mattered; he had laid his grief to rest and must look only to the future.

'Then what would your advice be in this matter? Should I go to Walsingham with my suspicion?'

'I know not what kind of a man Frampton is now, but I would simply warn you to take the greatest care. If Bevis was responsible for Harry's death, or any other kind of plot, he could be very dangerous.' Oliver smiled at Nick. 'Now, you must stay with us for as long as you please. I know my lady would be happy to have your company.'

'I shall stay until the morrow,' Nick said. 'But then

I must be on my way. Catherine will wonder where I have got to else…'

'And who is Catherine?'

'She is the lady I hope and intend to marry.'

'I must hear more of this,' Oliver said, clapping him on the shoulder. 'We must celebrate tonight, and I know my dearest wife will want to join me in congratulating you.'

Nick groaned as he swung himself into the saddle and waved goodbye to his host and hostess, who had come out to the sheltered courtyard of their home to see him off. He had drunk a little too heavily of Oliver's good wine the previous evening, and his head ached.

He smiled ruefully. It had been good to be with true friends, and he had relaxed the guard he habitually kept in place at court. There was definitely something to be said for the life of a country gentleman, away from the intrigues and politics of the palace.

Once he and Catherine were married he would take her to his home, but it might be necessary to visit the court from time to time. He would do so as seldom as he could, for he was weary of the life and wanted nothing more than to live with his love in peace and harmony.

Busy with his thoughts of the future, it was not until Nick had been riding for some time that he realised he was being followed, and only seconds later that someone fired at him. Thankfully the ball went wide, missing his head as it whistled by and embedded itself in the trunk of a tree.

Unprepared for the sudden attack, Nick decided that it was better to make good his escape than fight an unknown enemy. It took time to reload a musket and take further aim, but he was not sure if there was more than one rogue lying in wait for him. Bending over his horse's neck, he urged it on through the trees. If hard riding did not shake off the would-be assassin, he would turn and defend himself when he had the advantage. But for now flight might prove the wisest course.

After some time had passed without a sighting of his enemy, he knew that the pursuit had ended. Whoever had fired at him had taken the chance to wound or kill him in an ambush but was not prepared to give chase.

The question was, had it been merely some ruffian out to rob him or was there a more sinister reason behind the attack? And why should it happen now? Just after his visit to Oliver Woodville? Was someone afraid of what he might have learned from Oliver?

The back of Nick's neck had begun to prickle. He had been ready to accept that he might have been wrong to suspect Bevis Frampton of treachery. Now he was beginning to wonder if he ought to give the possibility more credence. Oliver certainly thought him untrustworthy, and Nick was almost sure that he was the man he had glimpsed in the shadows that night in Paris.

If there was a chance that Frampton was involved in this dark business, even as some kind of a go-between for the man Walsingham suspected of being behind various plots against the Queen, then it was Nick's duty to inform Walsingham.

If his life was in danger, might not Catherine also be threatened? Nick turned cold as the thought occurred to him. If he thought that, he would turn his back on this quest for Walsingham's traitor. Yet it seemed that he might be on the verge of unmasking him, and he had spent so many months in searching that it would be cowardly to be deterred from his course.

Nick sighed inwardly as he realised he had no choice. It was his duty to seek Walsingham out and tell him of his suspicions. And that would mean a delay of several more days before he could return to Catherine.

Chapter Eleven

Elizabeth's expression was stony as she waited for the girl to answer.

'Well, what have you to say to me, Mistress Catherine?'

'Only that we never meant to deceive you, Your Majesty. We have but recently discovered that we… like each other. Sir Nicholas intends to beg for an audience when he returns to court and then he will ask for your permission. We hope that you will allow us to marry quite soon.'

'I have been told you intend to run away together?'

Catherine felt faint as she saw the Queen's frown of annoyance. Her head was swimming and she wished that she might sit down, but she had not been invited to do so.

'Whoever told you that was lying.'

'Why should someone try to cause trouble for you?'

'I do not know, ma'am.'

The Queen was silent for a moment, her eyes intent on Catherine's face. She had always found the girl honest, apart from the lie she had told to protect her friend. That had been done out of loyalty, and loyalty was an attribute Elizabeth admired.

'You do not look well, Cat. Does something ail you?'

'It is merely a little dizziness, ma'am.'

'Your cheeks are pale. Go for a walk. Obviously you need some exercise. I shall think on what you have said to me, and when I have reached a decision I may send for you to discuss this matter again.'

Catherine curtseyed and left the chamber. Outside, she had to pause to catch her breath. What on earth was wrong with her?

She walked slowly towards the gardens. The Queen was right, she would feel much better for some air.

Passing Louise Montpellier in the passageway, she was aware of the other girl's sly look of triumph, but felt too ill to care. It was clearly Louise who had gone to the Queen with her malicious tales. She must be hoping that Catherine would be sent home in disgrace, or sent to the Tower as a punishment.

Oh, if only Nick were here! Catherine sighed, wishing that he would come back to her.

Why did he not come as promised? He had told her that it would be a short absence this time, but it was already almost two weeks.

Had he deliberately lied to her? No, he would not do that! She could not believe that he had meant to hurt her this time.

A tear slid from the corner of her eye, trailing down her cheek.

'Come back to me,' she whispered. 'Oh, my dear love, please come back to me.'

Where was Nick? Why had he stayed away from her so long? She needed him. She needed him so much!

But she was ill; she must go into the garden for some air.

'I thought you might like to know that a marriage has been arranged for Louise Montpellier.'

The Queen's announcement took Catherine by surprise. Several hours had passed since their first interview that morning, and Catherine had feared the worst. But it seemed that Her Majesty was no longer angry.

'Louise is to be married? You have given your permission?'

'I made Mademoiselle Montpellier welcome at court because of her unfortunate experience,' Elizabeth said. 'I understood that she had no family, but now a distant cousin has come forward, a gentleman from the Low Countries. He made a formal offer for her hand and I was pleased to grant his wish. Mademoiselle Montpellier does not belong with us. It is better that she should be married and leave the court. She will do so tomorrow.'

'I hope she will be very happy.'

Catherine was conscious of relief that the French girl would no longer be at court to torment her with her vicious whispers and malicious looks.

The Queen was watching her, her gaze narrowed and intent.

'You do not look happy, Cat. I have noticed of late that you are heavy-eyed. What ails you? Are you ill, or is it that Sir Nicholas has been too long from court?'

'I have not been sleeping well,' Catherine confessed. 'I do not know why.'

'If you continue thus I shall have my own physician attend you,' Elizabeth said. 'I would not have you ill. I cannot spare you, Cat. I miss your wit and conversation when I cannot rest. Besides, too many of my ladies leave me.' There was a flash of annoyance in her eyes, as though she was remembering Lettice's desertion.

Catherine made no answer. She was feeling desperately tired and her limbs were heavy, as though she suffered from some severe illness.

'You should go and rest,' the Queen said, dismissing her with a wave of her hand. 'You grow dull, Catherine. Where has your spirit gone?'

'Forgive me. I am tired.'

Elizabeth waved her away, and Catherine knew she had displeased her mistress. The Queen was in the mood to be entertained and Catherine could not summon the energy necessary.

She was wondering whether it would be better to rest on her bed or walk in the fresh air, but sleep did not bring her ease these days, for she had such terrible dreams. She could never recall them when she woke, but she knew that they made her cry out, for poor Jane had woken her more than once out of concern for her.

'I hope you are satisfied now!'

Catherine came slowly out of her reverie as she found herself face to face with Louise Montpellier in the narrow passageway. She had not noticed the French girl, but she was standing in her way, clearly angry and determined not to let Catherine pass.

'Please allow me to pass. I feel unwell.'

'I hope you catch the plague and die of it,' Louise said, her pretty face twisted with hatred and spite. 'It is all your fault. I know you did this. You told tales to Her Majesty and now she is making me marry Pietre. I hate him. I refused to marry him when he asked my father for me, and now I have no choice.'

Catherine blinked as she realised what Louise was saying. She did not want to marry her cousin, but the Queen had made it a royal command and Louise was being forced into a marriage she did not wish for. Despite her headache and the taunts she had been forced to endure from Louise these past weeks, Catherine felt sympathy for her.

'I am sorry,' she said. 'Please believe me when I tell you that I had nothing to do with this. I have not complained of you to Her Majesty, nor did I know that the marriage was not of your choosing.'

'Liar!' Louise glared at her angrily. 'I hate you! I hate you. I loved Nick and he would have married me if it had not been for you.'

She suddenly burst into tears and fled down the corridor. Catherine stared after her. Had she been feeling less ill she might have gone after Louise and tried to comfort her, but her head was spinning too much. She was afraid that if she did not go and lie down at once she might fall down, and she turned her steps towards the chamber she shared with Jane.

Each step she took was so difficult. Catherine's sight was blurred, and she had to place a hand against the wall to stop herself from falling. She felt so ill, so very ill. She must lie down; perhaps then she would begin to recover.

Nick, oh, Nick, she thought. Please come to me. I need you so.

Entering her bedchamber, she saw that Jane was there. Jane was staring at her, and she needed to pass her to get to her bed. It was almost too much effort to look at Jane. She could not see properly, and the room was spinning.

'Is there something wrong, Catherine?'

'I need…'

Catherine took a step towards her, gave a sigh, and collapsed into a heap at Jane's feet.

'Catherine!' Jane stared at her in dismay, realising that she was very ill. She had known for a few days that something was wrong, but Catherine had managed to keep going somehow, refusing to have a doctor. 'Oh, Catherine…' She bent over the unconscious figure, realising that there was nothing she herself could do to assist Catherine. 'Help. I must get help,' she said, standing up and running to the door. 'Help! Mistress Catherine is ill. Someone please help me…'

For three days Catherine lay in a deep sleep while the doctors shook their heads and disagreed about what ailed her. She seemed to be in a fever, and yet there was no sign of the sweating usually connected with such illness.

'Please, you must do something,' Jane begged but her pleas were met with resigned looks. 'She is so young. There must be a cure for what ails her.'

The doctors came and went, puzzled by an illness

that they did not understand, their only advice to wait and pray. Jane was her devoted nurse, for almost everyone was afraid that Catherine had some dread disease and would not venture near her, and then after the fourth day she woke and took a little water, complaining of a headache. On the fifth day she was able to sit up in bed, and that was when the Queen sent for her to be brought to a chamber nearer her own so that she might visit with her favourite maid of honour.

It was on the tenth day that Catherine discovered that she was feeling a little better.

'It was merely a little fever,' the Queen declared. 'I knew that once my own physician attended you, you would soon recover.'

Feeling weak and ill, Catherine could only smile wearily and agree. She was tired and listless, and wanted only to be at home. At last she dared to put her request to the Queen, and though it was obvious that Elizabeth was not best pleased, she was not denied.

Catherine felt too exhausted to weep or even think of Nick. If he had truly deserted her she did not wish to live, and if he loved her he would come to her when he returned from his journey. But he had promised to return long since.

Where was he? Why had he broken his promise to her yet again?

'You will soon be home.' Jane smiled encouragingly at Catherine as she opened her eyes and looked wearily about her. 'I know the journey has not been easy for you, but the Queen thought it best that you should go home to rest for a while.'

'Her Majesty was kind and thoughtful to send me home with an escort and you to accompany me,' Catherine said. 'Indeed, I am well enough, Jane. Just a little tired.'

'You were very ill,' Jane said, looking at her anxiously. 'When Her Majesty sent her own physicians to you we all thought you might die. It was not until you were taken to a chamber near the Queen so that she might visit you more easily herself that you began to recover your senses.'

'It must have been a putrid fever,' Catherine said. 'I cannot remember much about it, except that I did feel very unwell just before I fainted.'

'There were those who thought you might be with child,' Jane told her. 'I was so angry when I heard the rumours, Cat. The physician told Her Majesty that it was no such thing, and that you were still a virgin.'

Catherine's cheeks grew warm for shame that she had been examined by the physician while she lay unconscious, but she knew that they had been puzzled as to the nature of her ailment, and could find no cause for it. It was merely one of those fevers that science could not name, and she had been fortunate to recover as well as she had. It was true that she might easily have died, and due in part to Jane's care of her that she had lived.

'You are very kind to me, Jane.' Catherine sought her hand and held it. 'I do not know what I should have done without you these last few days.'

'You were kind to me when I first came to court,'

Jane replied. 'I know I must have seemed a foolish thing to you, for I was nervous and afraid of doing something wrong.'

'I merely thought you shy,' Catherine said and sighed. Those days seemed so far away now, and she had been so happy then, believing that Nick loved her. Where was he? Why had he not come to her? Did he not know that she needed him?

'Well, I have lost my shyness now, thanks to you, and a certain gentleman,' Jane said, her cheeks pink.

'You will not want to be away from court long,' Catherine said. 'Master Brooks will be pining for you, Jane.'

'You tease me,' Jane said. 'But I do not mind. I believe that Master Brooks does like me a little, and perhaps one day—but that cannot be for a year or two. The Queen has made it plain she does not encourage ideas of marriage in her ladies. She bid me remind you that you would be expected back at court once you were well again.'

'Yes, she told me herself.' Catherine sighed. 'I had hopes…but it seems they will come to naught and I shall have no choice but to return to court.'

The carriage was slowing now, and Jane looked out of the window. 'We are coming to a house,' she informed Catherine. 'Do you suppose we have arrived?'

Catherine had been too weary to look out at the countryside, but rousing herself now, she saw that they had indeed arrived at her home.

'Yes, this is my father's house,' she said, and suddenly she felt a surge of excitement as she saw someone come from the house. 'Father…oh, Father…'

Sir William came to the coach as the door was opened and the steps let down by a servant. He gave his hand to Catherine to help her down, looking anxiously at her pale face. It was clear that she had been ill, and he felt tightness in his chest.

'Catherine my dearest,' he said, his voice croaking with emotion. 'I have been anxious since Her Majesty's letter arrived. Are you better, my child? You look as if you should be laid on your bed, not travelling all this way.'

'I am very much better, Father,' she said, catching the note of censure in his voice. 'I begged Her Majesty to let me come home to you, though she was reluctant to part with me.'

Sir William put his arms about her, holding her tenderly for a few moments before turning to Jane to welcome her as she was helped from the coach.

'Mistress Howarth. I hear that you were my daughter's devoted nurse during the worst of her illness, and I must thank you for your care of her. I am deeply indebted and do not know how I may repay you.'

'I need no reward,' Jane said, dimpling with pleasure at his compliment. 'Catherine is my friend and I care for her.'

'You are welcome to my house at any time,' Sir William said. 'Come in, both of you. Catherine, will you take some refreshment or would you like to rest for a while?'

'I am a little tired,' Catherine said. 'But I shall take a glass of wine and biscuits with you and Jane, Father—then perhaps I may go up to my room and rest for an hour or so before we dine.'

* * *

Catherine stood at the window of her bedchamber, gazing out at the park and beyond to the ruins of an abbey that were just visible in the distance. It had been razed to the ground at the time of King Henry VIII, when the monks were turned out and the Church of England reformed. For a while no one had gone near it, and it was said to be haunted, but then the villagers had begun to carry away stones for their own houses and there was very little of it left now.

After two days at home, being cosseted by the faithful Martha, who clucked round her like a hen with a chick, Catherine was feeling rested from the journey. She had slept peacefully for two whole nights, and thought that it was the good country air which had restored her.

Jane Howarth was due to begin her return journey to London and the court that morning, and Catherine was about to go downstairs and see her off. She must find a little gift for Jane, something small that would not embarrass her but something that she might use and enjoy.

Catherine recalled a small gold pin that she had bought when first in London. It was fashioned in the shape of a flower and had a tiny ruby at its heart. It was the kind of thing that Jane might like.

Now where had she put it? Catherine looked in a little box on top of her counter, then remembered that she had last seen it in the coffer she had kept beside her bed at court. She opened the carved box, and lifting a small tray out found the pin she wanted. She was replacing the tray when she discovered the love charm that Lettice had given her. How had that got there? Jane had told her that she had thrown away a small pouch she had found beneath Catherine's pillow, and she had imagined that to be the charm Lettice had given her.

'I hope you did not mind, but I thought it smelled strong, and I threw it away when I packed your things,' Jane had told her.

Catherine had hardly listened at the time, but now she stared at Lettice's love charm. It had not brought Nick back to her, but perhaps she would try it one last time. She lifted her pillow and placed the charm beneath it, before turning to leave the room.

Jane would be ready to leave and she wanted to say goodbye to the girl who had done so much for her when she was ill.

'Are you going out, Catherine?' Sir William looked at his daughter anxiously. She had seemed better for a few days after she first arrived home, but now she seemed a little pale and tired. 'Have you been feeling ill again?'

'No, not ill—not as I was when I collapsed,' Catherine said. 'It is merely a headache, Father. I did not sleep too well last night. I think I shall go for a walk; the fresh air will do me good and clear my head.'

'That is a very good idea, daughter. Would you like someone to come with you?'

'No, there is no need.' Catherine smiled and went to kiss his cheek. 'Truly I am not ill, Father. It is merely a little headache.'

Sir William nodded, but looked after her anxiously as she left the room. She seemed quiet and almost listless, and he knew that something was bothering her, though she had made no attempt to confide in him. If she was not unwell, she must be anxious about something.

On her return from court, Helen had spun him a tale about Catherine having become entangled with Sir Nicholas Grantly, but he had sensed she was out of temper and had taken little notice. He had liked the younger man when they met, and could not quite believe Sir Nicholas the rogue his sister seemed to imagine.

Now he wondered if perhaps they had quarrelled. Was Catherine pining for Sir Nicholas, and just what was the situation between them? He decided that he would talk to Catherine when she returned from her walk.

Catherine knew that her father was anxious, and that he wondered why she was so unlike herself. She believed that she was over her illness, though she had had one of the dreams again since her return home. Her head ached a little, but it was nowhere near as bad as it had been for those last days leading up to her illness. She vaguely remembered the strong smell in the chamber she had shared with Jane, and wondered if that had contributed in some way to her headaches.

But what had caused that pungent odour? She recalled the pouch Jane had told her she had thrown away because it smelled strong—but where could it have come from? Had someone put it beneath her pillow?

Catherine's brow wrinkled in thought. Had whatever was in that pouch contributed to her illness?

The love charm had smelt quite pleasant. She had never noticed the change from one sachet to the next, because it was not one of her tasks to clean the room. A little chambermaid came in every morning to empty the pots and tidy their beds, but she was a gentle little thing and Catherine could not believe she would harm anyone.

Who would have wanted to make Catherine ill? She could think of only one person who might have done it. Louise Montpellier had hated her enough to try and upset her in any way she could, but where could she have got such a thing?

Like other women who had lived in the country for most of their lives, Catherine knew that there were many kinds of plants that could cause sickness or death, just as there were those that were used for healing. She herself knew how to make various simples and cures, and that some plants could cause violent death if the sap was somehow swallowed or rubbed into the skin.

Had someone wanted her dead?

The coldness trickled down Catherine's spine. Surely even Louise could not have wanted that?

She knew that the love charm Lettice had given her had been given in good faith, but her dreams had returned since she had placed it beneath her pillow once more. Even if it was not meant to harm, it was possible that something in the herbs was causing her headaches.

Catherine made up her mind that she would throw it away when she returned home. It had failed to bring Nick back to her, and she had started to feel less well since she had found the charm.

Lost in her thoughts, she had been walking for some time and realised that she had come to the ruins of the abbey. There was very little of it left now other than a flight of stone steps that led nowhere, and some tumbledown walls, moss and grass growing up between the rubble. But there was something about it that fascinated Catherine, and had done so since she had first come to it as a young girl.

She climbed the stairs to look out at the view afforded by her superior position, gazing about her with interest. A hawk was hovering in the sky before swooping down on a crouching rabbit. Shading her eyes against the light, she watched it as it took flight once more, its prey dangling from murderous talons. She stood there gazing out at the landscape for some minutes, and it was only as she was about to go down again that she saw something swirling about the bottom of the steps, which made her blood run cold.

What could it be? No, not again! Please not that again! As she watched, it seemed to creep up the steps towards her, sometimes shapeless, but growing to a point, gathering form and finally taking on the appearance of a man.

'No…' she whispered, as his hands seemed to reach out to her. 'No…please don't…'

It was the *thing* she had seen that day at Cumnor Place, and again briefly at the palace, but it could not be. Surely it was not real, but just an image from her dreams?

Yes, it was very like the dreams when the mist surrounded her and she could not breathe. In her dreams the blackness enveloped her and she knew that unless she could wake up she would die.

'No,' she whispered fearfully. 'Keep away! Do not come near.'

Her nostrils were assailed by a terrible stench like burning sulphur and her throat was constricted as she fought for breath

'Nick…help me…help me…'

She cried out for her love to save her, knowing that he was far away and could not hear her. But she needed him, she needed him so badly and knew that she was in grave danger. The feeling of evil all around her was so overpowering that she was terrified.

In her fear and confusion, she took a step forward, missed her footing and went tumbling down, rolling over and over to finally lie still at the bottom. Her eyes were closed and she knew nothing more, for a blow to her temple had robbed her of her senses.

For a moment the black shadow hovered over her, and then a horseman appeared on the horizon, riding at speed towards the ruins, and in an instant the shadow had vanished, disappearing like the morning dew in the heat of the sun.

Nick had set out immediately in pursuit of Catherine after being told that she had gone walking. He had stayed but minutes to greet Sir William and explain his errand, and had found Catherine's father only too eager for him to go in search of her. Sir William explained that he feared for her safety and had thought of going to look for her himself.

'For she seemed unwell this morning when she came down,' Sir William told him. 'I asked her to take someone with her, but my daughter has a mind of her own, sir.'

'I know it well enough,' Nick replied with a rueful smile. 'And I think I may be to blame for her unhappiness. I promised I would return to her long since, and she will think me faithless once more.'

'I believe she had a fever while she was still at court,' Sir William said a worried frown on his brow. 'She was attended by the best physicians, but they seem not to have any idea of what was wrong with her. It puzzled me, for Catherine was never prone to fevers. Even when she took it from her mother as a child she made a quick recovery.'

'They told me she had been very ill when I returned to court,' Nick said, 'and I have spared no time in coming to find her. You will excuse me, sir. I must not stay lest Catherine needs me.'

'Go and find her,' Sir William urged. 'I have been uneasy in my mind since she went out, though I do not know why. She has taken long walks since she was a small child, and most often goes in the direction of the abbey ruins. She has never come to harm, but I cannot rid myself of the fear that she is in some danger.'

Nick needed no further urging, and, armed with directions of the path she was likely to choose, set out at once.

Nick's alarm on hearing of Catherine's illness had grown as he had made the journey to her home in Cambridgeshire, though like Sir William he could not put a name to his unease. It was just there in his mind, haunting him, and had become overwhelming since he'd spoken to her father. It was almost as if Catherine was calling to him, begging him to help her.

If only he had returned sooner! But he had been torn between his duty and Catherine. He would never forgive himself if he had arrived too late.

He had made haste to communicate his thoughts, concerning the man he suspected of having spied on them that night in Paris, to Walsingham at the first opportunity.

'I caught but a glimpse of him in the shadows that first time, and though I thought I his face familiar I could not put a name to it. When I saw him again at Whitehall I was certain it was the same man. However, Oliver Woodville does not think Frampton capable of being the master plotter you suspect of being behind so many schemes against the Queen.'

'Frampton?' Walsingham frowned. 'The name is one I have heard before. Indeed, I suspected him of being one of John Dee's disciples, but they say he is a sickly creature. However, you may be sure that I shall have my agents keep a watch over him, Nick. I thank you for coming to tell me your suspicions.'

Nick had left again almost immediately. It was too long since he had seen Catherine, and he feared she would be angry. He was like to have to woo her all over again. But his fears of her temper had given way to another kind of anxiety, namely that he might lose her to death.

So many died of putrid fevers, and the physicians could neither explain the cause nor effect a cure; the weak failed and only the strong survived.

As he rode from London to Cambridgeshire one thought dominated his mind. Harry had been strong, but the fever that took him had been virulent, sapping his strength until he could no longer fight against it: unless it had not been a fever at all but some kind of subtle poison.

Had Catherine been poisoned? Nick did not know why the thought haunted him, yet he could not rid himself of the fear that she was in danger. But the question was, from whom or what?

Nick's feeling of unease intensified as he neared the ruins. He could see that it was but a few tumbled walls and a set of steps that led nowhere—and Catherine was standing at the top of them, outlined against the sky.

'Catherine,' he cried instinctively as he felt the prickling sensation at the nape of his neck. 'No! Catherine, no…'

He watched in horror as she seemed to start at something as if in fear, and then she fell, tumbling down and down until he could no longer see her. His heels kicked at his horse's flanks as he frantically urged it to greater speed. There was nothing he could do to save her from falling, nothing that he could do to break her fall, and his sense of impotence was hard to bear. His lovely, beautiful Catherine falling, perhaps to her death, and he too far away to help her.

His fear was so great that it almost choked him as he threw himself down and rushed into the ruins, to discover her lying on the third step from the bottom. She was so pale and still, and his heart felt as if it were torn asunder as he bent over her, believing her dead.

'Catherine my darling,' he cried in his agony. 'Forgive me. Oh, God, forgive me.'

He stroked her face, hardly daring to touch her, and then her eyelashes fluttered against her cheeks and she gave a little moan. Nick felt the tears sting his eyes as a surge of emotion rushed through him. He had thought her dead, but, God be praised, somehow she had survived the fall and lived.

'Catherine,' he whispered as he knelt by her side, gently brushing back her hair to reveal the place where she had hit her head as she fell. The wound was bleeding and he could see a gash where the flesh had been cut, but it did not seem deep. 'Catherine, can you hear me?'

Nick caught his breath on a sob. If he should lose her there would be nothing left in life, and he would never forgive himself for not being there when she needed him.

'Don't leave me, my darling,' he whispered. 'Oh, God, don't let her die. I beg you, do not let her die…'

Chapter Twelve

She was lying very still, making no response, but he knew that she was breathing. The blow to her head had clearly robbed her of her senses, but after a careful examination of her limbs, he discovered that nothing else was broken.

For a few moments Nick was tormented by despair as he gazed down at Catherine. This was his fault! Had he not been so caught up with affairs of state he would have been with her, he would have cared for her in her illness. If she lived he would give up his ambition and devote his life to making her happy, for he knew now that nothing and no one could mean as much to him as she.

She must live. She must! He could not bear it if she died.

He must get her home, but how best to do it? To carry her all that way alone would be difficult, and she could not ride on his horse, for the jolting might harm her. He needed help, but was reluctant to leave her even for a moment. As he looked about him, he saw

a young lad of perhaps nine or ten peering at him from
behind a pile of stones, and beckoned to him.

'Who are you, lad?'

'I be Ned, sir, son of the gamekeeper,' the youth
replied. 'I saw the lady fall and come running. That
be Mistress Moor. Be she hurt bad, sir?'

'Yes, I fear she is quite ill,' Nick said. 'Can you
ride, Ned?

'Aye, sir, been riding since I could walk,' the lad
bragged.

'Do you know where Sir William Moor lives?' Ned
nodded and Nick smiled. 'Take my horse. Go to Sir
William and tell him what has happened, say that Sir
Nicholas Grantly is with Catherine, and ask him to
send men to carry her home. Can you do that? There's
a guinea in my pocket for you if you make good speed
all the way there.'

'I can ride faster than the wind on a horse like that,'
the lad said with a grin.

Nick watched with some misgivings as Ned swung
himself up in the saddle. However, from the way he
handled Nick's horse, which admittedly was not the
high-spirited beast he usually rode, but a stout hunter
borrowed from Sir William's stables, it was plain Ned
was no stranger to the saddle.

Nick bent over Catherine again, kissing her forehead as the lad rode away. He took off his cloak and
placed it about her, because she seemed to be turning
cold. Then he gathered her up in his arms, feeling that
he could not just wait here for assistance. At least if
he could carry her a part of the way that would save

some time, and the sooner she was in her bed and a physician called to her, the better Nick would feel.

'Forgive me if I hurt you, my love,' he said. She had moaned a little when he lifted her. 'But I must get you home.'

Catherine could obviously not hear him, but he talked to her as he began the long walk towards Sir William's house. The countryside seemed flat and cheerless, a leaden sky threatening rain or worse. The wind was bitter, and Nick reflected on what might have happened had he not arrived when he did. In her state of unconsciousness, Catherine could easily have died before a search party was raised to look for her.

Never before had he understood what love could mean. At court he had flirted with her, teasing and pricking her pride, seducing her with his words of love, but now for the first time he realised how very precious she was to him—how empty his life would be without her. Worldly ambition was nothing without love and Catherine, his sweet Cat, was his only love.

'Such a foolish, stubborn girl,' Nick scolded gently. 'Why did you come to a place like this when you were feeling unwell?'

He frowned as he wondered what had made her fall like that. He had seen nothing, and yet she had seemed to start, as if she had suddenly seen something that frightened her. She could not have been aware of Nick, because he had ridden in from behind her, and the lad had come running after her fall. What had startled her enough to make her fall?

'I shall not forgive you if you die and leave me,' he went on, though Catherine had shown no sign of hearing him. 'Listen to me, my little Cat. I shall never let you go. You shall have no peace in your grave, for I shall call you forth by the power of my love. You must not leave me, my own dear love, for I cannot bear to live if you do not.'

A little sigh issued from her lips. Nick glanced down at her in sudden hope, but her appearance had not changed, she was as pale and still as ever.

Could she hear him? He could not be certain, but something told him to keep talking to her. Perhaps if he could somehow reach her, if he could let her know that he was with her, and that he loved her, she would come back to him.

'I do not know what made you ill,' Nick went on as if she were wide awake and listening to him. 'But we shall take more care of you in future, my love. No one shall hurt you again, I promise you. I shall be with you always, Catherine. I promise I shall never go away and leave you again. Only come back to me, darling. I love you so much, need you so very much.'

He did not know whether he talked to reassure himself or her, or merely to make the distance he must cover seem less far. Where had the gamekeeper's boy got to? In God's name, where were Sir William's servants? Surely Ned must have reached Sir William's house long before this? Or perhaps he had simply taken the horse and ridden off, never to be seen again.

Nick cursed himself for a fool in having trusted the lad. He must have been mad. Better to have fetched help himself! How much further was the house anyway? Catherine was not heavy, but the strain of his anxiety was exerting a fearful toll on his strength.

The house was almost reached when Nick saw a small army of servants issuing from the grounds. He was aware of frustration at the time wasted in gathering so many when three would have done, so that they might have carried Catherine home on some kind of a board. However, his arms were aching and he was beginning to feel the strain of carrying her so far when four of the men came rushing up to take his burden from him. Thankfully, they had brought a door on which to lay Catherine, and blankets to cover her, one of which he folded carefully to support her head as he walked beside her.

Sir William was about to mount his horse as the little procession entered the courtyard, and throwing the reins to his groom, he came quickly to Nick, who still walked beside Catherine.

'Thank God you found her so quickly,' he said, looking at her white face. 'She is not dead?'

'No, mercifully. She is alive but robbed of the power of her senses by a blow to the head, I fear. Her eyelids have fluttered and she has sighed, but I do not know if she can hear me, though I have been talking to her.'

Sir William nodded. 'The lad told me he saw her fall and was running to see what had happened when you came riding up and startled him. He was afraid that he might be blamed at first, for he has been told not to play in the ruins.'

'We must think ourselves fortunate that he was there, for I did not wish to leave her alone and unprotected,' Nick replied looking grim. 'I trust that you have sent for a physician?'

'Yes, at once,' Sir William laid a hand on his arm as he would have followed Catherine up the stairs. 'Leave her to the women now, sir. It is not fitting that a man should enter my daughter's bedchamber while she is being tended.'

'Catherine has done me the honour of agreeing to be my wife,' Nick said, a determined gleam in his eyes. 'Had I not been away on important business for the state, I should have been here long since to advise you of my intention towards your daughter.'

'I know you love her,' Sir William said. 'I suspected it from the start, and your manner when you arrived today was so agitated that I could not doubt your sincerity—but still you must leave her to the women for the moment, though I will not deny you the right to visit when she is decently settled.'

Nick stared after Catherine as she was taken up the stairway and out of his sight. His frustration and need was so urgent that he almost defied Sir William's spoken wish, but then, seeing that he was not the only one to watch anxiously as she was carried from their sight, he accepted that Catherine's father was right.

'I promised her I would never leave her again,' he said.

'She must be tended by her women,' Sir William said as he led Nick into the small parlour he used most often when alone. 'You must wait in patience until they call us, and then we shall go up to her. You are not the only one in this house who loves Catherine, sir.'

'I know it.' Nick smiled ruefully. 'But if anything should happen and I was not near...' His mouth thinned to a grim line. 'I should not easily forgive myself or you.'

'They will call us soon,' Sir William said. 'Take a glass of wine with me, sir, it may help to settle your nerves.' He went over to the oak buffet where some glasses and a silver wine jug stood on a tray. Pouring wine for them both, he brought a delicate Venetian glass back to Nick. 'This is good malmsey and will warm you while you recover your strength. I remember the night when my daughter was born and I feared to lose my wife. There are times when it is hard to be a man and wait, sir, but I fear it must be endured.'

'You lost your wife when Catherine was quite young, I believe?'

'Yes, of a putrid fever. We had but the one child, for my wife suffered too much the first time and I could not bear to see her suffer so again, though she would have endured it had I asked her for a son.' Sir William smiled. 'Some men long for a son to follow them, but Cat was always sufficient for me.'

'I hope you will consider yourself free to make your home with us when we are wed, sir,' Nicholas said, and then laughed wryly. 'I ought to have asked your permission, but in truth I do not think I could relinquish her if you were to withhold it.'

'Then it is as well that I have no intention of it,' Sir William replied and chuckled. 'From what I hear you are well matched. Besides, Catherine will have her own way, as she always has.'

Nick was amused as he caught the irony in the older man's voice. His lady had clearly been spoiled all her life long.

Nick liked Catherine's father, and he imagined they would deal well together in the future. He had spoken with confidence of a time when Catherine would be his wife, because he dare not let himself think otherwise.

His glass stood untouched on the mantel as he paced the room, his anxiety making him unable to relax. Where was that damned physician? In heaven's name, why did it take so long to do anything in this place?

They heard the physician arrive, and Sir William went into the entrance hall to greet him, Nick hard on his heels as they exchanged a few words before he went up to Catherine. The time that elapsed before he came down again was difficult to bear, and both men swung round in anticipation as he came at last to join them in the parlour.

'There is no change as yet,' the physician told them. 'I have bathed and bound her wound, but can find nothing more other than a few bruises. It is the blow to her head that has caused her to lose her senses, and there is nothing more that we can do but wait.'

'For God's sake, man!' Nick burst out. 'We knew as much when I brought her home. Have you no news for us? How long will Catherine be this way? Will she be well again when she wakes?'

The physician looked offended, addressing himself to Sir William.

'Forgive me, but there is no way of telling when she will wake, or how she will be. These cases are never the same, sir. Sometimes the patient will wake within a short time and be none the worse, but...' He shook his head gravely. 'If this condition goes on too long it may be that she will never be the same again.'

'Is there nothing you can do for her?' Sir William asked, as Nick seemed as if he might explode. 'What must we do until she comes to herself again?'

'Her ladies know how to care for her,' the physician said. 'Call me if she wakes, but I shall call in a day or so to see how she goes on.'

Nick swore fiercely as the man left, Sir William going with him into the hall to speak privately for a few minutes.

'We must find another physician,' Nick said on his return. 'The man is a fool!'

'No, I think not,' Sir William replied. 'I do not deny you the right to bring another doctor here if you wish, Sir Nicholas, but Browning is a good man. If he believed there was something he could do, he would do it. He told me that he heard of a case where a young lad lay without speaking for six months, and then recovered, though in that case the patient was able to swallow liquids and broth, and responded when spoken to. We must pray that Catherine will be as fortunate.'

'I wish you comfort of your prayers,' Nick said his frustration eating at him like a gnawing rat. 'But I intend to seek further advice. There is a doctor my mother swears by. I shall beg him to come to us with all speed. If I may employ one of your servants as a courier?'

'Of course,' Sir William inclined his head in sorrow. 'Use my house as your own, sir. And now, if you would care to accompany me, I intend to go up and sit with Catherine for a little while.'

Nick frowned, torn between seeing his love and doing something more useful. 'If you will forgive me, I have some urgent messages to send. Go up alone, sir, and I shall join you later.'

It was night when Nick entered Catherine's room. A woman was sitting by her, but she got up to allow him to take her place, moving to the far end of the room so that they were almost alone, though chaperoned.

Nick bent over the girl he loved beyond all bearing, stroking her forehead as she lay in the daze that had seemed to hold her mind since the fall. She felt cold to his touch and a terrible fear clutched at his heart.

'You must not die,' he said huskily, his voice caught with tears. 'If you die, my sweet Cat, then I shall have nothing to live for. Live for me, my beloved, I beg you, live for me.'

There was no response and tears slipped down his cheeks as he watched for any sign of her awakening but there was none and his heart was heavy as he slipped to the floor beside her bed, on his knees, praying as he had never prayed before.

At the far end of the room Catherine's serving woman stifled a sob, then left the room. Such devotion deserved respect, and she would not listen to Sir Nicholas praying for his love, for a man who loved, as he did, could never harm her mistress.

Nick did not even hear her go.

* * *

Six days had passed since Catherine's accident, and apart from a few sighs or moans, there had been little sign of life from her. Both Sir William and Nick were at their wits' end, and they could neither of them wait in patience for the arrival of the London physician.

When he finally arrived, towards the evening of the sixth day, Sir William had gone for a walk to relieve his anxiety, though Nick sat as he had for most of the intervening time by Catherine's bed. He got up with alacrity as the doctor was shown in by one of the women, going at once to greet him, his hand outstretched in welcome.

'I am glad to see you, Doctor Rowling.'

'Lady Fineden informed me of your urgent need, sir. I have not stayed in my efforts to reach you. Has there been no change?'

'She seemed to be more restless this morning,' Nick replied. 'Indeed, I thought for a moment that she might wake. But we have not been able to give her more than a little water and wine. I fear that if she does not soon wake she will die for lack of sustenance.'

'Indeed, the poor lady cannot go on in this state for long,' the doctor said, shaking his head over Catherine. He made a brief examination of the wound. 'I would not have said this was severe enough to cause Mistress Moor to remain in this state for so long. It seems to me that there may be another cause for her loss of senses.'

'What do you mean?' Nick frowned. 'I do not understand you.'

'I have had experience of this particular ailment before,' the doctor replied. He looked at Nick oddly. 'Do you trust me, sir?'

'Yes,' Nick replied, for he had tended Lady Fineden several times and she believed him a most excellent man. 'What have you to tell me, sir?'

'It may be that there has been some mischief here,' Doctor Rowling said slowly. 'I thought when Lady Fineden told me something of the case that it might be as well to come prepared. I have someone waiting downstairs who may be able to help us, but I must have your promise that you will not interfere before I ask him to come up.'

'What is this—some black art?' Nick looked at him suspiciously. 'Good grief, man, who have you brought me—a sorcerer?'

'The person I have asked to wait is a gentleman much skilled in fighting those who employ the black arts,' Doctor Rowling replied. 'If something of the kind has occurred here, he will know it as soon as he enters the room—but he will not do so unless you agree to let him do what he thinks right without hindrance.'

'You are asking me to let a stranger do whatever he will to Catherine?' Nick stared at him in stunned disbelief.

'Unless someone does something she will die,' Sir William's voice said from the doorway. 'I met your assistant on my way here, sir, and he has told me that I must allow him to treat my daughter or she will die. He says that he feels she is in great danger and he has arrived only just in time to save her.'

'Are you sure you wish to trust him?' Nick was doubtful. 'It may all be nonsense.'

'I assure you that I shall do only good to Mistress Moor.'

Nick saw that another man had now entered behind Sir William. He had feared some strange flaunting creature in flowing robes who would pretend to be what he was not, but was at once reassured. This man might have been mistaken for a very ordinary country gentleman. Dressed in rusty black clothes that most would call shabby, he might have been a modest parson.

'There is little time to be lost,' the newcomer said and ignoring Nick, who had still not given his approval, he walked up to the bed. 'Support her head for me, Rowling.' As the physician obeyed, he lifted Catherine's pillow and removed a small pouch, taking it over to the fireplace, where he tossed it into the flames, chanting a toneless litany as he did so. 'That was not helpful, and may have caused restless nights, though not I suspect the cause of this problem. Tell me, had this lady been very ill just prior to her accident?'

'She had a fever,' Sir William said. 'They told me she had been having bad dreams and became weak and dizzy just before she collapsed. She was ill for some days, though she was almost recovered when they sent her home.'

'I think she has been a victim of someone well versed in the black arts, but someone who was not able to gain direct access to her, for if he had then I believe she would already be dead of some foul poison. The charms he used were less deadly, for they had to be handled by another. He used them for two purposes, first to make her feel ill so that she became vulnerable and he was more able to penetrate her thoughts through her dreams…'

'How can that be so?' Nick exclaimed and was treated to a severe look by both Doctor Rowling and Sir William. 'I do not doubt you know your work, sir. I only ask how it is possible for someone to penetrate another's mind?'

'It is an art that takes much concentration and causes suffering to both the victim and the perpetrator. Done too often, it could cause the perpetrator to become ill himself, as do other favourite tricks used by creatures of this ilk.'

'What kind of tricks?'

'Appearing as a shadow of some kind to startle or frighten the victim. I have suspected it many times in the past, though it is impossible to prove. When a person is ill it is easier to frighten or startle them, and thereby cause an accident such as this lady suffered. In some cases the effect is so severe that the victim loses his or her mind, and may even seek to harm themselves.'

'Are you claiming Catherine is possessed by demons?' Nick demanded angrily.

'No, indeed, sir, that is a very different thing, and would need far more power than I think the man who did this to Mistress Moor possesses.' The stranger paused to let his words sink in. 'The second purpose of the poisons in that charm, and others he may have used, is to give the victim what we call mind pictures that come to her, even when she is not dreaming. As yet we do not have a name for these, and some would call them demons, but they have no substance or power; they are merely the tool of the man who wishes to harm his victim.'

'Good grief!' Nick exclaimed. 'Walsingham was right…'

He shook his head as the others looked at him. 'Forgive me, this is something I may not discuss with any of you, other than as it affects Catherine. But it may be that someone has tried to harm her this way because of her association with me.'

The grief twisted inside him. If Catherine had come to harm through him he would never forgive himself! He had been aware that he was dealing with evil, that he must take care for her sake, but had never truly believed it would touch Catherine.

'It would help to know who gave her that charm,' the stranger said. 'You must guard against such things in future, though if it has not worked this time he may not try again.'

'Why? If she was a danger to him before, that danger still exists,' Sir William said with a frown.

'As I explained, sir, it takes too much out of the perpetrator.'

'And he has other purposes for his evil powers,' Nick said, his gaze narrowing intently. 'If we believe you, sir, what more must we do?'

'There is nothing for you to do, sir. I would ask that I might be alone with Mistress Moor for a few minutes. I give you my word that she will come to no harm in my care. I shall do nothing that might affect her modesty or cause her shame.'

Nick was reluctant to leave, for though his trust had been partially won, he could not help being suspicious of someone who spoke of the black arts as if it were a normal practice. He was sceptical and feared this man might do his love some harm. Yet perhaps these things were true, and in his pride he had blinded himself to that truth.

'I have given my word that Mistress Moor will suffer no harm from me, sir. Unless you leave, I can do nothing more.'

Nick felt Sir William take hold of his arm, and looking into the father's eyes he saw his own doubts, fears and hopes reflected there.

'We must do as the gentleman asks, Nick. I believe it is Catherine's only chance.'

Nick allowed himself to be led from the room. Outside, Dr Rowling stood between him and the door so that he could not open it without permission.

Nick turned his back on them, looking out of the window at the frosty ground. The weather was as bitter as his thoughts. He could hardly bear this waiting, and he was torn by his hope that this stranger could help Catherine and the fear that he was a charlatan who would render her some harm. It was more than he could bear, to be thrust from her side by a stranger, kept from her while some secret ritual was carried out.

'I trust him completely, Sir Nicholas. I should not else have brought him here.' He felt the touch of a hand on his shoulder and turned to look at Rowling. 'If there is a way to save her, he will find it.'

'If she dies…' Nick could not go on, for he knew that Catherine was going to die if nothing was done. His hands clenched at his sides. What was going on in there? Why had he left Catherine alone with a stranger? He must be a fool! 'I should be with her…this cannot be borne!'

Dr Rowling held him back, as he would have torn open the door.

'If you do that it might be dangerous for her. I promise you he is to be trusted. I would stake my life on it.'

'Has he a name?'

'I call him Foxworth, he will own to no other, and I doubt that is his true name, but he is a good man, though some would burn him at the stake if they could.'

'If he harms Catherine I shall break his…' Nick ceased to speak as the door opened and the stranger appeared. 'Is she…' He could not go on, for his throat was tight and for the first time in his life he was afraid of breaking down in tears before others.

'She opened her eyes and asked for someone called Nick. I believe that must be you, sir?' The stranger caught Nick's arm, as he would have rushed into the room. 'She is sleeping. You will see no difference in her for a few hours, but believe me, this is a healing sleep.'

Nick did not reply as he went on into Catherine's chamber. At first he thought that there was no change, for she was still lying with her eyes closed, but then he saw that her natural colour had returned. He walked across to the bed, bending over to kiss her forehead as he struggled and could not hold back the moan that broke from him.

'She looks peaceful,' Sir William said coming up behind him. 'We should let her rest, Nick. You can come back to sit with her before she wakes. It will be at least five hours, so I am told.'

Nick turned back from the bed. 'I must thank him and apologise.'

'He has already left. I offered him money, but he told me he would need only his expenses and that I must pay Dr Rowling. He will take nothing from those he helps, for he says that his own power would be weakened if he allowed himself to be tainted by coin.'

Nick allowed himself to be conducted from Catherine's chamber once more, but he would not remain in the house and set off after the stranger, wanting to speak with him again before he disappeared.

'Please!' he cried as he caught up with him. 'I must thank you for what you have done, and apologise for doubting you.'

'Protect your lady and I shall be thanked enough,' the stranger replied, smiling oddly at him.

'What must I do to protect her?'

'Discover what either you or she has done to bring her to the attention of the creature who did this, and desist from it at once. If you represent no danger to him, he will not waste his energy or thoughts on either of you.'

Nick looked into his eyes and the stranger nodded.

'I was the danger and she but the tool of his displeasure.'

'I see that you understand, and you know what must

be done. And now I must rest, for these things take too much out of me. Excuse me, I would be alone.'

Nick watched as he walked away, and a short distance further on curled up beneath a hedge, where he appeared to fall straight into a deep sleep. A shiver went through Nick as he realised what could have happened to Catherine—and it would have been because of her involvement with him, because he had come too close to the truth.

He had taken pride in his rising popularity at court and his importance as a servant of the Crown, but that was all worldly ambition. It was true that his work for Walsingham had brought him satisfaction, but what was that beside his love for Catherine? Every honour in the land was not worth one hair of her head, and he would give up more—his own life—to keep her safe.

He must give up his work for Walsingham! He had passed on all the information he had gathered to those who would know how to use it, and from now on he must devote all his energy and time to keeping Catherine happy and well.

Catherine opened her eyes to see that someone was sitting beside her bed. She blinked, because the sun was shining in at the window and she could not immediately see who it was, and then she realised it was Sir Nicholas. What on earth was he doing in her bed-chamber?

'Who gave you permission to be here, sir?'

'Catherine…' Nick felt the tightness in his chest as

a rush of emotion almost overwhelmed him. 'Are you better, my love?'

'Did I say that you could address me in that way?' Catherine frowned. She pushed herself up in the bed, taking care to keep the covers over her breasts. She was wearing only a light bedgown, and it was most improper for Nick to be here with her. 'I seem to remember that you went away and left me!'

'I was delayed longer than I had hoped,' Nick said. 'I returned as soon as I was able. Please forgive me, my love. I promise I shall not leave you again.'

'You make too many promises you do not keep.'

'But I shall in future, you have my word as a gentleman.'

Catherine stared at him for a moment. She was feeling so much better than she had for a long time, although she was aware of a slight weakness of her limbs and thirst.

'May I have some water?'

'Of course.' Nick rose and brought a cup of water to her, placing his arms about her shoulders to lift her as she drank. 'Be careful that you take only a little at a time. Dr Rowling said that you must take things easily at first.'

'I am hungry,' Catherine announced, and looked at him as he put the cup down, lowering her against her pillows. 'You did not answer me, sir—who said that you could be here in my room?'

'I did, Catherine,' Sir William answered her from the doorway. 'You had an accident, my dearest, and Nick found you and brought you home. Had it not been for his prompt action you might have died.'

'Is that why I feel weak?' Catherine asked, sighing as she lay back against the pillows again. 'What happened to me?'

'Do you not remember?'

'No, should I?' Catherine frowned as she stared at them. 'I remember that I felt ill at court and the Queen sent me home, and then I woke up and Nick was here.'

'There is nothing in between that?'

'No, nothing at all.'

'You walked to the abbey and fell from the steps,' Nick told her. 'Something must have startled you, but you do not recall it?'

'I do not remember going to the abbey,' Catherine said. 'I am sorry, is it important?'

'Nothing is important except that you should get well again,' Nick said. 'The doctor told us that you would have to rest for a week or two, but that afterwards you would be perfectly well again.'

'I do not like lying in bed,' Catherine said. 'I shall get up and come downstairs as soon as I feel able.'

'You will do as you are bid,' Nick told her. 'The doctor said you must rest, and rest you shall.'

'And who gave you permission to order my days, sir?' Catherine glared at him. 'I have not yet decided whether or not to forgive you for deserting me—for the second time.'

'It was for the last time, Cat. I promise that I have done with all that. When we are married I shall never go anywhere unless you are able to go with me, at least only within the boundaries of our estate.'

'Have I told you that I shall marry you?' Catherine sighed and closed her eyes. 'Go away, Nick. I may forgive you when I feel able, but for the moment I want Martha. Ask her to come to me, please.'

'We shall both go and leave you to your women,' Sir William said. 'For you must be wishing us to the devil, I dare say.'

Catherine smiled at him. 'Not you, Father. You did not promise you would be back within a week, and then stay away for more than a month without a word of explanation.'

'Nick had his duty, daughter,' Sir William said. 'And he has scarce left your side to eat or sleep while you were ill, and that only at my insistence.'

'Catherine has a right to be angry,' Nick said and smiled at her ruefully. 'I pray that you will forgive me, Cat, for I cannot imagine a life without you.'

He followed Sir William from the room without giving her time to answer. Catherine stared after him, feeling close to tears. How provoking the man was! Had she felt less weak she would have made him quarrel with her so that they could make it up with kisses.

She smiled as she lay back against the pillows, alone for a few minutes before Martha came bustling in to make her comfortable. Apart from this foolish weakness she felt so well. It was as if a dark shadow that had been hovering over her had gone. Her last illness had been frightening, though she could no longer remember the bad dreams, only that she had had them. All memory of what had happened after her return from court had gone, and she could not wait to have her hair washed and brushed so that she felt herself again.

And she was very, very hungry!

Chapter Thirteen

'So we are agreed,' Sir William said. 'Catherine is never to be told what happened here that day, nor that she was the victim of some evil spell. It is as the stranger told me, she has no memory of what happened that day at the abbey, and it is best that she never does.'

'She will never learn of it from me,' Nick said. 'It almost seems like a nightmare now, and I cannot wait to put the past behind us and prepare for our wedding.'

Indeed, he had begun to wonder if the stranger had duped them all. Catherine had quite possibly been about to wake before he arrived that day. All that nonsense he had told them about a man who had the power to infiltrate another person's mind—how could it be true? Yet Walsingham believed that such a man might well exist, and many believed that people were often possessed by demons. Besides, everything the stranger had told them would happen had come about. Catherine was well, and she had no terrible memories to frighten her.

But Sir William was speaking again, recalling Nick's mind to the present.

'Her Majesty has sent word that she wants to see Catherine once more before the wedding. I have told her that I have given my permission, and she has accepted it—but she may want to keep you with her even after the wedding.'

'I do not believe that Catherine should return to court for a long time, if ever,' Nick said. 'Nor do I intend to myself.'

'I believe it would be the wiser course,' Sir William replied, 'and to this end I have written a letter telling Her Majesty that my daughter is not yet strong enough to travel to London, and that I fear she may suffer another breakdown if she attempts it.'

'Elizabeth will not demand that Catherine returns if she believes that she is not strong enough, but it would mean we must remain here for a while after the wedding.'

Sir William nodded in agreement. 'If you are prepared to wait before you take her back to your own estate I think we might go ahead with the wedding as soon as Catherine is well enough. Perhaps in a few months you could think of leaving, by which time the Queen will have forgotten you both.'

'I shall do whatever is best for Catherine,' Nick replied. 'Besides, it will give you time to decide whether you wish to make your future home with us or not.'

'We shall see,' Sir William replied. 'I do not wish to come between you in your early days of marriage, Nick, and so I shall go and visit my sister for a while.'

'There is no need,' Nick began but Sir William held up his hand. 'There is every need, Nick. A young couple should be alone for a few weeks. I shall return in a month or so and then we shall talk of the future.'

'We make our plans,' Nick said with a rueful smile. 'But as yet Catherine has not said that she will marry me...'

Once Catherine had begun to eat and drink normally she improved more quickly than anyone had expected. Within a few days she was able to move about her chamber without assistance, and when she insisted that she must come downstairs, Nick carried her.

'You take too much liberty, sir,' she told him crossly. 'I am well able to walk.'

'You shall not do so until you are stronger.'

'Do you mean to be so insistent on your way when we are married? If I should decide to marry you!'

'Only when it is for your good, Catherine.'

'Then I am not sure I shall marry you.'

'You might have missed your step on the stairs and hurt yourself,' Nick replied, a little smile about his mouth. It seemed that illness had not changed his love, and he was heartily glad of it. 'I do not want to have to delay our wedding because you are ill again.'

'You are very sure of yourself, sir.'

'That is because I love you and I believe you love me, even if you will not admit it.'

Catherine made no reply. The truth was that she could not wait to be truly well again so that they might be married, but she did not intend that he should have things all his own way.

As the days passed and the bitter winds of winter gave way to the milder tones of spring, Catherine was able to walk in the gardens again. Her father begged her not to go too far alone, and she obliged him by staying within the bounds of the formal gardens. She had no desire to visit the abbey ruins, for though she could recall nothing of what had happened to her there, she had developed an aversion to the place.

She was sitting on a wooden bench staring at a mass of violets that clustered about the root of an old tree, when Nick came upon her unawares.

'Why do you look so sad, Cat?'

She turned as he spoke and smiled. 'I am not sad, merely thoughtful.'

'Do your thoughts trouble you?'

'I was thinking of my father,' Catherine said truthfully. 'When we are married he will be alone, and although he does not complain I know he is not always well.'

'He does not have to be alone. I have assured him that he is welcome to share our home, Catherine.'

'You would allow that?'

'Of course. You must know that I would allow almost anything to make you happy.'

'But shall you not want to return to court? Surely you have work for the state—important work?'

'Nothing is as important to me as your happiness,' Nick said, and took her hand in his, his eyes dwelling on her face in a way that made her heart flutter, for she had never seen him look like that before. 'I have decided that it is time I took more interest in my estates, Catherine. We shall visit the court from time to time, of course, but our life will be spent mostly in the country.'

'Is that what you truly want?'

Catherine sensed that there was more behind this decision than he was telling her, but she did not ask. Instead she returned to her teasing mode to lighten the mood.

'What would you not allow?' Her eyes were brighter than he had seen them in a long while and he knew that she was teasing him, and that she was truly herself again. 'Shall you buy me all the new gowns I desire?'

'You shall have your own money and buy whatever you wish.'

'Then shall you give me my way in everything I ask?'

'If I think your request fair and reasonable.'

'And if I wished to take a lover?'

Nick's gaze narrowed, his mouth set hard. 'Then I should beat you and lock you in your room until you came to your senses.'

Catherine's laughter trilled out in delight. 'It is as well then that I wish for no other lover. It seems you will be a stern husband, Nick. I am not sure that I should marry you.'

'But you will,' he said and took her hand, tugging her to her feet and pulling her hard against him, his eyes fierce with possession and pride as he looked down into her lovely face. 'You will because we both know that for one to live without the other would be not to live at all.'

'Oh, Nick,' she breathed as she saw the fire leap up

in his eyes. 'You were gone so long and I needed you so much.'

'And then I almost lost you,' he said huskily. 'I do not know what I should have done if you had left me, sweet Catherine.'

'Now you know how I felt,' she whispered, a suspicion of tears in her eyes as she lifted her face for his kiss. It was a hungry, passionate embrace that left them both trembling. 'Never desert me for so long again, Nick.'

'I think that we should marry as soon as it can be arranged,' he said, touching her face with his finger-tips. 'I am not sure that I can wait much longer to make you mine.'

'You have become too familiar with my chamber,' Catherine teased. 'If I should wake and find you in my bed…'

'You are a wicked temptress,' Nick murmured. 'Tell me, are you well enough to marry me, Cat?'

'I am perfectly well,' she replied. 'You are almost as bad as my father, Nick. I am not a little girl or an invalid. I am a woman of natural needs and longings, who wants to be your wife.'

'Then you shall be very soon, my sweet rose of many thorns.'

'You make a beautiful bride, Catherine,' Lady Stamford said. 'I am happy to see this day, and I must tell you that I have revised my opinion of Sir Nicholas. After what my brother told me, I believe he does truly care for you and I have confidence that he will make you a good husband.'

'I thank you for your kind words, Aunt, and for coming to my wedding.'

'I could not do otherwise. As you know, Willis could not leave his wife, who is increasing again, and at least one member of your family besides your father must be here. William will return with me after the wedding to keep me company for a while.'

'Some of my friends are coming to the wedding,' Catherine told her. 'Jane Howarth, of course, because she did so much for me when I was ill. You remember Lettice, Aunt? She married James Morton.'

'How could I forget?' Lady Stamford looked sour.

'Lettice and her husband were under a cloud of the Queen's displeasure for some months, but Her Majesty has decided to forgive them. She has told Lettice that they may return to the court at some time in the future.'

'That is fortunate for them. I hope you are not thinking of doing so, Catherine? You would do better to stay at home and provide your husband with an heir.'

Catherine smiled inwardly. For once her aunt was telling her to do exactly what she wanted to do.

'Yes, Aunt. I believe you are right.'

Lady Stamford gave her a suspicious stare. 'I am not quite a fool, Catherine, and I shall admit that I was wrong to criticise Sir Nicholas as I did. Besides, I have often heard it said that reformed rogues make excellent husbands.'

'Nick will be the best of husbands,' Catherine said and smiled contentedly.

Catherine's wedding was not a large one, though they had invited their close neighbours as well as some

of her friends from court. However, Sir William had
caused a huge pavilion to be erected in the gardens
and it was here that all the people from the estate and
nearby village gathered to feast and wish her well.

The feasting and dancing in the house itself went
on until the early hours of the morning, but Catherine
and Nick had slipped quietly away long before that.

Sir William had decreed that the ancient ceremony
of the bedding was outdated and forbidden in his
house. His thoughtfulness and insistence that the
young couple should have privacy spared Catherine's
blushes, and there was no one to attend her as she
prepared for her wedding couch other than her devoted
Martha.

'You're as pretty as a rose, my dove,' Martha said
fondly as she finished brushing her hair. 'I shall leave
you now and say only that I know you will be happy
with such a fine man as Sir Nicholas for your husband.'

Catherine kissed her, for she had ever been a good
and faithful friend. Martha was to accompany her to
her new home, though that would not be for some
weeks yet.

She waited until she was alone, then walked to the
bed and drew back the sheets. She lay back against
the pillows, her lovely hair spilling over them, her eyes
closed.

He was here! He was coming to her; she sensed his
nearness but did not open her eyes as he stood gazing
down at her, and then she felt the touch of his lips on
her eyelids.

'Look at me, Cat,' he said and she obeyed. 'You have no need to fear anything this night. I shall not hurt you.'

'I do not fear you,' she said. 'I long for you beside me, Nick. I was merely savouring the moment you would come to me.'

Nick drew back the covers so that he might look at her, the delicious contours of her body barely hidden by the filmy nightgown. Yet he wanted more, and, as Catherine sat up, sensing his need, he pulled the nightgown from her, exposing the creamy tones of her skin.

'You are so lovely,' he breathed as he perched beside her on the bed, his fingers trailing reverently over the silky smoothness of her breasts. He bent his head to kiss them, flicking delicately at the nipples with the tip of his tongue, setting a flame of hot desire running through her. His tongue and mouth kissed and tasted her as he explored her feminine sweetness, awakening feelings and sensations hitherto unknown to her. 'I adore you, my lovely Catherine.'

She smiled and lifted her arms to him, inviting him to lie with her, her body responding eagerly to the feel of him close to her, thigh to thigh, breast to breast. So close were they that as they moved together it seemed natural to become one, joined together in the ancient dance of love. They moved in sweet rhythm, each seemingly aware of the other's needs, their loving neither hurried nor careless, but tender and in harmony as they reached the climax of their passion.

Afterwards, they lay talking for a long time, words of love and secret, funny, foolish things that neither had ever told to anyone else, the kind of things that only lovers share. And then Nick drew her into his arms again, and this time it was hungry, passionate and shattering, draining them so that they both slept entwined in each other's limbs.

Nick was the first to wake and leave their bed. He stood for several minutes gazing down at her. If she had been precious to him before, she was doubly so now. He would do nothing that might bring harm to her.

Going into the dressing chamber that led through to his own, Nick took out the letter that had reached him as he was about to leave for the church the previous day. He had read it but briefly and wanted to read it again more carefully.

Walsingham had written that he had received a preliminary report on the man that Nick had brought to his notice. His agents had told him that Frampton was a weak, sickly creature, who was more often laid on his bed than not.

> *He seems to have no friends, though that may be yet to discover. I shall continue to have him watched, but I think he is unlikely to be our man. My suspicions lie more and more in the direction of another, though for the moment I have no proof. I may not say more at this time, save that we have previously spoken of him, and that he has the trust of a certain person who must not here be named.*

Reading between the lines, Nick guessed that Walsingham was referring to the Queen's astrologer

Doctor John Dee. He had glimpsed the man once at court but had never met him, and could therefore have no opinion on the matter.

If Walsingham was right, he had been mistaken to suspect Frampton of plotting against anyone. And yet he recalled the stranger who had attended Catherine telling him that using the black arts could cause sickness in the perpetrator.

He shook his head as he read on. Walsingham was talking of using Nick's services in other ways.

> *I realise you would not wish to travel abroad often, but a man of your talents could serve in many ways, and I believe you might find the rewards to be high in time.*

Nick took up his pen, writing decisively of his decision to retire from public life. Walsingham and others must carry on the work they had begun, for Nick would not risk the happiness he had found with his beloved wife.

He sealed his letter and laid it ready with others to be sent by trusted messenger, then he went back to the bedchamber to lie beside Catherine and wait for her to wake.

'I shall miss you both,' Sir William said. 'But my mind will be at rest because I know you to be happy, Catherine.'

Four months had passed since their wedding, and Nick had decided it was time to take his wife home.

She was excited at the prospect of seeing his home for the first time, but sad to leave her father.

'Will you not change your mind and come with us?' she asked.

'You would be very welcome, sir,' Nick added his voice to hers. 'My home is also yours.'

'I know that a warm welcome awaits me,' Sir William said, smiling fondly at them. 'And be sure that I shall visit often. However, my sister has decided that she will take no more husbands and I have asked her to spend some time here. She grows tired of her son's noisy brood, though she loves them dearly. We shall go on well enough together, and I have good friends besides. Do not worry for my sake. Should I become weary of my own company I shall avail myself of your hospitality.'

Catherine knew there was no persuading him once his mind was set. She kissed him again, then went out to the waiting coach, leaving Nick to follow. She was sad to leave her father behind, but he had made his decision, and she had a new and wonderful life to look forward to.

'Oh, it is beautiful,' Catherine said, exclaiming in delight as she saw the red brick house Nick had had built in the shape of an E. 'So spacious and yet so comfortable.'

'My father's house was a draughty medieval manor,' Nick told her with a wry twist of his lips. 'When he died I decided that I would have it pulled down and rebuilt in the new style; the work was begun three years ago. I have made some improvements to my original design of late, and I hope you will be pleased with it, Catherine.'

'I think it will give me much happiness to be mistress here, Nick, but I should be happy anywhere with you.'

'There are many treasures inside that I sent back from my travels,' he told her. 'But it is a lovely day and I should like to walk with you in the gardens for a while.' He offered his arm, and Catherine took it, smiling up at him. 'If you are not too tired after the journey?'

'Not tired at all,' she assured him, though it was not quite true. She was feeling a little less energetic of late, but if what she suspected was true, she could accept the changes her condition would bring for all the happiness it would give both her and Nick.

They had been walking in the sunshine for some minutes when Catherine heard a strange noise. She looked at him in surprise.

'That sounded like a beast of some kind.'

'It is,' Nick said and laughed. 'Would you like to see your bear? I understand there are great changes in her.'

'In her?' Catherine stared in wonder. 'I had always supposed it was a him, though I do not know why I should.'

'I am assured that she is an adult female, and there I think is our proof…'

Catherine stopped and directed her gaze to the sight that Nick had indicated. A high iron railing had been erected to close off a large area of parkland. Within it she could see an adult bear, which looked healthy and content as it rolled on its back, and, playing contentedly about their mother, two very small cubs.

'Oh, Nick,' she cried. 'Is that my bear? She has given birth to two cubs? How wonderful!'

'I am glad you are pleased, Catherine. Ben has looked after her for you, and you must thank him another day. I think she might have died so sorely had she been treated if it were not for his tender care.'

Catherine looked at her husband curiously. 'Ben is the friend you told me of? I recall that you mentioned him when you spoke of buying the bear from her cruel master.'

'Ben is what many would call a simpleton,' Nick said. 'I rescued him from a travelling fair when he was but a lad. He had been beaten and starved, and so I brought him here and had him nursed back to health. He lives in a hut in these woods, and he takes care of all the wounded animals and birds he finds. He has no fear of any beast, and I have seen him gentle a maddened bull. Indeed, we have been grateful for his help with the domestic beasts many times. He told me at once that your bear was in cub, but I scarcely believed it possible. She must have been thus when I bought her, though she was painfully thin and ill.'

'And her cruel master was making her dance! I am so glad you rescued her, Nick. I wish we might do as much for all similarly afflicted creatures.'

'I did it for your sake, Catherine. I have no love for such sport, but as a man I tolerate it. There are many cruel truths to be faced in the harsh world in which we live, my love. Only when men come to see the evil of their ways will such things cease.'

'I know you cannot right all the wrongs of a hard world, Nick, nor would I ask it of you—but knowing that you think and feel as I do makes me happy. And I am glad our bear and her cubs have somewhere safe to live.'

'It is a fine sight,' Nick agreed, smiling as he watched the mother bear deliver a lazy swat at a tiresome cub. 'Young animals at play are amusing to watch.'

'As are children,' Catherine said, as they continued their walk beneath the shade of some dense trees that temporarily blotted out the sun. 'Tell me, husband, do you wish for a son or a daughter for your first child?'

'I have no preference…' Nick began and then stopped to stare at her. 'Catherine! Are you saying that you are…?'

Catherine laughed. 'It is my belief and my hope, though I am not quite sure yet. Shall you be pleased if the doctor confirms it?'

'Yes, of course—but should you be walking so far? What a brute I am to drag you out when you would rather rest!'

'I do not wish to rest,' she assured him. 'Time enough for that when I grow fat and ugly.'

'You will never be ugly.'

Her face glowed as she gazed up at him. 'When I am, remember your promises not to leave me. I would not have you gallivanting off to court as many gentlemen do at such times.'

'Believe me, nothing shall drag me from your side. Besides, I am determined to become a country gentleman and forget the court with all its intrigues.'

'Then I am quite content,' she said. 'Tell me, Nick—do I see a rose garden behind those hedges?'

Arm in arm, they strolled unhurriedly towards their rose garden. All that could be heard was the sound of birds and insects, and in the distance the squeal of a hungry bear cub.

For Catherine there were no shadows to haunt her, no terrible memories to spoil her happiness. Nick was there to love and guard her, and the future was secure.

If somewhere a man lay sick upon his bed, plotting in his evil malice against a Queen he hated and cursing the bodily weakness that laid him low, it was not their affair. England's future lay in the hands of others.

Catherine and Nick had passed through the shadows into the warmth of the sun, and for them it was only the beginning.

Turn the page for a preview of

THE ADVENTURER'S WIFE

from

Anne Herries

*The glorious autumn of
Elizabeth's reign...*

*With supporters rallying for her rival,
Mary Queen of Scots, and the Spanish
invasion fleet on the horizon, Elizabeth
turns to her secret service for help.*

Available May 2004
from Mills & Boon®

Chapter One

October...

Chapter One

October 1586

'You may rely on me,' said Sir Nicholas Grantly to the man with whom he was sharing a flask of good French wine in his parlour. 'Should Lady Hamilton find herself in need of assistance while you are in the north I shall be pleased to help in any way I may.'

Sir Christopher Hamilton was some fifteen years younger than his neighbour, a tall man, powerfully built, with the look of an adventurer about him from his years at sea in the fleet of ships commanded by the great Sir Francis Drake. His skin had a slightly bronzed appearance, his mouth, harsh in repose, could be merry when he smiled, yet it was his eyes that sometimes gave him away as a man of strong passions, for they could be as stormy as the Atlantic Sea. At the moment, however, they were soft and smiling.

'I knew I might rely on you, sir. You and Lady Grantly have been good friends to my mother these past years, and I believe I may speak plainly?'

'Of course. Something troubles you, Kit?'

'As you know, I have spent the past five years sailing in Drake's fleet, and we have dealt the Spanish a bloody nose or two; a dangerous business but one that has brought both wealth and honours. The knighthood Her Majesty was pleased to bestow on me for services rendered, and the introduction to Sir Francis Walsingham, which you yourself effected...' He paused, as if not quite sure how to proceed for the moment.

Nick nodded, understanding instantly. Having worked secretly for Walsingham in the past, he was instinctively alert as he guessed much that his friend might not say. 'Tell me only as much as you feel right, Kit. I am aware that sometimes it is unwise to speak too openly of these things.'

Kit nodded, his eyes darkening in thought. 'While my father lived I did not need to concern myself overly with the estate, but his death has left my mother in some part vulnerable. Neither Edward nor Jack are old enough to help her much, and indeed are sad scamps more likely to cause her worry than ease it. I think my late father's steward an honest fellow and I trust him, but I am uneasy...'

'You need say no more. I shall ride over from time to time to see all is well. How long do you expect to be away?'

'I am not certain.'

Kit hesitated, unsure of how much he ought properly to confide in his friend and neighbour. He trusted Sir Nicholas as much as any man he knew, but Sir Francis had insisted that their interview remain a secret.

'For it seems that I find a new plot against Her Majesty at every turn,' Walsingham had told him.

'And I believe that the girl's father may in some way be involved in a devious plan to rescue Mary of Scots and set her upon the English throne even now. With the discovery of the Babington conspiracy I have proved that Mary did indeed put her seal of approval on that devilish plot; she has been tried and found guilty of treason, and yet the Queen will not sign the death warrant, plead as I might for her to make an end to it.'

Kit had realised he was being asked to spy upon the girl who lived with his mother's kinsmen as their ward. She had been sent to them as a child of a few years as a surety for her father's good behaviour, and Kit knew that Beth Makepeace had come to love her as a daughter. For himself, he had seen the girl only once on a long ago visit to Drodney with his parents, and could hardly remember her—and yet it went against the grain to be asked to spy on someone who was almost family.

'You are to visit Mistress Makepeace at the castle of Drodney, I believe?' Nick asked, as Kit remained silent, apparently lost in thought.

'My mother thought the northern air might do me good.'

'But your wound has healed?'

'Aye, I am better, though the fever left me feeling low for a time. A change of air perhaps…'

Kit left the sentence unfinished, not liking to hide his true purpose from a man he respected. It was true that Lady Sarah Hamilton had suggested that a visit to her kinswoman might help her son recover his former zest for life, which had been dimmed both the sad loss of his father and the wound taken in an encounter with a Spanish treasure ship.

However, the real season for his journey was very different.

'It will not seem strange that you visit your kinswoman,' Walsingham had told him in their private interview. 'I am concerned that the girl is given more freedom than she should properly have, for she is hostage to her father's good behaviour.'

'Is that fair to the girl?' Kit had asked, his brows lifting. 'If the father is the danger, surely it would be better to imprison him?'

'Lord Angus Fraser is an important man among the Scottish nobility,' Walsingham replied. 'He is a Catholic and supported Mary after Darnley was murdered and she married that dangerous fool Bothwell. Had she not been so reckless she might even now be still upon Scotland's throne. If I could I would arrest Fraser, but it is beyond my power for the moment. He gave his bond that he would remain at his home in Scotland, but I know for certain that he has travelled to Spain at least twice in the past few years, and I suspect that he may have had a hand in the Babington plot, but was clever enough to keep his name out of it.'

'But surely with Mary safely imprisoned there is nothing that he or any other can do?'

'If Mary were dead…' Walsingham shook his head sorrowfully. 'But her Majesty will not put her hand to the warrant and until the traitor is dead, we shall always have those who would use her for their own ends.'

'You speak of Spain, I think?'

'Aye, King Philip of Spain has always had an eye for England's throne,' Walsingham replied. 'He would make Catholics of us all and bring back the stench of burning to England's fair land.'

'Not if Drake's band of sea captains have their way,' Kit said grimly. His time at sea had brought him into contact with men who had suffered at the hands of the Spanish Inquisition and what he had learned from them had made him staunchly Protestant. He made up his mind to do as Walsingham asked. It was for the sake of England and of all right-thinking men. 'But if you believe the girl represents a danger I will do what I can to help you in this matter.'

'The girl is no danger in herself, but I think the father may try to get her away before whatever plot he is concerned in comes to fruition, and I would not have him succeed.'

'I shall keep a watchful eye and send you word if I see anything that troubles me,' Kit had promised, and on that note they had parted, Kit to return briefly to his home to advise his mother of his intention to travel north to the castle of Drodney, which guarded the borders between England and Scotland, and to ask Sir Nicholas to keep a friendly eye on the estate.

'Should you ever need help yourself for whatever reason, you may come to me,' Sir Nicholas said, because Kit had been silent for some minutes and was clearly still bothered by something. 'You may trust me in an emergency—on your own part or that of the State, for I have been in Walsingham's confidence in the past. Had I not had private reasons for retiring from public life, I might still be one of his couriers.'

He might have said spies, for Walsingham was the great spymaster, and it was mainly due to his vigilance that so many attempts against the Queen's Majesty had been foiled these past years.

'Yes, I had suspected that might have been the case,' Kit said. 'I think there are many who have served in like cause. For the moment you will forgive me if I say nothing, but should the need arise I shall come to you, Nick.'

'I shall be happy to serve if I can,' Nick replied and smiled. 'And now you must stay to dine with us. Catherine would be happy to see you, I know, and young Lisa is over her fever at last. My boys are sad scamps, much like your brothers, Kit, but they would be thrilled to hear about your adventures. Young Harry has told me he intends to be like Drake when he is a man grown, and I believe he may, for he loves the sea. John is very different and I suspect that he may have a leaning to the intellectual…'

In good humour with each other, the two men went into the parlour where Lady Catherine Grantly sat with her needlework. Seeing the way she smiled at her husband, Kit thought that he had seldom seen such love in a woman's eyes, and he found himself envying his friend. If he could discover such a woman then he might be content at last to give up his adventuring and settle down. But a woman of Catherine Grantly's equal was not often met with, and Kit's own experience with women had not been a happy one. The woman he had offered for at nineteen had spurned him in favour of an older, richer man, and by so doing had set Kit's feet on the path to wealth and honour, for if he had married he would never have gone to sea.

His mouth curved in a wry smile as he recalled the spirited beauty he had loved as a youth. Madeline was married now to Lord Carmichael, a man much older than herself, and he believed that she took lovers to alleviate her boredom. She had hinted that she would not be averse to having Kit in her bed, and had his time not been promised to Walsingham he might well have taken her at her word!

His eyes sparkled with amusement at the memory. Madeline's chagrin at being turned down had wiped away any bitterness he might still have harboured over her rejection, for she had not been able to hide her disappointment.

The young Christopher Hamilton had been quiet and awkward, a very different man from the one who had returned rich, powerful and influential after his years at sea. Yes, had he been a vengeful man he might have taken pleasure from being the one to say no this time. As it was, he merely felt a fleeting regret for a pleasure that might have been. His mind was occupied with the things he had discussed with Walsingham and wondering what he might find at Drodney Castle. What kind of a girl was Anne Marie Fraser, and would he discover that she was involved in some kind of secret plot against the Queen?

'Do you think Anne Marie is happy?' Beth Makepeace asked of her husband as they sat over the fire enjoying a cup of mulled ale at the end of their busy day. 'She has been very quiet of late.'

'Anne Marie is a good, dutiful girl,' he replied. 'She has never been a trouble to you, Beth. The Lord knows she has been a blessing to us these past years, for we have been sent no children of our own, and the girl is like a daughter.'

'But she is not our daughter,' Beth said, looking anxious as she warmed her hands before the fire. 'You know I love her as my own, Thomas, but when Sir Francis Walsingham sent someone to interview her last year she was reminded that she is merely a hostage for her father's good behaviour. I believe that hurt her deeply, more than we might guess.'

'Aye, I have noticed something in her manner since then.

'Do you think they will ever allow her to marry?'

He was thoughtful for a moment before he answered, and then spoke with a heavy seriousness that frightened his anxious wife. 'It has been my fear that they will give her in marriage to a man she does not know and cannot love. I thought that might have been Walsingham's purpose in sending for a report on her life here.'

'Surely not?' Beth looked at him in alarm. 'The Queen is not so cruel. Pray tell me it is not so, husband. I should refuse to allow it!'

'You could do nothing if the order came from London,' Thomas Makepeace said, and leaned forward to hold his hands to the fire. They were gnarled and rheumatism and chapped from the cold, a testimony to the hardness of life at the castle. 'Anne Marie is our ward, not our daughter, much as we love her, and we must obey our orders.'

Outside the partially opened door of their private chamber, Anne Marie Fraser listened to their conversation. She was very still, her lovely face pale, her serious eyes reflecting both fear and anger. Over the years she had learned to hide her passions beind a demure manner, though sometimes her eyes gave her away. She had known since childhood that she was a prisoner here. As kindly as she had been treated, the fact remained that she was not free to come and go as she pleased, or to live anywhere else.

She has been a very small girl when the man came

to take her from her home and her nurse, who had wept bitterly at the parting. Anne Marie could not remember her mother, Lady Margaret Fraser, who had died soon after she was born, but she remembered Morag, who had nursed her from a babe, and of course her father.

Lord Angus Fraser was a big, heavily built man, black of hair and beard, with fierce grey eyes and a loud voice that had frightened her as a child. She was not afraid of him now, for she had seen him three times in the past five years; twice he had visited her in the presence of her guardians and once he had come to her when she was walking alone on the hillsides that surrounded the castle. There was a spot where she liked to stand and gaze out at the sea, which foamed and thrashed about the rocks below. She was allowed to walk on the cliffs alone, for there was no path down to the cove below; the face of the steep cliff was too dangerous for her even to attempt escaping by that route.

Anne Marie had thought of escape a few times since her father's last visit. He had told her that she must always remember she was a Catholic and a prisoner of the English.

'Your mother was French and I am a Scot,' Angus Fraser had growled. 'Do not allow these English dogs to indoctrinate you with their faith, daughter. They are heretics and would burn had I my way. One day Mary will take her rightful place on the thrones of England and Scotland, and I shall be at her right-hand. Then you shall be restored to honour at the wife of a Catholic gentleman of rank.' His eyes were very fierce as he laid a hand upon her arm. 'Do not let them marry you to a heretic, Anne Marie. Far better that you should die than accept such dishonour.'

She had promised that she would never marry other than as he directed and he had kissed her briefly on the cheek before taking his leave.

'One day soon I shall come for you, Daughter,' he had promised. 'My plans are not yet complete, but you must be ready to leave when I say. And the time will be soon now.'

Anne Marie had watched him walk away with mixed feelings. She had always known that she was not Beth Makepeace's daughter, but there was a part of her that wished she were. Beth had been kind and loving and Anne Marie had gradually come to love her. As she grew older and began to question, Beth had not prevented her from using the Bible and cross which had been her mother's. In private she was permitted to worship in her own way, though outwardly, she'd had to appear to accept the Protestant faith.

In Elizabeth's England there were many who did much the same. Queen Elizabeth had begun her reign with a show of tolerance towards the Catholics, but as the years passed and there were too many attempts against her throne, that tolerance had waned. There were fines for those who neglected to attend church on a Sunday, and other more severe penalties for those thought to have committed a traitorous act. Indeed there were many disadvantages to being a Catholic in England, for the chance of honour and high office was not often met with.

Anne's wandering thoughts were recalled as Beth Makepeace began to talk of her kinsman.

'It is many years since we saw Chistopher, husband.'

'Aye, he will have changed, I dare say. He will be a man now.'

'And knighted by Her Majesty…'

Anne Marie turned away, walking slowly up the worn stone steps to her own chamber at the top of the tower. The castle was old and had stood here for centuries, guarding the borders between Scotland and England, dealing with raiding parties of lawless Highlanders who came stealing cattle from the English villages about, and giving warning of any likely attack. In winter it was bitterly cold, the water she used for drinking sometimes freezing in the ewer overnight. There were no fireplaces in the bedchambers, and they slept beneath piles of coverlets and furs. However, Anne Marie was used to the discomfort, and though her hands sometimes became chapped with the cold in the worst of the winter, this was only late October, and the snow had not yet fallen.

It was wrong of her to listen to her kind guardians talking privately, she knew, but it was the only way she could learn of what went on in the wider world outside the castle. She had recently heard Beth speaking of the arrest of Mary of Scots, but she was not certain what that meant, as one of the servants had come along the passage and she'd had to move on.

Surely Mary, once Queen of Scotland but deposed after she married Bothwell, the man most people suspected of murdering her husband, the Earl of Darnley, had been a prisoner for many long years? She had fled to England after the Scottish lords had defeated her in battle, seeking sanctuary from England's Queen and begging her *sister* to help her.

For they were both women in a world that was too often at the mercy of men and sisters beneath the skin. At first moved by her plea and refusing to hand her over to her enemies, Elizabeth had wanted to help her regain her throne. However, her advisers cautioned against it and Mary had been kept under close house arrest, not quite a prisoner and yet not quite free.

Anne Marie had often thought of the poor woman who had been so full of life and gaiety when she first came to Scotland as a young widow of the French King. How sadly her life had turned out. In a short space of time she had gone from being fêted and spoiled in France, to a lonely prisoner. Her first mistake had been to marry the Earl of Darnley, a coarse brute of a man who had behaved ill towards her by murdering her secretary, Rizzio, and her second mistake had been to marry the man who had caused her downfall. Her third perhaps was to throw herself on the mercy of the Queen of England.

But what had happened recently that had caused Mary to be taken to the castle of Fotheringay? Anne Marie had tried asking Beth, but her guardian had refused to be drawn on the subject.

Entering her chamber, which was furnished with a truckle bed, a table, a chair and an oaken coffer for her clothes, Anne Marie went over to the niche in the thick stone wall that held her prayer book and the wooden cross she used for her devotions. She bowed her head and prayed for peace of mind and for Mary of Scots, but asked nothing more for herself.

In truth, Anne Marie did not know what she wanted of life. At almost twenty years of age, sixteen of which had been spent as a hostage at Drodney, she was a beautiful woman. Her hair was a very dark brown, long and straight, her eyes wide and clear, the irises a bright blue. Her complexion had a freshness that came from her habit of taking long walks no matter how inclement the weather, and though she was not much above a man's shoulder in height, she was perfectly formed.

Had she not been held hostage these many years, Anne Marie would have been married long since. At nearly twenty she would be considered quite old for marriage, and it was unlikely that she would ever find love or happiness. Even if a match was arranged for her, it would most probably be to someone she neither knew nor liked.

The prospect was not particularly pleasing and Anne Marie thought she might prefer to remain as she was now. Her father's promise to take her away had faded from her mind. It was many months since she had seen him and she thought that he had probably forgotten her. Besides, she knew that he did not love her—not as Beth Makepeace loved her. He was merely concerned that his enemies should not continue to use her against him.

Her prayers finished, Anne Marie walked over to the arrow slit that served as her window in the tower. As she gazed out at the night a shooting star suddenly flashed across the sky.

'I wish,' she said. 'Oh, I wish that something wonderful would happen. I wish that I was free…that I could fall in love…'

In another moment she was laughing at herself. She had made three wishes and only one would be granted if the old superstition were true. But of course it was merely nonsense. Nothing was likely to happen. She would stay here, forgotten, until she died.

* * *

The morning had dawned fine and bright. As Anne Marie left the castle for her walk, the sun was shining and there was a mild feel to the day. She smiled at the guard who stood sentry at the East Gate. He bowed his head in acknowledgement, allowing her to pass through without challenge. She could walk only as far as the cliff edge, for there was no way down to the sea below.

Sometimes Anne Marie was allowed to visit the village at the bottom of the hill at the west side of the castle, but only when accompanied by Beth and one of the man at arms. Sometimes she and Beth would gather herbs and wild flowers on the way, and on rare occasions Thomas Makepeace would ride with her and a groom in the hills and valleys about Drodney.

'You must be allowed your exercise, my dear,' he told her kindly. 'I like to see the bloom in your cheeks and the air will do you good.' But he was a busy man and she did not ride as often as she would have liked.

Her chief pleasure was in walking, reading and of late sketching. She had brought with her that morning a pencil and a tiny leather-bound journal with sheets of plain vellum that Beth had bought her as a birthday gift. Anne Marie used them sparingly, for both the pencil and the journal had been sent specially from London and were expensive.

Sitting on a cushion made of her cloak, Anne Marie stared out at the sea. It was that morning a curious dark blue topped with greyish white foam and she longed for a palette of colours so that she could capture the true essence of that angry water.

'What are you doing?'

Absorbed in her contemplation of the view, Anne Marie had not been aware of the man's approach. For

a moment her heart raced with fear, but then it stilled
as something stirred in her memory and she knew him.
He had visited the castle but once before when she
was a child of some ten years, but his image had
stayed in her mind because he had put her up on his
pony and taken her riding outside the walls of
Drodney. She believed he might have received a
scolding for taking her without permission, but he had
left the next morning and she had never known.

'I was thinking that I should like to paint the sea,'
she replied. 'To sketch it in pencil would not do that
colour justice.'

'No, you are very right,' Kit said, and sat down
beside her on a piece of rock, gazing out as she did
to the sea and endless sky. 'It is a magnificent view,
though somewhat daunting at times. Do you often
come here, Mistress Fraser?'

'I was not sure you would remember me.' Her eyes
widened as she looked at him; they were as cool and
clear as the autumn sky but a much deeper blue that
reminded him of other skies. 'I come most days. I am
allowed to walk here alone, you see.'

'And you are not allowed to walk to the village?'

'Not alone,' she replied, her tone more wistful than
she knew. 'When Master Makepeace can spare the
time he takes me riding, but that is not often.
Sometimes Beth comes with me to the village. Once
a month there is a market. It is possible to buy silks
and ribbons from the pedlars, but Beth sends to
London for most of our needs.' She handed him the
tiny journal. 'This was a gift for my birthday last year.'

Kit took the book and looked at the pages. There
were equisite drawings of the castle, the cliffs, the sea
and various people, including Beth and Thomas

Makepeace. Some were in pen and ink, smudged slightly to give them shading, others in pencil. He examined the pencil curiously, for though they had been produced in England for some years now, he had never handled one before. It was not more than a finger's length above its flat silver holder and he guessed that it had been much used.

'Have you no paints, mistress?'

'I am fortunate to have this,' Anne Marie replied. 'Until Beth bought it for me I had only a slate. She says that she will buy me some colours at Christmas, but she has very little money of her own and I fear paints are too expensive.'

Kit frowned as he returned the book to her, his eyes moving over her intently. He felt the injustice of her treatment, for there was surely no need to deprive her of such simple pleasures! Indeed, it was a sin to do so, for her life could not have been easy here.

She was dressed in a plain gown of black cloth with a white ruff at her neck, her only adornment a silver cross on a green ribbon. Her hair was covered with a neat black cap at the crown, but streamed down her back in heavy tresses.

Gazing into her clear eyes, he felt an odd sensation in his stomach and caught his breath. Damn it! She was lovely. Not exquisitely dressed, painted and adorned like the beauties of Elizabeth's court, but with a quiet, graceful beauty that moved him deeply. He was aware once more of dismay at the nature of his task, which was in truth to spy on her.

'I should go back,' she said, as if something in his look had disturbed her, and he offered his hand to help her rise. After the merest hesitation she took it and he bent to retrieve her cloak, shaking it before placing it about her shoulders. Gazing down at her he was aware of an urgent desire to kiss her, and had to berate himself mentally. She was no tavern wench to be tumbled in the hay! She smiled, a faint flush in her cheeks, as she said, 'I thank you, Sir Christopher. I was turning a little cold.'

'Will you not call me Kit as you did when we were children?'

'It might be frowned upon,' she said, her gaze clear and honest. 'How long do you stay with us, sir?'

'Oh, for a few weeks or so,' he said vaguely, made uncomfortable by those candied eyes. He had not expected to be so attracted to her, and it pricked at his conscience to know that he was here under a false flag. 'My mother thought the northern air might do me good, and it is many years since any of us visited Mistress Makepeace, though I believe my mother writes quite often.'

'Have you been ill, sir?' Anne Marie glanced up at him and he felt the pull of those eyes once more. His stomach churned and he understood that what he felt was desire—the desire to possess her, to touch that soft white skin and kiss those full, sweet lips.

'I was wounded in a battle with a Spanish ship,' he explained, fighting the fierce passion she had unwittingly aroused in him. What was wrong with him? He was like green youth, the sap rising as if he had no control. 'She was a merchant ship and loaded down with silver from the New World. Her crew put up a fierce resistance when we boarded her, and that was when I was wounded.'

'Are you a pirate, Sir Christopher?'

'I am what is called a privateer,' he replied with an odd smile. 'I sail under Drake's command and with the blessing of Her Majesty Queen Elizabeth. Our mission is to harry the Spanish and take what we can of the wealth they have stolen from the New World. In the first half of this century the Spanish were the most powerful nation on earth, but their ships are clumsy compared to ours. At sea we have the advantage of them, though they are fierce and oftimes cruel on land. If we did not do what we can to relieve them of some of their wealth they would become too powerful and represent a danger to England.'

'I have read in a pamphlet that they sometimes slaughter innocent natives of the New World. Someone told me that was lies, set about by those who hate them. Tell me, sir—what is your opinion?'

Kit felt his throat tighten with desire as he gazed into her eyes. He swallowed hard and averted his gaze as he replied, 'Let me assure you that what you read was true. Whoever told you that the pamphlet lied was misinformed. I have heard and seen things that I would not repeat in a lady's hearing, but which I found shocking.'

Anne Marie nodded, accepting his word. Her father had told her she was being fed lies by Beth but she had not quite believed him. She knew that he had friends in Spain, and suspected it might be from there that he was expecting help in his plan to rescue Mary of Scots.

Perhaps this man would tell her the truth? He seemed open and outgoing and she thirsted for news of the outside world.

'Have you heard of the arrest of Mary of Scots?'

Kit's nape prickled as she spoke. How could she have heard this? It was known only to a few and of very recent occurrence.

'That she has been sent to Fotheringay? I know it to be true, mistress. But how do you know of this?'

'I heard Beth speak of it to her husband but was not sure what was meant.'

'Few know of this, Mistress Fraser. Your guardians should be more careful in their talk.'

'It was but a chance remark I heard in passing.' He nodded but frowned, and she drew a deep breath. 'I would know why she has been sent there,' Anne Marie said. 'What has she done that she is so condemned? Until recently I believe she was given as much or more privilege than I.'

'And she betrayed that privilege,' Kit said sternly, remembering belatedly why he had come. 'She plotted with the traitor Babington to murder Elizabeth and take the throne of England by force. She is a vain, foolish creature and will no doubt forfeit her life for this latest treachery.'

Anne Marie's hand flew to her throat. Her eyes widened in fear as she saw his harsh expression.

'Surely she cannot have done anything so wicked?'

'I assure you it is proven by Walsingham. If the Queen was not a woman of conscience and compassion Mary would have been executed long before this for other crimes. As yet Elizabeth has stayed her hand, but I think it must come at the last.'

'God have mercy!' Anne Marie said and crossed herself. 'You may call it justice, sir, and perhaps it is—but I feel for Mary's plight. You have been accustomed to freedom and cannot know what it is like to be kept a prisoner for so many years. If Mary of Scots truly did what is said of her it was because it was her only hope of freedom.'

Kit's gaze narrowed as it centred on her face. 'Are you so unhappy, Mistress Fraser?'

A warm blush suffused her cheeks.

'I—I have been lucky in my guardians, sir. Mistress Makepeace has always been kind and loving towards me. I would not have you think me ungrateful.'

'But you long for freedom?' Kit looked at her profile as she was silent. Her expression gave no hint of her feelings and he guessed that she had learned to keep them in check, but a tiny nerve flicking in her throat told him all. 'I should not have asked such a question,' he said softly. 'Forgive me if you can.'

Anne Marie turned her eyes on him. There was a hint of accusation in their depths.

'There is nothing to forgive. It was but an idle question. The answer is that I have learned to long for nothing. I expect only what I am given, that way I am not disappointed.'

She gave the appearance of calm, a modest, emotionless creature without passion. Why did he not quite believe in this face she showed to the world?

Surely such beauty could not belong to a woman of so little passion? Kit was convinced that the picture she presented of modesty and compliance was not the true one.

They had reached the castle gate and passed beneath the old stone arch. Seeing Sir Christopher, the sentry saluted and stood to attention.

'Are you a person of importance these days?' Anne Marie asked, a hint of mischief in her eyes.

Kit laughed deep in his throat. She was not so emotionless that she had no sense of humour!

'Oh, I think not,' he murmured. 'The poor fellow must have confused me with someone else.'

Anne Marie stared at him in silence for a moment, and then her laughter rang out. It was clear and joyous, like the sound of tinkling bells, and so surprising that it shocked the man at her side. His stomach clenched and he was captivated by the charm of the woman thus revealed. How delightful she might be if she were not so restricted by her life at the castle.

Once again he felt an urgent desire to take her in his arms and wondered at himself. Why should this woman have such a marked effect on him? It was not often that he met a wench that made him burn as she did, and within such a short time of meeting her. Had he run mad, or was it simply too long since he had taken a woman to bed?

'Why do you stare at me so?'

Her laughter had stilled and there was apprehension in those wondrous eyes, as if she thought she had done something wrong and might be reprimanded for it.

'Your laughter pleased me,' Kit said, realising that he had been staring at her for several minutes. He was a damned fool and must control this urge. 'Forgive me if I offended, mistress. I meant not to be rude.'

'You were not rude, sir. I wondered if I had offended you?'

'I do not believe that is possible.' He smiled down at her. Beside him she was diminutive—the fairy sprite of many a poem! He knew a mad temptation to sweep her up on his horse and ride away with her. 'You are sweet company, Mistress Fraser. Would that I had words to tell you, but I am a common sea captain and do not have the gift of a silver tongue.'

'Oh, I think you rather an uncommon man,' Anne Marie replied, a little smile about her lips. 'I am fond of poetry but I have no talent for it either.'

'You have other talents,' Kit murmured. 'Not least your skill at drawing likenesses. Will you take mine, Mistress Fraser? I believe my mother would like to have it by her when I am away.'

'Are you often away?'

'I have been for some years past. I am not certain of the future. My father died a month before I returned from my last voyage. My mother was managing but ill, and I fear it may be too much for her. I am reluctant to leave her again too soon, though for the moment she is well enough and has kind friends about her.'

'I am sorry for your father's death.'

'As I was. When we parted he was in the best of health. It was a sudden chill. He was six and forty and seemed young for his age. I expected him to live for many years more.'

'My mother died when she was but twenty,' Anne Marie said, feeling the sting of tears. 'I never knew her, though she survived my birth by some months. She took a fever and was dead within hours.'

'That was a tragedy for you and your father. I believe your father did not remarry?'

'No, he has never done so. I think he…'

Anne Marie was silent all at once, lost in thought. She was not sure why Lord Fraser had not taken a second wife. He had always been a staunch supporter of Mary, but why remain unwed? Unless he had hoped…but surely not? He could not hope to take his place as Mary's consort when she became Queen?

It was a foolish idea and one that Anne Marie dismissed at once. There were other more important men who must have similar aspirations. If Lord Fraser was prepared to risk all on such a slender hope he was a reckless fool. No, no, she decided. His purpose was nobler. He wished to restore the Catholic faith to the people, and to see Mary in her rightful place.

'What do you think, Mistress?' he asked, as she remained silent too long.

Anne Marie was recalled to the present. Sir Christopher was looking at her curiously, as if he hoped to read her thoughts. She blushed and shook her head.

'Why nothing, sir. Nothing that would interest you.' Nor that she dared repeat to anyone. She hesitated as they entered the castle together. 'I think I must leave you now, sir. Mistress Makepeace will be waiting for me. It is my habit to report to her on my return. She likes me to help her in her stillroom. To be mistress of a castle is a big responsibility. There is no physician for leagues, and if anyone in the castle is ill the task of caring for that person falls to Beth, and sometimes in the village too. She hath some skill for it, and I help her where I can, for she has much to do.'

The castle was in fact like a small walled town, with its own blacksmith, carpenter, mason, farrier, bakery and a cookhouse for the men, besides many other small tradesmen who worked within the castle walls but lived in the village below.

'Go then,' Kit said and then laid his hand upon her arm, as she would have turned away. 'Do you walk every morning?'

'Most mornings if it is fine,' she agreed and lowered her gaze.

'Perhaps you would like to ride with me tomorrow?'

'We should need permission from my guardian.'

'I have not forgot,' he said with a rueful laugh. 'I

shall speak to Thomas and see if he will permit the pleasure—a pleasure as much for me as you, mistress.'

'If permission is granted I should very much like to ride with you, sir.'

Anne Marie turned away, a smile on her lips. If only she could go riding with him! It would be such a joy. Yet she must not, dare not hope for too much. It would be a bitter disappointment if Sir Christoper's request should be denied.

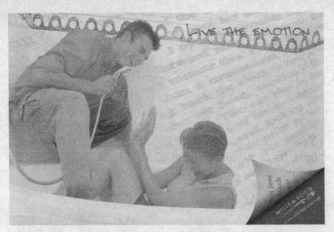

Modern Romance™
...international affairs
– seduction and
passion guaranteed

Medical Romance™
...pulse-raising
romance – heart-
racing medical drama

Tender Romance™
...sparkling, emotional,
feel-good romance

Sensual Romance™
...teasing, tempting,
provocatively playful

Historical Romance™
...rich, vivid and
passionate

Blaze Romance™
...scorching hot
sexy reads

30 new titles every month.

Live the emotion

MILLS & BOON®